"I didn't come up here to seduce you, if that's what you think,"

Meg insisted.

Rafe just looked at her for a long while. "You confuse the hell out of me, Specialist Mary Margaret Kavanagh, I'll tell you that much for nothing."

"You know," she said quietly, "I swear I won't tell anyone if you lose that chip on your shoulder for a few hours. As far as anyone else is concerned, your reputation as a five-star bastard will be unsullied."

"I could still shoot you and stuff your body in a hole, Kavanagh."

She smiled up at him and linked her arm with his. "But you won't, ex-Super Agent Blackhorse. You'll make me somethin̄ and then you'll tell me everything I w know."

"And why would I do that?"

"Because you're starting to like r

Dear Reader,

It's time to go wild with Intimate Moments. First, welcome historical star Ruth Langan back to contemporary times as she begins her new family-oriented trilogy. *The Wildes of Wyoming—Chance* is a slam-bang beginning that will leave you eager for the rest of the books in the miniseries. Then look for *Wild Ways,* the latest in Naomi Horton's WILD HEARTS miniseries. The first book, *Wild Blood,* won a Romance Writers of America RITA Award for this talented author, and this book is every bit as terrific.

Stick around for the rest of our fabulous lineup, too. Merline Lovelace continues MEN OF THE BAR H with *Mistaken Identity,* full of suspense mixed with passion in that special recipe only Merline seems to know. Margaret Watson returns with *Family on the Run,* the story of a sham marriage that awakens surprisingly real emotions. Maggie Price's *On Dangerous Ground* is a MEN IN BLUE title, and this book has a twist that will leave you breathless. Finally, welcome new author Nina Bruhns, whose dream of becoming a writer comes true this month with the publication of her first book, *Catch Me If You Can.*

You won't want to miss a single page of excitement as only Intimate Moments can create it. And, of course, be sure to come back next month, when the passion and adventure continue in Silhouette Intimate Moments, where excitement and romance go hand in hand.

Enjoy!

Leslie J. Wainger
Executive Senior Editor

Please address questions and book requests to:
Silhouette Reader Service
U.S.: 3010 Walden Ave., P.O. Box 1325, Buffalo, NY 14269
Canadian: P.O. Box 609, Fort Erie, Ont. L2A 5X3

Naomi HORTON
WILD WAYS

Published by Silhouette Books

America's Publisher of Contemporary Romance

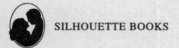

SILHOUETTE BOOKS

ISBN 0-373-07986-9

WILD WAYS

Visit us at www.romance.net

Printed in U.S.A.

NAOMI HORTON

was born in northern Alberta, where the winters are long and the libraries far apart. "When I'd run out of books," she says, "I'd simply create my own—entire worlds filled with people, adventure and romance. I guess it's not surprising that I'm still at it!" This RITA Award-winning author is an engineering technologist who presently lives in Nanaimo, British Columbia, with her collection of assorted pets.

IT'S OUR 20th ANNIVERSARY!
We'll be celebrating all year,
continuing with these fabulous titles,
on sale in February 2000.

Chapter 1

It was the kind of place he'd spent his entire life trying to avoid.

Small town bar, set back from the dusty street on a cracked surface of tarry asphalt tufted with weeds and dry grass and confetti sprinkles of broken glass. The windows were blank behind their jailhouse grillwork, as shuttered and private as a drug dealer's eyes behind reflective designer shades.

Great. Rafe eyed the place unhappily from the car, feeling the sweat trickle between his shoulder blades and soak into the stained upholstery of the seat. He was going to kill Dawes, he decided thoughtfully as he cut the engine. Silence fell around him, broken only by the chainsaw buzz of some insect in the tall, dust-grayed grass by the curb.

That wasn't the plan, of course. The *plan* had been to take Dawes and his blond girlfriend into custody and drive their sorry behinds back to Las Vegas and Tony Ruffio.

He'd known it had sounded too easy. Dawes had led him through three states and seven counties, in and out of towns no one had ever heard of, up hill and down hot, sunbaked dale, and he was by God going to pay for it. Okay, killing him was out. Tony had said he'd only pay for the recovery if the man were delivered into his hands alive and squirming. But there was nothing in the contract about dents and bruises.

Rafe flexed the fingers of his left hand, the network of scars webbing his knuckles bone-white in the harsh sunlight. Then he sighed. Hell, even that wasn't an option. He didn't have a lot of scruples left, but even he drew the line at punching out a little guy like Dawes.

Rafe looked at the bar again. Sighed again. And pushed open the car door and eased himself out into the heat-stunned afternoon. It was time.

The bar's neon sign buzzed, its glow feeble under a layering of dust. The parking lot surface was soft and it seemed to suck at Rafe's boots as he walked across it, the stink of hot asphalt hanging in the still air. The thought struck him that it was like walking across the foyer of hell, and he smiled at the irony. Even more ironic was the fact that he'd been born somewhere around here.

But that sure as hell wasn't anything he wanted to think about. He shook it off and forced his suddenly drifting mind back to the business at hand.

A brace of Harley-Davidsons sat to one side of the doorway, parked all in a row, as tidy and pristine and perfectly aligned as nuns in a choir.

That could mean trouble. He paused and did a quick check: Taurus PT 99 in the holster tucked under his left arm; Smith & Wesson in its leather, tucked discreetly into the small of his back; Walther double-action semiautomatic in his boot. The Taurus and the Smith & Wesson were licensed and legal as hell, the Walther a little thing he'd picked up while on a job in Oklahoma City a year back. It had fallen into his hands so tidily it had seemed ordained that he have it, so he hadn't bothered turning it in. He'd had the boot holster specially designed and was so used to it now he rarely thought about it. Except for times like this.

He flexed his shoulders once to loosen them, then pulled open the door and stepped inside.

From caution borne of habit, he stepped quickly to one side until his eyes adapted to the dimness, scanning the shadows for threat or motion even before he could fully see what—or who— they contained. The cold air dried the sweat on his forehead and across his back almost instantly, and he shook his left arm out, feeling the muscles start to tighten.

Heads turned, as they do in a place like that. Incurious eyes met his, then drifted away, dismissing him as unimportant. It brought the usual rush of automatic anger, but he ignored it. To everyone in here, as in most places, he was just another Indian, the next best thing to invisible. Which was handy for a man in his line of work.

Two farmers sat at a table to his left, peaked caps set on the backs of their heads, faces lined and grizzled from decades of staring at the sky. A salesman of some kind sat at another round table, tie loosened and hanging askew, a pile of papers scattered across the table. Two lanky Native kids were playing pool at a table in back, jostling and showing off, and an old man sat at the bar, staring morosely into the half-empty glass in his hand.

Only the bikers seemed to take any notice of him. They sat around a table to his hard right, all of them big and watchful, their leathers cluttered with studs and chains and coded patches. They eyed him warily, but he gave his head an almost imperceptible shake and they relaxed again.

But no Dawes.

Which was just the way he'd planned it.

This time, this close to his prey, he wasn't going to take a chance on losing them again. He'd almost caught them in Denver, and then again in Rapid City, but both times they'd taken off like startled hares before he'd gotten close enough to nab them. It was as though they had some kind of sixth sense, and he was tired of it. Tired of the hunt, the heat, all of it. So no more messing around. This time, he was going to set the trap and simply wait for them to walk into it, and in another two days he would be back on Bear Mountain, thirty grand richer, Reggie Dawes nothing more than an irritating memory.

Rafe chose a table not far from the door, far enough in shadow not to stand out, but not so far back it would look as though he was hiding. He eased himself into the gunfighter's seat, back to the wall, and gave the room another swift, calculating look. Everything seemed normal enough. But in this line of work, you just never knew.

The bartender was drying glasses and stacking them on a tray. He looked across at Rafe and lifted an inquiring eyebrow, and Rafe gestured toward the half-empty pitcher of pale draft in front of the salesman. The bartender came across with a pitcher of beer and set it on the table, then dropped a glass in front of Rafe. He was built like a small building, all shoulders and broad, beefy chest and no neck to speak of. A toothpick poked from one corner of his mouth. "This all?"

Rivulets of sweat ran off the pitcher and formed a pool around it, and Rafe swallowed, throat suddenly parched. "Get me another one of those full of ice water," he said tightly. "And another glass."

"Ice water." The bartender shifted the toothpick. "And another glass."

"That's right."

"You expecting company?"

"Could be." Rafe tossed a wrinkled five onto the wet tray. "And how about some peanuts or pretzels to go with that?"

The toothpick moved to the other side of the bartender's mouth and he gave the table a swipe with the dirty wet rag, then moved off, as light as a dancer on small, tidy feet.

Ex-fighter, Rafe found himself thinking. Not someone you want on the other guy's side in a brawl. There'd be heavy iron behind the bar, more than likely. Probably a sawed-off shotgun—something with minimal range but plenty of hitting power. And a baseball bat or ax handle. He looked like the kind of guy who would favor seasoned ash over raw firepower any day.

The pitcher of ice water arrived a minute or two later, frosted with condensation. The bartender set a glass beside the first one, then dropped a basket of pretzels in front of Rafe. "Knock yourself out, sport."

Dawes came in about thirty minutes later. He and the woman stood just inside the door for a moment or two and darted uneasy glances around the dim room, as frightened as mice. Rafe propped himself up on his elbows and unsteadily poured beer into the glass in front of him, managing to spill as much onto the table as he got into the glass. His feigned drunkenness had the effect he wanted. Dawes's gaze lingered for a scant few seconds before moving on, and Rafe felt the muscles across his shoulders relax.

It *was* Dawes, no doubt about that. Rafe had stared at the man's picture every night for two weeks, burning it into his memory, and now that he actually had the man almost within his grasp, he had to fight from walking across and grabbing him by the scruff of his scrawny neck and shaking him until his teeth rattled.

And the woman had to be Honey Divine.

Which was kind of an understatement, Rafe decided with awe.

He realized he was staring and hastily looked away. But then he also realized there wasn't a man in the place who *wasn't* staring at her. Even the drunk at the bar was paying attention, rheumy old eyes aglitter.

She was gorgeous, in a white-trash kind of way. Not the type of woman Rafe normally paid much attention to, but you would have to be a dead man not to notice her. She'd piled her hair onto the top of her head in a butter-blond haystack, probably in an attempt to get cool, and it teetered there precariously, trailing tendrils and wisps she kept brushing back from her cheeks. Her skin was that pale porcelain that seems to glow from some kind of inner light, although she'd managed to dim most of that glow with a thick layer of makeup she had no earthly use for.

Impressive little body, too, clad in electric-blue spandex tights and a long, loose-knit white pullover that kept slipping off first one creamy shoulder, then the other. Although the nightclub poster advertising her as Honey Divine, club singer extraordinaire, had hinted at considerably more than God had given her, without the glittering rhinestone-spangled evening gown, she looked small and tidy and compact, the awe-inspiring cleavage undoubtedly still back in Las Vegas with the costume that had created it.

Rafe had to smile. He'd kind of looked forward to seeing the real thing. Too bad they weren't.

He felt a little pang of disappointment and nearly smiled again, trying not to stare as she followed Dawes toward a table halfway down the room. Every head in the place swiveled as she clattered past on four-inch heels, and he could have sworn he heard a faint, collective sigh as she sat down and the sweater slipped off her shoulder again. She seemed used to it and simply tugged it up again, apparently oblivious to the hormonal havoc she'd left in her wake.

He'd give them five minutes, Rafe decided. Time to order a drink and relax and shake off any last nervousness. Then, as soon as they were off guard and unlikely to bolt for the nearest door, he would make his move.

This was a really *bad* idea.

Meg gave the dim interior of the bar another uneasy look, trying not to panic completely. The whole idea had been crazy to start with, she would admit that, but it had been going fairly well until now. And now…well, now things had completely gotten away from her, and she had absolutely no idea what to do next.

Problem was, she'd done such a good job of convincing Reggie that she knew what she was doing that she'd managed to convince herself, as well. She'd forgotten she was a complete fraud. That she had no training, no backup, no idea of how to pull this off.

"Reggie." Meg took a deep breath. "This is crazy. Tony's man is out there somewhere looking for us. For all we know he could be pulling into the parking lot right now. We should quit while we're ahead and get on a plane and back to Washington before—"

"Not without the disk." Reggie darted an uneasy look around the bar. He looked like a scared gerbil, hair slicked down, Adam's apple bobbing with nervousness, shoulders hunched. "The information on that computer disk is the best bargaining chip I have, Meg. You told me that yourself."

He had her there, Meg thought unhappily. Of course, she'd told him a lot of things. "And if your friend can't make it? If Tony's men found him first?"

"He'll make it," Reggie said stubbornly.

"Presuming you can trust him. Presuming he hasn't—"

''Charlie Oakes is a brother to me,'' Reggie reminded her, as he had about twelve times in the past hour. ''I'd trust him with my life.''

''You *are* trusting him with your life.'' Meg gave the bar another uneasy look. ''Worse, you're trusting him with *mine*.''

''This was your idea.'' Reggie gave her a baleful look.

''No,'' Meg said very reasonably, ''this is not my idea. My *idea* was to fly to Washington and turn you over to the Feds and let *them* get the disk from Charlie Oakes. This—'' she waved her hand to take in the entire bar ''—is *your* idea.''

Reggie just hunched his shoulders a little closer to his ears. ''He'll be here. I told him to meet us here at two-thirty, and it's only ten after. We have plenty of time.''

Plenty of time to get ourselves killed, Meg thought gloomily. How in God's name had she ever talked herself into this crazy plan in the first place? Maybe O'Dell was right. Maybe she wasn't cut out for this kind of work. Maybe she should just—

''I just wish I knew if Honey was okay,'' he fretted. ''Maybe I should call her just to—''

''No!'' Meg winced and lowered her voice. ''Reggie, just one phone call could be enough to jeopardize her life. She's safe with my brother—the guy's a cop, for crying out loud. One of Chicago's finest. No one will get close to her, I promise you that.'' The promise sounded thin to Meg's ears, and she prayed she wasn't lying.

When she'd thought up this lunatic scheme, she'd never given Reggie's pretty young wife much thought. Hadn't given Reggie much thought, for that matter. But now, after two weeks, he was more than just a name on a computer screen. He was flesh and blood, and he was scared. And he trusted her. That was the hardest part.

''You said if I gave O'Dell enough information to bring down not just Tony and the Vegas setup, but Gus Stepino's entire Atlantic City operation, he'd give me whatever I wanted. That he'd put Honey and me into witness protection and get us new lives. Maybe even hire me. You said—''

''I said *maybe* on the job,'' Meg muttered, squirming a little. What had she been *thinking,* telling him something like that?

She'd been frantic to get him to go with her, to believe her, to trust her…and she'd told him whatever he'd wanted to hear. "Reggie, I just said *maybe* on the job, remember. I'm not sure, with your record and all, that…well, that my boss can hire you."

Another lie. Spence O'Dell could hire anyone he damn well pleased, running his mysterious agency seemingly unencumbered by rules or other government meddling. The fact that Reggie had a history of—and a record for—fraud and embezzlement and an assortment of other vagaries didn't come into it at all. Heaven knows, O'Dell had worse working for him.

Her, for instance.

Just the thought nearly made her laugh out loud.

"Twelve more minutes," she said firmly. "If he's not here by two-thirty-two on the dot, we're leaving." To her surprise, he nodded glumly, seemingly impressed by the take-charge authority in her voice.

She looked around the bar again, wondering if the man Tony had sent after them was already here, watching them like a fox watching chickens. The bikers in the far corner had worried her at first, but they seemed oblivious to everyone around them, and she decided finally that they wouldn't be Tony's style. The harried-looking salesman didn't look like much of a threat. He was trying to eat a roast beef sandwich and drink beer and work a calculator and fill in a bunch of forms at the same time, dripping mustard on whatever he was working on. She gave the two farmers a long, hard look, but they didn't look like hired assassins. Nor did the two Native kids playing pool amid much hooting and laughter and good-natured jostling. That left the bartender—who didn't look like someone she'd want to tangle with at the best of times—and the man asleep at the table in the back.

Her heart had nearly stopped when she'd spotted him back there in the shadows. He was tall and wide-shouldered and looked like someone who knew trouble on a first name basis, unmistakably Native with strong, clean-cut features and black hair cut almost severely short. It was his worn leather jacket that had worried her. It was all wrong in this heat and she'd eyed it suspiciously, wondering what kind of weaponry it hid.

But he'd paid no attention to them, and after a couple of

minutes she realized he was too drunk to be a threat to anyone except himself. He was lying across the table, head in a puddle of spilled beer, arms thrown out as though to keep the table from spinning off into space. And for half an instant she almost envied him his complete lack of concern about present, past or future. Especially the future.

Hers seemed to be getting shorter by the minute.

Trying not to fidget, she looked at her watch. "Five more minutes, Reggie."

"He'll be here," he said stubbornly. "You said you'd do this my way if I agreed to come back to Washington with you, remember?"

"And I told you if you didn't come back with me voluntarily, you'd come back in handcuffs." Meg gave him a look she hoped was hard and unforgiving. "My people gave you five thousand dollars on the understanding that you'd bring us the information. And you disappeared, Reggie. With the money. My boss is *not* a happy man."

"I told you I was coming in," he muttered, not quite meeting her eyes. "But I had to make sure Honey was safe first. I—"

"You were making a run for it," Meg said shortly. "You had *two* tickets for Rome in your pocket, Reggie. Not one. Two. I haven't told O'Dell that, because if he finds out you tried to run out on him, he'll kill you himself and save Tony the trouble. I'm giving you the deal of your life, and you know it." Meg gave him her best government-agent glare, not seeing the need to tell him that she hadn't told O'Dell about the tickets because O'Dell didn't know she was here. Didn't know Reggie was here, either. Didn't know about any of it, in fact.

O'Dell thought she was on vacation. In England. Sightseeing. O'Dell did *not* know she was sitting in a smoky bar in the middle of God Knew Where, North Dakota—or maybe it was South Dakota, she was so turned around—with Reggie Dawes more or less in custody, waiting for delivery of a computer disk containing enough information to bring down one of the best-connected mobs on the Eastern Seaboard.

O'Dell was going to kill her.

If one of Tony's people didn't get to her first. If Gus Stepino—Tony's none-too-patient boss in Atlantic City—hadn't found out what was going on and killed her before that. She was going to have to start handing out numbers, she thought a little wildly.

The thought made her swallow hard. "Okay, Reggie. Time's up. We—"

"Excuse me, miss, but you wouldn't happen to have a sister in La Jolla, would you?"

Meg blinked. The salesman had appeared beside the table with no warning at all and was smiling down at her. It was a pleasant, open smile, set in a pleasant, open face, and he had sandy hair and freckles and his eyes were an unremarkable—but pleasant— shade of blue.

"I…what?" She stared up at him, wondering what on earth he was talking about. "La Jolla?"

"Sounds like a bad pickup line, I know," he said with an ingenuous grin, "but I swear you look just like a girl I used to date when I lived in—"

"Hey, anybody gotta match?"

How the man in the leather jacket had gotten from his table to theirs so quickly and silently when he was so drunk, Meg had no idea, but here he was, grinning benignly and a little vaguely at them all. He took an unsteady side step, as though the floor had moved under his feet, and lurched into the salesman, who stepped away with an exclamation of disgust.

"I don't smoke," the salesman said sharply. "Go on back to your table and stop bothering people."

"Not botherin' anyone," the other man said in a soft slur, grinning down at Meg. "I jus' wanna smoke." He held out a cigarette. "Wanna cig'rette?"

"No, thank you," Meg said quietly. "I don't smoke."

He looked perplexed. "Y'don't? How come?"

Meg had to smile. "Can't afford matches."

He looked at her for a moment, then gave a snort of laughter.

"Buzz off!" The salesman knocked the man's hand and the proffered cigarette away from Meg. "She doesn't want a cigarette, and she doesn't want to be bothered by some drunk."

"Not botherin' her," the man said with mild indignation.

"Look, you, I'm going to—"

"He's not bothering me," Meg said a bit sharply, wishing the drunk would wander off and sit down again before the salesman did something stupid. He was making noises like a hero, trying to protect her from some imagined danger, and she felt the old impatience rise. Fought it down as she tried to see past both men to the door beyond. She was starting to feel trapped, unable to see anything, her view of the door blocked by broad shoulders. Reggie felt it, too, and was shifting uneasily in his chair, as though getting ready to bolt.

"See?" The drunk smiled broadly at the salesman. "She says I'm not botherin' her."

"But maybe you should sit down," Meg said gently. "You don't look too…steady."

The grin widened, jaunty and irreverent and utterly charming. "A li'l drunk's all."

In spite of herself, Meg had to laugh. "Yeah, I can see that." The bartender had come around from behind his bar and was standing there, poised and ready, watching them intently. Meg shook her head very slightly and he relaxed after a heartbeat, then went back behind the bar, still watchful.

"Look, chief," the salesman said congenially, "take this and buy yourself some beer, all right?" He tucked a crumpled ten-dollar bill into the man's shirt pocket.

"Hey." The man plucked the money out of his pocket and gazed at it wonderingly, staggering a little to one side.

"Now, as I was saying," the salesman continued smoothly, turning back toward Meg, "you look just like this girl I used to know. Let me give you my card and I'll—" He started reaching inside his jacket, and in that moment, all hell broke loose.

Meg didn't even see what started it. One instant she was just sitting there, and the next the salesman went flying off to one side, the gun in his hand spinning away. Meg just gaped at it uncomprehendingly as it arced through the air in a perfect parabola, and she found herself wondering where on earth it had come from and why she felt so calm and why Reggie was shouting at her to get down, get down, get down…

In the end, she didn't have a choice. A large hand fit itself around the back of her neck and shoved, and the next thing she knew she was flat on her belly in a puddle of what she prayed was spilled beer, the wind knocked completely out of her. The big round table followed, landing on its side with a crash that nearly deafened her, wooden chairs and beer glasses and pretzels cascading across the floor. People were shouting and then she heard shots—two, one right after the other—and she gulped for air, blinded by tendrils of hair as the wig slipped, groping for her small handbag.

All wrong, she thought dizzily, this was going all wrong. *She* was supposed to be the one with the gun. She was supposed to be protecting Reggie, supposed to be—

Another two shots. Wood splintered right above her head and she sucked in a startled breath. Reggie…oh, God, where was Reggie…?

Frantic and completely disoriented, she started to sit up, desperate to find her handbag and the gun, desperate to—

''Stay—*down!*'' Another hand, or perhaps it was the same one, landed between her shoulder blades and shoved her flat, making her wheeze, and then someone was firing right above her head. It was heavy firepower and she could tell by the way the shots were spaced that whoever was using it was an expert, and then a beer glass lying just to her left exploded into shards and she recoiled with a yelp as broken glass sprayed around her.

Another shot, this one even closer, and suddenly something massive and heavy landed across her, driving the rest of her breath out of her in a gasp. She could smell leather and beer and cigarettes as the man's jacket fell open around her, wrapping her in his heat, and she tried to suck in her breath to scream for Reggie.

More shouts, crashes. A shotgun blast roared to her left, deafeningly close, and then, abruptly, there was utter silence. She could hear someone swearing a little distance away, and the rasp of someone's breathing against her ear. And slowly, she started to collect her wits.

Whoever was lying on top of her was heavy, all solid muscle and meat pressed a little too intimately against the full length of her body. She could feel his heart hammering against her back and wondered dizzily what on earth *he* was scared about, considering he was the one with the gun and she was the one lying flat on her face on a bar floor, unarmed and dazed, not having a clue what was happening.

"Reggie?" Her voice was just a wheezy squeak. She turned her head, but the blasted wig had tumbled down over her eyes and she couldn't see a thing.

"I'm okay." Reggie sounded shocked and scared. "I'm okay."

"All right, you jokers," someone bellowed above them. "Onto your feet, all of you! This is my bar, by God, and no one comes in here and starts shooting it up, understand me?"

"Meg? Miss Kavanagh? A-are you all right?"

"Yeah." At least she thought she was, Meg decided dimly. She was completely paralyzed, but nothing hurt outrageously and she didn't seem to be gushing blood all over the place. Of course, it was a little hard to tell, with this *behemoth* on top of her. She gave her head a slight shake, and the wig tipped even more precariously.

This hadn't been in the plan. Not a shoot-out in a Dakota bar with some unknown assailant. Not being pinned to the floor under about a ton of human male—who, by the way, didn't seem to be in any kind of hurry to get off her. Not completely losing control of things like this...

She rammed her elbow into the nearest part of the behemoth's anatomy and was rewarded by a grunt of pain. "Get *off* me, damn it! I'm a government agent and you're under arrest!"

This wasn't going according to plan, Rafe thought irritably as the slender female form under him gave another wriggle. Under different circumstances it wouldn't have been that unpleasant, but it wasn't doing much at the moment but distracting him. And he was getting the hell beat out of him, into the bargain. She had the sharpest elbows he'd ever encountered in his life, and seemed to have no qualms about using them enthusiastically. Plus, she kept yelling something about arresting him, which didn't make a lot of sense considering he was on top and had the gun.

She gave another muffled threat of some kind or another, but he ignored it, swearing through clenched teeth as she buried her elbow into his solar plexus. He wasn't getting paid enough for this, he thought wearily. No way was he getting paid enough.

"Okay, you jokers—I said on your feet! And keep those hands and guns where I can see 'em, 'cause this here shotgun can make an awful big hole in a man."

Rafe sighed. Maybe he was losing his touch. Maybe it was time to find a new line of work, because nothing about this whole case had come even close to going the way he'd planned it.

"Okay, okay," he growled, planting both hands flat on the floor where the bartender could see them. "Where's the guy who was shooting at me?"

"Down," the bartender said succinctly. "Bleeding all over my floor. You going to pay to have that cleaned up?"

"Yeah, yeah, I'll pay, I'll pay." Rafe swore under his breath again. "I'm going to get up now, so keep your finger off that damn trigger."

"Just don't give me no reason to do otherwise," the bartender rumbled. "Come up slow. That skinny little runt down there beside you have a gun?"

"N-no," Reggie stammered. "I—I'm an accountant."

Rafe didn't see where that made a difference, but it seemed to satisfy the bartender, who motioned Reggie up with the barrel of the shotgun. Honey Divine was still wriggling and swearing underneath him, and Rafe eased himself off her gingerly, wondering how long it would take the bruises on his ribs to fade.

The bartender was watching him intently, and Rafe got up slowly, hands well outstretched, giving the man no reason to feel threatened. "I'm a cop," he lied. "ID in my hip pocket."

The bartender gestured with the shotgun. "Get it out. Slow."

Rafe reached behind him and under the jacket slowly. The Taurus brushed his fingertips but he left it there, easing his wallet from his jeans pocket instead. He held it up, then flipped it open and tossed it onto the nearest upright table. The bartender picked it up, read it, looked at the ID picture and then at Rafe, then nodded after a moment and lowered the shotgun. "Nevada? You're a long way from home."

"Special assignment," Rafe lied without missing a beat. According to that forged ID he was with the sheriff's department.

"And this guy?" The gun barrel gestured toward the salesman. He was sitting on the floor looking rumpled and sullen, clutching his upper arm with his hand. Blood trickled through his fingers.

"No damn idea," Rafe replied quite honestly. He gave the man a long, hard look, running the bland features through a mental mug book. Nothing. Whoever the guy was, he was new to the equation.

The bartender grunted. "So he just started shooting at you for no reason at all, is that what you're saying?"

"He wasn't shooting at me, he was shooting at *him*." Rafe nodded toward Reggie, who was still sitting on the floor looking shaken and pale.

"And you decided to do your civic duty and stop it."

The bartender sounded skeptical and bored with the whole thing, and Rafe sighed again, deciding it was time for a bit of embroidery. "I was sent here to bring this man back to Nevada." He gave Reggie another nod. "There's a warrant out on him. Fraud and embezzlement."

The bartender grunted again. "What did he do?"

"Scammed a whole lot of little old ladies out of their life savings."

Reggie gave an indignant yelp of protest.

"Which doesn't explain why someone was trying to kill him."

"If someone scammed your old granny out of her life savings, wouldn't you be out for blood?" It sounded so plausible, Rafe almost believed it himself.

"That's absolutely preposterous!" Honey Divine had managed to catch her breath finally and was sitting flat on her bottom on the floor, glaring through tangles of hair, one shoulder distractingly bare. She pulled the sweater up impatiently, then shoved the mound of blond hair out of her eyes. "Mr. Dawes has done no such thing!"

The bartender lifted an eyebrow. "And you are…?"

"Special Agent Mary Margaret Kavanagh," she enunciated

very clearly into the expectant silence. Her hair had tipped over one eye again and she gave it a shove, then swore with unlady-like exasperation and reached up and pulled it off entirely.

"He scalped her!" The drunk at the bar—who apparently hadn't moved throughout the entire melee—stared at her in stupefaction. "The Indian scalped her!"

Rafe gave the man an evil glare that made him recoil, and the bartender just snapped, "Shut up, Claude," without even turning around. But even he seemed taken aback at the sight of a woman sitting on his barroom floor with her hair in her hand. "Special...what?"

She gave her head a shake and her own hair—masses of it, tangled and as red as a fire engine—tumbled around her face. Then she got to her feet, teetering a trifle unsteadily on those four-inch heels, retrieved her small handbag and rummaged through it. "Special Agent Kavanagh," she repeated impatiently. "And Mr. Dawes is in *my* custody." She found what she was looking for and pulled it out, walking across to hand it to the bartender. "You can call the number there on my ID and confirm it."

Rafe looked at her, narrow-eyed. "If you're FBI, lady, I'm Clark Kent."

"I'm not FBI," she said crisply. "I'm with a special agency that specializes in—" She stopped and glared at him. "Who did you say you were?"

Rafe paused very slightly, selecting and rejecting a dozen explanations in the space of a heartbeat, trying to fix on the one that would get him out of here with the least amount of trouble and explanation. Government agent. Just his damn luck. What the hell else could go wrong today?

"His ID makes him for a Nevada cop," the bartender spoke up.

"I doubt that." She looked at Rafe evenly. "I'd be very surprised if you're in law enforcement, Mr....?"

Again, he thought it through. "Blackhorse," he replied after a moment, deciding this much truth couldn't get him into too much trouble. "Rafe Blackhorse."

"And you're obviously not drunk."

Rafe managed a tight smile. "Wallpaper."

"Excuse me?"

"People see a drunk Indian, they don't see him at all. He blends into the scenery, like wallpaper. It makes for good… camouflage."

"That's very cynical, Mr. Blackhorse."

Rafe smiled coolly. "Just experience, Agent Kavanagh."

Her eyes narrowed very slightly. "You're the man who's been following us."

Reggie Dawes made a gurgling sound.

"That's right," Rafe said after a split second, deciding to stick to the truth as far as he could. It was hard to concentrate, with those aquamarine eyes locked on his, but he forced himself to hold her gaze. "I'm taking Dawes back to Nevada."

Another gurgle from Dawes.

The woman simply smiled. "I don't know what the Nevada sheriff's department wants with Mr. Dawes, but they'll have to take it up with the Justice Department."

"Tony sent him," Dawes piped up from somewhere behind Rafe. "And this guy over here…this guy's from Atlantic City."

Special Agent Mary Margaret Kavanagh said a word that Rafe was pretty sure wasn't in any special agent manual. She stepped by him and walked across to where Dawes was peering down at the salesman from a safe distance.

"His name's Pags Pagliano, and he's muscle for the Atlantic City operation."

"One of Gus Stepino's men?"

Dawes nodded, Adam's apple bobbing wildly. He was pale and damp, and he swallowed audibly. "Th-that means he got tired of waiting for Tony to take care of it and sent his own guy after me."

"Terrific." Kavanagh did not look happy.

And Rafe had to sympathize. If Stepino's men got Dawes first, he was out a cool thirty grand.

"We're leaving," she said abruptly. "Now."

"Not with Dawes, you're not," Rafe told her flatly.

Kavanagh looked around at him coolly and opened her mouth

to reply when Dawes stepped in front of her. "W-what about Charlie?"

The salesman—Pagliano—snorted. "Don't hold your breath waiting for him to turn up, Reggie."

"You killed him?" Dawes's voice ended on a squeak.

Pagliano just smiled a feral little smile. "Your best friend sold you out. Three grand, Reggie. That's all you're worth, can you believe it?" The smile widened. "Gus would have paid ten times that, but Charlie's such a moron he only asked for three." He gave another snort and shook his head in disgust. "Moron."

Dawes looked sick. "I don't believe you. Charlie wouldn't do that."

"How do you think I found you so quick? You think I stumbled into this little rat hole out here in Nowhere, North Dakota, by accident?" His tone made it clear he didn't think Charlie Oakes was the only moron of his acquaintance.

Kavanagh had gone a shade or two paler herself, and Rafe wondered how long she'd been on the job. First solo case, maybe. Which could mean she would be easy to bluff, if he played his cards right. But it could also mean she might not bluff at all, too worried about getting it right, about making points with her boss, to risk messing up. He swore, using another word or two that wouldn't show up in any government manual.

"Well, Agent Kavanagh," he said carelessly, "I'll leave Pagliano in your capable hands while I get Dawes back to—"

"Not on your life." She turned those amazing aquamarine eyes onto him again. "I don't know who you are, Mr. Blackhorse, but I doubt very much you have ever worked for Nevada law enforcement. And you're not taking Reggie Dawes anywhere."

"You don't think he's a cop?" The bartender swung the barrel of the shotgun almost casually toward Rafe.

"I'd be very surprised, but I'll let your sheriff sort it out. Tell him we'll be in contact."

The bartender blinked. "Where are you going to be?"

"En route to Washington." She shoved her ID back into her handbag, then pulled out a business card and a pen and started writing something on the back of the card. "When the sheriff gets here, have him call this man at this number. He'll verify everything I've told you and will arrange for someone to come out and collect Pagliano. He can deal with Mr. Blackhorse then. And call an ambulance for Mr. Pagliano, will you? I'd like him alive when we try him for attempted murder.''

Rafe managed not to swear out loud. So much for wondering what else could go wrong. ''Look, honey, this isn't—''

''Special Agent Kavanagh,'' she said crisply. ''Honey Divine is Mr. Dawes's wife.''

''That's not what—'' He caught himself. Just about the last thing he needed right now was a lecture on political correctness.

''Hold it!'' The bartender's voice rattled a nearby tray of glasses. ''Nobody's goin' nowhere till Sheriff Haney gets here. I'll let *him* figure out which of you's telling the truth and which ain't.''

''Oh, for—'' Kavanagh caught herself, eyes glittering with subdued anger. ''All right. Fine. Have it your way.''

Rafe eased his breath out on a long, weary sigh, thinking of his thirty thousand dollars winging its way south even as he was standing there. It had sounded like easy money—once.

Chapter 2

It took pretty much the whole day and a multitude of lengthy phone calls to convince Sheriff Dobbes Haney that she wasn't kidnapping Reggie, that the Beretta in her handbag was registered, and that she wasn't wanted on a half-dozen warrants for who knows what kind of mayhem. And that Special Agent Mary Margaret Kavanagh was, indeed, exactly who she said she was. He didn't seem happy about it. And after the last phone call, this one to Virginia, during which he seemed to do more listening than talking, he was even less so. But he did finally tell her she was free to go about her business. Suggesting—strongly— that she do whatever it was Special Agents from unspecified offices in Virginia do outside *his* jurisdiction.

That was fine by Meg. She couldn't get far enough away fast enough.

But by then it had been almost eight o'clock, too late to do anything but drive to the nearest town big enough to have an airport of any size and wait for the earliest flight eastbound.

Which was why she was sitting in a cheap motel room at a little after midnight, listening to Reggie brush his teeth in the bathroom between their connecting rooms and wondering what in heaven's name she was doing with her life.

Maybe her sister was right, and this obsession about finding Bobby's killer was getting out of hand. She could be married right now. Was *supposed* to be married right now. Living in Marblehead in a big overwrought Tudor, discussing lawns with the landscaping people and wallpaper with the interior decorator and choosing names for their first child. If she'd married six months ago, as planned, this would be a suite at a luxurious hotel, not a ratty room in the Dewdrop Inn. And the man brushing his teeth in the bathroom wouldn't be a skinny little accountant for the mob, but Royce Bennett Packard of Packard Industries.

Meg closed her eyes and tried to conjure up the image of Royce brushing his teeth, to no avail. *Did* Royce brush his teeth? She imagined he must, they were such perfect teeth. Like everything about Royce—the country club tan, the health club physique, the gentleman's club portfolio. Not a hair, a molar or an investment out of place.

She wondered, very idly, what he would have thought if he'd seen her today. Not just the spandex and the wig and the four-inch heels—those would have rendered him speechless on the spot. But the rest of it: her lying flat on her belly on a barroom floor in the middle of a gunfight, a fifteen-round semiautomatic Beretta pistol in her handbag and a hundred and eighty pounds of good-looking Nevada cop on top of her.

Not pleased, she decided. Royce's vision of the future Mrs. Packard did not include guns, bullets or cops of any variety.

And then, to her annoyance, she found herself thinking about that good-looking Nevada cop. If that's what he was—the cop part, not the good-looking part. As skeptical as she was about the first, the second was beyond argument.

The last she'd seen of Rafe Blackhorse, Haney had told him to park himself in a chair and wait, and Blackhorse had done just that. He'd apparently spent the afternoon asleep in a wooden chair that he'd tipped back against the wall in the booking room, long legs stretched out, booted feet resting comfortably on a desk, ankles crossed, looking as relaxed as a cat.

"Miss Kavanagh?"

Meg looked up as Reggie poked his head hesitantly into her room.

"My pajamas are in my other suitcase, and it's in the car."

"Forget it, Reggie. You're not setting foot outside this motel until tomorrow morning."

He managed to look both contrite and indignant. "But I always sleep in pajamas."

"Well, you're not sleeping in pajamas tonight."

"But—"

"Reggie, we nearly got killed this afternoon because of you, so I'm not feeling as generous as I could be, all right? No pajamas."

"It's not my fault we nearly got killed," he said prissily. "You *are* supposed to be protecting me, after all. It was up to you to—"

"All right!" Meg threw her hands up to stop him. "All right, I'll *get* your pajamas!" She got to her feet and grabbed the car keys from the nightstand, then paused and turned back to the bed and dug the Beretta from under the pillow. She tucked it into the back waistband of her jeans and headed for the door, jabbing her finger at Reggie as she walked by him. "You sit down and stay out of trouble. I've told the manager if he puts through any calls from either of these rooms without my go-ahead, I'll have his head on a plate. So don't even *think* about trying to contact Honey. And I'll be just outside, so there's no point in trying to make a run for it."

He looked hurt. "I wouldn't do that."

"In a pig's eye you wouldn't," she replied uncharitably. "I wish you'd get it into your head that Spence O'Dell is your only hope of getting out of this alive, Reggie. But if you make another run for it, he'll let Stepino kill you just on principle and make his case some other way."

Leaving him standing there to mull this over, she turned off the lights both inside and outside the room, then pulled open the door and stepped out into the cold North Dakota night. She closed the door behind her and stepped well away from it, tucking herself into the shadows under the open stairway to the second story. There were a handful of cars in the parking lot and she scanned the dimly lit area for movement.

She'd been careful when she'd found this place, doubling back a couple of times, keeping Reggie out of sight when she'd registered and telling the manager she was traveling with her senile old aunt, which explained the no-phone rule. She'd taken every precaution in the book, but she was still jumpy as she eyed the parked cars.

Pagliano had almost gotten them that afternoon because she'd been careless. That wouldn't happen again, but Pagliano wouldn't be the only hired gun out here on Reggie's trail. Gus Stepino obviously figured that Tony Ruffio and *his* hired gun weren't up to the job and was taking care of it himself. So odds were there were others out here hunting for Dawes, all working independently, all stone killers, all very, very good at what they did.

She, on the other hand, had the requisite month of generic agency training under her belt, plus another month of field agent training done on the sly and without O'Dell's knowledge. Had this been an authorized assignment, she would be out here with no less than six months of special training behind her, and she sure wouldn't be alone. She would be with at least two others, relegated to fetching coffee and standing guard while learning everything she could.

If she didn't get herself or anyone else killed after a few of those jobs, and if O'Dell was in an expansive mood, she might then be assigned as second agent on a case, working closely with a mentor who would be testing her every step of the way, watching for weakness, for flaws, for anything that could be a problem. And after maybe a year of that, if she was very good and very lucky and was still alive and still interested, she *might* get assigned a solo job.

Might, because regardless of how good she was, she was still a woman. And O'Dell didn't like women field agents.

There had been two in twenty years. Now there were none. And O'Dell made no bones about the fact that he intended to keep it that way.

Which was why she was out there half trained and without a

clue, determined to prove she could handle the job if it killed her.

Bad choice of words. Meg shook her head and gave the parking lot another searching look, then walked across to her rental, wishing she had eyes in the back of her head. No wonder Bobby used to be so darned jumpy when he was home. Now and again she had walked up on him without warning and he'd nearly leapt out of his own skin, hand going instinctively to where his gun would be had their father allowed them in the house. Now Bobby was dead, and she was the one leaping at shadows. Little wonder everyone wished she would marry Royce Packard and concentrate on charity luncheons and babies.

She unlocked the trunk of the car and raised the lid. Reggie's suitcase had slid toward the back and she couldn't reach it without practically crawling in after it. She rested one knee on the bumper and leaned way forward, balanced precariously on her belly and one braced arm, wondering for the umpty-millionth time why everyone in her family had inherited their father's height except her. Bobby used to say it was because she was the youngest and by the time she was born, all the tall genes had been used up. And Maureen always said—

"That's one hell of a tantalizing view, Special Agent Mary Margaret Kavanagh. But if I were one of Stepino's men, you'd be as dead as last night's halibut."

For his pains, Rafe damn near lost her.

One instant she was teetering over the lip of the car trunk, rounded little bottom upthrust and perfectly showcased by the loving caress of soft denim and moonlight. And in the next, she'd shot off sideways, moving faster than he'd ever seen a woman move.

He caught her, but not without effort, and he swore savagely at himself as he fought her up against the side of the car, where she couldn't turn on him. Mistakes like that could get a man real dead, and he didn't like what it said about his concentration. This whole job had been a series of mistakes from beginning to end, and if he ever got Dawes to Las Vegas and got his thirty grand, he was going to call it quits for a while, because he was by God losing his touch.

Kavanagh was struggling like a tiger, but he had the advantage of surprise, weight and height, and she wasn't getting very far. He'd wedged her against the side of the car where she had no room to fight, and had shoved one foot between hers and forced her legs apart. He'd pressed his forearm diagonally across her chest, holding her against the car, and had wrapped his hand around her throat so she was instinctively focused on prying his fingers away from her windpipe instead of trying to claw his eyes out, which he suspected would be her first choice if he gave her time to think about it.

She was panting for breath and he could feel her heart pounding against his arm, the pulse in her throat racing under his fingers. "I'm not here to hurt you," he told her quietly. "Quit fighting and I'll let you go."

The moonlight made her eyes glitter and he nearly smiled at the ferocious anger in them. "You're outgunned, honey. Give it up. I caught you fair and square."

She gave another furious wriggle and he just leaned against her slightly, rocking his left thigh against her pelvis so she was pinned against the car. He smiled down into her eyes. "You're the most fun I've had standing up in a long time, Irish. Keep wiggling around like that and we could be well on our way to a second date before we've even traded phone numbers."

She went as still as stone. And as pliant. Every inch of her— and there weren't that many—was nearly vibrating with outrage, and again he found himself nearly overwhelmed with the urge to laugh.

"Let. Go. Of. Me." The words held raw fury, but she *had* stopped wiggling around, to his faint regret. She was standing very still now, eyes snapping with rage, all fear long gone. "If you don't let me go, you're going to spend the rest of your eternal life in the worst, rat-infested prison in—"

"Where's your gun?" he interrupted calmly.

She stopped in midthreat. "What?"

"Gun. Beretta, if I overheard Haney right. Where is it?"

"Inside."

But she said it a bit too quickly, and he just smiled down at her tolerantly. "I don't think so, Irish." Slowly, he ran his free hand down her flank, fingertips brushing hot, bare flesh where her sweatshirt had ridden up. It made his belly tighten and he smiled as he moved his hand down her stomach and thigh, back up again.

She wasn't hiding anything in those jeans but a well-placed dimple or two, he was already sure of that. He settled his hand on her bare waist, wondering if he wasn't perhaps enjoying this just a little too much, and ran the flat of his palm up and around her rib cage. Her skin was hot velvet and she started to fight, then thought better of it and went still again, small chin set with anger.

The gun was in the small of her back, the metal warm to his touch, and he eased it free of her waistband. "Okay," he told her agreeably as he eased his weight away from her. "I'm going to let you go, and I don't want you doing anything reckless. I don't want to hurt you, but I'm sure not going to stand here and let you try to rip out my eyeballs, either."

She smiled malevolently. "It wasn't your *eyeballs* I was thinking of ripping out, Mr. Blackhorse."

In spite of himself, he gave a snort of laughter. "You've got brass ones, lady, I'll give you that much. But I'll still break your arm if you try anything stupid."

He could see her thinking it over, testing the threat for truth, anger and resentment warring with good sense. He held her there a moment or two longer, until he could tell by her eyes that good sense was winning, then he released her abruptly and stepped well back, bracing himself.

There was a heartbeat of time when Meg actually contemplated going for him. But she took a deep, ragged breath of cold air instead and forced herself to stay where she was, her desire to maim him for life counterbalanced by an equally strong desire to stay alive. There was something about the cool watchfulness in those dark eyes that made her think his threat to break her arm wasn't entirely idle.

So she satisfied herself with swearing at him instead, calling him a couple of choice things, not surprised when he didn't turn a hair. By the look of him, he'd been called worse over the years. She tugged her sweatshirt down and combed her hair back with her fingers, praying he couldn't see how badly her hands were shaking. "Was there a point to this exercise, or is being obnoxious something you do for fun?"

To her annoyance, he just grinned lazily. "Well, I can't say it *hasn't* been fun." The grin widened suggestively and he let his gaze rove from hair to ankle and slowly back up again. Then his eyes met hers, cool again. "But, yeah, there's a point. I want Dawes."

Meg just stared at him. Then she snorted. "Yeah, well, I want world peace and a cure for cancer, Mr. Blackhorse, but I don't see *them* happening tonight, either. Reggie Dawes is in *my* custody. If you want him, you're going to have to take your turn. You can put in a request with my boss and maybe in fifty years—when we're through with him—you can take him back to wherever it is you're from."

"Nevada."

"Whatever." She put her hand out. "My weapon, please."

His smile was pleasant. "I don't think so. Not until I have Dawes."

"You're not getting Dawes."

"Yep." He shoved her Beretta into his belt. "I am." Then he turned and walked toward the motel room door.

Short of bringing him down with a volley of bad language, there was nothing Meg could do but scramble after him. He turned the knob and shoved the door open, and Meg found herself holding her breath, but Reggie was nowhere to be seen and the connecting door between the rooms was closed. Blackhorse stepped inside and Meg came in on his heels, not giving him a chance to lock her out.

Think! Damn it, no agent of O'Dell's would just stand by and let this happen. Then again, no agent of O'Dell's would have been caught as easily as she'd been, either.

"Where were you hiding?" she asked very casually, her mind going like a windmill. "Just for future reference."

"Halfway up the stairs," he said just as casually, giving the room a quick but thorough glance. "You're new at this secret agent stuff, aren't you?"

"What makes you think that?" Her voice was sharper than she'd intended.

"No other explanation for why you're still alive."

"I stayed one step ahead of you for a week," she said with annoyance. "So I can't be that bad."

"I didn't say you were *bad*." His gaze held hers momentarily. "Just inexperienced. You looked around you out there, but you never looked up. I was right above you the whole time. If I'd been on Stepino's payroll, I'd have taken you out with one shot to the head."

Meg swallowed, knowing he was right but resenting the fact that he took it so matter-of-factly. *I* am *inexperienced,* she felt like shouting at him. *So give me a break! Let me take Reggie back to the people who want him so my boss will let me be one of his agents and I can find out who killed my brother!*

Did any of O'Dell's agents get what they wanted by bursting into tears when things got tough?

The thought almost made her laugh. O'Dell's agents, to a man, were walking advertisements for testosterone and macho heroics. Bullets and balls, the old agency joke went.

"So, where is the little guy?"

"He's not here," Meg said instantly, praying that Reggie was listening from the other room and had the sense to hide. "I'm not as inexperienced as you seem to think I am. Reggie's in a safe place. Sorry to have led you on this wild-goose chase, but that *was* the point." She smiled ingenuously, praying he took the bait.

And for a moment she thought he might. He glanced around the room again, frowning now, looking undecided. Then he shook his head. "No, I don't think so, Special Agent Mary Margaret Kavanagh—that's a hell of a mouthful, by the way. Mind if I just call you Irish for short?"

He was prowling now, peering in the closet, behind the drapes, glancing around at her now and again as though not entirely sure she wasn't going to haul out a Mack Ten and start blasting away at him. Meg watched him silently, heart hammering against her ribs as she strolled casually toward the table where her handbag lay.

"You wouldn't let the little weasel out of your sight, for one thing," Blackhorse was saying. "And for another, I was on your tail ten minutes after you left Haney's office, and you came straight here."

"You weren't on my tail."

He just shrugged. "You were good, I'll give you credit. Better than most, in fact. If you don't get yourself killed before you get some experience under your belt, you'll be pretty damn good."

"I am pretty damn good."

"You're not bad." He smiled as he said it, swinging his head around to look at her. His gaze drifted to her handbag, maybe three feet away now. "You wouldn't have another gun in that thing, would you?"

Meg let her eyes widen with innocence. "Of course not."

He laughed. "I'll tell you one thing for nothing, Irish—you can't lie for spit. That's something you're going to have to work on if you want to be successful at this secret agent business."

"Will you stop calling me a secret agent!" Trying to distract him from the handbag, she strode across the room angrily. "I'm a government agent! Law enforcement of sorts. Or at least a lot closer to it than you are."

"Uh-huh." He didn't seem impressed. "Well, let's see what you've got in here." Still keeping an eye on her, he grabbed her bag and upended it over the bed. A variety of things spilled across the faded bedspread, but the thing both of them looked at for a silent moment was the small, satin-blue Targa semiautomatic pistol.

Rafe smiled. He looked at Kavanagh, but she just gazed back at him stonily, and he wondered what other armament she had stashed throughout the room. He took a couple of steps backward and rapped on the connecting door. "Come out of there, Dawes." Silence answered him and he hammered his fist against it. "I said come out, Dawes."

"He's halfway to Canada by now," Kavanagh said impatiently. "Once he knew you were here, he'd have been out the door and gone."

Rafe ignored her and tested the knob on the connecting door.

It turned easily and he pushed the door open gingerly. The other room was pitch-dark, drapes drawn, lights off. The back of his neck prickled and he gave the door a shove with the toe of his boot. "Dawes? I know you're in there, so stop playing games and—"

He sensed more than actually saw something move in the darkness, something coming straight at him, and he recoiled instinctively. The suitcase flew by him, inches from his face, and Rafe swore and dropped like a stone, grabbing for the Beretta even as his mind took in two separate images: Reggie Dawes taking aim with another suitcase, and Kavanagh diving for the gun on the bed.

He took Dawes out first, ducking under the suitcase that came cartwheeling through the doorway and grabbing the little guy by the front of his T-shirt. Dawes gave a squeak of terror as Rafe pulled him into Kavanagh's room, then shoved him ferociously. Dawes hit the wall with a thump and slowly slid to the floor, eyes glazed, down for the count. And in the same motion, using the momentum to spin him around, Rafe had the Beretta out and aimed.

And found himself staring into the barrel of the Targa. She'd landed on the bed on her shoulder and had rolled onto the floor, snatching up the small gun as she did so. And now she was kneeling between the bed and the wall, looking a little pale, as though unnerved by her own wild heroics. But unnerved or not, her hands were rock-steady. That damned pistol was aimed square at his chest, and it didn't waver so much as a hair.

"Okay." He blew out a tight breath and straightened very slowly, the Beretta trained on her. "This could get interesting."

"Put the gun down."

He very nearly laughed. "I was going to say the same thing."

"I'm not playing around here!"

Rafe let his smile fade deliberately. "Honey, neither am I." He let her think about it. "I know you think you're doing the right thing, Irish, but you're way out of your league here. Put the gun down, come out from behind there, and we'll talk."

She gave him a searing look, but did get to her feet and walk around the end of the bed, her weapon still aimed at his chest. "I won't ask you again to put that gun down."

He smiled coolly. "You haven't got the stones to kill a man in cold blood, Irish. I'll bet you've never even fired that thing at anything but a paper target." It was a wild guess, but he could tell the instant the words were out of his mouth that he was right.

Faint apprehension flickered across her face, gone in an instant under steely determination. "There has to be a first time."

"Do you have any idea what it's like to kill a man, Irish?" he asked softly. "Ever seen what a bullet can do to a human body at this range?" He dared to take a step closer to her. "Know what it's like to look in a man's eyes and watch the life leak out of him?"

"One more step, and we'll both get the lesson of a lifetime."

Rafe smiled again. "You're not going to pull that trigger, sweetheart, and we both know it. No way you're going to kill me."

Her eyes narrowed very slightly and Rafe's heart stopped.

Then she took a deep, unsteady breath. "Well, maybe not." She looked at him thoughtfully. Then, without shifting her gaze from his, she dropped her aim with unnerving swiftness to a point about eight inches below his belt buckle. "But I bet I can hurt you bad enough that you'd wish I had."

Rafe felt his belly constrict and had to fight to keep from dropping his hand protectively over his groin.

The apprehension in her eyes had turned cool. "Put the weapon down, Mr. Blackhorse. If you're the legitimate cop you'd have me believe, you're not going to shoot me, either."

"And if I'm not?" He said it belligerently, wishing—not for the first time today—that he'd never left Bear Mountain. No amount of money was worth this kind of aggravation.

Kavanagh lifted one delicate eyebrow and smiled. "Then, Mr. Blackhorse, I'd say the question isn't whether or not you're going to kill me, but whether you can kill me quickly enough to keep my finger from pulling this trigger as I'm going down and doing you a very painful and extremely inopportune injury."

Rafe nearly winced. He was tempted to just walk across and

grab the Targa out of her hands and have done with it. Odds were she wouldn't shoot, but then again...if that gun went off— even accidentally—the damage would be a hell of a lot more than just *inopportune*.

Swearing under his breath, he swung the Beretta away from her. He cleared the chamber and released the clip, and tossed both onto the table nearby.

She didn't lower her own weapon so much as an inch. "Take the other weapon out of the holster under your left arm and put it on the table as well, please."

Rafe thought of arguing with her, then just did as she asked, staring at her challengingly as the Taurus landed on the table beside the Beretta.

"Thank you." She smiled a disarmingly sweet smile. "Now take the other gun out and put it on the table with the others, please."

"Other gun?"

"The Smith & Wesson, Mr. Blackhorse. It's in the waistband of your jeans in the small of your back, and I'd like it on the table."

Rafe's teeth grated together and he balked for a moment, then swore savagely and wrenched the weapon from his jeans and put it on the growing pile of hardware. He held his arms out to either side, forcing himself to smile. "Anything else you'd like me to take off?"

"I guess that would depend on whether or not you have anything else I'd be interested in seeing."

He let the smile widen and dropped one hand to his belt buckle. "Guess there's one way to find out."

She smiled tolerantly. "Don't think a threat to drop your jeans is going to get me so flustered you can get this gun away from me, Mr. Blackhorse. I have five brothers, and I can assure you that I'm immune to adolescent male humor."

Rafe was half tempted to call her bluff but then had the distinct feeling that all he would accomplish was making himself look like twelve kinds of a fool. This day had gone badly enough already without winding up standing there with his jeans around his ankles and a gun pointed at the part of his anatomy nearest and dearest to him.

He contemplated a half-dozen options, discarding all of them as too risky. Which was pretty ridiculous, considering he wasn't up against a handful of Navy Seals or a squad of Green Berets but one small, very inexperienced government agent. He remembered what she'd felt like in his hands out by the car, all soft curves and satin skin and lithe muscle. Easy prey. He should have taken her out by now. Should be halfway back to Las Vegas with Reggie Dawes. Money in the bank. He eased his weight onto his left foot, trying to make it look casual.

Reggie moaned just then and she looked at him with concern. "Reg, are you all right?"

And, in the end, it was just that easy. Distracted, she let her attention waver for just that critical instant, and that was all it took. Rafe pivoted on his left foot and brought his right up high and fast, knocking the gun cleanly out of her hand, then swung around to grab her by the wrist before she could go after it. She responded faster than he'd anticipated and he nearly got a karate chop across the face for his trouble, but he blocked the blow awkwardly.

"Damn you!"

She sounded more astonished than dangerous, and Rafe had to grin. "That's lesson number two, Irish. When you've got your gun on a man, *never* take your eyes off him."

"A mistake I won't make twice," she said through gritted teeth.

Rafe's eyes narrowed as he watched her trying to decide what to do next. Oddly, he found himself hoping she wouldn't try anything, because if they kept this up long enough he was going to hurt her without even meaning to, and that seemed like a shame. "If I was serious about taking you out, sweetheart, you wouldn't get a second chance. Just what agency *are* you working for, anyway?"

"Does it matter?" She gave her head a toss to get a tangle of hair out of her eyes, scanning the room, looking for the advantage he had no intention of letting her have.

"Whoever it is, they have no damn business sending you out

solo before you're ready. Or are they *trying* to get you killed? Is that it? You tick someone off who wants a little payback?''

''Miss Kavanagh?'' Reggie sat up just then, blinking blearily and rubbing the back of his head. ''Miss Kavanagh, did you hit me?''

''Reggie, are you okay?'' Kavanagh hurried across and knelt beside him. ''Do you know where you are, Reg? Do you know *who* you are?''

''Of course I know who I am,'' he replied indignantly.

''You're not bleeding or anything.''

''It hurts,'' he muttered petulantly, giving Rafe an affronted look as he rubbed the back of his skull. ''I could have brain damage.''

''Somehow,'' Rafe drawled, ''I find that hard to believe.'' He walked across to the bed, still keeping an eye on Kavanagh.

''Come on, Reg, sit over here. I'll get you a glass of water.'' She helped him up and into one of the chairs. ''Are you sure you're okay?''

''He's fine,'' Rafe put in impatiently. The pile of things he'd dumped out of her purse still lay in a mound on the bed, and he rifled through it until he found what he was looking for.

''Hey!'' Kavanagh turned just in time to see what he was doing and took an indignant step toward him. ''You have no right—''

''Lady, not five minutes ago you were threatening to shoot off body parts I've become very fond of. I think I have a right to know just who the hell you are.'' Rafe flipped open the slim leather identification wallet. The picture was hers, and he had to smile. Typical first-year operative photo ID. They all had the same overly serious expression, trying to look blasé and tough as nails at the same time and winding up looking like kids playing cops and robbers.

Then he saw the agency name on the plasticized card and felt his heart stop for one long, disbelieving moment.

He blinked, not quite trusting his eyes, and moved closer to the reading lamp on the table by the bed, turning the gold shield to catch the light. But there was no mistake.

He remembered to start breathing after a moment or two, too

many emotions racing through him to make sense, mind spinning. Remembered the last time he'd seen this same gold shield. Remembered lying in the dust, blinded by the sun, knuckles bruised, jaw half-broken where—

"I'll be damned," he finally breathed, straightening to his full height and looking across the room at her. "And just how the hell is old Spence O'Dell, anyway?"

She blinked. "You know O'Dell?"

Rafe's laugh was tight. "Oh, yeah, I know O'Dell." He took a deep breath, the tangle of emotions surging through him separating out into strands now, each as bright as hot gold. Rage so strong it burned. Disappointment. Betrayal. And, brightest, hottest, of all, the hurt of memories he didn't want to remember. He saw Stephanie's face then, just a flicker really, a searing ghost image of laughing eyes and dark swirling hair, the remembered scent of her perfume. He shut his eyes tight and fought it down and away, back into the vault beneath his heart where he kept her memory stored, safe from prying.

When he opened his eyes again, Kavanagh was still standing there, an odd expression on her face. "I know you." She was looking at him intently, her eyes scanning his face. "You were an agent once. You used to be one of O'Dell's men."

"Once." Rafe bit the word off, almost daring her to say the rest.

"They…" She paused, as though trying to remember. "They talk about you. At the Agency. I thought…I thought you were dead. That's why I never made the connection. Your name was familiar, but…" She gazed at him curiously. "I thought you were dead."

"Not yet, no thanks to that bastard O'Dell." Rafe took another deep breath, annoyed at how shaken he was. It made him feel vulnerable, as though he'd been caught out in the open with no cover.

O'Dell. He let his mind toy with the name deliberately. Was he behind this? The Feds would be watching Ruffio, that went without saying. He'd known that when he'd taken the job but had decided it was worth the risk. If he really admitted it, in fact, he'd counted on his history with the Agency to protect him from any real suspicion. But maybe he'd underestimated O'Dell. Maybe the man wanted revenge. There were stories about O'Dell. About how he didn't like it when one of his trained agents ran amok. Maybe he'd been sitting back in the shadows all this time. Watching. Waiting for a chance to slip the noose around ex-Special Agent Rafe Blackhorse's neck and tighten it....

Shrugging his shoulders to loosen them, he prowled across to the window and tugged aside the lime-green curtain. The parking lot was still, bathed in moonlight. The scattering of cars and pickup trucks glittered with dew, and nothing moved until a high-legged dog trotted into view, slat-sided and wary. It moved toward the garbage bin at the back of the lot, pausing now and again to lift its ugly muzzle and sniff the night. Then, apparently feeling safe, it started rummaging through the garbage scattered on the ground.

Not that the stray's behavior meant O'Dell wasn't out there. No one worked at the Agency for long without hearing the stories. They still wove epic tales about O'Dell's three tours in Vietnam. Of how he could stay stone-still for hours at a time without so much as blinking, of how the Vietcong had called him The White Tiger because of the way he could slip ghostlike through jungle so thick you couldn't see a foot in front of you and never disturb a leaf. The man was a legend. Staking out the Dewdrop Inn in the wilds of South Dakota—or North Dakota, or wherever the hell they were—wouldn't be much of a challenge.

But, in spite of his suspicions, Rafe found himself relaxing slightly. Odds were that Kavanagh's involvement in this was just coincidence. There was no reason he could think of for O'Dell to be stalking him. They'd pretty much written each other off two years ago. Had put Paid to any debt between them. Any friendship.

It gave him a cold, empty feeling, for some reason. More loss than anger. It was strange how feelings changed with time. Once, he couldn't even think of O'Dell without being half blinded by rage. Now...hell, now he didn't even give a damn. O'Dell's memory had joined all the others, just one more in the collection of things he rarely thought of anymore. Part of a life he'd survived, barely, and had walked away from, as alien to the man he was now as kindness would be to that stray dog out there.

He shook off the thoughts impatiently, not liking the morose turn they were taking, and turned around to find Kavanagh standing not six feet from him, the Beretta in her hand pointed at his belly.

Chapter 3

"This game of musical guns is getting tiresome, Mr. Blackhorse. Can we just agree that neither one of us is going to shoot the other and enter into a dialogue that *doesn't* include bullets and threats?"

Blackhorse seemed to consider it for a moment. Then to Meg's relief he gave a snort of laughter and nodded, tipping his head back and rotating both shoulders to loosen them. "Hell, why not, Irish. I'm kind of interested in seeing where you're going with this, anyway."

She lowered the gun and shoved it into its holster. "The only place I'm going is Washington. *With* Reggie Dawes."

Blackhorse gave another of those harsh, abrupt laughs. "And this is your idea of a 'dialogue,' Special Agent Kavanagh?"

Meg shrugged. The race of adrenaline had eased and she was feeling the aftermath now, her heartbeat a little unsteady as she walked across to the bed and picked up her purse. She started shoving her things back into it, trying not to think of what might have happened here tonight had Blackhorse been just about anyone else.

O'Dell was right: she wasn't agent material. She would have

been dead two or three times over had he been one of Ruffio's men. Tomorrow, after she'd handed Dawes over to the Agency rep in Washington, she was putting in her resignation. Then she was going back to Boston and marrying Royce Packard and raising babies and busying herself with social luncheons and charity functions and being the perfect society wife, her brief foray into the dark world of secret agentry well behind her.

And Bobby? Well, Bobby's death would stay the mystery it was. She should just be glad she hadn't added her own to it, because her parents couldn't go through that again. Burying one child was more than any family should suffer. Burying two— the second death as futile and meaningless as the first—was a cruelty she hadn't even thought of when she'd started this stupid escapade. She'd done it because, of all her much-loved siblings, Bobby had been the closest. Had been her champion and her mentor and her best friend, and he was dead and she wanted to know why and now—

"Damn!" Meg clenched her teeth as her eyes filled with unexpected tears. "Damn, damn, *damn!*" She scythed her arm out and swept everything from the night table—water glass, clock radio, lamp and all—taking some small satisfaction as the lamp shade went flying across the room and the glass bounced off the wall, spraying cold water.

"Miss Kavanagh?" Reggie sounded tentative. "Are you all right?"

"Yes!" Meg drew a deep, calming breath, keeping her back to both men. She wiped her cheek surreptitiously with her fingers. "I'm fine, Reg."

She turned around to find them both staring at her with matching expressions of astonishment.

It was Blackhorse who broke the tension first. He laughed— a real laugh this time, not his usual cynical bark—and then walked across to the table and started putting his weapons away. "You're a real break in routine, Special Agent Mary Margaret Kavanagh, I'll say that much for you. Either O'Dell's mellowed since I last saw him, or you're one of a kind." He shoved the Smith & Wesson into the holster in the small of his back and gazed across the room at her, mouth tipped aside slightly in a bemused smile. "I wish I had time to hear your story, Irish."

"No story, Mr. Blackhorse," Meg replied wearily. "It's been a long day, and I'm tired. And we still have a situation to resolve. I'm not giving you Reggie, and you say you aren't leaving without him, so we obviously have a problem."

Blackhorse shrugged amiably. "I get paid to retrieve things, Irish. Sometimes those things are people. I'm good at what I do. But if people discover that I failed to retrieve Reggie Dawes here and take him back to the people who hired me, my reputation takes a hit. Not only do I lose my money for *this* job, people are going to think twice about hiring me in the future. This is an assignment to you, Agent Kavanagh. But it's my livelihood."

Meg looked at him curiously. "So I was right. You're not a cop."

He shrugged again. "Sheriff Haney didn't strike me as the kind of man who'd take to my line of work all that well."

"That line of work being a low-rent bounty hunter."

Something dark flickered across his high-boned features and his eyes narrowed slightly. In the unshaded glare of the fallen lamp, his features were blade-sharp and hard, as uncompromising as stone. And he was big, she found herself thinking uneasily, remembering the solid weight of him on top of her that afternoon. There wasn't an inch of him that wasn't muscle or bone, and he moved like a cat. If push came to shove, there was going to be very little she could do to stop him from taking Reggie.

She took a deep breath and released it slowly, trying to think her way through this. She was very aware of Reggie sitting behind her, looking more miserable and frightened by the passing minute, and thought of her promise to him to keep him safe. Thought of his wife, Honey, and the trust in her eyes when Meg had convinced her to go into hiding. *I'll take care of Reggie,* she'd promised. *Trust me, and I'll keep your husband safe....*

"If you take Reg back to Vegas, Ruffio will kill him, you know that."

"Ruffio just hired me to find Reggie and bring him back,"

Blackhorse said evenly. "Why is none of my business. I'm not getting paid to ask questions."

"This isn't a retrieval, it's murder," Meg said angrily. "That thug in the bar this afternoon was trying to kill Reg. He would have killed you, too, if you'd gotten in his way. Are these the kind of people you work for now, Mr. Blackhorse?" She looked at him searchingly, seeing nothing but emptiness and cold in his dark eyes. "What happened to you, anyway? How did you go from being one of O'Dell's top agents to...to *this.*"

Again there was a flicker of something deep in his eyes. "You don't want to go there, Kavanagh," he said very softly, the chill in the words trailing frost through his voice. "I'm here doing a job, just like you."

"Not like me. I'm paid by the Agency to bring people to justice. Or, as in Reggie's case, to protect him from those people who don't want justice done. From what I can see, you're a bottom feeder. One step down from that gun-for-hire that came after us in the bar. At least he was honest about what he does. You kill people and can't even admit it."

She thought for one split second that he was going to come at her. Every muscle in his lean body seemed to coil and go taut, and the emptiness in his eyes vanished under the heat of raw anger. Then he seemed to catch himself and he eased his weight back and away from her, breathing quickly, teeth bared slightly.

A little surprised she was still alive, Meg took a couple of backward steps, her hand on the comforting bulk of the Beretta. "Reggie, we're leaving. Now." She swallowed. "Mr. Blackhorse, I may not be a very good field agent yet, but I've got good instincts about people. You're no killer."

"Willing to bet your life on that, Irish?" he asked softly.

"Yes." Meg swallowed again, the sound loud in the stillness. "If you were, I'd be dead and you'd be halfway back to Vegas with Reggie by now. I don't know what happened to you, but you must have been a good man once or O'Dell would never have hired you. I'm gambling that there's still enough of that man left somewhere that I can walk out of here with Reggie, and you're going to let us go."

"Pretty big gamble."

For some reason, Meg found herself smiling. "After I deliver Reggie to Washington and get back to Virginia, I'll make sure O'Dell knows you were instrumental in bringing him back in one piece. After all, you probably saved my life in that bar this afternoon. There could be a reward in it, if I can pull the right strings. That'll make up in part for what you lost by not fulfilling your deal with Ruffio."

"Presuming you're going to get out of here alive...." Rafe made it sound as close to a threat as he could manage, but his heart wasn't in it anymore. He was weary of taunting her, weary of the sparring and banter.

He was tired and his left shoulder was aching and his knees hurt and he felt old and worn down. Kavanagh's barbed little shots had hit closer to home than he cared to admit, and the spots she'd taken aim at with such uncanny accuracy hurt, too, as though her words had been dipped in poison.

He wanted to get away from her, he realized. Back up to Bear Mountain, where no one ever bothered him. Away from her and those unnervingly clear aquamarine eyes that seemed to see too much.

He had his mouth half open to tell her to take Reggie and get the hell out before he changed his mind and shot both of them just on principle when he heard it. It wasn't even a noise as much as the suggestion of a noise. A scuff, maybe, like that of a rubber-soled shoe on concrete.

Kavanagh heard it at the same instant. He could see her eyes widen as she fumbled for the Beretta. Common sense told him she was okay, to watch out for his own hide and let her take care of hers, but instinct propelled him across the room so he was between her and the doorway, his Taurus in a two-handed grip. Dawes had reacted with instincts of his own and was curled up on the floor between the bed and the wall, both arms wrapped around his head like a kid shutting out a nightmare.

"Will you get out of my way!" Kavanagh whispered furiously. "I can't get a clean shot with you in the way!"

"Shut up and stay back," he whispered just as furiously, shouldering her out of the way. "You're not ready for this!"

"And who's paying you to play Joe Hero? Get *out* of my—"

There was a knock at the door and Rafe heard her suck in a startled breath. Looking pale and frightened but grimly determined, her grip on the Beretta letter-perfect, she eased herself away from him and cat-footed across to take up a position against the wall beside the door. Rafe eased himself across to the other side, moving silently on the carpet, pausing to take a swift glance through the peephole in the door.

Two men that he could see, neither taking any particular pains to hide themselves. Rafe held up two fingers so Kavanagh could see them, then indicated that there might be others out of his line of sight. She nodded tightly.

"Agent Kavanagh?" The voice was muffled by the door, but clear. "Meg, it's me, Matt Carlson. Adam Engler's with me. O'Dell sent us to bring you and Dawes in."

Meg's breath left her in a huff and she closed her eyes for an instant, knees nearly buckling with relief, then she swung the Beretta down and reached for the doorknob. Her fingers just grazed it when Blackhorse came hurtling at her and knocked her back against the wall with a thud that nearly jarred her teeth loose.

"It's okay," she tried to wheeze. "I know them...they're—"

There was a sharp voice outside the door, and in the next instant it exploded inward, the doorframe splintering right beside her, shards of wood flying like shrapnel. Something large catapulted into the room and hit the floor somewhere out of the line of Meg's sight. Blackhorse swore and shoved her against the wall again just as someone else swung through the door, gun glinting in the unshaded lamplight.

"Government agents!" someone roared. "Nobody move!"

And for a moment, no one did. In the end, it was Meg who moved first. Still trying to get her breath back, her ribs feeling bruised where Blackhorse had slammed into her, she gazed at the tableaux of men and guns spread out in front of her.

It had been Matt Carlson who'd come bursting through the door first. He'd hit the carpet on one shoulder and had come up in perfect shooting stance, his weapon trained on Blackhorse's belly, staring at the Taurus that was pointed right at him. Adam Engler had followed him in and had his weapon trained on Meg.

He recovered first. Swearing, he swung his Beretta around so he was covering Blackhorse. "Government agents! Put the gun down! Put it down!"

Blackhorse didn't so much as blink. "I've got your partner covered," he said coldly. "Try to take me out, he's dead."

"Put the weapon down! Put it down *now*."

They might have stayed like that for another hour, bellowing threats and counterthreats at each other like the well-trained government operatives they all were until someone either backed down—which was unlikely—or got shot. Which *was* likely, considering all the testosterone in the room.

It would have been funny, except for the very real possibility of someone getting hurt. Meg holstered her Beretta and said very gently, "Guys, it's okay. I'm okay. This is Mr. Blackhorse, a…cop. Rafe, these are O'Dell's men. Now will you all *please* put up your weapons before you hurt each other?"

Blackhorse's eyes narrowed. "You sure you know them?"

"Positive. Mr. Engler brings me latte every Friday morning, and Mr. Carlson and I share a passion for crossword puzzles."

"You'll vouch for this guy?" Carlson sounded skeptical.

Meg paused, rubbing her sore ribs, tempted for one rash moment to deny it just to pay the man back for all the aggravation he'd given her. Then she sighed and nodded grudgingly. "Yeah. I'll vouch for him."

It took another moment or more, but finally all three of them relaxed slightly, trading hostile glares as they put up their weapons and holstered them, still prickly and watchful.

Blackhorse took two steps across to her, face like a thundercloud. He jabbed a finger into the air an inch from her face, making her blink. "Did you sleep through basic training, lady?" he bawled. "You never—and I mean *never*—open a door until you've verified who the hell's on the other side."

Meg bristled. "I *knew* who—"

"You knew squat! You thought you recognized another agent's voice, but you didn't verify it. He could have been out there at gunpoint. There could have been a dozen explanations—

none of them innocent—and you *and* your man Dawes there could be dead right now!''

"Hey, fella, where the hell do you get off talking to her like that?'' Carlson gave Blackhorse a shove, his face pugnacious.

Furious, Meg pushed past Carlson to glare up at Blackhorse. "Who do you think you are, anyway? You came here to take Reggie for yourself, and now you're lecturing me on how to—''

"You obviously need *someone* lecturing you on how to stay alive, because—''

"Hey! Back off!'' Carlson pushed his way between them again. "One more word outta you, buddy, and—''

"You want to take this outside, pal?'' Blackhorse loomed toward Carlson, his eyes hot with anger.

"Enough!'' Meg's shout cracked through the room like a pistol shot and everyone stared at her, startled into momentary silence. She ran both hands through her tangled hair, tempted to start pulling it out by the roots. "You guys sound just like my brothers! I've spent most of my life listening to them argue over who has the right to tell me what to do, and I stopped taking it from them and I'm sure not going to stand here and take it from *you!''* The last word was all but a shout and she caught herself and took a deep breath to calm down. "All of you back off, understand? Just…back off!''

"Hey, Meg,'' Carlson said, clearly hurt. "I never meant anything by it. I was just—''

"Trying to take care of me, I know,'' she said with forced patience. "Matt, what are you doing here? How did you know where I was?''

"We were in the air fifteen minutes after your call came in this afternoon,'' Engler said, eyeing Blackhorse suspiciously. "We choppered in and met with Sheriff Haney—who is *not* a happy man, by the way. I strongly recommend you don't go back there anytime soon.''

"I wasn't planning on it,'' Meg muttered. "Although it wasn't *me* who shot up the bar.'' This with a hostile look at Blackhorse.

"Anyway, we tracked you here.''

Meg's heart sank. She'd been quite proud of the way she'd

covered her tracks, but apparently she'd left a trail a mile wide. "How?" she asked wearily. "Where did I go wrong?"

Engler just looked at her. "The phone call, of course."

"What phone call?" Meg wheeled around and looked at Reggie, who was trying to make himself invisible. "Reggie, what phone call?"

He shrugged, not meeting her eyes. "Well, um…when you went out to the car, I…um…found your cell phone, and…um…"

"He called your brother in Chicago, wanting to talk to Honey. Grady called the Agency, saying something didn't sound right and wanting to know what we were doing about it."

Meg winced.

Engler looked across at her. "Meg, what did you think you were doing, coming after Dawes yourself? O'Dell's fit to be tied."

She winced again. "He, uh…knows by now. I guess."

Carlson laughed. "Oh, yeah, he knows. He doesn't *believe* it, but he knows." He laughed again. "I've seen O'Dell mad before, but I've never seen him like this. You have gone down in the annals of Agency history, Meg. I wouldn't give two cents for your future, but they'll be talking about you for decades. You've elevated the lowly computer gnome to new heights. Trouble is, now every gnome in the place will want to play field agent and the rest of us will be out of work."

Meg flushed slightly. "Look, I…uh…"

"Gnome?" Blackhorse had been listening to all this intently, and he looked at her now, eyes narrowed. "You're a *gnome?*"

"I am a Computer Information Retrieval Specialist," she said a trifle defensively.

Blackhorse just stared at her, seemingly unable to comprehend what he was hearing.

"She's one of the best," Carlson said blithely. "Although after O'Dell's finished with you, Meg, you'll be lucky to have a job counting paper clips. Everyone thought you were on vacation, then we get this phone call from some hicksville sheriff in South Dakota—"

"North," Engler put in. "North Dakota."

"Whatever. This sheriff says he has someone in custody who claims to be one of our agents. That said agent was involved in a shootout in a bar involving a Nevada cop—" this with a distasteful glance at Blackhorse "—a thug called Pags Pagliano and a pipsqueak calling himself Reggie Dawes." This elicited a huff of indignation from Reggie, but Carlson ignored it. "I happened to be closest to O'Dell's office when the call was routed through to him." He winced at the memory. "As I said, Engler and I were on a chopper fifteen minutes later and another team was dispatched to your brother's place to pick up Honey."

"Is she okay?" Reggie hovered in the background worriedly.

"She's fine," Meg snapped. "I told you, my brother's a cop."

"She's fine," Carlson echoed. He looked at Meg with a shake of his head. "O'Dell's mighty peeved about that, too, Meg. You know how he hates it when we get civilians involved. You should have sent Honey to an Agency safe house instead of involving your own family."

"There wasn't time."

"Not to mention the fact you didn't have the authority," Engler said calmly. "Seeing as you're out here playing field agent games you haven't been trained for, on an assignment that doesn't exist."

Meg flushed again. "The only way Reggie would come with me was if I could guarantee Honey's safety. I knew sending her to stay with Grady was as good as putting her in any safe house. Maybe better."

"Wait a minute." Blackhorse held up his hand like a traffic cop. "Run that by me again? She's out here on an assignment that doesn't exist?"

Carlson gave him a dark look. "What police force did you say you were with? Nevada? Kind of out of your jurisdiction, wouldn't you say?"

Blackhorse ignored him. "You're saying you clowns let a gnome with no field training come out here and—"

"I took the training!"

"—handle this non-assignment all on her own, without adequate backup or—"

"She didn't tell anybody what she was doing," Carlson protested. "She was on vacation! It wasn't until—" He caught himself abruptly. "Hey, don't I know you? I know you from somewhere."

Meg had her mouth open to tell Carlson exactly who Blackhorse was, then subsided, recalling the expression on Rafe's face when he'd spoken about the Agency. Rafe gave her a quick look, seemingly surprised by her silence.

"Special Agent Rafe Blackhorse," Engler said suddenly. He stared at Rafe in blank disbelief. "You're dead!"

"You're kidding!" Carlson took another look at Rafe, staring hard at him. "Well, I'll be...it *is* you! But Engler's right. You're dead."

"Do I *look* dead?" Rafe asked sourly.

Carlson flushed. "I was in the West Coast office when all that went down. I just heard that you—" He bit it off.

"Ate your gun," Engler put in helpfully. "Guess the story wasn't true, then, huh?"

"Guess not, Einstein."

It gave Meg such a jolt that she simply stared at Rafe, trying to remember everything she'd heard about him. Suicide? Surely she would have remembered *that*. "I heard..." She frowned, struggling to haul the memory up from the depths of her mind. "I heard it was in the line of duty."

"They always say that," Carlson said. "O'Dell doesn't like it when his agents off themselves. Figures it reflects badly on him. So unless you commit hari kari in front of the Lincoln Memorial at high noon with press and television, it's kept pretty quiet."

"You've been alive all this time," Engler said quietly, as though not quite believing it. "Why all the secrecy?"

"It was a cover story of some sort, wasn't it?" Carlson put in with sudden understanding. "And you've been working for O'Dell all this time. So that's why you turned up here, helping Meg." He grinned with relief.

Engler was still staring at Rafe. "That true? You still on the payroll?"

"Wish I'd known that beforehand, because I don't mind tell-

ing you, I was a little scared of what we were going to find."
Carlson scrubbed his fingers through his short, brown hair.
"Ruffio and Stepino have both got their soldiers out looking for
Dawes. I was sure you were dead."

"You're hell bent on seeing someone dead, aren't you?" Rafe
muttered. "And I'm not working undercover. Agent Kavanagh
and I just sort of ran into each other, is all. I quit the Agency
cold two years ago."

"But you were taking care of her." Engler just stared at him.

Rafe glanced at Meg. His gaze held hers for a long moment.
"She was taking care of herself just fine. I was ready to pull
out when you guys showed up."

"But..." Carlson looked from one to the other of them,
clearly puzzled.

"Mr. Blackhorse is a...private investigator," Meg put in
smoothly, ignoring Rafe's raised eyebrow. "He...um...became
embroiled in the situation when Pagliano tried to kill Reggie this
afternoon, and he kindly offered to...assist me."

Reggie was looking shell-shocked. "I don't understand any
of this," he whispered. "You mean she isn't an agent at all?"

"She's an Agency employee, just not a field agent," Engler
said with a disapproving look at Meg. "She had no authority to
bring you in, and no business being out here without proper
training."

"I *had* the training," Meg repeated heatedly. "Okay, so I
didn't *complete* it, exactly, but I didn't need the underwater dem-
olition stuff or the advanced military armament stuff or all that
pilot or parachute training stuff, either. And, okay, I didn't spend
two years as an intern, playing second banana to the agent in
charge. But I found Reggie when no one else could. And I
convinced him to come in. *And* I was bringing him in just fine."

"But...why?" Carlson shook his head. "That's what I don't
understand, Meg. You've never said anything to me about wanting to be a field agent. And you know how O'Dell feels about
women in the field."

"I wanted to prove he's wrong," she said flatly. "The man's
twenty years behind the times! If I can *prove* I can do the job,
he can't keep me out. I'd been following Reggie's case from

the beginning, and when he disappeared with O'Dell's money and no one was able to find him, I decided it was the perfect opportunity. It only took me a couple of days to track him down with our computers, and I…'' She shrugged and looked at Reggie. ''Reg, I'm sorry. I've been lying to you, but it really *was* for your own good.''

''So does this mean I'm not really in custody?''

''No!'' Carlson and Engler exclaimed in unison, and Reggie sat down, looking gloomy.

''It was crazy,'' Carlson muttered. ''You could have been killed, Meg. Why not just put your application in and see if—'' Abruptly, he stopped. Frowning, he blew his cheeks out, looking at her sadly. ''Oh. Bobby.''

''My brother died in the field,'' Meg said with quiet intensity, ''and I want to know why.''

''Meg…'' Engler lifted his hand, then let it fall to his side again. ''Damn it, Meg, we've been over this a hundred times.''

She lifted her chin slightly. ''And like I've said a hundred times, Adam, I don't believe that Bobby got sloppy. That he lost his edge and it got him killed. Something happened out there that night.''

''I was on Bobby's team,'' Engler reminded her gently. ''Nothing happened that night that wasn't in my report. And I've been over it and over it with you.''

''Except you weren't with him the night it happened.'' Meg looked at him evenly. ''He was set up, Adam. I know that as certainly as I know you don't want to believe it. Bobby was a good field agent. He told me that he suspected someone on the team was dirty and you've admitted he talked to you about it!''

''And I told him he was wrong,'' Engler said gently. ''Meg, your brother had been working deep under cover for almost six months. Things…happen to a man who's been out of touch with the real world for that long. He's so used to suspecting everyone he's working with that he starts to see conspiracies and threats around every corner.''

''Bobby was the most grounded, *real* person I've ever known. He was *not* imagining things!''

''Meg, I don't know what happened to Bobby that night, but it was no double cross. No one blew his cover. I'm sorry he's dead—he was a good agent and a friend of mine. But O'Dell's closed the case down because there's no evidence to keep it open. Good men die stupid deaths, Meg. I'm sorry, but it happens.''

''Not to my brother, it didn't,'' she said with quiet intensity.

Engler started to say something, then thought better of it and subsided, frowning.

''He was double-crossed,'' Meg said savagely. ''By one of *our* agents. Then he was murdered to keep him quiet. O'Dell won't investigate because he doesn't believe me, but I darn well intend to find out who killed Bobby if it's the last thing I ever do. And if O'Dell won't make me a full field agent, then I'll quit and do it on my own!''

Engler exchanged a quick look with Carlson, and Meg bit back an angry oath, knowing they were thinking the same thing everyone else at the Agency thought. Word had it that Bobby had slipped up and gotten himself and another agent killed, and that she couldn't accept the truth. That she'd come up with this preposterous idea that it had been another agent who had double-crossed and ambushed Bobby and his partner. Conspiracy plot, they called it behind her back, smiling knowingly amongst themselves. Even O'Dell was tired of listening to her.

She shook her head angrily and stalked across to the bed, starting to shove her things willy-nilly into her small suitcase. ''Reg, saddle up! We're leaving.'' She shot Engler a cool look. ''I presume you two are here to escort Reg and me back to Washington.''

''Well, actually, Matt's going to take Reg to Washington.'' Engler managed to look mildly embarrassed. ''My orders are to escort you back to Virginia ASAP. From this room to O'Dell's office, no stops between.''

''I'm not going back to Virginia until I know Reg is safe. I gave my word.''

''No problem. There's an Agency jet sitting on the tarmac out at the airport with its engines hot and two more agents aboard for backup. I'll let you walk on and buckle him in, if you like.''

"How are you and I getting back?"

"Military chopper." Engler smiled slightly. "O'Dell's private stock. You're getting the royal treatment."

"O'Dell's little joke, giving me the royal treatment to my own firing squad." Meg mustered up a rough smile. She looked at Rafe for a moment, then walked across and held out her hand. "Well, Mr. Blackhorse, it's been…instructional. I won't say it's been a pleasure, exactly, but I appreciate your help. And I'm sorry about your…arrangement with the other party. Give him my regrets, will you?"

To her surprise, Rafe actually smiled. His hand folded around hers, warm and incredibly gentle. "It *has* been a pleasure, Special Agent Mary Margaret Kavanagh. Like I said, you're one of a kind."

"CIR Specialist Mary Margaret Kavanagh," Meg said with a sigh. "And I meant what I said about appreciating your help, even if it wasn't exactly what you intended. I'll keep all your advice in mind. In case I ever need it again. You ought to think about billing O'Dell for your in-field training services."

His fingers tightened slightly, encasing hers in gentle warmth. "You take care of yourself, *Agent* Kavanagh."

Then he drew his hand from hers slowly, letting his fingers linger on hers for a moment before releasing them completely.

She nodded again, then just smiled and gathered up her suitcase, glancing around the room to make sure she had everything. Carlson was helping Reggie get his things together in the other room, and she could hear them squabbling already.

She walked outside with Engler, taking a deep breath of night air.

"Hey. You. Engler."

Rafe's voice caught Engler just as he was opening the door of his rental car for Meg. He stiffened and Meg saw his hand move fractionally toward his weapon.

She looked around sharply. Rafe was just standing there, tall and calm-eyed in the moonlight, hands loose at his sides.

Engler turned slowly. "What?"

"Tell O'Dell she did just fine out here. Handled herself better than most men I've seen with twice the training."

Engler looked as surprised as Meg felt. She stared at Rafe in amazement.

"She stayed one step ahead of me for almost a week, and when I did catch up to her, she drew down on me like an old-timer, cool as water. Tell him that."

"Yeah, okay." Engler looked at Meg with renewed respect. "I'll tell him that."

Rafe nodded, then touched his forehead in a lazy salute, his eyes holding Meg's. "S'long, Irish."

"I...yeah..." she stammered, feeling suddenly flustered for no reason. His gaze was as warmly intimate as a caress, as though they'd been sharing a lot more than barbed threats half the night, and she sensed more than saw Engler look at her curiously. "I, um...so...long."

"Well, if that doesn't beat everything." Carlson had joined them in time to hear the whole exchange and was standing there with his mouth open, watching Rafe stride away. "Meg, you just got a five-star recommendation from a legend! Man, wait'll O'Dell hears about this!"

Chapter 4

Mary Margaret Kavanagh was still on his mind three weeks later.

And Rafe was not happy about it.

It was irritating as hell to be thinking about her at all, for a start. But to have her on his mind here, up on Bear Mountain, really ticked him off.

Until now, he'd managed to keep the outside world from intruding up here. His fortress from reality, his sister had called it. She'd used a lot of phrases like that once, shouting them at him as though trying to pierce armorplate with words. But it wasn't a fortress, just a quiet retreat from the clamor and clang of a world that seemed increasingly irrelevant.

Up here there was nothing but him and the sky and the wind and the mountain itself, its granite roots planted deep in the planet's heart. It was silent, save for the moan of the wind and the occasional scream of an eagle, and as clean as bone, scoured by that ever-present wind.

Everything was reduced to its simplest form, all softness and artifice and weakness gone until only the core remained. Even the stunted trees had been stripped of nonessentials until they were more like polished stone than living things, gray and hard and elemental, all but unkillable. Tree-thing at its most fundamental level, like the rock and the sky.

Like him.

It had saved him, this mountain. Like the rocks and the twisted trees, he'd been scoured down to his most elemental self until all that was left was hard and pure. He'd come up here almost two years ago intending to kill himself. Eight months before, he'd drunk himself into a stupor and had stayed that way, trying to blot out the memories. But it had never worked. And finally, too exhausted by guilt and pain to go on, he'd decided to stop even trying.

He'd had some plan, he supposed, although he'd never been able to remember it. Later, he'd found the unloaded pistol where it had dropped from his bourbon-numbed fingers, so maybe that had been it. Whatever he'd planned, he'd managed to screw it up, too drunk to put thought into action. Instead, he'd fallen into a pile of boulders near the summit and had lain there for days, drifting in and out of consciousness, soaked by rain and heavy dew at night, burned dry by an unforgiving sun during the day.

He still had no idea how long he'd lain there. Long enough to kill most men, he suspected. Long enough to kill him had he not been so pickled in bourbon. He remembered licking dew from stone, the taste bitter in his mouth. Remembered waking once and seeing clumps of blueberries hanging just above him, growing where no blueberries grew. Knowing they were nothing more than a hallucination, he reached up with fingers that seemed unattached to his body and picked them and ate them, the juice as sweet as wine. Remembered finding apples. Like the blueberries, they were out of place and out of time—it was spring, not fall, and there wasn't an apple tree for a hundred miles in any direction. But, hallucination or not, he ate them and they were sweet.

He remembered watching the slow spiral of an eagle as it hung in an updraft a hundred feet above him, giant wings unmoving. He talked to it; he remembered that, too. Babbling things he'd never spoken aloud before, shouting his rage to the sky. He remembered screaming threats to God and man alike.

Remembered retching dryly for hour after hour, stomach cramping so painfully he could hardly breathe as the wind and sun worked eight months of cheap booze from his system. Remembered weeping finally, exhausted and empty and at the end.

He'd simply let go then, he remembered. Content to lie there and drift into a final sleep, relinquishing control to whatever forces had kept him alive that far. Something had been there, with him, at the end. Real but not real, just a presence half-seen, a Spirit Warrior keeping silent, still watch. And thus watched, he'd slept finally, slipping down into that kind of deep, dreamless renewing sleep that had eluded him for the better part of a year.

He'd awakened just before dawn, chilled to the bone, and had sat up slowly, sober for the first time in months. Everything was still, the crystalline air so pure and cold it hurt to breathe. The sky was the color of skim milk, still dotted by stars and streaked with peach in the east, and he had sat there, shivering uncontrollably, and had realized with surprise that he was alive. Purified inside and out by wind and rain and sun, as smoothed and polished and hard as an obsidian blade.

The sun had risen, warming him a little, and he'd gotten unsteadily to his feet, feeling as delicate and untethered as a cloud, and had stumbled light-headed and shivering down to the trailer. He had no idea where the key was—he'd locked it up after Stephanie had been killed and had never been back—so he just pried the door open and rummaged around until he found some clean, dry clothes. Then he'd gone up to the spring, stripped naked and dived into the icy water, coming up sputtering and breathless and shocked fully awake.

He'd gathered his old clothes up into a pile and burned them, then had cut his hair and burned that, too. He'd made it a ceremony of sorts, tossing a little tobacco into the flames to thank whatever spirits had held him back from dying, smiling at his own whimsy.

His pickup truck was still in a ditch about a mile down the trail where he'd run it into a tree. He'd winched it out, driven it up to the small meadow where the trailer was and cleaned it up, tossing out the empty bottles and then scrubbing out the stink of vomit and stale sweat and despair.

He'd started running the next day. It had nearly killed him at first. He would run twenty feet and stagger the next twenty, pouring with sweat and cursing with the pain as every muscle in his body knotted. But after a week or two the twenty feet stretched to fifty, then a hundred, and then he suddenly broke through and was running like a deer. He ran without thought or purpose those first few months, just pounding down the miles like someone trying to outrun his own demons, and maybe that was what he had been doing.

The healing started sometime during those months. His mind became as lean and healthy as his body, and soon he'd found himself thinking of the future again. Not long-range. Just a day or two at first. But, as with his physical endurance, that got stronger with time and practice, as well. Soon he was planning a whole week ahead, then the week stretched to a month, and somewhere along the line, without even realizing when it had happened, he was thinking in terms of years.

But until now, those thoughts had been solitary ones. Simple things, mostly, like what kind of water pump to buy when he realized the old one was finally beyond repair, and the best direction to angle the woodshed to keep the snow from blowing straight in, things like that. Now and again he would take on a retrieval job, adding his fee to the pile of fifty-dollar bills hidden behind the paneling in his bedroom closet, but mostly he stayed to himself up here.

There was always something to do. Repairing leaks in the trailer's sunbaked hide alone was almost a full-time job, the generator needed regular tune-ups, and there were books to read and wood to chop. It was a simple life, physical and free of the complexities and confusions and complications of the outside world, and he liked it just fine that way.

Until Mary Margaret Kavanagh had starting turning up in his thoughts for no reason he could figure, and suddenly things weren't the same at all.

Swearing under his breath, Rafe turned the key in the truck's ignition. The engine caught instantly and he gunned it a few times, listening carefully. He'd spent the better part of the morning tuning it up and was finally pleased with the way it sounded, although there had been nothing much wrong with it in the first place. He'd blown out the fuel line, replaced a couple of hoses and put in new spark plugs, and short of stripping the thing down to basics and starting all over again, there wasn't much more he could do.

Filling time. Trying not to think of *her.*

He refused to let his mind wrap itself around the syllables of her name. He'd been doing *that* a little too often, too. Her name was like a line of poetry or a bit of music he couldn't get out of his head, and now and again he would realize he'd been running it over and over in his thoughts like some tribal chant, the rhythm of the words almost hypnotic.

Mary Margaret Kavanagh.

Hell of a mouthful. Maybe her parents had hoped she would grow into it.

He grinned in spite of himself, letting himself savor the memory of her in those spandex pants and that white sweater that kept slip-sliding off one smooth shoulder, then the other, and those wide blue eyes. And maybe even better was the memory of her in the motel later that day, round little backside upholstered in soft denim, small breasts no more than a tantalizing hint under her sweatshirt, sex appeal less blatant but no less potent.

His grin widened before he could stop it and he gave his head a weary shake. Sex wasn't something he thought of a whole lot. Mainly because if he thought about it too much he was tempted to *do* something about it. And although there were women aplenty down in the world who would have been more than glad to help take the edge off—some for free, others not—there was something too clinical in that kind of release for his taste. So except for a lapse of judgment or two, he stuck to cold showers and hard work.

Sometimes it worked. Sometimes it didn't.

Lately, it didn't seem to be having the desired effect at all. He'd taken up running again, but even that didn't always work, and sometimes he just took care of it himself with the wry thought that, as far as sex went, anyway, things had been a lot simpler when he'd been drunk twenty-four hours a day.

He would be minding his own business, thinking about something else altogether, and suddenly he'd find himself remembering the way she'd felt against him when he'd held her captive against the side of her car that night, cat-supple and erotically curved and contoured. About the heat and satin of her skin against his fingers and the taste of her breath, the scent of her hair. At night the remembering would translate itself into dreams so hot and graphically sexual that he would wake up in physical pain, on fire with a want so fierce it felt like being flayed alive.

And sometimes on those nights the physical want would get all tangled up in an aching want of a different kind, and then the memories would surge over him no matter how hard he tried to keep them at bay. Those were the nights when he would get up and run for hours, because it was either run or stay there in the dark, with the thought inching ever nearer that all it would take was one bullet and a steady hand to stop all those memories for good.

And thinking things like that was less productive than thinking about Mary Margaret Kavanagh. Rafe swore at himself again—out loud and with considerable feeling this time—and gave the ignition key an angry twist to shut the engine off. He swung out of the truck and walked around to slam the hood down, then started putting his tools away.

Three, the old three-legged dog he'd found in a ditch last year and had never gotten around to getting rid of, was barking at something down the road and Rafe shouted at him to shut the hell up, in a foul mood suddenly. The barking paused, then resumed again, and Rafe swore at the old dog under his breath. And then he heard the car.

It startled him, getting caught flat-footed like that. Swearing, he grabbed his tool kit and headed for the trailer at a fast run. He'd gotten sloppy. And that damned woman had something to do with it! She'd knocked his timing and instincts all to hell and gone, and here he was halfway to being ambushed on his own mountain and his head was *still* full of her.

The old silver Airstream was comfortably cool and it took a

moment for Rafe's eyes to adapt from full sunlight to dimness, but he didn't need to be able to see to find what he was looking for. The rifle was in the cabinet where it was supposed to be and he grabbed it—no need to see if it was loaded—and walked back to the open door, staying just inside.

There was only one way to approach the trailer and that was straight across the hot, bright clearing. Anyone coming that way would be in full sunlight, half blinded by the glare of the sun off the trailer, and wouldn't see Rafe until he was ready to be seen.

The car growled up the last slope and eased itself into the open, wallowing across the ruts like a scow in heavy water. It was coated with dust, and flares of drying mud covered its flanks and grill, and there was a nasty dent on the left front where the paint had been scraped off. It settled to a stop about sixty feet from the trailer and after a moment the driver turned off the engine. Rafe stayed motionless, waiting to see what was going to happen.

Odds were it was nothing. Some lost tourist—he got one or two a year—or climbers or hikers who either hadn't seen or had ignored the No Trespassing signs at the bottom of the road. Or some New Age guru looking for magic rocks or the secret to enlightenment or some blasted thing. He never quite knew what it was they expected to find up here, but he usually humored them long enough to give them some enlightenment of his own—specifically, the meaning of those big Private Property signs nailed to trees along the road—and then sent them on their merry way.

But when the driver's door finally opened and the tall figure eased himself out into the harsh late-morning sun, Rafe was certain he was imagining things. It had to be a trick of the light, he decided calmly. Nothing else would explain what he thought he was seeing.

But then the man by the car reached up and pulled off his sunglasses and Rafe felt his safe reality crumble and dissolve. Suddenly light-headed, he pulled back from the open door and leaned against the wall of the trailer, eyes closed as he tried to catch his breath, fighting a barrage of images and memories that came up out of nowhere.

He subdued them by sheer force of will and dragged in a deep breath, then opened his eyes and stepped toward the door again, his hands clammy on the rifle barrel.

The intruder hadn't moved. Rafe stepped through the door and down the two wide steps and strode toward him, rifle aimed squarely at the man's belly.

Spence O'Dell's mouth quirked faintly in what might have been a smile in any other man. He ignored the rifle and inclined his head slightly in greeting. "I see you haven't done anything to improve that road. If anything, it's worse than it was two years ago."

"I told you if you ever set foot on my property again, I'd kill you," Rafe said with quiet menace. He lifted the rifle.

O'Dell didn't look as though he cared one way or the other. He gave Rafe a hard, impatient look and walked right by him without so much as a glance at the rifle. "You might be doing me a favor, ever think of that?" he growled as he strode toward the trailer. "I want a cold beer and an explanation, Blackhorse. You can start with the beer."

It was tempting, all right. Rafe eyed O'Dell's narrow back and fantasized for a moment about planting a bullet squarely between those arrogant shoulders. Could almost taste the raw pleasure he would get from taking the man down. God knows, he'd thought about it often enough.

But in the end, O'Dell made it too easy. Swearing savagely, Rafe swung the rifle barrel down and strode after the other man.

Not waiting to be invited in, O'Dell walked up the steps and into the cool depths of the trailer. Rafe stayed outside for a moment or two, tempted to get into the truck and just drive off. It didn't matter where to. Just away. From here. From O'Dell. Then he swore again and walked up and into his own home. Not a damn thing had changed. He'd learned the hard way that trying to put O'Dell off when he wanted something was like trying to stop an avalanche with your bare hands. You either went with it, or you got run over. And O'Dell didn't seem to give a damn which way it went.

O'Dell had the door to the small propane fridge open at the moment and was staring unhappily at the sparse contents. "No beer."

"I'm a damned alcoholic, remember? Quote and unquote."

O'Dell spared him a tolerant glance, then continued contemplating the nearly empty fridge. "I called you a damned drunk. There's a difference."

"From this side of the bottle, maybe." Rafe put the rifle back into the cabinet and closed it securely, out of temptation's reach. His shoulders were knotted and tight and he was having trouble breathing. He flexed his left hand convulsively, aching to put his fist through something, to tear the door off the hinges, to kick the wall in.

O'Dell's grunt could have been assent or disagreement or nothing at all. Then he reached in and helped himself to a soft drink. He tossed it at Rafe without warning, smiling that almost-smile as Rafe fielded it deftly, then grabbed a second one for himself. "Reflexes still pretty good."

Rafe didn't bother answering.

O'Dell pushed the fridge door closed with his elbow and turned and walked across to the small chrome and Formica table hinged to the wall. He slid into the built-in bench seat and ripped the tab off the can, then took a long swallow of the cold drink. Leaning well back, he rested his elbow on the back of the bench and simply stared at Rafe, saying nothing.

Rafe stared back. O'Dell downed another swallow of soda after a minute or two, his eyes never leaving Rafe's. Then he let his mouth lift to one side in a grim half smile. "You still hate my guts, don't you."

"I don't even think about you, O'Dell," Rafe lied. Those odd gray eyes of O'Dell's had always unnerved him slightly and he tore the tab off the soft drink can just for the excuse to look away.

"I did what I did for your own good."

Rafe managed a humorless smile, not saying anything. How often had he heard those same words when he'd been a kid? He'd been in and out of foster homes from the time he was four, and the words had been a common refrain back then, right before he got the hell beat out of him for one thing or another. Talking back, not listening, fighting. Sometimes for nothing more than being Native in a white man's world.

He shook himself free of the memories to find O'Dell studying him and he forced himself to stand there unconcerned, pretending to read the label on the soft drink can.

"You sober?"

The question came softly, almost as an afterthought, and anger surged through Rafe before he could catch himself. "I haven't touched a drop in nineteen months, you bastard."

O'Dell didn't say anything for a long while, just sitting there with his eyes slightly narrowed, as though testing the words, the very air around them, for truth. Then he nodded slowly. "I'm glad to hear that."

Rafe snorted. "Who are you kidding, O'Dell? You never gave a damn about me."

"You're alive, aren't you?"

It was typical O'Dell, more challenge than question, fraught with sixteen layers of meaning that you could take in any of a hundred ways. For some reason it disconcerted Rafe and he found himself thinking of those days he'd spent on the mountain, the sense that someone had been there with him. Blueberries and apples where blueberries and apples didn't grow.

But the idea that O'Dell had been there, hovering over him like some hawk-faced maiden aunt, was so preposterous it didn't even warrant serious thought. "What do you want, O'Dell? You didn't come up here to ask after the state of my health."

O'Dell took another long swallow of soda. "I hear you're working for Antony Ruffio."

"He hired me to do a job."

"Retrieving Reginald Howard Dawes." His gaze held Rafe's. "That's the word you used, wasn't it? *Retrieving?*"

Rafe rubbed the back of his neck wearily. "Quit dancing, O'Dell. Spit it out."

The skin tightened around O'Dell's mouth and something cold and hard flickered across the stone-gray surface of his eyes. He set the soft drink can onto the table. "Antony Leo Ruffio is under Federal and Agency investigation, and your name has come up more than a couple of times. For some reason I can't quite understand, Specialist Mary Kavanagh swears your presence was unrelated to the cases pending. And even Mr. Dawes has stated strongly that your involvement was incidental.''

''You already know I'm not involved with Ruffio or I'd be in a basement room in headquarters right now being debriefed with a cattle prod.''

O'Dell looked pained. ''You're a civilian now, Blackhorse. I can't touch you.''

Rafe snorted.

Even O'Dell seemed amused by the lie. One corner of his mouth quirked a scant quarter-inch, then subsided. ''I want to know where Kavanagh is.''

The question just hung there for a moment and Rafe blinked, feeling off balance. He'd just been thinking about her and now here was O'Dell saying her name, and it was disconcerting as hell. ''I—what do you mean, you want to know where she is?''

O'Dell's eyes darkened. ''English suddenly become your second language, Blackhorse?''

Rafe flushed. ''How the hell would I know where one of your agents is?'' For the life of him, he couldn't bring himself to say her name aloud, half-afraid that if he did he would conjure her up right there in front of them.

And then, abruptly, the import of what O'Dell was saying hit him dead center. He eased himself out of his slouch, eyes narrowing. ''What are you saying, O'Dell? That you've lost her? That you sent the woman out half trained and—'' Rafe bit the sentence off abruptly, aware that O'Dell was looking at him with an oddly speculative expression. ''How would I know where she is?'' he growled, tipping his head back and taking a long swallow of the soft drink. ''She's your gnome.''

''She's gone.''

Two words, but they landed in the bottom of Rafe's belly like lead. He shrugged, reminding himself somewhat forcefully that he didn't give a damn. Not about O'Dell, the Agency, missing persons *or* Specialist Mary Margaret Kavanagh. All five foot nothing of her. ''She shouldn't be too hard to find. Just look for a firecracker with red hair and a bad temper, and you'll have found her.''

''So you're telling me you haven't seen her?''

''Why the hell would I...?'' Rafe's eyes narrowed. ''So you haven't just misplaced her somewhere. She's really missing?''

''Five days.''

Rafe shook his head slowly, reminding himself again that he didn't care. ''Sounds to me as though you're losing control of your own organization, O'Dell. You've got computer gnomes running around playing field agent, and now you're telling me you've *lost* one of them.''

To his surprise, the shot seemed to hit its mark. A faint flush touched the sharp planes of O'Dell's cheekbones. ''Kavanagh is...'' O'Dell seemed to be gritting his teeth.

Rafe had to smile. ''Unique,'' he said without even thinking about it.

O'Dell glanced at him sharply. Then he nodded almost wearily. ''God, yeah, you got that right.'' He gave a quiet snort of rough laughter. ''After she got back to Virginia, I tore a strip off her a mile wide. Anyone else would have crawled off and that would have been the end of them. But not her. Not Specialist Mary Margaret Kavanagh.''

Rafe had to fight to keep from laughing. So O'Dell was doing it, too. Repeating the damned woman's name like some sort of incantation, as though there was magic somewhere in the rhythm of the syllables.

He gave himself an annoyed shake. ''Look, O'Dell, this is all very interesting, but it doesn't have a damn thing to do with me. Kavanagh and I crossed swords for a few hours, that's all. I don't know where she is. Ordinarily I'd enjoy watching you squirm, but I've got things to do.''

O'Dell just looked at him thoughtfully. ''She told me you saved her life in that Dakota bar.''

Rafe shrugged carelessly. ''Maybe, maybe not. Impossible to tell. Pagliano took her by surprise, but she's got reflexes like a cat. She's better than you think she is, O'Dell. Better than she thinks she is.''

''Which won't keep her alive if she gets in over her head.''

Rafe fought down an unreasonable jolt of concern. Shrugged again, twice as carelessly. "None of my business. I'm out of all that now, remember?"

O'Dell gave another one of those noncommittal grunts.

And then, in spite of not giving the slightest damn about either O'Dell *or* Mary Margaret Kavanagh, Rafe heard himself say, "She's looking for her brother's killer."

O'Dell's head came up, eyes narrowed. "And you just happen to know that."

"She was talking with Carlson and Engler about it, that's all. I wasn't paying that much attention." Which was a lie, Rafe realized. He could remember every word she'd said.

"And you haven't seen her since Dakota?"

"Now who's having trouble understanding plain English?" Rafe asked testily. "No, O'Dell, I haven't seen the woman since she got into Engler's car in South Dakota."

"North," O'Dell put in almost absently. "It was North Dakota."

"Whatever."

"She thinks you know something."

Rafe looked at him, confused. "About what?"

"Her brother's death."

Rafe started to say something, then shook his head. "O'Dell, you're making less sense than that three-legged dog out there." He nodded toward the door where Three was visible in the dusty yard, snapping at invisible bees. "Kavanagh was a pain in the butt, but she didn't strike me as crazy."

O'Dell smiled roughly. "Funny, she said the same thing about you." Then he sighed and ran his fingers through his short, steel-gray hair in a distracted gesture Rafe had never seen before. "Six months ago, Bobby Kavanagh and another agent, Damon Christopher, were killed."

"Christopher?" Rafe frowned. "He was just a kid."

"Twenty-four," O'Dell said tightly, his eyes like stone. "I put him with Kavanagh because Kavanagh had ten years of street cop experience under his belt when I recruited him."

"Chicago?"

O'Dell gave him an odd look and Rafe made an impatient

gesture. "Just a lucky guess. Grady's with Chicago PD, and I just figured odds were…" He let the words trail off, realizing he was digging himself deeper by the minute. Why the hell couldn't he just keep his mouth shut? Why was he acting as though he cared, when—

"Sounds to me," O'Dell said very quietly, "as though the two of you did a little more than just cross swords."

"Look, O'Dell, it doesn't mean anything, okay?" Rafe held his hands up. "She was talking, I was listening. I don't know anything about her brother, and I don't know where she is."

O'Dell didn't say anything.

"You believe her," Rafe said suddenly. "She swears that her brother was set up. That someone on the case with him—someone at the Agency—was involved. And you believe her."

O'Dell's eyes were like ice water. "Bobby Kavanagh was killed because he got sloppy, and Christopher died alongside him. There is nothing to his sister's suspicions."

"Then why don't you just cut her a little slack?" Rafe smiled carelessly. "If there's nothing to her story, let her do what she needs to do for her own peace of mind. She'll come around to the truth eventually." Rafe's smile widened slightly. "Unless that's what you're afraid of. *Is* that what you're afraid of, O'Dell? That she'll discover the truth?"

"The truth may not be anything she wants to find," O'Dell replied calmly, not taking the bait. "Bobby was her big brother, and she thought the sun rose and set on him. She believes he was double-crossed because she needs to believe it. Any other explanation—that he got sloppy, that he got himself and the agent under his care killed because he was hotdogging or because he wasn't as careful as he should have been—just isn't something she's willing to accept. And as for why I don't cut her some slack…" O'Dell's smile was thin. "Even gnomes have to be able to follow orders. If she can't do that, she's no use to me." His eyes held Rafe's. "You of all people should know that. There's no room in my Agency for people who can't follow orders."

"If you'd done your job, I wouldn't have had to do it myself," Rafe said hoarsely. He didn't want to go there. Didn't want to replay that whole nightmare again. He tossed the soft drink can into the sink and turned away, stomach churning. "You got what you came for, O'Dell. Now get the hell off my mountain. And stay off. Next time you step into my gun sight, I might not resist the temptation."

He walked out of the Airstream then, not waiting for an answer, out into the still, dry heat. O'Dell had nothing to say he was interested in hearing and he suddenly needed to get out and into the open, the trailer too small, the air hard to breathe. The sky was like a dome of hard, fired enamel, so deeply blue it hurt to look at it, and the air smelled of summer and mountains and pine pitch. Stephanie suddenly seemed very close simply because it was the kind of day she'd loved. He had the strange feeling that if he turned quickly enough, she would be there, laughing up into the sunlight without a care in the world, dark eyes filled with mischief and promise and that kind of love that just went on forever.

Or as far as forever went. Which wasn't very far at all, Rafe thought dully. Not half far enough.

"It wasn't your fault."

It was O'Dell's voice, but the words echoed Rafe's own thoughts so closely that it took him a distracted moment to realize that O'Dell had followed him outside.

"And it wasn't mine, either." O'Dell appeared beside Rafe, staring across the patch of grass to the rocky hillside beyond, and past that to where the mountain fell away abruptly and there was nothing but sky and the long, heat-hazed sweep of countryside far below them. "Sometimes you can do everything right, and things still go wrong," he said with uncharacteristic quiet. "Sometimes it's no one's fault."

Rafe turned his head to look at the other man. "Don't make the mistake of thinking that two years has made a difference," he said very softly. "I respected you once. We were even friends—once. But I'd have killed you that day as easily as I killed Gillespie if you hadn't brought backup. The only reason you're still alive is because I didn't want anyone else hurt."

"Killing me wouldn't have brought Stephanie back," O'Dell replied with trademark brutality.

"No, but it would have made me feel better."

O'Dell looked at him, his eyes as merciless as agate. "Your wife and baby died because the world isn't always a fair place, not because of something you—or I—did or didn't do. Quit playing the martyr. And quit blaming me."

Rafe heard the words but refused to let them touch him. It was just more of O'Dell's double-talk, more of the confusion of words the man used to weave his version of subverted truth out of the lies in a lifetime of lies. "You promised you'd protect her. You were supposed to have been there, O'Dell. But you wanted Gillespie, so you used Steph for bait. Just like you use everybody."

He stared at O'Dell, but O'Dell could have been carved from granite for all the emotion he revealed. "How the hell do you live with yourself, O'Dell?" he asked softly. "I counted on you. I *believed* in you. Steph's dead because I trusted you to come through for me, but when I needed you, you weren't there." He swallowed, throat thick with unspoken grief and fury. The words felt as though they'd been jammed there for years, and he had to swallow again, fists clenching and unclenching. "And later…you weren't there for me then, either. I needed you, O'Dell. But I wasn't any use to you by then, was I? I was just a sorry drunk, so you cut me loose."

Still, O'Dell didn't say anything. If anything, his expression was even colder and more remote, and Rafe took a half step toward him, fists clenched.

O'Dell turned his head slowly to meet Rafe's gaze. "Take a swing at me if it'll make you feel better," he said quietly. Too quietly, maybe. "But be prepared to go the whole distance this time. I let you take me down once because you were half-drunk and blind with grief and I figured maybe I owed you that much. But I paid any debt I had to you long ago. I didn't kill your wife and unborn son—the job did. If anyone's to blame for Stephanie's death, it's you. The day you married her, you made yourself vulnerable. And you put her at risk."

His thin lips twisted in a parody of a smile. "But you already know that, don't you? That's why you blame me—because it's easier to blame me and the Agency and Gillespie and the whole damn world than it is to blame yourself.''

The words slammed through Rafe like physical blows and he roared with pure rage and stepped toward O'Dell, already swinging. And walked into what felt like a concrete wall.

Something hit him on the side of the jaw with all the subtlety of a pile driver and he was driven back, seeing stars. He staggered to keep his feet, nearly going down and not even clear on what had happened. Then something hit him again, behind his right ear this time, and he did go down, dropping to his knees like a felled tree, dizzy with pain. He bellowed something and lunged to his feet, swinging blindly at shadows as he sensed more than saw O'Dell move toward him. His fist sailed through empty air and the follow-through swung him half around, and in the next heartbeat, O'Dell's fist buried itself almost gently into his solar plexus.

Rafe folded over with a groan, gagging as he tried to suck in a breath, and felt O'Dell's hand fit itself around the back of his neck. O'Dell shoved and Rafe went to his knees heavily, dizzy with pain and unable to catch enough breath to even swear properly.

"If Kavanagh turns up, call me," O'Dell said from above him, sounding unruffled and calm.

"No...phone..." Rafe gasped. Retching dryly, he closed his fist around a handful of dust, but before he could do more than think about throwing it into O'Dell's eyes and beating the hell out of him—presuming he could catch his breath and collect his wits and get to his feet before O'Dell shot him—a booted foot landed across his fingers.

"Quit while you're ahead," O'Dell said with what could have been gentle humor. "Here." A cell phone landed in the dirt in front of Rafe. "You know the number."

The foot withdrew. Rafe started to heave himself to his feet, but O'Dell pushed him down again gently. Rafe heard him sigh and then O'Dell was kneeling beside him, one hand around the back of his neck, the other on his shoulder.

"It's over, Rafe," O'Dell said very quietly, his voice little more than a whisper. "Let it go."

"You son...of...a...bitch," gasped Rafe. "Get...off my... mountain!"

He could have sworn he heard O'Dell chuckle. The hand on his shoulder gave a squeeze; then, before Rafe could figure out what to make of the gesture—as unlike O'Dell as a chuckle would have been—it was gone. And an instant later, O'Dell was on his feet, striding toward his car.

Rafe staggered to his feet and took a stumbling step after O'Dell, but it was too late. O'Dell was already in the car, slamming the door closed.

He started the engine, then paused to look out the open window at Rafe, his eyes oddly troubled. "I don't like it when my men fall in love, Blackhorse. I tell them straight up—like I told you when I recruited you twelve years ago—that falling in love is a one-way ticket out. I made an exception in your case, because for you it was different. For you, it was like finding your way back into the human race, and I figured it was worth the risk. But I was wrong. I should have taken you out of the field the day you told me you were getting married. Maybe if I had..."

He paused, a frown creasing his forehead, and let his gaze drift past Rafe to the mountain and the sky. Then he seemed to come back from wherever he'd gone and met Rafe's eyes again, his expression shuttered. "Take care of yourself, Blackhorse. And if Kavanagh turns up here looking for help, you might consider keeping her around. A man could do a hell of a lot worse."

And then he put the car into gear and drove off in a cloud of dust, leaving Rafe staring after him in angry confusion.

Chapter 5

Someone was stalking her.

Meg had suspected it for days, but now she was sure of it. That black Oldsmobile with the tinted windows was still behind her.

She gave her rearview mirror another quick glance. He'd had to drop back once she'd turned onto this secondary road, where there was little traffic to give him cover, but she knew he was still back there somewhere.

The fact that he'd dropped way back without worrying about losing her meant he had a good idea where she was going, which was reassuring in a weird kind of way. At least it meant her suspicions had been right and that she *was* on to something. That was the good news. The bad news was that whoever she was on to might not be too happy about it.

Then again, it might not mean a darned thing. It might just be O'Dell being O'Dell.

She wouldn't put it past him to send someone out to drag her back to Virginia just to prove he could do it. He hadn't believed a word of her promise to stop rocking the boat—not surprisingly, considering she'd been lying through her teeth at the time. But what she couldn't figure out was why he hadn't just fired her on the spot.

After she'd gotten back from Dakota, he'd spent almost forty-five minutes reading her the riot act, chapter, verse and paragraph. It had been classic O'Dell, and when she'd tottered out of his office afterward, the whole place seemed as astonished as she was that she hadn't been terminated. Figuratively, if not actually literally.

People had given her a wide berth after that, as though afraid they might be caught in the backwash of O'Dell's legendary fury. But she'd gone back down to work in Gnome Alley and a few days later it was as though nothing had happened.

And for a while, nothing did. Then, after two weeks of searching, she'd found the files she'd been looking for, and things had started to fall together. But not all the way. She'd gone as far as she could with the information she'd found, and that was when she'd booked off some sick leave to come out here to see if she could find the rest.

But first, she had to find Blackhorse.

She swore at him for the hundredth time that morning and retrieved the scrap of paper she'd shoved onto the dashboard. Frowning, she again tried to make heads or tails out of the directions the old man at the Weasel Creek General Store had scribbled down for her. He'd used a worn-down carpenter's pencil to write with and his hands had been so shaky the paper had ripped in a couple of places, but the hen-scratches were all she had. Something Mountain...Bean Mountain, maybe? Watch for the turnoff exactly six point three mules west—make that six point three *miles* west—of Indian Pile Road and if you hit Turnip Creek, you've gone too far.

Sounded simple enough. She'd found Indian Pile Road, which had turned out to be Indian *Pipe* Road, about six miles back, and now was watching for the turnoff. Which wasn't marked, the old man had cheerfully told her. Adding, just as cheerfully, that Blackhorse didn't like unannounced visitors and was as likely to shoot her as not.

At exactly six point three miles, Meg spotted what could have been a side road. *Not marked* was an understatement. She stopped the car and looked at the rutted trail unhappily.

Then, shaking her head at her own folly, she turned the nose of the car toward the break in the trees and eased it across a makeshift wooden culvert that creaked alarmingly.

Once on the other side of the culvert, she stopped the car and eyed the trail—calling it a road was laughable—with growing unease. Not a good idea. Not without four-wheel-drive and a small army to back her up. But there had been recent traffic along it, which was reassuring. She could see tire tracks, and they looked fairly fresh.

And she didn't have an army.

Touching the Beretta like a talisman, she took another deep breath, then gently pressed her foot onto the gas pedal and guided the car into the narrow set of ruts. I'm going to get to the bottom of this, Bobby, she whispered as the car wallowed through a pothole of muddy water. I won't let you down, I promise.

The rifle shot cracked through the evening's stillness just as Rafe set another piece of seasoned poplar onto the splitting block. He straightened slowly, eyes narrowing as a second shot followed the first. And then, at a well-spaced interval, a third.

He shifted his grip on the ax and went very still, listening. About a mile away, he estimated. It was hard to tell, this time of day. Sounds carried all over the place when the air was still and cool, and it could have come just as easily from somewhere down along Indian Pipe Road as on his mountain.

Poachers. Kids plinking beer bottles. Drunks killing road signs. Could be a dozen things.

Except the back of his neck was still prickling, and he knew why without even thinking hard. A good sniper spaced his killing shots like that: calm, steady, unrushed, taking deliberate aim at his target before squeezing off a shot.

He'd been on both ends of a sniper's rifle, and the sound was buried in his subconscious with a hundred others, part of his hunter-prey instincts, fine-tuned to keep him alive.

It was those instincts that made him move now. He eased himself into the shadows of the trees, walked quickly around to the trailer and went inside. It was dark, and he left it that way, moving around the familiar contours of furniture as easily as he would in broad daylight. There was probably no need for a weapon, but he grabbed the rifle out of the cabinet and checked it, then eased himself back out into the cold evening air.

He found the car about two miles down, tucked under the overhanging boughs of an old pine tree in one of the few spots where you could pull off the road. There was nothing remarkable about it—rental tags, an airport parking sticker on the windshield, an empty paper coffee cup lying on its side on the dashboard. Nothing to make him suspicious at all, aside from the fact it was on *his* mountain and seemingly abandoned.

And the bullet holes, of course.

There were two of them, and they were so new that the paint was still flaking off around the one in the rear panel on the driver's side. The other was in the windshield, the passenger side, and the nonshatter glass was crazed and sagging slightly. It took him a moment to find the third one. It had gone through the left rear tire, leaving it as flat as they come, and he looked at it for a moment, frowning, then tried the driver's door.

Locked. Wishing he'd brought a flashlight, he peered through the window but couldn't see anything beyond the fact that there was no body inside. Which didn't say there wasn't one in the trunk. Gritting his teeth, he tried that, too, almost relieved to find it solidly locked as well.

He whispered a heartfelt "Damn it to hell" under his breath, then quickly searched the ground around the car, not expecting to find anything to give him a clue as to what had gone on here but giving the area a thorough once-over anyway. Nothing. The grass was too damp and springy to hold a footprint, and there was nothing else to give so much as a hint as to who the car belonged to, who had shot it full of holes or where the driver was.

Which meant he had at least two strangers out here on his mountain, Rafe thought irritably as he straightened and eyed the heavy bush surrounding him. One doing the shooting, and one getting shot at.

In spite of himself, he thought about O'Dell's visit five days ago. And a hot-tempered computer specialist with hair the color of live flame who didn't know when to quit.

He swore again, almost wearily this time, and headed back to his trailer.

And for some reason he didn't even bother trying to figure

out, when he got back to his trailer and found it blazing with light, he wasn't even surprised. It had just been that kind of a day.

Whoever the intruder was, he'd made himself right at home. A mug half-full of lukewarm coffee sat on the table, and both camp lanterns were lit, hissing quietly as they filled the front half of the trailer with a welcoming glow. And Three, watchdog extraordinaire, was lying flat on his back, legs akimbo, snoring like a walrus.

Rafe swore as he stepped over the sleeping dog and stood there for a moment, rifle held loosely and at the ready. And then he realized the shower was running and swore again. He was going to kill the man, sure as hell. Right here, right now. And worry about the consequences later.

Not, in all likelihood, that there would be many. The line of people wanting O'Dell dead would circle the planet twice over and included everyone from presidents on down.

But the instant he pushed open the door to the tiny bathroom, he knew it wasn't O'Dell. The shower was going flat out, filling the room with steam, but it was the perfume of herbal shampoo and English Lavender soap that brought him up short. The scent wrapped warm moist tendrils around him, making his belly constrict as a flood of vivid memories made his breath catch.

He could see her in the metal shower stall, just a blur through the heavy plastic curtain, and he froze instinctively. But then he realized that she hadn't heard him come in. Had no idea he was there, watching her.

She hummed like a contented cat while she lathered her hair, and he found himself holding his breath, unable to take his eyes off the shadowed apparition of female curves and indentations standing just a step or two from him. He felt disoriented, having dreamed this sort of thing so often that the reality of her being here—naked and apparently quite at home in his shower—didn't even seem that out of place. It was as though all those erotic night thoughts had coalesced into form and substance and he'd brought her here somehow, all sleek, wet flesh and laughing eyes, waiting for him....

Rafe caught the thought right there and killed it dead. Putting his imagination firmly on ice, he shook off the rest of the fantasy and brought himself back into the here and now with brutal efficiency.

Not giving himself time to think too much, he reached out and yanked the curtain aside on its metal rings. "Like to tell me what the hell you're doing, Agent Kavanagh?"

She reacted so quickly he didn't get more than a glimpse of soapy skin and a few tantalizing curves before she'd snapped the curtain closed again. "Hey! Do you *mind!*"

"Yeah, as a matter of fact, I do mind." He was tempted to pull the curtain open again but realized his motives weren't half as pure as he would like to think they were. And he didn't have to *see* her to yell at her. In fact, it was probably just as well that he couldn't see her, he thought a bit desperately. Because yelling at her was about the last thing on his mind right now, and what *was* on his mind wasn't anything he was proud of.

"You're in *my* shower, lady!" he finally bawled. It sounded pretty lame, but it was the best he could come up with, considering his mind seemed to be off on a tangent of its own.

"O'Dell said you were smart," she muttered ungraciously. "Darn it, you made me get shampoo in my eyes!" There were some other mutters. "And I wouldn't be in your blasted shower if you hadn't shot my car up so I had to walk the rest of the way through the mud and...bugs!" One edge of the shower curtain was pulled back and he found himself pinned by a ferocious blue gaze. "You've got a hell of a nerve, Blackhorse. Shooting at a government agent is a Federal offence."

"Government agent, my—"

"You could have killed me, you idiot!"

"Don't give me any ideas," Rafe growled just as ungraciously. "And you're wasting hot water, damn it. You've got thirty seconds to get the hell out of my shower before I haul your backside out of there myself."

Her eyes widened slightly, more with fury than fear, and Rafe had the sudden image of her coming at him with a bottle of shampoo, deliciously naked and slippery with soap and—

He wheeled away. "Twenty seconds and counting, sweetheart."

To his surprise, there was silence. "I need a towel," she said finally, sounding subdued.

He opened his mouth to tell her to use the one hanging on

the side of the stall, then realized it had been there a while. A long while, in fact. Wincing, he reached up and opened the small cupboard built into the bulkhead above the shower and pulled out two clean towels, wondering when he'd last done laundry. And then wondering why he gave a damn. The woman was lucky he didn't haul her out buck naked and send her packing.

He stood in front of the shower curtain, trying not to look. Not that there was much to see, just an indistinct pink blur through steam and water trickles and old plastic. But his imagination didn't need any help filling in the details, and he had to take a deep breath. "Towels." His voice sounded strained.

A small hand attached to a slender arm reached past the curtain. "Thank you."

He wanted to touch her, he suddenly realized—so badly he could taste it. Just like in all those forbidden dreams, he wanted to run his hand up that silken arm to the sweep of wet shoulder behind it and then—

He shoved one of the towels into her hand and draped the other one over the curtain bar, and then he got the hell out of there.

He was still unsettled when she came out of the bathroom a few minutes later. She was rubbing her hair with one of the towels, and Rafe felt his belly constrict as she walked through the small kitchen area toward him. Where she'd found the flannel shirt, he had no idea—the last time he'd seen it was in his own closet—but she wore it with a casual elegance worthy of any designer gown. The long tails almost came to her knees back and front, and she'd had to roll the sleeves up ten or twelve times, but it was still as tantalizing as all get out. Her legs and feet were bare, and he could see droplets of water beaded in the delicate hollow of her throat and found himself wondering what she was wearing under it, if anything.

Seeming unaware of the tantalizing picture she presented, she gave her hair one last rub, then draped the damp towel over her shoulder and stood there in the middle of his trailer, filling the place with the scent of lavender and more erotic possibilities than he'd ever imagined.

Except the look she was giving him was anything but erotic. It was ice-cold and about as friendly as barbed wire. "You really are a piece of work, Blackhorse."

Rafe grinned in spite of himself. He didn't want to grin—hell, under the circumstances he should have half killed her by now. But instead of knocking her feet out from under her and putting her in a stranglehold and teaching her some manners, he just found himself standing there grinning like a fool, thinking it had been a long time since he'd seen anything quite so pretty on Bear Mountain. Or so angry.

"It's great to see you again, too, Special Agent Mary Margaret Kavanagh." He wrapped his tongue around her name, nearly laughing at the sheer insanity of it. After five weeks of fantasizing, here she was. For an instant or two he was almost ready to forgive O'Dell the subterfuge.

Almost.

"So, Irish, what the hell are you doing up here?" He smiled benignly, almost curious as to how it was going to go down. Almost. "They don't have showers where you're from?"

She gave him a withering look. "Don't start with me. There are laws against things like this. Even out here in this godforsaken part of the country, you can't just shoot people's cars up because it strikes you as a good idea." She saw the rifle just then, propped up against the wall by the door where he'd left it. Eyes narrowing, she strode toward it purposefully. Rafe stiffened instinctively but made himself stay where he was. She snatched it up and ran the bolt smoothly. "And you're going to pay for the damages to that rental car, mister, because if you think I'm going to let them hit me up for the inflated insurance charges, you're—" She seemed to suddenly run out of steam. "This isn't even the right caliber rifle, is it?"

"Nope."

Her shoulders sagged and she leaned the rifle against the wall again, looking decidedly subdued. Almost frightened. "It wasn't you. I'd hoped…"

It was so well done he found himself almost believing her. Almost. Then he reminded himself a little brutally why she was here, all shower-damp and tousle-haired and seductive, and gave himself a mental shake.

"You can give the innocent act a rest, Specialist Kavanagh. Or is that Agent-in-Training Kavanagh now? Is that what you're getting out of this? O'Dell's promise to let you train as a field agent?" He managed a humorless smile. "He won't go through with it, you know. He'll play you along for as long as you're useful, then drop you from the training program on some excuse and send you back to Gnome Alley, and that'll be the end of your new career.''

His voice was tight and rough, and Rafe turned away from her abruptly, pulling open the fridge door. For the first time in nineteen months, he found himself wanting a drink. But he shoved the thought aside and grabbed the jug of cold milk instead. He lifted it and took three long swallows, then wiped his mouth with the back of his hand and shoved the jug back into the fridge.

She didn't say anything. She was just standing there as though uncertain as to what to do next, and for an instant he almost felt sorry for her. O'Dell, being the bastard he was, probably hadn't really briefed her. He would have told her what she was supposed to do and then dumped her up here, leaving her to make it up as she went along.

Rafe looked at her for a moment or two, half tempted to play it out for as long as he could. She was too new at the game to know he was stringing her along, and he could give her the fright of her life before sending her back to O'Dell. It was tempting. She was as beautiful as they made them, and he could almost taste her mouth, the sweetness of her shower-damp skin, could feel the silk of her...

Too tempting. So tempting, in fact, that he decided to end it then and there before his imagination got him into a world of trouble.

So instead of walking across and drawing her into his arms and carrying her into the tiny bedroom and seeing just how far she was willing to take the charade before her nerve broke, he just smiled tolerantly at her. "Okay, Irish, let's get it over with. How's it going down? You give some signal and drop that shirt, and suddenly we're knee-deep in agents, right? Then I get the choice of being charged with—oh, hell, any number of things. Assault. Kidnapping. Attempted rape. Whatever. *Or...*'' He paused, feeling the anger flirt through him. "Or I agree to do some dirty little job for O'Dell. That about it?''

She was staring at him as though he'd just beamed down from another planet. "O'Dell? You think that *O'Dell* sent me?'' She gave a sputter of laughter. "O'Dell would *kill* me if he knew I was up here. And as for this…'' She waved her hand to take in the entire trailer. ''This, Agent Blackhorse, was just a bad idea.''

Rafe's eyes narrowed very slightly. She was either a hell of a better actor—and liar—than he'd thought, or she was telling the truth. And if she was telling the truth, that changed the whole ball game into something else altogether.

But what were the odds of that? That she would wind up here, just out of the blue like this, a handful of days after O'Dell's visit?

''So you're telling me this is all just coincidence?'' he drawled, watching her eyes. ''That O'Dell comes up here with some cock-and-bull story about you going renegade on him, and—''

''O'Dell was here?'' He could have sworn she paled. *''Here?''*

''Damnedest thing, isn't it?'' He smiled pleasantly, humoring her. ''Then, not five days later, you turn up.''

''But why would he come *here?*'' she said, more to herself than to him. She started pacing, rubbing her arms with her hands, looking bleak and uncertain. ''That doesn't make any sense. There's no way he'd have made the connection, unless—'' She went dead still, eyes focused on an invisible spot on the wall. ''Unless he knows what I'm looking for. But that—'' Again she stopped, appearing not to even be aware he was still there.

Rafe watched her impatiently. ''Look, Irish, I'm not buying this for—''

''Did he ask you about my brother?'' She turned her head to look at him, her eyes bright with intensity. ''Did he mention anything at all about Bobby? About how he died?''

Rafe didn't like the way this was going. He'd been in the business for a long, long while, and he knew when someone was hiding something. Especially someone as inexperienced as Kavanagh. It was in their eyes and voice, in their gestures, the way they held their bodies. It was an instinct he had. And it was rarely wrong.

Every instinct he had was telling him now that Mary Margaret Kavanagh was telling the truth. Which was crazy.

Frustrated and angry, he shook it off. ''So I'm supposed to believe that you thought I was the one who shot at you, but you still broke into my trailer, stripped naked and got into my shower? That about it?''

To his surprise, her cheeks flooded with color and she ducked her head, fingers automatically clutching the throat of the shirt closed. ''I, um…I'm sorry about that. It's just that I was pretty sure you were bluffing and wouldn't actually hurt me and I was—well, I was mad. I came up here intending to shoot back, if you want the truth. But you weren't here. I waited for a while, but I'd come through some sort of bog and was soaking wet and covered with mud and slime and I stank, and then there were all these gnats and mosquitoes and things and—'' She shrugged.

Then she looked up finally and met his gaze evenly. ''I'm sorry.'' She managed a look that could pass for contrite. ''I had no right breaking into your home, and I apologize. It's just that I figured you owed me a shower and a cup of coffee, at least, and I guess…'' She shrugged again. ''O'Dell doesn't have anything to do with my being up here, Mr. Blackhorse, I swear that. In fact, I rather doubt I even work for O'Dell anymore. The last time I saw him, he was pretty annoyed. And if he suspects I came up here, then he knows I'm not on sick leave. And if he knows that…'' She sighed, shoulders sagging again. ''I'm probably fired.''

The damnedest thing was, Rafe found himself believing her. Almost.

''And you didn't shoot at me?'' She sounded hopeful.

''Why would I do that?''

Another shrug. ''The old gentleman down at the Weasel Creek store said you might. That you don't take well to people coming up here.''

''I don't.'' He felt unsettled and off balance and found himself almost wishing O'Dell was up to his old tricks. At least then he would know what to expect. And what to do about it.

''Whoever put those three rounds into your car came up here looking for you.''

''But that's—'' She paled slightly. ''That's impossible,'' she added in a half whisper.

Rafe snorted. He expected it to elicit some sort of angry comment, but she said nothing, hugging herself again as though chilled, shoulders rounded as she gave the door an uneasy glance. Rafe felt the back of his neck tingle very slightly.

''Like to tell me what you're doing up here? And who you've brought up onto my mountain with you?''

She looked back at him, shaking her head slowly. ''I...I don't know. You said *three* rounds. How did you know my car took three rounds?''

Rafe smiled faintly. He dug the three brass shell casings out of his shirt pocket and tossed them onto the floor at her feet.

She paled again. ''Where did you find them?''

''Where your sniper left them.''

''*My* sniper?''

''He wasn't up here shooting at me, darlin'.''

She didn't say anything, and he smiled humorlessly, then shrugged away from the wall where he'd been leaning all this time. ''For future reference, like to tell me how you bypassed the security system and got through the door locks?''

She didn't meet his eyes. ''I...um...''

In spite of himself, Rafe had to give a snort of laughter. He had the whole place rigged like a fortress, everything state of the art, locks unbreachable, codes impossible to crack. Except to one of O'Dell's gnomes, of course, to whom *unbreachable* and *impossible to crack* were no more than minor irritations. His opinion of her rose a notch or two even while he was cursing her under his breath.

''Your dog gave me a fright. But he didn't give me any trouble.'' She looked across at Three, who was lying flat on his back, feet twitching in doggy dreams as he slept the sleep of the righteous.

''And if he had? What else do you have in your little secret agent bag of tricks? Strychnine?''

She sucked in an indignant breath. ''Of course not! I'd never hurt an innocent animal! What on earth do you think I am?''

''Trouble, Special Agent Mary Margaret Kavanagh.'' He gave her a steady look. ''I think you are a whole lot of trouble.''

At that precise moment Meg couldn't even argue with him and mean it. She had no real idea what she was even doing up here, she realized. It had seemed clear yesterday. Even this morning, she'd thought she had things under control. But now it felt as though it was all unraveling, and she had no idea how to stop it from just falling apart around her.

Rafe had walked across the small room and pulled open a

tall, shallow cabinet built into the hardwood paneling near the door. She caught a glimpse of at least two more rifles, one with an infrared nightscope, a brace of handguns, a couple of automatic weapons she couldn't readily identify, other than the fact that they were highly lethal and highly illegal. He settled the old hunting rifle into its slot, then closed the cabinet. She heard the click of automatic locks, the subdued beep of an alarm system kicking in.

"Do you get a lot of unwanted company up here?"

He gave her a cool look as he walked by her and back into the tiny kitchen. "Not twice."

Meg winced. This was going to be tougher than she'd anticipated. Then she found herself thinking about what he'd said. About finding the bullet casings. They were still lying on the carpeted floor where he'd tossed them, and she knelt down and picked them up, fingering them. If she'd been a real field agent, she would practically know her would-be assassin's hat size just from these things alone. But she wasn't a real field agent. She turned the casings over in her fingers, learning nothing.

"Why would O'Dell need to blackmail you into working for him?" she called to him thoughtfully. She realized he was watching her from over the kitchen counter and looked up, half-afraid of what she might see in his expression.

But his face was carefully blank. "When does O'Dell ever need a reason for doing anything?"

She thought about that for a moment, then decided not to risk an answer. Truth was, he was half-right. O'Dell might have his reasons, but she was sure she would never be in on them. Whatever was going on between him and this man, it didn't have anything to do with her. And she would be very smart to keep it that way.

She stood up finally, still looking at the shell casings. "You said sniper. Why a sniper, specifically? Why not just someone with a rifle and a bad attitude?"

"The way the shots were spaced. And the way he was set up. He'd taken some time to scout out a location—lots of cover, good view of the road, perfect shot angles. Whoever it was, he's good."

"But he left these." She held out her hand; the casings

gleamed in the light from the camp lantern on the table. "I thought the first rule was to collect your casings."

Blackhorse just shrugged. "Part of the warning, I figure."

"So you don't think he was trying to kill me."

He smiled very faintly, but the humor didn't come anywhere near his eyes. "And what do *you* think, Special Agent Kavanagh?"

His use of the title he knew she'd never earned irritated her, but she decided to ignore it. "I think if he'd wanted me dead, I'd be dead." She tipped her chin up, staring right at him. "Problem is, Ex-Agent Blackhorse, that brings the blame back to you. No one knew I was coming here. How would someone know to set an ambush for me?"

"Well, that's the big money question, isn't it, Irish?" His voice had taken on a friendly tone she didn't like at all. "So maybe, before I toss you out of here, you'd like to tell me the rest of your story so I know who's after your hide and if any of it's going to rub off on me."

It surprised her to realize she didn't want to tell him anything at all. It seemed thin, suddenly. Tenuous and farfetched. Everyone else thought she was crazy, including the mighty Spence O'Dell. Blackhorse wouldn't be any different. And she was tired of being told she was imagining things. Just get what you came for and get out of here, she told herself tightly. He doesn't have to know why you need the information. He doesn't have to know what you suspect.

Meg opened her mouth to bluff her way through it, then saw something in his expression that made her hesitate. "Someone's been following me," she finally admitted. "I spotted him in Denver five days ago. Then Albuquerque. When I flew out here, I thought I'd lost him. But there's been a car behind me all day. Oldsmobile. Black. Tinted windows. I thought at first it might be O'Dell. But that's not O'Dell's style."

To her surprise, it made him smile. At least she thought it was a smile.

"But I don't see—" She rubbed her arms, suddenly wishing she'd pulled on something more substantial than this cotton shirt. "The car was behind me. Whoever took those shots at me was already up here, waiting for me. It couldn't have been the same person."

He was looking at her in a speculative way she found even more unnerving than one of O'Dell's stares. O'Dell used silence like a weapon, just sitting there letting you fidget and think and imagine the worst until you finally broke and told him everything he wanted to know. But this was even worse.

She shivered suddenly.

It seemed to amuse Rafe. "There's a trail that runs straight up from Indian Pipe Road. It's not easy to find, but it's marked on some maps. Whoever was following you came up that way and got ahead of you. All he had to do was dig in and wait."

"Oh." Her voice sounded small.

"I don't know what kind of a mess you've gotten yourself into, Specialist Kavanagh, but I'd be mighty grateful if you took it the hell away from here." He smiled coolly. "The only reason I'm not hauling you down to the county sheriff's office and charging you with trespassing and breaking and entering and a half dozen other things is that I kind of feel sorry for you. I've seen O'Dell when one of his people crosses him. I figure the worst I could do to you would be a picnic compared to what he's going to do when he finally catches up with you." The smile widened. "You might want to think about moving to some faraway place, Specialist Kavanagh. Changing your name. Plastic surgery might be an idea, too. Not that it'll help, of course. He'll find you eventually. He always does."

"Like he found you?" she snapped, tired of his attempts to frighten her. "What are you running from, Ex-Agent Blackhorse? What made *you* go renegade?"

It was one of those moments that could go either way, Rafe decided quite rationally. Either he was going to kill her, or he was going to pretend he hadn't heard her. And from the expression on Meg's face, it was clear she was no more certain of which it was going to be than he was.

In the end, he just turned away without saying anything at all, not trusting his voice. He heard her swallow, the sound overloud in the stillness, and hoped she was thinking long and hard about how close she had come to seeing eternity up close and personal.

Anger ebbed and surged through him, fierce one moment and inconsequential the next, and he swore between his teeth. As annoyed by that as by any of it—the fact she was here, the fact she'd gotten by him and into his trailer without his even knowing it, the fact he hadn't already thrown her out into the approaching night without a second thought, all of it—he walked across and opened a panel beside the door. It was set into the tongue-and-groove paneling so skillfully that it was invisible unless you knew where to look, unbreachable unless you knew what exact spot to touch. Not that any of that had stopped Kavanagh, of course. O'Dell's sweet-faced wunderkind gnome. He wondered what else she'd discovered.

The panel popped open soundlessly, and he turned the perimeter security alarms on, running a swift systems check as he did so to make sure everything was working as it should be. He probably didn't have to bother with it, but *someone* had been out there stalking Meg. He was pretty sure whoever it had been had hightailed it and was halfway back to Weasel Creek by now, but he hadn't stayed alive this long by being careless.

He looked around at her. She was standing turned half-away from him, between him and the lamp, and the light was shining through the cotton shirt in ways he doubted she was aware of. He couldn't see anything at all, just a hint of hip and long thigh, the soft curve of a breast, but it made him swallow hard. Anyone else and he could have ignored it, but with her...

He drew a careful breath. All those damned dreams had left their mark. He'd made love to her a dozen times in those dreams. Two dozen. He knew her by heart. Or at least his imagination thought he did. His hands thought he did, aching to touch, to caress, to explore. His mouth thought he did, aching to sample, to kiss, to taste. And his body sure as hell thought he did, aching to stretch out along hers and feel her taut and willing against him, and—

A surge of pure, unadulterated desire made his stomach knot and he clenched his teeth, forcing the torrent of vivid images out of his mind. "Don't you have any damn clothes?"

It seemed to startle her, and she looked around at him. "What?"

"Clothes." He walked by her roughly, taunting himself with her closeness. The air around her was filled with the scent of her skin and hair, and he felt light-headed for a moment, wondering if this *was* just some more bizarre version of the dreams that had been haunting him for weeks now, ever since South Dakota.

"North," he said aloud, gritting his teeth. "*North* Dakota." Get rid of her, his mind whispered ferociously. Get rid of her *now*.

Meg stared at his retreating back as he walked into the tiny bedroom that ran across the back of the trailer. "Of course I have clothes," she finally said, more out of exasperation than any real understanding of what they were discussing and what North Dakota had to do with any of it. "I rinsed out my jeans and sweater and hung them outside to dry."

"Which should only take a week or two," he growled, appearing again as suddenly as he'd vanished.

Meg looked at him in confusion. Then she realized that the sound she'd been listening to for the past few minutes was rain drumming on the metal skin of the trailer. "Oh." She frowned. "Maybe I should bring them in, then."

"Maybe you should put them back on and get the hell off my mountain," he muttered ungraciously.

"But…"

Without even looking at her, he pushed the door open and vanished into the night, leaving her standing there with her mouth open in protest. The three-legged dog lifted his head and looked at the door, then lay down again, giving his tail a couple of absent beats, as though glad no one was suggesting he go for a walk.

Rafe was back a minute or two later, bounding into the trailer and giving himself a shake, spraying rainwater. He tossed a soaking bundle of clothes onto the floor at Meg's feet. "I'm not running a hotel. You had your shower and made your point." He nodded his head in the direction of the door. "*Hasta la vista.* Don't slam it on your way out."

She stared at him, stricken. "But—"

"You've got about an hour of daylight left. I advise you to make the best use of it, because changing that flat in the dark won't be a picnic. Neither is driving that road at night, but I figure you should have thought of that before you came up here." He gave the door another nod. "Now get the hell off my mountain before I decide to finish what your sniper friend started."

Meg started to feel panicky. "But I haven't even had a chance to—"

"I don't know how, and I don't know why, but this has got something to do with O'Dell. I can smell it. I told him if he ever came up here again, I'd kill him. You can tell him for me that goes for any of his people, too. Now get!"

"I told you, O'Dell doesn't have—"

"Lady," he said in a deceptively soft voice, "you're running out of daylight." He turned and headed toward the bedroom again.

"I need to talk to you!"

"You need to get off this mountain." He didn't even bother looking around.

"It's about your wife!"

Chapter 6

The words seemed to hit him like a physical blow. Meg saw him almost stagger and put his hand out as though to steady himself. There was a sudden silence, and she swallowed. Even the old dog seemed to sense something was wrong. He lifted his head and whined.

Rafe turned. Slowly. "What the hell did you just say?" His voice was barely a whisper.

Meg swallowed again. She'd wanted to get his attention and had said the first thing that popped into her head. But now that she *had* his attention, it didn't look like anything she wanted at all. Wishing she could take the words back, she fought the impulse to turn and bolt. He was moving back toward her, looking deceptively relaxed.

"What did you say?" he repeated almost conversationally.

"I—I said I need to talk to you. About a case you were on."

"No." He shook his head slowly, looking at her with the coldest expression she'd ever seen in her life. "No, you said something about my wife."

"I—" Meg took a deep breath, forcing herself to stand still as he neared. The trailer was smaller suddenly. Too small. She glanced at the door. "D-details. I need to check some details with you, that's all. A-about the case. And about your...about your wife's death." She swallowed, almost paralyzed by the expression in his eyes. "Murder. Her...murder."

"Get off my mountain, Miss Kavanagh," he said very softly. "You're a long way from Virginia now. A long way from O'Dell's protection. I could kill you and *no* one would be able to prove it, do you understand that? I could make you, your car, all of it just disappear."

Meg wasn't even breathing. There was something in his eyes, something so deep and so cold and so deadly that she didn't doubt for a moment that he was capable of doing exactly what he threatened.

Even if she'd wanted to say something, her tongue was frozen. Rafe just stared down at her for another chill half second or two, then he eased his weight back and turned away from her.

Meg didn't move so much as a hair until he'd walked the few feet down the narrow corridor past the bathroom, where tendrils of scented steam still hung in the air, and into the bedroom. The door was a beautifully woven Navajo blanket that had been draped to one side. It fell closed behind him, and only when he'd vanished from her sight was Meg finally able to breathe again.

She felt stiff and half-frozen, and she started to shiver suddenly, her teeth chattering. Closing her eyes for a moment, she struggled to get her heartbeat steadied. It had been insane, coming up here. *He* was insane. They said he'd tried to kill O'Dell two years ago. She'd put that down to rumor and the almost mythic way people still talked about him, but now she wasn't so sure.

She thought about the rest of his file—what little she'd been able to dig out of archives. It had been a warrior's file, filled with commendations and glowing appraisals and even a letter from a president. But there were gaps. Things missing. Details that didn't add up. That wasn't unusual—O'Dell found his agents in some strange places, many of them unsavory, and probably the majority of the personnel files had gaping holes and parts that were sealed to all but the highest security clearance.

But security clearance was no challenge to someone like her. Even O'Dell's security. She'd breached the sealed section of Rafe's files in about thirty seconds flat but had been left more puzzled than ever. He was a lone wolf; she'd figured that out. A cowboy. Although he'd been partnered with a number of good agents while he'd been with the Agency, he'd done most of his work alone. Undercover, mostly. Dangerous, dark stuff that was never fully detailed in the reports.

She'd wondered as she'd read through the file if he'd been one of those shadowy agents whose existence was always strenuously denied. Even Bobby had talked about them, laughing, but with something in his voice that had made her wonder if he knew more than he let on. Hired guns, the rumors went. Assassins. Stone killers. Word had it that they were O'Dell's elite cadre. Ex-mercs. Renegades from this nasty little war or that who'd liked the killing and couldn't leave it behind. Retired Special Forces types who just never fit back into the real world after years of black ops.

Whatever he had been, whatever he was now, one thing was clear: Rafe Blackhorse was the kind of serious trouble she didn't need.

The problem was, he was also the only person who could help her.

It would be dark in another half hour. Rafe stared out the small window without really seeing anything, avoiding his own reflection in the darkened glass while watching raindrops slant across it, blown almost sideways by the wind. It was days like these he'd loved most, once. Driven indoors by the weather, using it as an excuse to stay in and light the little woodstove, he and Stephanie would curl up on the sofa together, wrapped in a big wool blanket.

Cocooning, Steph had called it. Snug and dry and warm, they would talk quietly while the rain pounded the thin metal skin of the trailer and the wind made the whole place shudder. They'd talk about the past and the future. About the kids they'd planned to have—he always said three was a good number, but she'd always argued that three meant a middle child, always caught between, so four was better.

They'd talk about the house they were building. The bathrooms, anyway. He swore no one needed more than one bathroom, and she argued that if they were going to have four kids, they were going to have at least two bathrooms—preferably three—and that was all there was to it. And a laundry room. She'd been adamant about that damned laundry room.

Even now, almost three years later, it made him automatically smile. Their ancestors, he'd remind her regularly, had made do with a rock and a river. None of their ancestors, she'd always shot back without missing a beat, had juggled husbands, babies and busy teaching careers while finishing advanced degrees in history and education *and* raising hell on a routine basis as an outspoken activist for Native American rights. If he wanted to use a rock and a river, he was free to do so. She, on the other hand, had found an advertisement in some survivalist magazine for an old-fashioned wringer washing machine that ran off a small gas engine and had decided it would do fine. Although, as she'd then pointed out smugly, she *would* forgo the matching propane dryer just to prove that twenty years of big-city living hadn't turned her into a complete marshmallow.

And so he'd added another bathroom to the floor plan and shoehorned a small laundry room into one end of what had started out as a big porch and mudroom—another thing she'd sworn she wasn't living without. It was still out there, past the rain and the trees and the rocks. Just a skeleton of studs and planks and lost dreams now, Steph's bathroom and laundry room unrecognizable, the whole thing untouched for over two years. He'd thought once of burning the thing to the ground just to get it out of his line of sight, it and the memories it drove through his heart like sharp, thorned things. But he'd been too drunk to even strike a match properly back then. And once he'd sobered up, he'd just never gotten around to it. He never went out there now. Never looked at it. And some days he never thought of it at all.

Light bloomed as the blanket across the door was pulled aside.

Then it fell closed and the room was dark again, and Rafe felt his shoulders tighten. She didn't say anything, but he knew she was in the room with him. The darkness was suddenly filled with her, a warm female presence that seemed to wrap around him like a tangible touch, filling his nostrils with the scent of roses and his mind with a swirl of images.

He took a deep breath and released it, flexing his shoulders slightly to unknot them. He didn't bother looking around. "What the hell is it going to take to get you to leave me alone, lady?"

She was silent for a long while. Long enough for him to wonder if she was there at all or if his imagination had just run riot again. It seemed to do that a lot when it came to this woman. Then he heard her sigh.

"I'm sorry." It was just a whisper. "I didn't mean to…"

He waited for her to finish the thought, half-curious as to what she hadn't meant to do. Tempt him to commit wholesale murder? Remind him of a past he'd put to rest long ago? Remind him he hadn't been with a woman in what suddenly seemed like forever and that his anger at her was as much raw, unapologetic lust as it was honest fury at her prying?

He heard her take a deep breath and found himself almost smiling. Damned if she didn't have some serious backbone.

"I just need some information, and then I'll leave and you'll never see me again."

"I could break your neck and stuff your body under a rock and accomplish pretty much the same thing with a lot less aggravation."

"You could." But the way she said it made it fairly clear she thought the possibility was remote.

He gave her a sharp look, half expecting to find her smiling. But she wasn't. She was just standing there in the dimness of the unlit room, her expression troubled as she looked back at him.

"I'm sorry for intruding into your grief. And I'm sorry for disturbing a lot of private memories. But—"

"What the hell do you know about it?" He held her gaze challengingly.

"Not nearly enough," she said very quietly. "That's why I'm

here. To find out everything you can tell me about what happened.''

''And why would I do that?'' He turned his head to stare out at the storm again, both hands on the window frame, arms braced. He was watching her in the rain-dark glass, knew she knew he was watching when her reflected gaze met his dead-on.

''I think I know who killed your wife.''

The words didn't make any sense for a moment or two. He'd been expecting her to ask about her brother or about O'Dell or the agency or something. Or about the case, maybe. The one he'd been on when—

''Gil Gillespie killed my wife.'' He was surprised at how calmly he was able to say it.

''Gillespie pulled the trigger,'' she said just as calmly from the darkness behind him. ''But he was just the muscle, not the brains. He admitted as much before he...died.''

''Before I killed him.'' For some inexplicible reason, it made Rafe smile, although God knows there was nothing about that day that was remotely amusing. He met her troubled gaze on the dark, wet glass of the window again. ''Don't tell me O'Dell left that little fact out of the file, Agent Kavanagh. That's the one that got me fired.''

He heard her draw another deep, slow breath. ''No. No, he didn't leave that out of the file.''

''Doesn't it scare you a little?'' he taunted gently. ''Being up here, alone, with no transportation and no backup, half-naked, with a killer?''

He clearly saw irritation flicker across her face. ''I've worked for the Agency for three years, Mr. Blackhorse. You're not the first *killer* I've met, and I doubt you'll be the last.''

Her chin tipped up slightly, and Rafe had to smile again. Part of it was bravado, he reckoned, but not all of it. Again, without even really thinking about it, his estimation of her rose another notch. He gave a snort of honest laughter, surprising himself a little. ''Hell, if Spence O'Dell doesn't scare you, nothing will.''

''Spence O'Dell scares the living daylights out of me,'' she said quietly.

''And me?'' He turned around then, fixing her gaze with his.

He distinctly heard her swallow, but she didn't move a hair. Even when he walked toward her, slowly, letting her think about it, she didn't so much as blink. One tough little cookie. And stubborn. O'Dell had been right about her.

''No.''

He heard the lie in the single word and smiled faintly, close enough to her now that she had to tip her head back to meet his eyes. Still, she held her ground. ''You *should* be afraid, Special Agent Mary Margaret Kavanagh,'' he said in a half whisper, finding himself a little dizzied by the scent and warmth of her. The *reality* of her. ''You sure by God should be…''

And then, no more intending to than fly, he kissed her.

Not much of a kiss, but it still startled the hell out of him. Her, too. He heard her breath suck in, and she went rigid, her hands flying up to rest on his chest. But not pushing him away; he still had enough conscious thought left to make note of that. She didn't push him away at all. Her touch was more one of support than defense, as though she was afraid of falling or something, and she went very, very still as he lowered his face to hers. He saw her eyes widen with surprise, and then his lips brushed hers, warmth on warmth, and it was too late for second thoughts.

She was unresponsive for a moment or two, too surprised even to knee him. Then her lips parted slightly and he tasted her breath in his mouth, sweet and slightly minty, and he realized she had no intention of kneeing him at all. Still not knowing what the hell he thought he was doing, he kissed her lightly, then again, feeling her mouth soften in that way a woman's mouth does. He caught her lower lip between his and felt more than heard her breath catch slightly, nibbled the bow of her upper lip, kissed the corner of her mouth. She tipped her head back a little and he cupped her face in his hand, wondering what he was doing. What they were doing.

She kissed like a teenager on her first date, sweetly and a little hesitantly, seemingly startled when his tongue slipped into her warmth and sought hers. She responded after a moment, delicately but evocatively, and he felt his body respond to just that simple a taste of her. And then she was kissing him quite seriously, her mouth moving under his with slow, sensuous intent, and he came close to losing it entirely.

He wrenched his mouth from hers, swearing breathlessly, but for the life of him he couldn't push her away. He squeezed his eyes closed and rested his forehead on hers, teeth clenched, heart hammering, his arms sliding around her of their own accord. She seemed to be having as much trouble breathing as he was, and he realized she was gripping his shirt with both hands now, making no effort to pull herself free.

"Damn," was all he managed to get out finally.

"I had dreams…" she whispered unsteadily.

Dreams? Rafe wondered dizzily. He'd had dreams. About her. About them. About—

"Oh, God! I'm sorry!" She seemed to realize very suddenly where she was and what was happening, and she snatched her hands from his shirtfront and stepped back abruptly. She looked up at him, eyes wide. "That was completely unprofessional of me, Mr. Blackhorse, and I am *so* sorry. I just…it just…oh, this is so embarrassing!" She covered her mouth with her fingers, looking horrified. "This…I can't imagine for a minute what I thought I was—"

"This," he said shortly, taking her by the shoulders and pulling her toward him. "This is what you were doing."

And then he was kissing her again. But this time it was for real, no teasing, no gentle brushing of lip to lip. This kiss was hard, deep and wet, straight from the gut and points south, as full of hot sex and erotic promise as a rumpled bed. To his faint surprise she didn't buck or scream or tear herself away. Instead she sort of melted into his embrace and her mouth softened under his, welcoming, responding with a reckless abandon that made his head spin. He wondered very faintly if she had any idea at all of what she was doing to him physically and then realized he was hardly keeping it a secret. Had in fact cupped her taut little bottom with his hand without knowing it and was pressing her against him.

She was wearing panties and maybe a bra under the shirt, he realized, but nothing else. Her skin was hot and still shower-moist and he could feel the fullness of her breasts against his chest, the softness of her thighs as she adjusted herself slightly to cup him.

He damned near lost it entirely then. He moved against her and she gave a faint whimper, and he came *this* close to picking her up and swinging her around and laying her across the bed that was no more than three short strides away. Those filmy panties would be off in an instant, and he would be out of his jeans and inside her before either of them could catch their breath and there would be nothing but her soft cries as he—

And that was where he caught it, but barely. It took more willpower than he'd dreamed he had, but he pushed her away from him abruptly, swearing a blue streak, and took a shaky step backward. He gave her his best glare, praying she didn't see the desperate want beneath it.

"Consider that a final warning, Agent Kavanagh," he managed to get out. "Now get those clothes on and hit the road." And with that, having to get away from her, away from temptation, he spun on one heel and stalked out of the room, shouldering his way past the blanket so roughly that the tacks holding it up flew out, hitting the paneled wall like hail. It dropped into a colorful heap behind him, but he didn't even look back.

Meg didn't even start breathing again until she heard the trailer door slam closed. It brought her into the here and now with a jolt, and she swallowed and put her hand up, touching her lips with astonished wonder.

The whole thing had caught her so by surprise that she was still a little dazed. What in God's name had *happened?* She'd been kissed, she knew that much. Very thoroughly kissed, in fact, with an intensity and hungry passion she'd only dreamed about.

"Wow." She took a deep breath. "That was…interesting."

Interesting wasn't even close to it, actually.

Problem was, she didn't have a lot of time to contemplate the full range of emotions whirling through her. She had to make a decision, and fast. Stay here and risk…well, heaven knew what. Or call it quits while she was ahead and get out. She could spend the night in her rental car, change the tire in the morning and be on a plane bound for Virginia by nightfall.

Except it wasn't that easy, of course. This wasn't about taking a risk or staying safe. It wasn't about her at all, in fact. It was about a killer going free or being brought to justice. It was about Bobby. It was about the truth.

She swore wearily and let her hand fall to her side. O'Dell had been right about her. She really *didn't* know when to quit.

In the end, she took part of Rafe's advice and got dressed. She picked up her jeans and shirt from the heap where he'd dropped them, but they were sopping wet. Icy rainwater poured off them as she carried them down to the bathroom and dumped them into the shower stall, and she took a moment to mop up the mess she'd made before heading back into his small bedroom. She rummaged through the small closet and dresser until she unearthed an ancient pair of jogging pants about three sizes too big, a well-worn white T-shirt, and a heavy white and royal blue sweatshirt. It fell almost to her knees, but she didn't care. After rolling up the cuffs on the jogging pants about thirty-seven times, she was able to walk without tripping, and she shuffled back into what passed as a living room and contemplated her situation.

Perilous, if Blackhorse was to be believed. She doubted he would actually hurt her, but she did take the time to dig the Beretta out from under the sofa cushion where she'd hidden it before taking that ill-fated, and ill-advised, shower. It didn't do much to reassure her, but it was better than nothing. She was hungry but didn't feel like trying to find something to eat, cold but didn't want to try to light the woodstove. So in the end she just curled up on the sofa to wait.

There was a heavy Hudson's Bay blanket tossed across the sofa back, and she pulled it around her, wondering if she was doing the right thing. Not by staying—given that it was pouring rain and blowing a gale out there at the moment, she would have been crazy to do otherwise. But asking Blackhorse for help. To her, it was just another Agency case, full of half clues and tantalizing hints masquerading as facts. But she'd learned long ago that what files said was often less important than the things they didn't say. That the truth often lay in the hissing silences in the debriefing tapes, in the gaps between reports, in the lines between the lines. But to Rafe...

She sighed, snuggling down a little farther into the warm folds of the blanket. To Rafe, the Gillespie case represented a career that ended in disgrace, and a happy marriage that ended in death and the end of everything he dreamed of. Did she have the right to dig that all up again? To ask him to relive those terrible days just to fill in some detail that might not even make a difference?

She didn't even realize she'd fallen asleep until she woke up, feeling disoriented and groggy. The room was dark except for the flicker of flames and she pushed herself up onto one elbow and gazed around sleepily, trying to get her befogged brain kicked into gear.

There was a fire burning in the small potbellied woodstove beside the sofa, filling the room with welcome heat. Blackhorse was sitting sprawled in the armchair across the coffee table from her, one booted foot braced against the paneled wall, one on the wide chrome fender of the stove, staring at the flames as though fascinated by them. He was holding a coffee mug in his right hand while his left hung down by the side of the chair to absently stroke the dog's silken ears as it slept beside him, and he seemed a million miles from here. And her.

Strong profile, she found herself thinking. All sharp angles and hard planes. There was little softness there, little gentleness. He wore his hair very short, probably more for ease of care than stylishness, but it suited him. Good shoulders, but she already knew that. Those shoulders had been the first thing she'd noticed about him in that Dakota bar.

And his hands. He had good hands. Well proportioned and wide through the palm. A working man's hands, competent and strong. And warm. She recalled the feel of those hands on her when they'd been in the bedroom earlier. They'd known exactly what to do, those hands. And somehow she suspected that the rest of him knew exactly what to do, too.

Meg felt herself blushing hotly, remembering some of the dreams she'd been having lately. If the poor man had any idea of the things they'd been up to in the blessed privacy of her overheated imagination during the past few weeks, he would be out the door and halfway to the Canadian border. Those darned dreams were why she'd all but lost it when he kissed her. He'd just done it to scare her off, but she'd burst into flame like a match in gasoline at the first touch of his mouth, and if he hadn't come to his senses and stopped when he had…

Just the thought of the possible consequences made her heart go all silly and erratic. Truth was, she was halfway to having a serious crush on this guy. She didn't know if it had happened in Dakota or in the weeks between, but somewhere along the line, all her hormones had gone into overdrive where Rafe Blackhorse was concerned.

Rafe chose just that moment to turn his head and catch her looking at him, and her cheeks flooded with heat. Trying not to look guilty, she cleared her throat. "I…um…" She took a breath and tried again. "I'm not leaving until my clothes are dry," she said all in a rush. "And until I get some answers."

He just turned his head to stare at the flames again, as though not even hearing her.

She was making a complete hash of it, she thought with despair. He was her one last hope to put the pieces together, and she was messing up completely.

"What happened earlier…" he said out of the blue, his voice strangely rough. "That wasn't part of it, was it?"

Meg went very still. Her cheeks started to burn again, and it took all her willpower not to sink into the folds of the blanket and pull it over her head in embarrassment. "No," she managed to say finally, her voice almost as strained as his. "That…I don't know what that was."

"Do you want to go to bed with me?"

They could have been talking about almost anything, she thought in a daze. The weather. Wall Street. Anything. "I…" Her voice gave out entirely and she had to swallow. "I, um. That would be nice," she said very properly, wondering who in God's name had taken over her body while she'd been asleep, because this was not the Mary Margaret Kavanagh she'd been a few hours ago. "But I'm not sure that this is a good time. I mean…'' She lifted her shoulders in a futile shrug, then let them drop. ''I—I don't know what I mean, actually.''

He smiled a little grimly then, but to her relief he didn't seem to be laughing *at* her. ''I haven't been with a woman in…'' He blew his cheeks out, thinking hard. ''Damned if I know the last time, actually. But it's been a while. A long while.''

''Does…that make a difference?'' She tried to sound very offhand about it, as though she were perfectly used to having this kind of conversation with a man she barely knew.

He turned his head to look at her quizzically, and she hastened to add, ''Aside from the obvious urgency, I mean.''

''Obvious urgency.'' Something that might have been a smile flirted around his mouth. ''You, uh…noticed that, did you?''

''It was a little hard to—a little *difficult* to miss.''

He chuckled. ''Damned hard. To miss.'' He gave her an amused glance, then looked away again. ''I've been thinking about you a lot, Specialist Kavanagh. Since South Dakota.''

''North,'' she corrected automatically. ''It was North Dakota.'' She wet her lips, wondering if this was just part of one of her more bizarre dreams. Since it might be a dream, in fact probably *was* a dream, she decided that answering him wouldn't get her into too much trouble. ''You have?''

''Oh, yeah.'' He gave her another of those lazy glances. ''You're not an easy woman to forget.''

Meg didn't know quite how to take that. Tidal waves, earthquakes and snakebites weren't easy to forget, either.

''I've thought about you once or twice, too,'' she heard herself saying after a moment. A lie, she heard her mind mock. A thousand and one times, more like.

''Really?'' He seemed interested, half turning in the chair to look at her curiously.

She shrugged, feigning a calm she in no way felt. ''I wondered if you had managed to explain to your client how you lost Reggie Dawes. That…sort of thing.''

''Uh-huh.''

''Did you?'' she asked a trifle desperately. ''Explain, I mean?''

"I explained it, but I'm not sure my 'client' bought it. But we came to a mutually beneficial agreement."

"What kind of agreement?"

"We agreed to not kill each other." He smiled faintly at her expression. "How's Dawes doing, anyway? The little rodent squeal?"

Meg gave him a disapproving look. "Mr. Dawes gave over two hundred pages of testimony, yes. That, along with information gathered from other sources, will ensure that Gus Stepino will go to jail for two or three lifetimes."

"And Dawes?"

"He and Honey are deep in the witness protection program— O'Dell's, not the government's. They've effectively disappeared."

"If Reggie can stay honest."

"Reggie will stay honest. Honey will make sure of that."

"Have sex with me."

Meg blinked, wondering frantically how she'd missed the shift in the conversation. "Now?" Her voice broke on a squeak.

He shrugged. "Why not?"

"Well, I…" Too stunned to move, she just sat there, frozen, and watched him unfold to his feet. He was wearing a roomy sweatshirt that was a twin to the one she had on, and he casually pulled it over his head. His chest and abdomen were corded with muscle, silk-smooth and bronze in the firelight, and Meg felt her breathing go all ragged as he dropped his hands to the fly of his jeans.

"Oh m-my," she managed to stutter. "I—oh dear, I'm not sure this is a good idea, Mr. Blackhorse."

"Rafe," he said easily, popping the snap of his waistband free. "I think, under the circumstances, Special Agent, that you can start calling me Rafe."

"I—I'm not a Special Agent," she whispered as his hand went to the zipper tab. "I—I'm just a gnome."

"Gnomes like sex, don't they?" The zipper sounded very loud as he started to ease it down.

"I…I guess they do." She closed her eyes for an instant.

The zipper stopped its downward slide. "You *guess*?"

"I mean, yes," Meg hastened to assure him, caught, suddenly, between two horns of a very sharp dilemma. "Of course they do."

Rafe didn't say anything at all for a very long time. The silence grew until it almost hummed with expectation, and when Meg couldn't stand it anymore, she dared to finally look up at him. He was staring down at her with a look of thoughtful speculation.

Then abruptly, he gave a snort and pulled the zipper firmly closed, shaking his head. "Man! Just my luck. O'Dell's gotta have fifty gorgeous women working for him down there, and *I* pull the virgin."

"I am *not* a virgin," Meg snapped. The lie, bursting out of her mouth like that, astonished her, but she didn't even contemplate retracting it.

"Not physically, maybe," he growled. "But you're as virgin as they make 'em when it comes to an afternoon of hot sex with no strings attached and no morning after regrets. When *you* make love, you make love."

Meg just stared at him in growing astonishment, realizing he was serious about changing his mind. "And what, exactly, do *you* do when you make love?"

"I wasn't planning on making love to you this afternoon. I was planning to—" He caught himself. "Have sex," he amended after a moment. "Just sex. No love. No…"

"Strings." The word was crisp. "For your information, Super Agent Blackhorse, I'm perfectly capable of enjoying an afternoon of hot sex without strings or attachments or—or any of that."

"Uh-huh." His voice was heavy with disbelief.

"I've done it lots of times," she said with more indignation than prudence. "*Hundreds* of times, even."

"Bull."

Meg glared at him. "So you're saying you'd take me to bed if I'd gotten around a bit more, is that it?"

"Pretty much."

"That is so…so sexist!" Meg pulled the blanket tight around her shoulders, her cheeks flaming.

He pulled on the sweatshirt. "Maybe. But I can guarantee you'll be thanking your Irish luck come morning." He gave her a hard look. "There are a lot of good reasons they told you in basic training why having sex with another field agent is grounds for immediate dismissal."

"You're not a field agent."

"Neither are you, but that's not the point." He managed another of those grim little smiles. "Danger is the most powerful aphrodisiac known to man, Irish. Come through a hot assignment in one piece and all you can think about is sex. Problem is, that's all it is—sex. If both partners understand that, you can have some good times. And when it's over, neither side gets hurt. But if one partner mistakes sex for love or commitment or something meaningful…" He shrugged.

"You're saying that if we have sex, I'll fall in love with you?" Meg arched one eyebrow. "Got a pretty high opinion of yourself, cowboy."

"I'm saying you don't need me messing up your life," Rafe said quietly. "We got a few sparks going, I won't deny that. Between here and Dakota…" He shrugged again. "It's not all that unexpected, is what I'm saying. Getting shot at can stir up some pretty powerful emotions. But it's not real. And I may be a five-star bastard, but even I draw the line at taking advantage of some new agent's first gunpowder rush."

She felt like throwing something at him, but there was nothing within reach. Which was probably just as well, she realized, as she just sat there and silently seethed. The truth was, she had no idea why she was so angry. He was right—she *would* be thanking him and his blasted self-control in the morning. And as soon as her annoyance wore off, she was going to feel like a fool. But right at the moment…

"Fine," she said through gritted teeth. "I'm glad we got that cleared up. And now that we *have,* perhaps you'd like to answer some questions for me about the—"

"You're mad."

She drew a deep breath, ready to deny it heatedly, then let it out again with an exasperated sigh, scooping her hair back from her face with both hands. "I don't know what I am. I didn't come up here to seduce you, if that's what you think."

Rafe just looked at her for a long while. Then he gave a snort of soft laughter and shook his head. "You confuse the hell out of me, Specialist Mary Margaret Kavanagh, I'll tell you that much for nothing."

Meg thought about it for a moment. "I confuse myself at times." Then she sighed. "Do you have any food in this place? I haven't eaten since breakfast." She pushed the blanket off her shoulders and stood up, giving the three-sizes-too-big jogging pants a hitch to hold them up. She caught sight of Rafe's face as he stared at her and jabbed her finger toward him. "Don't say a thing! You told me to get dressed, I got dressed."

"Good thing I'm such an honorable guy. If I had decided to take you to bed, it would have taken me a week to find you in all that gear."

"Lucky thing for you that you didn't." She smiled sweetly at him. "I'd hate to slow a man down when he's in a gunpowder rush."

He laughed then, surprising her slightly. It seemed to surprise him, too, because he frowned a moment later and made his face all hard and serious again, as though annoyed by his momentary lapse.

"You know," she said quietly, "I swear I won't tell anyone if you lose that chip on your shoulder for a few hours. As far as anyone else is concerned, your reputation as a five-star bastard will be unsullied."

He looked at her sharply, and she shrugged. "It was just a thought."

"I could still shoot you and stuff your body in a hole, Specialist Kavanagh."

She smiled up at him, linked her arm with his and tugged him toward the kitchen. "But you won't, ex-Super Agent Blackhorse. You'll make me something to eat, and then you'll tell me everything I want to know."

"And why would I do that?" he asked amiably, not taking his arm away.

"Because you're starting to like me." Her smile widened. "I'm the most fun you've had standing up in a long while, remember?"

Chapter 7

The crazy part was, she was probably half-right.

Rafe found himself thinking about that while he opened a can of meatball soup and plopped the mess into a saucepan. He banged the pan down on the propane stove and lit the burner. There was half a loaf of suspicious looking bread in the fridge, and he unwrapped it and sniffed it, decided it was still edible if he cut off the moldy bits, and tossed it onto a plate.

"Don't do a lot of quality entertaining up here, do you, Mr. Blackhorse?"

"Rafe," he reminded her easily. "And no, I don't. I shoot most visitors. Those I don't shoot, I run off." He spared her a dry, sidelong glance. "You're a rare exception."

"And don't think I'm not honored." She peered distastefully at the bread. "I think this green stuff is trying to communicate."

"Give it a rap with the bread knife. That usually quiets it down."

"The Agency field training course teaches an agent how to live rough. But I think this exceeds the parameters." Rafe glanced around in time to see her skewer the bread with the knife and carry it, at arm's length, to the door. Before he could stop her, she'd tossed it out into the night. "I don't eat anything that's still moving," she said calmly as she turned around and caught him watching her. "That green stuff was moving."

"We're eating the soup bareback, then. That was the last of the bread."

"I hope so." She wiped the knife with a towel. "Although I suspect we just started a new life-form out there." She tossed the knife onto the table and then turned and started pulling open cupboard doors at random, pausing now and again to give the jogging pants a hitch as they threatened to slide over her slender hips.

Rafe watched her for a moment, then tossed the spoon down and walked into the bedroom. He stood there, arguing with himself, then swore sulfurously and wrenched open the tiny closet. There was a box on the shelf, shoved way back, and he hauled it out and tossed it onto the bed, steeling himself before removing the lid.

He'd expected a wafting of familiar perfume, a flood of memories, but to his surprise he felt nothing as he gazed down at the few garments folded inside. They smelled faintly of cedar shavings. Taking a deep breath, he pulled out the faded jeans.

When he got back into the kitchen, Meg had pulled a variety of things out of the cupboards and was industriously tossing ingredients into a bowl he didn't even know he owned. She was muttering to herself, frowning as she measured this and estimated that. Finally she seemed satisfied with the results and gave her head a decisive nod, glancing up at him as he walked into the room.

"Biscuits. A little thyme and a pinch or two of oregano would help, but they'll do as is."

"Here." Rafe shoved the jeans toward her. "These should fit better than those jogging pants."

Meg stared at the jeans, then tentatively reached out and took them. "You're...sure?" she asked quietly.

"If I wasn't, I wouldn't have given them to you," he replied gruffly. "You're going to break your damn neck in those things you're wearing."

She opened her mouth as if to say something more, then

wisely shut it again and just nodded. Silently, she slipped past him and down the hallway and into the bathroom.

Rafe was still cursing himself when she came back. He held his breath and looked at her, but, again, there was no stirring of memory, no haunted sense of déjà vu. Just a knockout redhead in a pair of old jeans and an oversize sweatshirt that hung halfway to her knees. She'd had to roll the cuffs up a time or two, but they seemed to fit her pretty well otherwise.

Meg looked at him uncertainly. "Are you okay with this?"

"I'm okay with it. They're just jeans, okay? No big deal."

"She must have been tall." She gestured at the rolled-up cuffs.

"Stephanie?" He thought about it. "Not especially. Five-seven, maybe."

Meg laughed quietly. "From down here, that's tall."

Rafe grinned, feeling something loosen under his breastbone. "Hell, from down there a grasshopper would be tall. Ooooph!" He laughed, rubbing his rib where her elbow had connected. "Are you cooking or what?"

"You must miss her a lot." Meg didn't look at him as she said it, seemingly preoccupied with pouring milk into the bowl. "I noticed that picture beside the bed. She was very beautiful."

"Yeah." Rafe's chest felt tight again. He stirred the soup, wondering why he was doing this to himself. He should have thrown the damned woman out into the rain when he first found her in his shower. Thrown her out and locked the door and put her out of his mind once and for all. Because this wasn't going to lead anywhere but straight into trouble; he knew that without even thinking about it. And he didn't need trouble. He'd left trouble behind a long time ago.

"You haven't asked me yet who I think was responsible for her death."

Rafe didn't turn around. "Gillespie was responsible. And Gillespie's dead. That's all I need to know."

He knew she was looking at him, could feel her questioning gaze burning into his back, but he refused to look around.

"Do you have a cookie sheet? I need something to put these biscuits on, then you'll have to show me how to light that oven."

They ate by lamplight. And in silence. Meg seemed withdrawn and thoughtful, eating the hot biscuits and soup without comment. To his surprise, it bothered Rafe a little. He kept alternating between resenting the hell out of her just for being here and wanting to make her laugh again. It didn't make a lot of sense, and he resented that, too.

He kept thinking that maybe he should have just taken her to bed and gotten it out of his system. She was a big girl. She could have handled an afternoon of sex with no strings attached. It would have done them both a world of good.

"They say he was hotdogging."

Rafe looked at her. Meg was staring into the bowl of soup, stirring it absently with the spoon.

"Or that he just got careless. That he messed up somewhere and blew his own cover and got himself—and his partner—killed."

"It happens."

"Not to my brother." She said it flatly, as indisputable fact, and raised her eyes to look at him. "Bobby was one of the best. The job was his life. It wasn't a game to him, or some macho testing ground. He was deadly serious about every assignment, and he had no patience for hotdogging or carelessness or anything less than one hundred percent. Especially with a partner. He might risk his own life, but he'd never risk someone else's."

"Not knowingly maybe, but there are about a million things that can go wrong when you're working deep cover, and most of them can kill you. Your brother knew the risks going in. So did his partner."

"God, you sound like O'Dell!" Meg slapped the spoon onto the table and shoved the bowl back violently, sending a tidal wave of soup over the edge. "Glib Platitudes 101. Do they make you memorize a manual full of them before you graduate to being *real* agents?"

He had his mouth half-open to ask her what the hell any of this had to do with him—or with Gillespie—then remembered in time that he didn't care and didn't want to know. "You still haven't told me who came up here gunning for you today. And if he'll be back."

"I told you, I didn't know." Her voice held a distinct edge. "Someone who doesn't like me investigating Bobby's death, obviously. Someone who's afraid of what I'm going to uncover."

"If your brother was working deep cover, he was working with something big. That makes it—the people he was working with—dangerous. Odds are they're not going to just sit back while you poke a stick in their nest and stir it around." He leveled a hard stare at her. "Odds are that they'll poke back. I'd leave it alone if I were you, Irish. I doubt you have any idea what you're getting into."

"That's why I'm up here." She met his stare with one of her own. "I read your file after I got back to Virginia. You were good. You were *very* good. There's not a lot about this business you don't know. You know the Agency. And you know O'Dell."

Rafe's eyes narrowed slightly. "What's O'Dell got to do with it?"

She hesitated for a second. "I don't know. Maybe nothing. Maybe everything. There's just…" She shook her head, frowning. "He's blocking me at every turn, that's all. You'd think he'd want to know what happened to Bobby. That if there *is* a bad operative in the group—and Bobby was sure there was— that O'Dell would want to know. But he…" She gestured vaguely. "He doesn't even seem interested. Which makes me wonder if…"

Now they were *really* talking about things he had no interest in, Rafe thought irritably. So he was even more irritated when he heard himself ask, "If…"

She started to say something, then stopped. Thought about it. "If he's involved somehow. If he knows what happened but doesn't want it formally investigated because he doesn't want something uncovered."

Rafe just stared at her. "Let me get this straight. You think Spencer O'Dell was involved with your brother's death?"

She shrugged. "Like you said, stuff happens. Why should O'Dell be any more immune to temptation than anyone else?"

What she was saying was insane. Unthinkable. O'Dell? Easier

to believe the sun would come up in the west tomorrow morning. Sure, he hated the man's guts. But to even think…

"God Almighty." He gave his head a shake. "I'll tell you one thing for nothing, Kavanagh—you've got more guts than any five men I know."

"I'm not saying O'Dell *is* involved," she said tightly. "But if he's not, he's in my way. You know what the Agency is like—everyone thinks the man is God's boss. He's red-flagged the case, effectively closing me out, and everyone's too terrified of him to bend the rules."

Rafe arched one eyebrow lazily. "None of which kept you from trying."

She ignored the jab. "I did as much as I could in Virginia, but it's not enough. I need more information. I need the keystone that'll make everything else make sense."

In spite of himself, Rafe had to grin. Damned if O'Dell hadn't met his match this time. It would almost be worth hanging around just to see O'Dell's face when she—

He caught the thought before it got him into even more trouble. But in spite of himself, in spite of not wanting to ask the next question, it was out before he could stop it. "What about your brother? He think O'Dell was involved?"

She shook her head impatiently. "Bobby was like everyone else. He thought the sun rose and set on the man."

"But he thought *someone* from the Agency was bad." Damn it, it was like he had no control over his own mouth. Even as his brain was saying *leave it alone,* the words just kept popping out.

"Yes." She broke off a bit of biscuit and stared at it thoughtfully.

Questions kept loping through his brain, and finally he gave up any pretense of trying to ignore them. "You two sounded pretty tight."

She just nodded. Then her shoulders drooped a little, and she looked up at him with an expression of such loss and sadness that it was almost palpable. "I'm the youngest. Bobby's… Bobby was two years older than I am, and I was his kid sister and he was my big brother and it was always sort of us against the rest of the family, you know?''

He didn't, but he wasn't getting into that. Without even wanting to, he thought of his sister. Of the distance gaping between them, the distance he'd done nothing to bridge in spite of her attempts to play at being a family. He had a half brother someplace, too. Montana. And for all he knew, there could be a half dozen others, full siblings, half, quarter. Scattered across the country like windblown seeds, taking root where they finally landed. Or, like him, not taking root at all.

He shook it off, not liking the direction his thoughts were going. ''And you talked with him. Knew what he was doing.''

''Of course.''

''So he was breaking cover on a routine basis to make contact with you.'' He said it evenly, wanting her to think about it.

Meg shook her head impatiently. ''You're talking about two well-trained operatives here, Rafe. He did *not* blow his cover by making contact with me, I can guarantee it.'' She lifted her head to give him an angry look. ''Do you really think I'd jeopardize my brother's life by being careless? Or that he'd jeopardize mine?''

Rafe thought, fleetingly, of the laughter in Steph's eyes that last morning he'd seen her. He hadn't planned to jeopardize her life, either. But in the end, that was exactly what he'd done. ''Not intentionally, maybe,'' he said quietly. ''But all anyone investigating him would have to do was take a second look at you, at where you work, and it would set alarm bells ringing.''

She gave him that kind of long-suffering look people usually reserve for dealing with slow children. ''I hardly go around with a neon sign across my chest advertising I work for O'Dell,'' she said with exaggerated patience. ''Gnomes work under tight cover as a matter of course. After all, we're more vulnerable— and more important—than you field agents are.'' She smiled faintly. ''You guys are just the muscle. *We* are the brains. O'Dell makes very, very sure that we and the information we carry around in our heads are kept secure.''

To be honest, he'd never thought about it before, but it made sense. Then he realized he was listening to her as though he gave a damn. Which he didn't. "I'm not in this equation any-more, remember?"

"His cover story was unbreakable," she added, ignoring his interruption. "That's the first thing I looked at, to see if someone had screwed up and left a loose end to unravel. But CoveOps had made him and his cover story airtight. Everything was in place. They had a history for him that went back to before he was born, and there wasn't a weak spot or inconsistency in it. And I *looked,* trust me."

"If Covert Operations made the cover airtight, then the breach was with him or Christopher."

"The breach was not with him or Christopher."

Rafe could have sworn the room temperature had just dropped by about twenty degrees. He let a beat or two go by. "Okay, presuming you're right—" he paused just long enough to let her know he sincerely doubted it, but not long enough for her to launch into another defense of her brother "—and presuming it was someone in the Agency who blew their cover, the big question is who? And why?"

"I don't know. Exactly."

"Uh-huh."

She flushed. "Just because I can't tell you his name yet doesn't mean he doesn't exist."

"Yet."

"Yet." The word was as sharp and succinct as a neck snap-ping.

He leaned back in his chair and settled a lazy stare onto her. "And you somehow think I give a damn."

"I think you might. After I explain what—"

"I don't." He gave her a long, unsmiling look.

"Does the name Baxter Pollard mean anything to you?"

"I've heard the name."

"Baxter Pollard is a wheeler and a dealer. Real estate. Cor-porate acquisitions and mergers. Venture capital. He's constantly in motion, buying this, selling that, making money by the box-car. Owns two or three high-rise office buildings in Manhattan, a casino in Windsor, Canada, a hotel in New Orleans. In the last year alone he's bought—and sold again, at enormous profit—a small independent film company in New York, four or five office buildings, property in Arizona and California, an Alaskan gold mine, a Los Angeles recording label, and a string of funeral homes. Those were just the deals that hit the newspapers. He's very fluid, with a convoluted set of interlocking but independently run corporations and numbered companies. All very aboveboard and legal. To the casual eye.''

''Uh-huh.''

''The IRS has been snooping around him for years but have never found anything. There is a strong suspicion that he's laundering money for someone—gambling, drugs, who knows. He just seems to have a lot more cash on hand than looks right. The FBI put together a task force to look into his deals last year, but even they came up empty. They came to O'Dell last year and asked us to put some people on it. *We* came up with nothing.''

''So the guy's clean.''

''The guy's not clean.'' Her mouth curved around a self-satisfied smile.

''And you found something.'' In spite of himself, Rafe had to smile. Her obvious excitement was well controlled but electric, and he felt himself caught in its current before he could even stop himself.

She nodded, cornflower-blue eyes sparkling. ''Oh, yeah. I found something. He's damned good, I can tell you that. It's not surprising the IRS and FBI couldn't unravel it, because the money trail is all but invisible. He's got a team of the best lawyers and financial wizards that money can buy, and they're giving him every nickel's worth, because there is no way you can follow the trail using normal search procedures. The information is there, it's just not available to most people.''

Rafe knew better than to ask her how *she'd* found it. He'd long ago stopped being surprised by the information O'Dell's computers and their operators seemed capable of ferreting out. He'd never really known where the money for all of O'Dell's electronic toys came from—he suspected the entire Agency was funded from monies syphoned secretly out of some military budget—but the millions of dollars the man had to play with bought him the best there was. Some of it was probably even legal.

And then there were the gnomes. All of them were frighteningly brilliant, most with strings of degrees after their names long and complex enough to start their own languages. But not all of them. Many were hackers and phone phreaks, some recruited after their attempts to access Agency computers brought them to O'Dell's attention, others while they were sitting in jail after getting caught. At least one young hotshot had been brought on board at the ripe old age of fifteen after nearly shutting down the Pentagon's entire military complex, spy satellites and all. Everyone from the President on down thought he should be shot; O'Dell gave him a jillion-dollar budget and all the toys he could dream of. The kid was nineteen now and could probably bring the entire world to its knees with a couple of keystrokes.

"How come the rest of your gnome-kind couldn't put it together last year?"

She just shrugged. "The team O'Dell put on it wasn't as motivated as I am."

"You think Pollard was involved in Bobby's death."

"Directly, no." She paused, almost delicately. "But he knows Charlie Sweetgrass. In fact, they're some sort of shirttail cousins."

Rafe just stared at her.

She raised one eyebrow. "Charlie Sweetgrass? Also known as Gordon Harper. Also known as—"

"Wapiti." The word scratched Rafe's throat as though barbed. "That's impossible."

She sighed, as though expecting exactly this kind of reaction. "The actual blood trail is almost too faint to follow, but they are related somewhere along the way. Somebody's fourth cousin married somebody's great-granduncle's third wife's half sister sort of thing." She made a motion with her hand as though shooing flies. "It gave me a headache and wasn't that important, so I didn't bother with DNA testing or anything."

"How the hell—" Rafe caught himself. If she said it was possible to run DNA tests on New York financier and corporate heavyweight Baxter Pollard and a small-time hood from outside Detroit named Charlie Sweetgrass, it was possible. It was also possible—no, make that highly probable—that it was utterly illegal, and he didn't want to know the details.

"Which doesn't necessarily mean squat."

"No, it doesn't. But in this case, it *does*. Maybe coincidentally—it's possible they don't even know they're related by blood—they've been in business together on and off. Mr. Sweetgrass ran one of Mr. Pollard's businesses for him three years ago, in fact."

Rafe felt his stomach tighten. "The Arrowhead Casino?"

"Yep."

Rafe shook his head decisively. "No way, Irish. The Arrowhead was Native owned and run. They were using it to launder money from illegal sales of liquor and cigarettes to Canada. That's why I was working the assignment in the first place."

"Yes, I know. You spent almost six months working undercover as Greg Crow, infiltrating the Mohawk Casino Corporation." She made another impatient gesture. "I know all about that. The Corporation was supposed to be supporting Native rights issues by building casinos on reservations land to give local tribal bands financial independence, but it was actually little better than a down-home version of the Mafia. They built the casinos, all right, but they were also involved in smuggling, gunrunning, prostitution, intimidation, protection and any other type of thuggery they could invent."

"And you're saying Pollard was involved?"

"At arm's length. The Mohawk Corporation needed start-up funds. Pollard needed someplace to launder drug money coming in from his South American cocaine connections."

"So why are you telling me this? Use it to take Pollard down, if you've got enough on him."

"I have enough. But I'm not interested in Pollard. It's Sweetgrass I want. Except he's not Charlie Sweetgrass anymore. He's Jackson Chilende now. Supposedly from the Honduras or someplace, although he's as Honduran as you are."

"Well, you know us redskins. We all look alike to you white folk."

"Don't be snide," she said coolly. "You've used your ethnicity to good advantage over the years when it suited you, pretending to be everything from Mohawk to Mexican."

"When it suited O'Dell, you mean," Rafe growled. "And you're a hell of a lot more *ethnic* than I am, honey, between that red hair and the Mary Margaret Kavanagh moniker. I'll bet you even have a shamrock tattooed on your—"

"Don't start with me," she said with a hint of heat in her voice and eyes.

"Or is it a leprechaun?"

The glint in her eyes was starting to look dangerous. And Rafe was starting to enjoy himself for some reason he couldn't even begin to fathom. Making Mary Margaret Kavanagh mad wasn't something he suspected was a good idea, but for the life of him, he couldn't seem to keep his mouth shut. "Remind me to have a look later."

She was blushing, but she slogged on resolutely. "I want to see everything you have on Charlie Sweetgrass. In fact, I want to see your entire assignment case file, beginning to end."

Rafe shrugged. "They're in the Agency files."

"The other case notes. The ones you *didn't* hand in when you made your report and were debriefed."

Rafe kept his face expressionless. "What makes you think there were other notes?"

"There are *always* other notes," she said evenly. "All you field agents are the same. You always have two sets of reports and notes—the set you put in the files, and the set that details what really happened. I want the set you held back."

He shook his head. "Not me, Specialist Kavanagh. You read my personnel files. I was one of O'Dell's fair-haired boys, remember?" He grinned. "I always went by the book, you should know that."

She used the word she'd used to good effect in that bar in North Dakota, and it made him smile. "That's a pretty grown-up word, Irish. Your brothers know you talk like this?"

"My brothers are the ones who taught me words like that one, and I have a whole repertoire of them I've never even used yet. So unless you want me to *start* using them, you'll hand over those files and save us both a lot of wear and tear.''

''So what's Charlie Sweetgrass aka Jackson Chilende doing that's got you on him like a hound on a scent?''

''He was my brother's primary contact, the guy Bobby was supposed to meet the night he was killed.''

Something wafted across Rafe's internal radar, just a single blip, but it was enough to make his eyes narrow. ''Charlie Sweetgrass was my primary contact.''

''Exactly. And you were supposed to meet him the night you were ambushed and nearly killed, if you recall.''

He recalled, all right. He still saw that damned riverside warehouse in his dreams, sweet with moonlight and as innocent looking as a baby's smile. He'd walked into gunfire from three sides, and it had been pure dumb luck that he hadn't been hit as he'd dived and rolled for cover. He'd come up firing, but it was way too late. They'd had the advantage of surprise, position and firepower, and he'd taken one long, hard look at his situation and called it quits, throwing his weapon down even as he sprinted for the riverbank.

How they hadn't hit him, he still didn't know. There were about seven of them, all spraying automatic weapons fire like there was no tomorrow, but he made the river with nothing more serious than a bullet crease across the top of his left hand, and then he'd dived hard and deep into the black, murky water.

He brought himself back to the present with an effort, realizing Meg was watching him with a small frown between her brows. He thought about what she'd said, trying to grab the loose ends and pull them together.

''It seems a little coincidental, wouldn't you say, that Sweetgrass was the primary contact for both you and Bobby? And that you were both ambushed after he set up a meeting with you?''

More than a little coincidental. Rafe's internal radar was screaming like a banshee. He ignored it with an effort. He feigned a careless shrug. ''Maybe so, maybe not. Sweetgrass always was an ambitious little bastard. If you're right about Pollard's involvement with the Arrowhead, I can see Sweetgrass making himself part of the organization.''

Meg frowned impatiently. ''That's not what I mean.''

''I know what you mean,'' Rafe told her smoothly. ''But you still haven't told me how Sweetgrass or Chilende or whoever he is this week managed to crack my cover as well as your brother's. Are you saying he's got another shirttail cousin in the Agency?''

Impatience made her eyes sparkle. ''That's because I don't *know* how he did it. I just know he did. There's no other explanation for how he managed to get the better of two of O'Dell's best agents. He had to have gotten the information from inside, there's no other answer.''

''You took this to O'Dell?''

She hesitated just long enough to give him the answer. He swore, using the same word she had but with considerably more expertise.

''I didn't have time! And besides, what if *he's* the leak?''

Rafe didn't even bother holding back his snort of laughter.

''I don't want to believe it, either,'' she said quietly. ''But stranger things have happened. I'm leaving my options open. Isn't that what you superagents are taught to do? Always leave yourself a way out?''

''Preferably not one that leads over a cliff.'' He pushed his chair back and got to his feet. ''Go back to Virginia and tell someone who cares, Kavanagh.'' It was harsher than he'd intended, and he could see the tiny flare of disappointment in her eyes. It made him hesitate, even though he didn't intend to do that, either. ''Look,'' he said more gently, ''I can't help you. I've been out of the game for two years, and that makes me a dinosaur. Anything I might have known is ancient history. If you're serious about not trusting O'Dell, go to Washington and tell someone there.''

Why he added that, he had no idea. There were plenty of people in Washington who would dearly love to see O'Dell brought down, his rogue agency disbanded, his people scattered, his secret budget appropriated, the very ground he'd walked on plowed under and sewn with salt. But there wasn't one of them with the stones to do it.

"I'm going out to check the perimeter." He said it without even thinking, falling into the vernacular as easily as any agent still on the payroll. It made him swear under his breath, and he pulled his leather jacket on angrily, in a foul mood suddenly.

"Do you think he's still out there?" she asked quietly from behind him.

"You'd better hope not," he muttered through his teeth as he keyed open the security lock on his stash of weapons and grabbed the nearest rifle. "Because if he is, I'm going to shoot him. And if I shoot him, I'm shoving him into the trunk of *your* rental car. And then I'm shoving you in with him and calling O'Dell and telling him to come up here and take you both off my hands." He spared her an angry glance. "I had a quiet, uneventful life up here once. I'd like it to get quiet and uneventful again real quick. Am I making myself clear?"

"Crystal," she said with a sigh, not looking half as intimidated as he thought she should be. "I'll reset the security system after you've gone, so don't come in without warning or I might shoot you." She smiled up at him as sweetly as a nun. "And that would put a crimp in your quiet, uneventful life, wouldn't it?"

Rafe just glared at her. "You're a pain in the butt, Kavanagh. It's *my* trailer, remember? *My* security system."

"Be careful, okay?" The concern on her face looked sincere.

He had his mouth open for a hostile reply, then shut it again and simply nodded. It felt strange, hearing those words. He couldn't even begin to remember the last time someone had worried about him. It felt…odd. Good odd, maybe. He couldn't even be sure of that. Which was another thing, he told himself with considerable annoyance as he pulled the door open and stepped out into the night: He couldn't begin to remember being this damned *confused,* either. She was making him crazy. And, worse, he was almost starting to enjoy it.

In the end, he did exactly what he'd sworn up and down that he wasn't going to do. By the time he got the flat tire off her car and the spare on, he was soaked to the skin and in a worse mood than when he'd started, if that was possible. He rationalized it by telling himself that fixing her flat was a small price to pay for getting her the hell off his mountain, but he knew he was lying even as he thought it. She wasn't going anywhere tonight.

Maybe not tomorrow, either, unless the rain let up. The storm had turned the twisting, rutted trail down to the highway into a sluice, the foaming water a foot deep in places and moving like a freight train. It had washed the whole mud track out in places and sent loosened boulders tumbling like pebbles, and he knew from experience that there would be one or two trees down. It might take him a couple of hours to make the road passable again, or it might take him a week. He wouldn't know until the weather cleared and he had a chance to look at it.

Either way, Mary Margaret Kavanagh was going to be underfoot for a while longer.

Just the thought of it made him break into a sweat.

Chapter 8

She was asleep again when he got back to the trailer, curled up on the sagging old sofa with nothing but a tangle of fire-red hair showing from the folds of the Hudson's Bay blanket. Three was curled up beside her as though he belonged there, not even bothering to open his eyes when he heard the door open, and Rafe looked at them both for a moment or two, thinking they were a fitting pair. Both of them seemed to think he should consider himself lucky to have them. And neither seemed to find his ongoing threats to throw them out especially worrying.

He swore silently under his breath at what was starting to look like a determined invasion by both dog and woman, then put the rifle away and rearmed the perimeter alarm system. He would deal with it in the morning.

In the meantime, he was going to bed.

What he *wasn't* going to do was fall into the trap Meg had set for him and spend the night thinking about Charlie Sweet-grass and the coincidences that connected him to two cases three years apart and what that might mean. Grimly, Rafe eased himself into the tiny closet that passed for a bathroom and started brushing his teeth, staring into his own eyes in the small round mirror above the sink. He'd known good agents to wind them-

selves up like cheap watches trying to connect the unconnect-
able, getting so focused on what wasn't there that they missed
what was.

Fact: Steph and Bobby Kavanagh were dead. Fact: Charlie
Sweetgrass was a fast-talking career criminal whose illegal ac-
tivities took him far and wide. Fact: coincidences happened.

Meg was following the wrong trail.

Rafe realized he'd stopped brushing and was just staring unseeing at his own reflection, chasing some random thought, and
hauled himself back to the here and now with a rough curse. He
spat out a mouthful of toothpaste and rinsed his mouth and the
brush, then stepped out of the bathroom. And found himself
face-to-face with Meg.

She looked half-asleep, that mad riot of hair all tangled and
unruly, eyes a little puffy, cheeks flushed. She was grasping the
blanket around her like a shawl, and when he materialized in
front of her she just stared at him for a sleepy moment, then
shuffled to one side.

There was nothing to do but edge by her. Or try to. The
passageway to the bedroom—no way could you call it a hall—
was barely wide enough for one, and the instant Rafe tried to
slide past her he realized he should have gone into full retreat
the instant she'd appeared.

She sort of got all jammed up against him, and even through
the heavy wool blanket and the jeans and the shirt, she felt good.
All womanly curves and soft bits and tantalizing indentations.
And she smelled like a good dream made you feel, the scent of
warm female skin and hair making him suddenly light-headed.

"Was everything okay out there?"

Gazing up at him curiously, she seemed to be unaware of
their intimate embrace, pressed so tightly against him that he
swore he could feel her heart ratcheting against his chest.

"I, uh…yeah." He swallowed. Close. My God, she was so
close he could see the faint scattering of freckles across the
bridge of her nose. Could see the even fainter pulse in the hollow
of her throat, the skin there slightly moist. Soft.

"Thank you for bringing my stuff in." She made a gesture—
as best she could in her confined position, anyway—and he saw
she was carrying a toiletries case.

"I, uh…" He swore at himself and planted his hands firmly

on her shoulders, pushing past her almost roughly. "It's no big deal. Don't think I'm inviting you to stay or anything. I just don't want you using my toothbrush."

It made her smile, which puzzled the hell out of him, because he could have sworn he'd used his fiercest voice. She should have been terrified. But instead of looking frightened, she just gave him one of those sweet smiles that seemed to light her up from inside, and he felt himself go all hollow and stupid.

"Well, thank you anyway. My case notes are in the leather folder on the coffee table, by the way. If you want to look at them…"

"I'm not interested," Rafe snapped. "I told you I'm not interested, didn't I?"

"You did," she said very agreeably. "But since I'm here and the notes are here, I thought you might—"

"The only reason you're still here, lady, is because the road's half washed out. But come tomorrow, you and your case notes and your questions are history, got it?" He drilled her with a ferocious look.

"Of course." She smiled that sweet smile again, nearly sending every thought in his head to the four winds. "If you'll excuse me, I'll brush my teeth and go to bed. You don't have an extra pillow, do you? That cushion on the sofa feels like it's filled with gravel. Then, in the morning, after you've told me all about your old case and if the road is passable, I'll leave."

Rafe opened his mouth to tell her there was no way in hell he was telling her anything about anything, *ever,* and that she was leaving at first light whether the road was passable or not. But he just let his breath out noisily instead. The woman was impossible. *All* women were impossible most of the time, of course—any man over the age of five knew that for a fact—but this particular one seemed to be impossible *all* of the time.

He started out looking for the spare pillow and wound up making up his own bed with clean sheets instead, relieved at some level that he even had clean sheets. If she slept in here, he wouldn't be falling over her every time he turned around. That was the plan, anyway. Somehow he suspected it wouldn't keep her out from underfoot for long, but it was a start. And if he slept on the old sofa, he was pretty sure he would be uncomfortable enough to keep his imagination on hold, which wouldn't be a bad idea, either.

He hadn't even finished thinking that when she appeared in the doorway in a swirl of scented steam, dressed in something that made his mouth go dry. It wasn't that erotic, as erotic went—just a plain-Jane blue wrap of some kind—but it was made out of some slithery, silken fabric that hit all the right places in all the right ways, and it took some effort to keep his mind on what he was doing and not on what he would like to be doing.

"I'll give you these jeans back now. Thanks."

Rafe nodded and took them from her.

"Is that pillow for me?"

She was gazing at him hopefully, and Rafe realized he'd just been standing there, jeans in one hand, pillow in the other, his mind off on some tangent all of its own.

"I…yeah. No." He shook his head, irritated at how easily she managed to rattle him. "I'm taking the sofa and you're sleeping in here. It's…safer that way."

"Safer?"

Her eyes held what he could have sworn was amusement, and he frowned, wondering what the hell was wrong with him. His mind seemed to be in third gear, every thought an effort, and he kept finding himself staring at her mouth instead of answering her, remembering how it had melted under his.

"Safer," she half whispered.

He blinked. "Yeah." His voice was hoarse. "If someone tries to break in."

"I…see." She drew a deep breath that sounded as unsteady as his own breathing felt. "Of course. I…I understand."

Did she? he wondered dimly. Did she have even the slightest idea of what she was doing to him? It seemed impossible that she could and still be standing there, gazing up at him with those wide sky-blue eyes, lips slightly parted, seemingly fearless.

"Oh, damn," he heard himself whisper as though from a long distance away. "What the hell are you doing to me, Specialist Mary Margaret Kavanagh?"

Those eyes, which seemed only inches from his now, widened very slightly. "Me?"

''Yeah,'' he muttered roughly, tossing the jeans onto the bed and dropping the pillow as he reached for her. ''You.''

She gave a soft inhalation that was more sigh than protest as his arms went around her and he dropped his mouth down to those soft lips that had been driving him insane all evening. They were warm and silken, and she tasted of peppermint, and as her mouth opened slightly beneath his and he felt the tentative touch of her tongue, no more than the touch of a butterfly's wing— there, then gone, then there again—he knew with resignation that he was halfway to lost.

Meg didn't know why she wasn't surprised to find herself in Rafe's very competent embrace again, but she wasn't. It seemed as natural as breathing, which was an odd thing, considering she barely knew him and was not in the habit of kissing men she didn't know. Truth be told, she wasn't even in the habit of kissing the ones she *did* know, as Royce was only too happy to point out at every possible opportunity. Then again, she thought through a pleasant haze, if Royce kissed like this, she would have married him months ago.

Because if there was one thing Rafe Blackhorse was good at, it was kissing. His mouth just sort of claimed hers, but in a delicious, sensual kind of way, his tongue slip-sliding against hers with a slow, coaxing rhythm that made her breath catch and her toes curl and everything in between just sort of go all melty and hot.

She hadn't actually intended to kiss him back. Not at first, anyway, thinking in a vague, far-off kind of way that it was certainly inappropriate, all considered. And the truth was, she suspected she might not be very good at it. Royce never seemed especially appreciative of her efforts, anyway, kissing her in that dry, antiseptic way he had that always made her feel as though he found the entire process a little distasteful.

Rafe, on the other hand, made it quite clear that he found the process very much to his liking. His mouth moved on hers, sucking, teasing, leading her on, and she found herself responding without even thinking about it. His hands were moving, too, one caressing her back in long, slow strokes that molded her against him, while the other cupped her head.

He was vitally aroused, Meg realized with delicious shock, her entire body electrified by the erotic promise in the touch and taste of him, in the soft growl he made as he ran his hand down and around her bottom, in the sound of her own shuddery little gasp as he moved strongly against her.

"I want..." she managed to moan against his mouth. "Oh, Rafe, I want...."

"I know," he whispered back, his voice ragged. "This is *not* a good idea, Specialist Kavanagh...." He slid his hand between their straining bodies and wrenched the belt of her wrap free, then pulled it open. "In fact, it's a real bad idea."

"Agency policy says we shouldn't be doing this," she moaned in agreement as he caressed her ribs and hip over the satiny fabric of the teddy she'd put on under the robe. She gave an impatient wriggle, and then his hand was under the fabric, on her, trailing fire. He caressed her ribs, his thumb just brushing the underside of her breast, and then he ran his thumb over her breast, brushing the nipple, and Meg nearly died on the spot as molten fire ran from her breast to that aching spot between her legs.

"I'm not an agent anymore," he groaned against her mouth. "Policy doesn't count...." He pulled away slightly and dropped his mouth over her breast, suckling her through silk, his tongue rhythmically circling her swollen nipple.

Meg moaned right out loud, squeezing her thighs together as the heat there threatened to explode completely. She cupped his head with her hands and pressed him against her, so breathless she wondered if she were going to faint from sheer pleasure. "Me...me neither," she finally managed to gasp. "I'm... probably...fired...anyway. Oh...oh, my!"

He was sliding one warm hand down the back of her thigh, then back up, slowly, tantalizingly, fingers gliding up under the loose leg of her tap pants to cup her bottom fully in his palm. He pressed her against him, then eased his hand down slightly and around the back of her thigh so his fingertips touched her, a delicate, fleeting caress that was gone almost before it started, and Meg bit her lip, hard, against another moan.

The faint thought fluttered across the surface of her mind that if she was going to stop him, now would be the time. Now *had* to be the time. Another moment more and it was going to be too late for either of them. And yet, even as the thought faded, she knew it was already too late. She was aching with want, half-mad with it, and there was no way in heaven she could pull away, even if she wanted to. And she didn't want to. All she wanted was...

"...more!" It was a soft cry, her voice so thick with desire that she didn't even recognize it, and she shuddered as he nudged her teddy up and started kissing her stomach, tongue delving into the mysteries of her belly button for an astonishing moment before finding her breast again.

She wasn't aware of him picking her up, and yet he must have, because there was suddenly nothing under her bare feet but air, and she wrapped her legs around his, unable to get close enough to him. And then she was tipping over backward, still cradled in his arms, and in the next moment she was on her back on the bed and Rafe was on one knee beside her, his sable-colored eyes glittering slightly in the dim light as he gazed down at her.

He asked the question without saying a word, and she replied just as wordlessly. And it was just that easy, Meg thought wonderingly as she watched him ease himself back and onto his feet. His hands dropped to the zippered fly of his jeans and he stripped quickly, never taking his eyes off her. She felt dazed and sleepy and she stretched sinuously, arching her back, knowing but not caring that both her breasts were bared. Rafe's eyes narrowed slightly, and Meg smiled, loving the way he was looking at her, his gaze as hot as a tangible caress.

"My God," he whispered finally, "you really are beautiful." He put one knee on the bed, then the other, straddling her, and reached up slowly to rest his hands on her hips. Then he ran his hands up her ribs, taking the teddy with them, and eased it over her head. Not touching her with his hands, he lowered his mouth to her left breast and started kissing it, just lightly, grazing her with his teeth and tongue before settling his lips around the nipple and tugging it gently.

Meg lost her breath and most of her reason and made some sort of soft moaning sound of assent that made him laugh. He ran his parted lips to her other breast, giving it the same loving attention as his fingers ran down her ribs again and caught the elastic of her tap pants, then worked them slowly down over her hips. As he slid them down her thighs, he drew his mouth down as well, across the flat of her belly to the soft concavity below. Then lower still.

Meg's breath left her in a soft sigh and she closed her eyes, thighs falling open of their own accord, wondering fleetingly where on earth her modesty had gone. The same place her willpower had gone, she decided, and then in the next instant she thought she well and truly *would* faint right then and there.

The first silken, gliding touch of his tongue teased her. The second opened her. The third found her. A sensation of such pure pleasure shot through her that Meg gave a choking little cry and tried to wriggle away from him, but he caught her by the hips and pressed her firmly against the bed and dipped his mouth toward her again.

"Rafe!" Terrified of losing control completely and making an utter fool of herself, she managed to half sit up and take his head between her hands. "No...not...that...please...."

"Meg..."

"I...I can't," she gasped. "I'll...I'm afraid...."

He laughed softly and rolled onto one shoulder, pulling her against him. Then he rolled again, carrying her with him until she was on her back again and he was on one elbow, kissing her deeply and slowly, his fingers touching her gently where his mouth had been only moments before. He drew his lips from hers slowly, nuzzling her throat, her ear. "It's been a long time for me, Meg. Too long. There's no way I can hold out long enough to make it good for you."

"B-but..."

"Shh. Be still. Be still...."

"But..."

"Shh..."

And then it was too late to even attempt to stop him, and after a moment or two of shyness, she didn't even want to. Kissing wasn't the only thing Rafe knew how to do.

Finally, lost in a haze of desire she couldn't even begin to fight, she simply gave in to it, focusing on the silken, slippery glide of his tongue and lips, the intimate intrusion and withdrawal, the growing urgency of her own body as that nowfamiliar aching tension drew tighter and tighter and more and more focused.

And broke, suddenly, catching her so by surprise that she

cried out in startled dismay, not wanting it to end and yet needing it to end so badly that she could think of nothing else. It pulsed through her like molten fire, one throbbing wave of sensation so pure and strong it tore a groan of raw pleasure from her before she could stop it.

Rafe was murmuring something to her, words she couldn't make out, and she wanted desperately to answer him, but she felt so shattered and stunned by the power of what had happened that she couldn't do more than just sob his name. He slipped his hand between her thighs and she tried to turn away, feeling too sensitive to tolerate his intrusive touch, but he just pressed his hand against her with a slow rhythmic pressure that eased her through the trembly little aftershocks.

And after a while, after the most cataclysmic part had eased enough for her to catch her breath and collect her thoughts, she realized his mouth was on hers, gently this time, just nibbling kisses that traced her lower lip, then her upper one. She put her hand on his cheek and gazed up at him in wonder. His skin was as smooth as sun-warmed stone, and she traced the angle of his cheekbone with her fingertips as he smiled and lowered his mouth to hers and kissed her slowly and deeply and with enough latent erotic promise to light up every nerve ending in her body.

"That," she whispered finally, "was incredible."

Kissing her lightly, he lifted himself onto his elbow and pulled open the drawer on the small bedside table and dug something out.

A moment later, he pressed a condom into her palm. "Do you…?"

Meg stared at it in sudden panic, then handed it back to him as though it had burned her. "I think you'd better do it."

To her relief, it made him laugh. Not seeming concerned or even curious about her hesitation, he swiftly tore the package open and took care of matters himself. He gave her an amused sidelong look as he realized she was watching him. "Specialist Kavanagh, you look a bit apprehensive. Not having second thoughts, are you?"

"I…" She stared at him. Last chance, some tiny voice whispered. Be sure, Mary Margaret, because there'll be no turning back past this point. And then, very suddenly, she realized she didn't have a second thought in her head. "No." She laughed softly and reached for him, tugging him gently down to her. "No second thoughts at all. But…could you go a bit slow? I don't want to miss even a moment of this."

A puzzled expression crossed his features, then he just smiled. "Slow as I can, sweetheart. But I'm not making a whole lot of promises."

But it *was* slow. At first, anyway. Slow and lazy and deliciously exciting, his every touch a symphony of sensation and delight. He seemed able to touch her all over all at once, using his mouth and tongue and sly fingers to caress and explore and tease. She'd made up her mind right at the very beginning to pay close attention to every detail, and at first she did just that, exclaiming with surprised pleasure at every new touch and sensation.

But it wasn't long before she forgot to concentrate on what he was doing, and not long after that she forgot to even breathe as his caresses became more and more intimate, more and more arousing. He was whispering things to her, too, forbidden erotic things that made her moan in shocked delight, and then he was kissing parts of her she never knew *could* be kissed and doing things she'd never dreamed could be done. All reason and thought vanished in a steamy haze of sexual desire and abandon, and she lost touch with everything but Rafe, with the taste and scent and feel of him, with the thud of his heart against her, the heat of his hands and body and breath.

And then, dimly, dimly, she became aware that he was easing himself between her thighs and that the sweet, urgent pressure there was suddenly centered and real and insistent.

"Wait…!" Somehow she got the word out, panting against his mouth as she clung to him. "I want…" Rafe was kissing her throat and neck, his fingers tangled in her hair. "I don't…want to miss…any of this.…"

He chuckled against her ear, his breath hot and rapid. "Oh, I don't think you're going to miss—" He paused suddenly, going utterly motionless against her. Then, slowly, he drew back to look down at her. "Kavanagh…?"

"D-do you think you…could call me…Meg?"

His eyes narrowed very slightly. "When I called you a virgin earlier…I didn't mean that literally, right? I mean…" He swallowed, a hint of desperation in his eyes. "Please tell me you're not really…"

"Do we have to have this conversation right now?" she whispered urgently.

Rafe laughed, the sound a rough gasp. "Oh, yeah! Right now is a real good time."

"But—" Meg gave an impatient wriggle under him, making him groan out loud. "But I don't want to talk. I want to do this." She kissed his chin. "We can talk later."

"Megan." The one word was half plea, half warning.

"If I tell you I'm a virgin, are you going to get all stupid and heroic and leap out of this bed to protect my virtue, or are you going to stay and finish what we've started?"

It made him grin. "I'm not sure I'm that much of a hero."

"Good." She took his face between her hands and held his gaze with hers. "Don't you even *think* about doing the honorable thing, Rafe Blackhorse! I want you at your dishonorable best, do you understand me? I want you to make love to me. Right. Now."

To her everlasting relief, he didn't seem inclined to argue. He smiled a slow, incendiary smile, filled with amusement and promise, and lowered his mouth to hers. Lips just brushing hers, he whispered, "But you don't want to miss even a moment of the occasion, is that what you're telling me?"

Meg nibbled his lower lip and slipped one of her legs across the backs of his. "I'm twenty-seven years old and a virgin, and I'm about thirty seconds from finally—*finally*—making love for the very first time. You're damn right I don't want to miss a moment of it!" She laughed very softly, running her hands down the muscled sweep of his back, his skin like hot satin under her fingers. "As occasions go, it doesn't quite rank with man landing on the moon or the turn of the millennium, but it's right up there."

Rafe laughed. "In a little while, Mary Margaret Kavanagh, after I've finessed my way through this *occasion* to the best of my abilities, I want to hear how on earth a woman who packs as much raw sex appeal into five foot nothing as you do managed to reach the grand old age of twenty-seven without ever having tasted the forbidden fruit."

"Later," she murmured against his mouth. "You were finessing, remember?"

"Mmm." Another chuckle rumbled through him, and he started kissing her again. "Okay, one step at a time, nice and slow, so you don't miss a thing. First, I'm going to do this...."

Meg's eyes widened slightly as he whispered something wickedly explicit.

"And then I want you to do this...."

Another suggestion, as deliciously, as wickedly, explicit as the first. Meg moaned softly.

"And then," he murmured, "I'm going to do...this...."

It seemed in that moment as though the very universe shuddered to a stop, as though every star in the sky held its breath. There was a pressure, a hesitation, and then a long, slow silken slide of pure pleasure that made her sigh. And then still more, filling her with him until she sobbed with inexpressible pleasure.

"Are you taking note of this, Agent Kavanagh?" he murmured against her ear. He pressed himself against her gently, rocking his hips very, very slowly. "I won't go so far as to say I'm the world's leading expert or anything, but I would venture to say without a hint of modesty that this is pretty much as good as it gets."

"That was...this is...incredible." Meg drew a deep and unsteady breath, wanting to capture this moment indelibly. "Thank you," she whispered. "This is...this is even better than I dreamed it would be...."

"Don't put too much pressure on me now, sweetheart, or I'll get performance anxiety and ruin it for both of us."

It made her laugh, as she suspected it was supposed to, and she relaxed into the soft warmth of the mattress to gaze up at him. "I hope this isn't going to be *too* arduous. After all," she added with a slow smile, "you're going to have to show me how to do everything. And help me with all the good bits."

He grinned. "Tough job, babe, but someone's gotta do it, right? I'm honored to be of assistance on this auspicious *occasion.*"

"Feel free," she whispered against his mouth as she drew his head down, "to finesse yourself to your heart's content."

And that, she decided much later, was exactly what he did. She had no idea how long they lay like that, laughing quietly in the darkness, kissing and being silly. But in a little while she realized that Rafe was moving gently in the cradling heat of her thighs and that she was moving in concert with him, just a lift of her hips, a tightening of thigh muscles, a soft sigh of pleasure at each long, slow silken thrust of his body. She had unfolded around him like rose petals to the sun's warmth, embracing him, welcoming him, taking him easily at first, then urgently, then with greed as something caught fire within her, filling her with a honeyed heat that grew with every caress, every move.

She hadn't expected the insistent urgency of her own body, and at first she tried to ignore it, telling herself she was expecting too much from this first time, that he'd already pleasured her, that it wasn't right to hold him back. She even gave a wriggle or two that she hoped he might interpret as satisfied completion just to make it easier for him, but he didn't even seem to notice. Instead, he seemed to understand exactly what she needed even when she didn't understand it herself, seemed to know where and how to touch her, how to move, how to time his rhythms with the deep contractions growing within her.

She felt as though she was drowning in a haze of pleasure, every nerve ending on fire, the taut urgency at her core pulled so tight she was half-wild with it. She was vaguely aware of Rafe's voice against her ear, urging her on, whispering things to her, of his fingers in her hair, of one hand cupping her bottom and lifting her against him time and again, adjusting her unsteady movements to his.

And then she was right *there*, right on the very edge, and she knew it was all right, that it wouldn't elude her, that Rafe would make sure it didn't. He did something then, a shift in his movements, a pressure of flesh on flesh, and it was exploding up through her like a juggernaut, ripples of pure sensation that went on and on, enveloping her, driving all thought and awareness from her.

She cried out, or at least she thought she did, heard something far, far away that might have been her own voice cresting with raw pleasure. Rafe had gone very still, his body pressed deeply into her, and she clung to him breathlessly as the ripples of satisfaction echoed from toe tip to the ends of her fingers, every cell in her body vibrating like a fresh-plucked harp string.

"Now you?" she finally whispered, when the last of the aftershocks had rippled away.

"Oh, yeah," Rafe whispered back, his fingers tightening in her hair. "Now me...."

It seemed like hours went by before Rafe remembered to start breathing again. He was still lying within the silken embrace of Meg's body, panting, his heart going like a jackhammer, wondering for half a moment or two if lightning had struck the trailer.

Not lightning, he reminded himself through a daze. Just Mary Margaret Kavanagh.

Admittedly, he reminded himself as he tried to catch his breath, it had been a while. But he'd had sexual droughts before and never had them end quite this spectacularly.

This hadn't just been great sex after going without for a while. This had been great sex, period.

He could feel Meg's heart beating against him, the rhythm steady and strong. It had been a long time since he'd lain on this bed with a woman. It had occurred to him when they'd first tumbled across it that he might regret it later, that the memories might come flooding back, the past tarnishing the pleasure of the present. But they'd been too caught up in mutual need for reason to have any power over him, so now he let the thoughts wash through him slowly, testing them for pain as they came. May as well face the music, he thought. May as well face the past.

Sadness, maybe. Wistfulness, certainly. A sense of loss. But, oddly, that was all. And even the loss wasn't as painful as it might have been, just an awareness that he'd loved a woman once who was no longer here and would never be here again. It wasn't that he loved her less in this moment, he realized with surprise, as much as that the love seemed to have settled into a quiet place in his heart, solid and certain but at peace.

He kissed Meg's damp cheek and she stirred slightly, murmuring wordlessly. To be honest, he'd been afraid that he'd been fooling himself. That he'd convinced himself he wanted to make love with Meg when in his heart he'd just been chasing ghosts. But he hadn't lost her. Not even in those last few moments, when he'd lost what little control he had left and just let himself go, he'd been keenly aware that it was Meg he was making love with, Meg's lips he'd kissed, Meg's body he'd pleasured, Meg's laughter and soft voice he'd wanted.

He was moving on. Letting go. And strangely enough, it didn't feel even half as frightening as he'd thought it might.

Gently, he eased himself off her and turned onto his side, cradling her against him. She snuggled into the curves of his body, one leg over his, arm across his chest, purring like a cat.

"You're smiling." Her voice was slurred, and her eyes, heavy-lidded, left no doubt that she was well and truly pleased with herself. "That means it was good, right?"

Rafe smiled and traced the curve of her cheek with his thumb. "I think we could say that."

"Really?" Her smile blossomed.

"Very really."

"You're not just saying that?"

"Quit trolling for compliments, Kavanagh."

The smile widened. "So you're saying that the effort you put into this *occasion* wasn't entirely wasted?"

"What do you think?"

She took a deep breath and let it out on a long, happy sigh. "I think," she said after a moment's consideration, "that when I get back home, I am going to kill my brothers. All of them. The entire male contingent of the Kavanagh clan is toast."

"And the reason for this wholesale mayhem is…?"

"Sex, of course." She traced the bow of his lower lip with a fingertip. "Or the lack of it, in this case." She sighed. "I have five of them, remember. Six, when Bobby was alive. Six brothers. Six *big* brothers."

She said it as though it explained everything. And when he thought about it, Rafe realized that it probably did. He thought of his own kid sister. "Pretty hard on your boyfriends, were they?"

She arched one beautiful eyebrow. "My brothers have terrorized every man who ever dared look at me twice. They have this…this *routine* they do. They act all friendly and nice and get the guy off-guard, then they take him out for what they call a 'talk.' The last fellow who survived one of their 'talks' didn't get the cast off his arm for eight weeks. The one before that moved. Sold his condo, packed up and moved to California without even telling me where he was going. I found out a week after he'd left when his mother happened to mention it.''

''Must've been rough.''

''I'd decided I was going to die a virgin. Never get married. Never have children.'' She sighed again, still tracing the outline of his mouth with her finger. ''Not,'' she added as a sudden afterthought, ''that I'm suggesting I want to marry you or anything. I mean, this is just a…an opportunity that came up, and…'' She blushed. ''What I mean is, I didn't come up here planning for this to happen. I don't want you to think I was stalking you or something.''

''But you did dream about me.''

The blush deepened. ''Well, I…'' She tucked her face against his throat. ''This is so embarrassing. Yes, I will admit I had a couple of rather…um…explicit dreams. And you did happen to be in them. But—''

''So did I.'' He nuzzled her temple. The hair there was damp and tangled, and he kissed her, tasting salt. ''Since South Dakota.''

''North,'' she murmured. ''It was North Dakota.''

''Whatever.'' He kissed her ear, then the soft downy spot just under it. ''You put me through five weeks of hell, Mary Margaret Kavanagh. Every time I closed my eyes, you were there. I'd come to bed at night and lie there and think about you and spend some long, uncomfortable hours. And cold showers. A *lot* of cold showers.''

''Which explains our lack of restraint, I guess.'' She smiled against his chest and started kissing him lightly. ''Not that I'm complaining. But I am still going to kill my brothers. I could have been doing this for years and years if it hadn't been for them.''

''Years and years.'' Rafe smiled as her kisses ran along the ridge of his left shoulder.

''Mind you, maybe it's a good thing they did.'' She nipped his shoulder and let her fingers trail delicately down his rib cage. ''Given my behavior this evening, it's possible I might have become insatiable. I might have gone right off the deep end with this sex business, doing it all the time.''

''All the time.'' Rafe ran his hand down to cup her bottom,

pressing her gently against him. "I like the sound of that. But you're going to have to give me a minute or two to catch my breath."

"Oh, that's okay." Her hand made an interesting foray south, fingers trailing magic. "I'm sure I can entertain myself for a while. I *have* read all the books, you know."

"*All* the books? That sounds...dangerous."

"Well, there's only so much you can learn from reading. In the end, it still comes down to practical application." Her smile widened wickedly. "And practice, of course. Plenty and plenty of practice."

"Feel free." Sprawled on his back, one leg drawn up, feeling lazy and sated, Rafe smiled at her.

"Hmm." Her laugh had a husky catch to it as she curled around and started kissing his chest and abdomen, then his belly, her lips coaxing sensations from him he'd all but forgotten. "I can't believe all the intriguing possibilities there are to this. Just endless variations and complications and explorations..."

Rafe swallowed and closed his eyes. "I'm not going anywhere," he breathed, thinking that was probably the greatest understatement of his life. "But I should warn you that it might take a while."

"Mmm, that's fine." She blew a warm breath into his navel, the tip of her tongue trailing sweet promises south. "That'll give me the opportunity to scope out the terrain without getting too sidetracked, so to speak."

"So...to...speak." Rafe swallowed again.

"I've read all sorts of interesting things," she said after a moment or two, fingers gliding downward. "*This,* for instance, is supposed to give a man a great deal of pleasure, if the Oriental texts are to be believed...."

Rafe nearly lifted off the bed. "Holy...catfish!" Struggling to catch his breath, he collapsed against the pillow again. "Read a lot, do you?"

"Oh, yes." She was kissing his belly again, tongue lapping wetly in ever-widening circles. "There are literally dozens of texts on this way of pleasing a man, for instance. I've never been too clear on the exact methods, I'll admit, not being too clear on the exact nature of the anatomy involved. But...well, nothing ventured, nothing gained."

Rafe gave a gasp of laughter and caught a fistful of hair to hold her head still. "Meg, you don't have to do—"

"This?" she whispered. And started to do it.

Rafe's protest got lost in his groan of surprised gratification. He pressed his head into the pillow, wondering if it were possible to forget to breathe. "Meg...oh, Meg..."

"Hmm." Her chuckle had definite salacious—and pleased—overtones. "Well, my goodness. It seems as though the books were right. That certainly got a reaction, didn't it?"

"Oh...yeah," he managed to get out. "What else...did... your books...say?"

"Oh, tons of stuff," she replied quite happily, settling down to some serious work. "I'm not sure I'm going to get it right the first time, you understand, but there's only one way to become proficient at something like this, don't you think?"

And Rafe, swiftly losing his mind, could only moan in agreement.

Chapter 9

It didn't seem possible, Rafe thought somewhat fatuously, that a man could spend the kind of night he'd spent and still have energy left over to seriously contemplate doing some of it again.

He smiled around his toothbrush, eyeing his own reflection in the mirror above the bathroom sink. Given the fact that he'd gotten no sleep to speak of, he showed a surprising lack of wear and tear. A scratch on his shoulder, a love bite on his neck and a pleasant afterglow, but no lasting damage. Not so bad for a guy as badly out of practice as he'd been. Some things you just never forgot, he guessed.

He'd made love to Meg for the last time no more than half an hour ago, and he was still a little shaken by the intensity of it. He'd turned to her in the half-light of dawn, and she'd come to him with a knowing smile that belied her inexperience of the day before, opening for him, taking him into her with that whispery groan he'd come to love, her body fitting to him, enfolding him, mastering him. After a night of experimentation and exploration, they'd come full circle to the simplicity of him between her thighs, moving strongly and certainly, not saying anything, neither of them needing words for what they could read in each other's eyes.

Their rhythms had been perfect, point and counterpoint, quick thrust, long, slow glide, slow withdrawal, relishing every vibrant, electric moment of contact. Even the end had needed no words as he adjusted himself instinctively to her needs, already in tune with her, with what she liked and needed. Somewhere during the previous hours she'd lost the last bit of shyness, and this time she just let go completely, knowing he was watching her and seeming to get even more pleasure from that.

She'd cried out time and again, asking him for more, letting him play her body with a virtuoso's skill, with no hesitation or holding back. And at the end he'd asked her what she wanted, and she'd told him and he'd given it to her, and she'd given that long, soft cry of pleasure and arched under him, head thrown back, small breasts arched toward him, as she took her release fully and with delight.

And then it had been her turn. She'd coaxed him onto his back and had slipped astride him and had ridden him like a strong, wild Celtic goddess, flaming hair tossed back, supple body moving like witch-fire on his, taking and giving in equal measure. She'd been so intent on making it good for him that she'd been caught up in it herself, and they'd come to the crest and over it and down the long, breathless slope on the far side together, his body so deeply buried within her that he couldn't tell her heartbeat from his, her breath from his.

And he wanted her again, he thought with wry amusement. Just thinking about her made his groin stir, and he laughed at himself and shook his head at his own badly compromised will-power.

But more than the sex, he wanted *her*. Here. With him.

The thought took him by surprise, and he stared into his own eyes in shock. Where the hell had that come from? The sex was great—the sex, he amended, was incredible, might as well get that straight right now—but that was all it was. Sex. A day, a couple of days. Whatever they could steal from the world. Then she would go back to her life and leave him with his, and that would be the end of it.

No forevers, Blackhorse, he reminded himself deliberately. You tried for forever once. Forever doesn't happen. Just the here and now counts. And don't forget that, he added ferociously. Just the here and the now.

With that sorted out, he turned and padded back to bed.

Meg didn't know what woke her. She was sound asleep one moment, exhausted and as sated as a cat that had overindulged on canaries and cream, and wide-awake the next, every sense fully alert.

Holding her breath, she listened carefully, trying to figure out what had startled her awake. It was still very early. The light coming through the wide window in the end of the trailer above them was watery and pale, and the sliver of sky she could see was solid gray. It had stopped raining finally, but she could hear the pitter-pat of rain dripping off the trees around the trailer.

But there was no other sound. Nothing. She lay listening to the silence for another few minutes, then decided she'd imagined whatever it had been. Or maybe it had been part of her dream, a complex tangle of images she couldn't quite remember.

Rafe was still sleeping soundly beside her, his breathing deep and steady, features chiseled and strong in the pale light, and as she gazed at him, something suddenly pulled so tight beneath her breastbone that it hurt to breathe. She'd been half-afraid that when morning came she would discover that the whole night had been nothing but an erotic dream. That she would waken to an empty bed and empty arms, every part of her aching for his touch.

But last night had been no dream. Her skin still tingled with the remembered imprint of his caresses, and just thinking of the way he'd turned to her again and again during the night made her breathing catch. As did the memory of her own uninhibited responses, the last of her shyness vanishing sometime during the night under his very skillful ministrations. She should be thoroughly ashamed of herself, she thought with amusement. But in reality she felt completely wonderful.

She was just about to roll onto her side and tuck herself into the welcoming curve of his body when she heard something—

really heard it this time. A scratching, almost, on the outside skin of the trailer, as though something metallic had skidded lightly along the wall.

Her heart skipped a beat and she sat straight up, telling herself it was just some animal. A porcupine, maybe.

Something moved in the open door of the bedroom and her heart rate soared; then she huffed out a breath of relief as Three came limping in, his ears cocked. He whined quietly, and Rafe stirred, muttering something.

Meg put her hand on his shoulder. "Rafe?"

He came awake instantly, dark eyes clear and alert, although he'd been deeply asleep only an instant before.

"Something's outside," she whispered.

Not saying a thing, he eased himself from between the warm sheets as silently as a wraith, naked flanks gleaming like copper in the pale gray light. Three whined softly again, and Rafe silenced him with a whisper and slipped from the bedroom.

Telling herself it was nothing, Meg pulled the sheet around her bare shoulders and sat as still as stone, straining to listen. Three turned awkwardly to stare after Rafe, every muscle in his body taut, then he spared Meg an uneasy look, as though wanting her to assure him that everything was all right.

And then Rafe was back, materializing out of the shadows, and all it took was one look at his face to know it wasn't all right at all.

"We have an intruder," he told her softly. "I don't know how the hell he got past the perimeter laser triggers and the proximity trips without setting off every alarm in the place, but he did."

"Then how do you know…?"

"Infrared scans show someone's out there, but I don't have them hooked up to the audio alarms. I figured by the time someone got that close, he'd have set everything else off and I'd have plenty of warning." His expression made it clear he wouldn't make that mistake again.

"So it's not an animal." She was slipping out of bed even as she asked it, heart hammering against her ribs. Rafe shoved a handful of clothing at her and she took it wordlessly.

"The perimeter triggers are man-height, and the only way through them is to disarm them."

"So whoever it is knows alarms."

"Knows alarms and wanted to come up on us nice and quiet."

"Do you have any idea who it—?"

"None. But between us we have a few options." He smiled without humor. "Whoever took that shot at you yesterday may have decided to come back and finish the job when he realized it didn't scare you off. I can also think of one or two people who'd like to see me go down hard."

"Wonderful." Meg shoved down an automatic jolt of panic as she wrenched her jeans up over her hips and zipped them, then pulled on a turtleneck sweater, not wasting time with a bra. Rafe was getting dressed just as quickly, but he paused long enough to toss a heavy wool sweater at her, and she pulled it on, too.

"Where are your boots?"

Meg's heart sank. "Outside. They were caked with mud, and I left them on the steps."

Rafe swore, then looked around the bedroom. He grabbed a pair of woolen socks from a drawer, then followed them with a pair of beaded moccasins. "Put these on. Weapon?"

"Living room. Under the sofa cushion."

"Stay here. Keep clear of the window, and don't make any noise. And keep that damned dog quiet."

Again he vanished, to return in under a minute with her Beretta in one hand and his own Taurus PT99 in the other. Meg's heart was hammering so rapidly her mouth was dry and she was shivering. She looked at him questioningly.

"I don't know what or who we're up against," he said in a low, tight voice, "but we've got to get out of this trailer. The walls have no stopping power, and we're trapped. So we're going out the window, and we're going fast and quiet. Keep low and head for the trees, and regardless of what happens, do not—repeat, *do not*—stop."

Meg's mind reeled. "But—"

"Head for the store down at Weasel Creek if we get separated. The old guy down there knows me. He'll help you get to the nearest airport.''

''But—''

''Head straight to your brother the cop's place and stay low.''

''Damn it, Rafe, will you stop giving me orders and tell me what—''

''And one last thing.'' He cupped her chin in his palm suddenly and tipped her face up. His gaze searched hers for an eternity that couldn't have lasted more than a heartbeat, his dark eyes filled with a tangle of emotions. Meg felt her heart cartwheel to a stop, and then he dropped his mouth over hers and kissed her with a slow and exacting thoroughness that left her completely breathless. ''It's been a hell of a pleasure, Mary Margaret Kavanagh.''

''But—''

Ignoring her protest, he lightly pushed against the window. It swung up on its hinges and he took a swift look outside, then shoved the window fully open and eased himself through the opening. Three was whimpering steadily now, as though afraid they were going to leave him behind, and Meg swore under her breath. Rafe whispered urgently at her to get the hell out now, that he would catch her, and she shoved her Beretta into the back waistband of her jeans and braced both hands on the sill, then swore again and turned away.

''Kavanagh!''

''In a minute!'' Telling herself that Rafe was just being overly cautious and that there was no real danger from whoever was out there, she bent down and slipped her arms around Three and boosted him up onto the bed. Off balance, he nearly fell on his face, but she got her arms around him again and lifted him up to the window. ''Take him!''

''What the...?'' Rafe swore vividly. ''Kavanagh, put that damn mutt down and—''

She shoved her head out the window and glared down into Rafe's angry, upturned face. ''He goes or I don't!''

''For the love of—'' He snapped his teeth across the protest. ''Give him to me, then!''

Somehow or other Meg managed to get the old dog up to the

window and more or less through it, and Rafe did the rest. He grabbed Three out of her arms and hauled him through the window and dumped him unceremoniously onto the ground. Three sneezed violently and struggled to his feet, seemingly none the worse for wear.

"Sometime today would be nice, Kavanagh!"

Meg braced her hands on the edge of the window opening and pushed herself through and Rafe's hands settled around her waist, pulling her through and around effortlessly. He dropped her onto the ground and then shoved her toward the trees.

Or where the trees would be if she could see them. The mountaintop was cloaked in heavy gray cloud as thick as flannel, and Meg hesitated, disoriented and blind.

"Go!" Rafe gave her another none-too-gentle shove, and she stumbled forward, sucking in a frightened breath as something dark and spindly loomed in front of her. But it was just a tree, and as soon as she reached it she could see the others crowding behind, dark limbs groping out of the sodden cloud like skeletal arms.

They half walked and half ran maybe fifty yards into the trees before Rafe stopped her. He shushed her question with an abrupt gesture and she went motionless, every muscle as taut as wire as she strained to hear something that might tell her if they'd been followed. Three whimpered softly and pressed against her legs, shivering in the icy air, and Meg put her hand on his head to quiet him.

Nothing. The constant patter of water dripping off spruce boughs, but utter silence beyond that aside from the hammering of her own heartbeat and the rasp of her breath in her throat.

There was a muffled *pop* in the distance, back where the trailer was, and Meg held her breath. She didn't think it had been a gunshot, but the cloud distorted everything so badly she couldn't be sure.

"Stay here."

Rafe started back in the direction they'd come, the Taurus in a two-handed grip as he edged his way cautiously through the cloud-shrouded trees. Meg's instinct was to go with him, but instead she went down on one knee beside Three and whispered at him to stay in a voice so ferocious he whimpered and huddled against her. Her breath left white streamers in the cold air and she was shivering again, her eyes aching with the strain of trying to see through the pale velvet enveloping them. Everything looked distorted and strange and threatening, and when she spotted the glow through the trees it took her a long puzzled while to realize what it was.

The trailer was on fire.

"Oh, my God..." Meg swallowed again, half strangled by sudden raw panic. Whoever was out there had ignited the trailer, probably thinking they were still inside. Maybe even still asleep.

Three whimpered again, and Meg hugged him tightly, refusing to think about the consequences had she not awakened when she had. Or if Rafe hadn't anticipated a trap and gotten them out. Whoever was out there meant business, and that meant the danger was still very real. The minute he—or they—realized she and Rafe had escaped being burned alive, the hunt would start. All she had was her Beretta and a full clip of fifteen rounds. Rafe's arsenal was going up in flames even as she was thinking about it, leaving him with the Taurus. Three was more a liability than an asset. And the truth was, she wasn't much better, with just enough training under her belt to make her a danger to everyone, Rafe and herself included.

She swore again, then nearly died on the spot when the thick cloud in front of her swirled and darkened as something big moved through it. She raised her weapon, heart in her throat, and then Rafe materialized right in front of her, freezing as he stared down into the barrel of the Beretta. Then he relaxed with an oath and knelt on the wet ground beside her.

"The trailer's burning."

She nodded. "I don't suppose it was an accident? The propane tank or something?"

His expression was grim. "Gasoline. Whoever was out there soaked the whole place with gasoline, then tossed a match down. The place is going up like tissue paper. If you hadn't wakened up when you did..."

"Did you see anyone? Get an idea of how many there are?"

He shook his head. "They want us dead, that's the only thing

I know. I don't know if the plan was to burn us alive or pick us off as we came out the door, but whoever it is isn't messing around with a warning this time.''

"This time." Meg looked at him. "So you think it's the same person who tried to frighten me off yesterday?"

"I don't know, Irish. Doesn't seem likely, but I don't know. If I had to guess, I'd say it was Gus Stepino's work, but maybe that hornets' nest you've been stirring up is bigger than you suspected."

Meg felt sick. If it did have something to do with her investigation into Bobby's murder, Rafe had paid with everything he owned. She thought of the small framed photograph of Stephanie that had hung on the bedroom wall. Would he ever be able to replace it? That, and who knew how many others? And all the other things collected over the years, more precious for the memories than actual cost.

"I'm sorry," she whispered, touching his shoulder.

"It's done," he said flatly. He checked the clip on his Taurus, swearing under his breath. "Twelve rounds. You?"

"Full fifteen."

He knelt there for a moment longer, not saying anything, staring in the direction of the trailer. Then he stood up abruptly. "Okay, this is how we're going to do it. The hiking trail down to the main road isn't far from here. You and the mutt are taking it and heading for Weasel Creek at double speed. Tell old Jonah I said he's to drive you to Abbotville—there's an airstrip there. You can hire someone to fly you to Denver, and from there you're home free."

Meg waited for him to continue. When he didn't, she stood up slowly and looked at him. "That's it? I leave, you stay?"

He gave her a steady look. "You got a problem with that?"

"Yeah! What if this guy isn't after you at all?"

"I don't give a damn who he came up here after. He tried to kill me, and he burned me out. That makes him mine."

Meg tried not to shiver, but the coldness in his eyes was chilling. "I'm not going anywhere until I find out if whoever's out there is after you or after me. Because if he's after me, I want to know who it is and what he knows about Bobby's murder. This might be the break I need.''

Rafe stared at her as though not quite believing what he was hearing. ''The break you need? Lady, in case you hadn't noticed, someone just tried to roast us alive.''

Meg glared right back. ''Don't try to bully me, Blackhorse. I didn't listen to my brothers when they told me to stop my investigation, and I didn't listen to Spence O'Dell when he told me the same thing, so I have no idea why you think I'd listen to *you*.''

As arguments went, it probably wasn't the best one in the world, but it was all she had. Meg held his stare with grim determination, refusing to back down an inch and praying he couldn't tell that under the bluff and bravado she was scared to death.

She thought for a moment that he was going to explode right then and there. But instead he just bared his teeth and wrenched the Beretta out of her hand, replacing it with his Taurus. ''I am going to kill O'Dell if I ever see him again,'' he said conversationally. ''I know he sent you up here to drive me insane, but it's not going to work.'' She opened her mouth to hiss a protest, but he silenced her with a look. ''You've got twelve shots. If it comes down to a fight, space them out and make every one count. I don't know if we're up against one person or twenty-one, and this damn fog doesn't help. But it doesn't help who-ever's out there, either. You stay here and hold your ground. And don't shoot me by mistake, okay?''

''If I shoot you,'' she whispered furiously, ''you can believe it won't be a mistake! How am I supposed to do anything stuck out here?''

Rafe closed his eyes and counted to ten. Slowly. He'd met only one other woman in his entire life who could argue like this one did, and that had been Stephanie. Well, his sister wasn't much better, but she was a lawyer, so you expected her to argue with every word you said just as a matter of course. There must be something about him that attracted beautiful argumentative women. Three out of three wasn't normal odds for any man.

''Yes, darling.''

Meg blinked. "I beg your pardon?"

"It would just be nice if once in a while you said, 'yes, darling' and did as you were told, that's all. But I guess the chances of that are slim to none, huh?"

"Damn straight."

For some reason it made him smile, although there was little enough reason for it. He wanted to catch whoever was out there and find out what was going on, and he didn't want to be worrying about Meg while he was doing it. Odds were she could manage to take care of herself just fine, but if it was Stepino getting a little payback for the Dawes mess, he'd probably sent in some serious muscle and Rafe had enough experience with mob muscle to know they would be as dangerous as snakes. He had the advantage of knowing the terrain, but they would have the firepower.

What worried him, though, was the possibility that it wasn't mob payback. Or any of a handful of other enemies he'd made over the years. If Meg had stirred something up within the Agency, they might be facing a team of highly trained specialists with orders to terminate with extreme prejudice.

"Okay, Kavanagh. You want in, you're in." He gave her his best secret agent glare, hoping she couldn't see the concern under it. She was gazing up at him trustingly, drops of rainwater jeweling the tangle of red hair framing her small heart-shaped face, and he could see her shivering with cold and damp. That delicious little mouth was within kissing range, full lips parted slightly, but he ignored it as best he could. He was in danger of losing it with her, he realized with a sinking heart. If they made it out of this alive—and there was no reason to believe that, with a little caution, they wouldn't—he had to get rid of her, and fast. Because for the first time in a long, long time he was starting to feel things again. And that was the last damned thing he wanted.

"Hello? You in there?"

He gave himself a little shake, realizing he'd been staring at her. Not meeting her eyes, he pretended to check the Beretta. "I'll give you five minutes to work your way around to the right. There's a deadfall close to where the road enters the clear-

ing. Set yourself up there so you can see anyone trying to leave.
If you can take them out quietly, do it, but if you can't, let them
go without giving up your position. We need to know how many
people are out there. And watch your back.''

She had paled slightly, and he hesitated, wondering if he
wouldn't be smart to just sling her across his shoulder and get
the hell down to Weasel Creek before whoever was out there
even knew they were in the clear. She would never forgive him,
of course, but it wouldn't be the first time he'd had a beautiful
woman mad at him. And with his unflagging luck with women,
it probably wouldn't be the last.

''I'm going to circle left, drive them toward you if possible.
Once we know what we're up against, the rest should be easy.''

She smiled faintly. Or tried to. But he could see she was
scared and uncertain, and again he hesitated.

''Count five, right?'' She swallowed and adjusted her grip on
the smooth Brazilian walnut grip of the Taurus. She must have
seen some of his indecision on his face, because she smiled
again. ''I can do this, Blackhorse. I outsmarted you in Dakota,
remember.''

Rafe snorted. ''Count five.'' He blew his breath out and flexed
his shoulders. ''Go.''

She got.

And left him standing there alone in the eerie drift of low
hanging cloud, feeling a sudden and inexplicable sense of loss
that didn't make any sense at all.

Meg found the deadfall with no problem, a tangle of old fallen
trees hidden behind new growth that gave her good cover, and
tucked herself into it. Problem was, she couldn't see a blessed
thing. The low-hanging cloud blanketing the top of the mountain
was even thicker now, and she had a sight line of maybe ten
feet in any one direction.

She heard the first two shots almost immediately and held her
breath, weapon braced. There was something that sounded like
running footsteps off to her right and she braced herself, waiting
for someone to come charging toward her, but nothing happened. Then, a minute or two later, she caught the faint silhouette of two ghostly shadows moving stealthily toward the clear-

ing, but they were gone almost before she convinced herself they were real. She had to fight to keep from going after them, driven half-wild with inaction and the frustration of not knowing what was going on.

There could be a dozen people in any given direction and she would never know it. And where was Rafe? Why hadn't they settled on some sort of verbal signal before splitting up so they could track each other's location? It was driving her nuts just sitting here, eyes nearly crossed with the effort of trying to peer through the shroudlike banks of cloud surrounding her, straining to hear something that would tell her what was going on.

Something moved just to her right again, and she swung the Taurus in an arc, its unfamiliar balance and weight throwing her aim off. But it was just Three, hobbling awkwardly through the undergrowth, looking wet and miserable. She hissed at him to lie down and he dropped to his belly, then started to crawl toward her, shivering and whimpering.

In spite of knowing he could have given her position away, Meg was glad to see him. He crept close and pressed himself against her, and she dared to drop her hand to his head to reassure him. And brought it away wet with blood.

It startled Meg so badly she just stared at her outstretched palm for a horrified moment, then collected her wits and turned to look down at the old dog to see how badly he was hurt. He gazed back at her trustingly, and it took her another long moment to realize that the blood soaking the thick fur on his neck and back wasn't his at all.

Rafe. A wave of raw panic washed through her. She closed her eyes and fought it down, her mind wheeling. Every bit of field training she'd ever had left her in that stomach-churning instant, and she just knelt there, feeling sick and dizzy and terrified, her mind as empty as a blank sheet of paper.

But then, almost as suddenly as it had left her, it came back. She went through a quick mental checklist without even realizing what she was doing, while another part of her mind started firing options and possibilities at her, and yet another told her in a cold voice that sounded suspiciously like Spence O'Dell's that if she wanted to live, she was going to have to do better than this.

It was that last bit that snapped her fully back into the here and now. She pushed the worst of the panic down and slammed the lid on it, then took a deep breath and started to think. First, the blood might not even be Rafe's. Second, rushing off into forty-seven different directions in a blind panic wouldn't accomplish a thing beyond getting herself shot.

"Three!" She kept her voice low. "I hope you make a better tracker than a watchdog, because I want you to find Rafe. Can you do that?" He gazed up at her intently. "Can you find Rafe?"

She didn't have a clue how you told a dog what you wanted him to do, so she just said Rafe's name a few more times, making the word a question, and to her amazement, Three seemed to understand. He slapped the ground with his tail, then turned himself around and started to crawl out of the deadfall. And Meg, praying that she was doing the right thing and not walking squarely into a trap, followed.

And nearly walked squarely into Spence O'Dell instead.

It startled her so badly that she dropped soundlessly to her belly and clapped her hand across Three's muzzle to keep him quiet, literally not even breathing.

It was O'Dell, all right. There was no mistaking that handsome, coldly arrogant profile, even from this vantage point. He must have heard something, because he turned sharply and stared intently into the trees beyond her, but the cloud, as thick as porridge, was obviously hampering him as badly as it was her. After a heart-stopping moment or two, he turned away again and started talking softly into a cell phone.

Meg closed her eyes and waited for her heart to restart. Then she took a deep, calming breath and stared down the slight slope to where O'Dell was standing. He wasn't alone. Another figure stepped out of the swirling fog to join him, then a third, limping slightly, and Meg pressed herself tightly into the wet grass, her mind careening like a runaway horse.

This wasn't what she'd expected. This was so far from what she'd expected, in fact, that she was having trouble getting her mind around it. Had O'Dell set fire to the trailer?

No. No way. Burning someone in a locked trailer or shooting

them when they came stumbling out, blinded by smoke and heat, was a coward's trick. And while she'd heard O'Dell called a lot of things in the three years she'd been with his Agency, no one had ever called him a coward. If he wanted you dead he would walk up and kill you where you stood without a word, looking right into your eyes as he did it.

Damn, damn, *damn!* Now what? Every instinct she had was screaming at her to stay quiet and not show herself, while three years of Agency training was telling her that O'Dell was the good guy, the one to trust, the one who would make sure she and Rafe were safe.

Except Rafe could spit farther than he trusted O'Dell. And as far as she was concerned, O'Dell had done nothing to find Bobby's killer.

Maybe because he already knew who it was.

The thought made Meg's heart stop. She pressed herself even more tightly against the ground, feeling icy rainwater soak through her jeans and sweater and the shirt under it.

"...he is?" One of the two men with O'Dell looked around uneasily, the weapon in his hands moving to cover the woods around them.

"Gone." That was O'Dell, his voice vibrant with anger. "This whole thing was a screw up from the start, Matsui, and I am not a happy man, you got that?"

From the man's expression, he got it only too clearly. Meg frowned. She knew the name. Matsui. Matt Carlson's old partner from the West Coast. What was he doing out here, a thousand miles from his home base?

"And that blasted Kavanagh woman?" This from the third man. She didn't recognize him, but there was something about him, something about the way he held himself, the way he kept scanning the treeline, his lean face alert and watchful, that made the back of her neck prickle.

He wasn't an active, front-line operative, she knew that for a fact, because she knew the personnel files inside out. That meant O'Dell had brought him in from the outside, or there was a pool of manpower at the Agency that no one but O'Dell knew about. And without wanting to, she found herself thinking about those rumors of a secret squad of stone killers commanded by and answerable to no one but O'Dell. Black Ops so dark even the Pentagon's secret elite knew nothing about them.

"Gone, too, if she knows what the hell's good for her," the first one, Matsui, said angrily. "I'm telling you, if I ever get my hands on her—"

O'Dell's snort cut him off. "Give it up. She's been running rings around you for weeks."

The other man, the one with the limp, looked at O'Dell evenly. "You've lost control of it, you know that, don't you? Cleaning it up now is going to get real dirty. You should have called me in weeks ago."

"I called you in when it was time," O'Dell said in a voice like cold ice. "It was under control."

"Was." The man held O'Dell's stare without flinching. "She's a loose cannon, O'Dell. Uncontrollable. I told you that a month ago. You should have let me take care of it then."

"Just take care of it now." O'Dell gave him a hard look, then turned away without another word. "We're wasting time out here. Blackhorse is long gone, and the woman with him. We'll get them when they come up for air. Do you have the surveillance in place?"

"Affirmative. But it cost me valuable manpower. The woman's got five brothers and a sister, plus parents, and they're spread around."

"It'll pay off. When she gets in trouble, she heads for family."

"Blackhorse is the one I'm worried about," Matsui said. "Your report stated categorically that he wouldn't get involved, but we know for a fact that he's helping her. The woman I can handle, if I can ever catch her. But Blackhorse..." He shook his head. "Bastard's sly and quick and as mean as a snake when he's backed into a corner."

"Leave Blackhorse to me," O'Dell said with quiet intensity. "The only thing you two need to worry about is taking Kavanagh out, and doing it quick and clean and with a minimum of fuss." O'Dell gave the surrounding trees one last probing look. "We're wasting time. Let's move."

They faded into the drifting fog and vanished before Meg even realized they were on the move, and then they were walking past her, no more than maybe fifteen feet from her, and her heart nearly stopped. To her everlasting relief, Three seemed to understand the danger and lay utterly motionless under the pressure of her hand. She could feel him trembling, but he stayed still and silent until the three men had vanished down the trail and into the fog without so much as a backward glance.

This was turning into a nightmare.

Meg fought off another tidal wave of panic. If O'Dell was involved, that hornets' nest she'd been stirring was bigger and more deadly than she'd ever dreamed. She had no way of knowing what side of things he was on—hers, theirs, his own—but she did know she couldn't risk trusting him until she was certain. Bobby had trusted the wrong person. And Bobby was dead.

But what she had to do right now was find Rafe.

Slowly, moving with a caution born of stark terror, she eased herself to her feet. "Three, find Rafe," she whispered. "Rafe. Find Rafe."

Three whined and struggled to his feet stiffly, then started limping toward the trees on the far side of the clearing. It was raining again, just a fine mist that was more cloud than actual water, but it seemed to soak right through to the center of her bones, and Meg shivered violently as she followed him.

The first thing she saw was the burned-out frame of Rafe's pickup truck. And the second thing she spotted was the blood trail. It was faint, nearly washed away by the light rain, but it got heavier as she followed it cautiously. She wasn't sure it *was* Rafe, she reminded herself with false calm. There might have been a fourth person up here, someone who got here before O'Dell and his crew, who torched the trailer, and it might have been this person and Rafe she'd heard exchanging gunfire. Rafe might have gotten the drop on him and not gotten hurt at all. He might just be lying low, waiting for O'Dell to leave. There were a dozen explanations for those shots, for the blood.

And yet, when she found him, she realized with a sinking feeling that she wasn't surprised at all.

Chapter 10

The bullet had creased Rafe's skull on the left side, leaving a ragged gouge that made her stomach cartwheel. He'd bled like a gored bull, his clothing and the ground around him soaked with it, and she whispered a heartfelt prayer as she dropped to her knees beside his still form and put her fingers on his jugular.

His pulse was uneven but strong, and she breathed a sigh of thanks. ''Rafe?''

He groaned and tried to roll onto his back.

''Lie still.'' Meg pulled up the heavy sweater Rafe had given her and tugged the tail of her shirt out of her jeans. Using her teeth and simple brute force, she ripped the entire bottom part of the shirt off, then tore the strip in half, folding one half to make a rough pad. She placed it over the gouge in his scalp and lifted his hand to it. ''Hold that. Tight.''

He muttered something and let his arm drop, and Meg swore at him and slapped his cheek with the back of her hand. ''Rafe! Wake up and help me!''

His eyes flicked open, filled with pain and confusion but also, to her relief, a healthy dose of anger. ''What th' hell...?''

''Hold this.'' She pressed his hand against the pad of fabric again, then started winding the second strip around his head to hold the makeshift bandage in place. Do you know who you are? Who I am?''

"You hit me, Kavanagh," he muttered ungraciously. "Is that how you're gonna treat every guy who makes love to you?"

"If you're any example of the kind of men I'm going to be attracting from now on, very probably," she muttered back.

He attempted to sit up again, then sagged back to the ground with another groan.

"Lie still," Meg told him urgently. "Be still. I've got to get this bleeding stopped before—'' She gritted her teeth, not wanting to think about it. "We're okay for the moment. They think we got away." Meg tied another knot in the bandage to keep it tight. "I heard them talking. They don't even know you've been hit."

His eyes, glazed with pain, held hers. "Damn shot came out of the fog before I even knew someone was there." He managed a wry smile. "Some hero, huh. I'm s'posed to be watching out for *you,* not th'other way 'round."

"Well, I owe you for saving my skin in that bar in Dakota, anyway." She forced herself to smile carelessly. "But right now our priority is getting off this mountain. You've got a head like a cast-iron skillet, but there's a possibility you've got a concussion and I want to get you to a hospital." Before you go unconscious again and I can't move you, she added to herself. Before night falls and we wind up huddled here in the wind and rain, without shelter or food, until you die of exposure.

"Truck…"

"Burned."

He swore through clenched teeth. "Brand-new starter motor…"

For some reason it made Meg laugh. She shivered again and looked around. It was raining harder now, the drops hard little pellets that stung her cheeks.

As though reading her mind, Rafe shivered violently. "Snow…we're going to get snow."

Meg's oath was unimaginative but heartfelt. Then she got to her feet and looked down at him. "Okay, hotshot, time to be a hero. I can't risk leaving you up here while I get help. And I can't carry you down. So you're going to have to get on your feet and stay on them.''

Rafe managed a painful grin. ''Anyone ever tell you you're bossy as hell?''

''All the time. Now stand up.''

Somehow, with her help, he struggled to his feet and managed a few unsteady steps.

''Are you going to be able to do this?''

''I can do this,'' he got from between clenched teeth. ''Bastards burned me out. Shot me. I've got a little payback of my own to do.''

''It'll keep. Right now we've got to get down to Weasel Creek without breaking our necks or freezing to death or getting shot.'' She slipped her arm around his waist. ''You said something about a shortcut. A hiking trail. I don't know if the road up here is being watched, but I wouldn't be surprised if it is. And we're in no shape to fight our way out of an ambush.''

She had no idea how they made it down. It started to rain heavily a few minutes after they started down the steep, root-snarled path, and then the rain turned to snow, making the twisting, narrow trail even more treacherous. Bruised and half-frozen, they slipped and stumbled over rocks and fallen trees, half-blinded by blowing sleet and swirling, low-slung cloud, and they were soon soaked to the skin and covered with mud. Three was trying desperately to keep up with them. She could hear him panting and struggling somewhere behind them, and there was a minute or two when Meg would have laughed out loud if she'd had the breath to spare. If O'Dell could see them now, he would laugh himself silly: one burned-out ex-agent with a dent in his head, a three-legged dog, and a computer gnome who didn't know when to quit. Some odds.

When they were about halfway down, the snow turned back into a heavy, drenching rain, and by the time they staggered out onto the shoulder of Indian Pipe Road, they were too cold and exhausted to even talk. Rafe, still dazed by the blow to his head, was shivering uncontrollably from exposure and shock, his flannel shirt and jeans too wet to provide any protection from the cold.

And then, just about when Meg was wondering how much longer she could keep him on his feet, the miracle she'd been praying for drove out of the rain and stopped right beside them in the form of a rusted-out pickup truck that looked old enough to have belonged to Moses. She recognized the old man from the Weasel Creek General Store—Jonah—and nearly burst into tears of relief.

He helped Rafe into the truck with no questions, accepting Meg's explanation that they'd had an accident without a glimmer of curiosity. He just shifted the wad of chewing tobacco in his cheek and spat into the ditch, then lifted Three onto the truck bed while Meg climbed in beside Rafe.

He lived behind the store in a tiny clapboard house that appeared to be the same vintage as the truck. But it was dry and almost clean and looked like a piece of heaven, as far as Meg was concerned. And when he helped her get Rafe out of the truck and inside without asking a single question, she could have kissed him on the spot. Together they half carried, half dragged Rafe into the bedroom and lowered him onto the bed. Meg pulled his muddy boots off while Jonah covered him almost tenderly with a ragged gray blanket, and when she tried to stammer her thanks, still so cold her teeth were chattering, he just waved her off and told her gruffly to stand by the woodstove until she thawed out.

He brought her a dented tin mug of steaming hot coffee and tossed another old blanket onto the floor for Three, who had crept so close to the stove that wisps of steam rose from his fur.

"Looks like you folks had yourselves some difficulty."

Meg nodded and took a sip of the coffee. It was so strong it made her eyes water, but she forced herself to swallow it, grateful for its warmth. "Yeah. We're in a bit of trouble. Actually."

"Thought as you might be." He gave her a sidelong look. "Some folks in here this mornin' asking if I'd seen a little bit of a gal with red hair hereabouts lately."

"Did they say what they wanted?"

"Nope. Asked them that, but they wasn't inclined to answer."

His eyes were the color of sun-faded denim, milky with age, but they held hers evenly. "Said they was with some guvmint office, but they didn't look like no guvmint folks I ever seen. Looked like bad news to me. 'Specially the one in charge. Coldest eyes I've seen." He nodded toward the bedroom "The young fella in some kind of trouble?"

"No." Meg wearily scooped her filthy hair back from her face. "I'm the one in trouble. Rafe got mixed up in it by accident." She shook her head slowly. "It's my fault he's hurt."

Jonah chuckled. "Excuse me, miss, but that young fella in there, he's got a mind of his own. Ornery cuss, right from the day he and his woman moved up there. He ain't about to get mixed up in nothin' he don't want to get mixed up in, so don't go blamin' yourself."

Meg forced herself to smile. "I appreciate that, but I know better."

"Think you do, maybe," he said gently. "But I've know'd that boy since he and his wife came up here five, six years ago. When she died, he went to pieces. Spent most of a year tryin' to kill hisself with bad bourbon. When he crawled up out of the bottle, he shut hisself off. Hardly comes down off that mountain 'cept now and again. His sister came up a time or two, but he ran her off like he runs everybody off, and I ain't seen her in, oh, goin' on a year."

Meg didn't say anything, and Jonah smiled. "Ain't nobody ever stayed up there overnight, 'cept you. I see the way you're all fretted over him. Woman frets like that when she cares about a man. Fact you were there all night, fact he came down here with you, even hurt and all, tells me you ain't just ordinary folk to him. A man like that, he don't get close to folk easy. If he's helpin' you, you'd best believe he's doin' it from wantin' to, not outta some kindness. Man like that ain't got much kindness left."

He walked slowly to the table and set his empty coffee mug on it. "There's venison stew in that pot on the back of the stove. Been cookin' since yesterday so's to be tender. Help yourself to some, then try to get some inside the young fella. Can't heal on an empty belly. And he needs the heat."

Meg nodded, suddenly so exhausted she felt drugged. "I don't know how to thank you, Mr....?"

"Jonah's fine," he said gently. "That boy in there done me a good turn a year back when I had me some trouble. I owe him." He nodded. "I got to open the store. You stay here as long as you need. When you're ready to move on, there's a car out back you can have. Belonged to my granddaughter. She'd dead now. Been meaning to get rid of it, but..." He shrugged. "You eat something now."

He turned and walked stiffly toward the door, pausing to pull on a heavy sheepskin jacket before venturing out into the rain. Meg let her shoulders slump, then took a deep breath and turned back toward the stove. The pot of venison stew was simmering gently, and when she lifted the lid, the smell of sweet onions and stewing meat and broth made her mouth water. She found a clean bowl and scooped a generous ladleful of stew into it, then grabbed a spoon and headed into the bedroom.

Rafe hadn't moved. She found another blanket and put it over him, then sat on the side of the bed and touched his cheek with the back of her hand. His skin was hot, but not dangerously so. And when she checked the rough dressing on his head, she was relieved to see the deep gash had stopped bleeding.

"Hey." His voice was ragged.

Meg forced herself to smile. "Jonah was telling me you did him a good turn last year. Keep doing people favors, Blackhorse, and you're going to ruin that hard-ass reputation you've been working so hard to create."

A smile shadowed his mouth. "Don't believe it. I got well paid for helping Jonah. I don't do anything for free."

"Does that mean I can expect to be billed for the effort you extended on my behalf last night when you divested me of a certain encumbrance?"

"I figure that was a mutual effort," he said with a weak attempt at a grin. "I divested you of your virginity, and you divested me of the possible damaging side effects of long-term celibacy. I'd call us even on that."

In spite of everything, it made Meg laugh. "See if you can manage to sit up and eat some of this stew."

He shook his head slowly and closed his eyes. "Maybe later."

Meg opened her mouth to argue, then just nodded and set the bowl aside. "I'll hold you to that."

"We in the clear?"

"For the moment. But we need a plan, Rafe. We can't just hole up here forever."

The smile brushed his mouth again. "Right at the moment, Irish, spending forever holed up with you doesn't strike me as a bad idea." He opened his eyes and held her gaze. "In case I don't get a chance to tell you again, last night was pretty spectacular. If I didn't feel like I'd been hit by a runaway locomotive, I'd suggest you get out of those wet clothes and slip under these blankets for a while."

Meg was bemused to feel herself blush. "I might just hold you to that, too, so don't promise me anything you're not willing to deliver on." On a whim, she tipped forward and kissed him gently on the mouth. "In the meantime, you need a hospital to have that thick skull of yours looked at. Jonah has a car we can borrow."

"No hospital." Rafe touched the dressing on his temple, wincing. "They're legally required to report all gunshot wounds. And the minute we're in the system, we're sitting ducks."

"But, Rafe, that—"

"Not as bad as it looks, trust me. I've had worse. Couple, three days of rest and I'll be ready to rock and roll."

"Rubbish. Bobby got nicked on the shoulder two years ago and was out of action for weeks. I'm in the business, remember? Save the heroics to impress the civilian girls."

It made him grin fleetingly. "And what does it take to impress you, Mary Margaret Kavanagh?"

"I'd tell you, but I embarrass easily. But you can put your salacious little mind to rest. I was impressed."

"By anything in particular?"

She blushed, but put her mouth close to his ear and whispered her reply. He gave a bark of laughter and Meg smiled, then let it fade as she gave the door an uneasy look. "I want to have a look around outside. I wouldn't put it past O'Dell to have this place staked out, too."

"O'Dell?" Rafe looked at her in confusion. "O'Dell was here?"

Meg just looked at him. "That's who was up at the trailer. O'Dell and two other agents. I thought you—"

Rafe swore dully. "I never saw a damn thing. Just a figure in the fog. I came up on him with no warning and he got off a shot before I did, then he ran before I hit the ground."

Meg frowned. "That doesn't sound like O'Dell."

"Isn't." Rafe shook his head slowly, swallowing. "Wasn't O'Dell. I know his style. He doesn't shoot unless he's got a hard target, and if he targets you, you're a dead man. He'll track you 'till you drop."

"So someone else was up there."

"The agents with O'Dell: You know them?"

"One. Matsui, from the west coast office. I didn't recognize the other one, but I'll lay odds he's Special Ops. All those guys give me the creeps, and this one wasn't any different."

Rafe swore again. "What the hell have we fallen into?"

"The man with O'Dell, the one I didn't recognize, was saying that O'Dell should have brought him in weeks ago. That the cleanup was going to get messy."

Rafe looked at her sharply. "What are they cleaning up? Us, or Bobby's murder? Or something we don't even know about?"

"They're after me," she said quietly, deciding he didn't need to know the details of what she'd overheard. Even she didn't understand the full implications, and Rafe didn't need anything else to worry about. "But I don't know what's going on, Rafe. None of it's making sense. Setting fire to the trailer isn't O'Dell's style, either, so I think we're definitely dealing with at least two groups of people."

"And both seem to want us dead," he said with a grim attempt at a smile. Then it faded and he looked at her seriously. "You need to get the hell out of sight, Meg. Head for your brother's place in Chicago, and lay low for a while."

Meg shook her head. "O'Dell's got my whole family staked out. He knows that's the first place we'd go."

"Some place he wouldn't think to look, then."

"Not without you. You're in as much trouble as I am by now."

"Maybe. But I can handle O'Dell. You can't."

"Yeah, right, with a hole in your head you can see daylight through." Meg gave him a disgusted look. "Bobby was *my* brother, Rafe. If O'Dell was involved, I'm going to take him down. Myself."

Impatience flickered across Rafe's strong features. "Meg, don't be—"

"What? Stupid?" She stood up and glared down at him. "On a good day, you probably *can* handle O'Dell better than I can. But you're not having a good day, Rafe. And won't be for a while. You're in this because I was careless enough to get you involved, but this whole mess is my problem, not yours."

"This whole mess became my problem when somebody burned down my trailer and tried to put a bullet through me," he grated. "So don't even think about trying to take these guys down without me."

"Rafe…!" Meg caught the rest of her tirade and swallowed it. Logic wouldn't work on this kind of male bullheadedness, she knew that from twenty-odd years of living in a houseful of it. And besides, as much as she hated to admit it, he had a point. "I'm going to check on that car Jonah says we can use—let's just hope it's in better shape than his truck. In the meantime, you'd better get some rest."

She didn't like leaving him, but she wanted to make sure the car would actually run. And she also wanted to scope out the terrain, not liking how vulnerable they were here. Although it did have one advantage—no one in their right mind would think to look for them here in the open like this.

To her relief, the car was a three-year-old Ford that looked immaculately cared for. Jonah had given her the keys, and she popped the hood and checked the carb, plugs, wiring and hoses, and found everything shipshape, gratified that something seemed to be going their way for a change. She decided to top up the gas tank later and settled for checking the oil and tire pressure, finding that they, too, were fine. Things were definitely looking up.

She was halfway back to the house before she realized someone was there. There was a big late-model Chrysler sedan sitting at the gas pump, looking out of place here in the middle of nowhere, and she stepped out of the line of sight and eyed it uneasily. It was probably nothing. Just a couple of tourists who'd taken a wrong turn somewhere.

But then she saw someone slip around behind the house, and every instinct she had clicked into action. She had Rafe's Taurus in her hands without even thinking about it, and she cat-footed around the woodpile and a machine shed until she could see the back of the house without being seen herself. Whoever it was, he was being as cautious as she was. She caught a glimpse of him, then he vanished around the far side of the building.

Meg hesitated, her heart in her throat. And then, very suddenly, she'd had enough. Swearing under her breath, she moved quickly and silently toward the opposite side of the house, planning to meet him head-on and catch him by surprise.

Her plan worked almost too well. He was moving faster than she'd realized and reached the corner a split second before she did, but while he was caught by surprise, she had her weapon up and trained fully on him before his had even cleared the leather holster under his left arm.

"Don't!" Meg's voice was clear and steady. "Don't do it. Please. I really don't want to have to shoot you, sir. But I will if you pull your weapon, I swear it."

O'Dell eased his hand out from under his dark trench coat and sighed, looking resigned and vaguely bemused. "Miss Kavanagh. You are an endless source of surprises."

"What are you doing here?"

"Hoping to find you."

"Where are the others?"

"Others?"

"Matsui and the other man, the one with the limp. Where are they?"

O'Dell hesitated just a fraction of a second too long. "Gone. I'm here alone."

"You're lying. Sir." Meg wet her lips. "Where are they?"

An annoyed frown creased his forehead. "Matsui's on a chopper heading back to Virginia."

"And the other one?"

"Right here," a soft, dangerous voice said from right behind her. "I've got a Walther double-action pointed at the back of your head, Agent Kavanagh. Put your weapon down. Slowly."

The hair on the back of Meg's neck stood up, but she held O'Dell's cold, gray gaze without flinching. "No."

O'Dell looked startled. Then vaguely amused.

"Do it," the voice behind her said. "Now."

"My weapon is trained on Mr. O'Dell's heart. Odds are excellent that if you shoot me, I'll squeeze the trigger by reflex as I'm going down and he's a dead man."

This time she didn't imagine it. There really was a flash of amusement in O'Dell's stone-colored eyes. "I have definitely underestimated you, Miss Kavanagh. Something I rarely do."

"Yeah, well, life's full of learning experiences. Now please tell him to put his weapon down before this gets messy. I've had a real bad morning so far, what with someone trying to burn me alive, and I pretty much don't give a damn who I shoot at this point."

His gaze flicked over her shoulder. "Put up your weapon, Jarvis."

The man swore ferociously. There was an electric pause, then Meg heard the rasp of steel on oiled leather, and an instant later the man walked around and turned to face her, his lean face dark with anger.

"Jarvis, this is Mary Margaret Kavanagh, the Computer Information Retrieval Specialist I was telling you about. Miss Kavanagh, this is…an old friend."

"You don't have friends. Sir." Meg looked at the other man coldly. "There's a Rick Jarvis in Special Ops. That would be you, I suppose."

He inclined his head slightly in acknowledgment, never taking his eyes off her.

"And you were brought in to…clean up."

"So, you heard that, did you?" O'Dell sounded bored. "I had the feeling up on that mountain this morning that something wasn't right. Where's Blackhorse?"

"I have no idea," she lied smoothly. "He's no concern of mine. I was up there looking for information he didn't have and was already leaving when you set the trailer on fire. He went one way and I went another.''

O'Dell's eyes narrowed fractionally. ''For what it's worth, we got there after the fire was set.''

''But you came looking for me.''

''Yes.''

''I'd ask you why, but I doubt you'd tell me the truth. I'm not sure you even *know* the truth anymore. Sir. I think you've spent so long telling lies for a living that you've forgotten how to do anything else.''

Something flickered across O'Dell's hawklike features, and his mouth tightened fractionally.

''I *could* take her out,'' Jarvis said conversationally. He held Meg's gaze, his eyes filled with lazy arrogance.

''Even think about it, Slick, and I'll kill you where you stand.'' Rafe stepped from around the corner of the house with a Winchester pump action in his hands, looking like he would love nothing better than to use it on someone. ''O'Dell, this is getting real old. Any reason I shouldn't finish you both off right here and be done with it?''

''Not offhand,'' O'Dell said mildly. ''Except this has nothing to do with you. Kavanagh's opened a can of worms, and I'm trying to get the lid back on before anyone else gets hurt. But that's Agency business. And as you've told me more than once, you don't work for me anymore.''

''And this can of worms...it have a name?''

''It...might. That's what I'm trying to pin down.''

''By killing Meg. And me. Or was I a happy accident?''

O'Dell made an impatient gesture. ''As I just told Miss Kavanagh, that wasn't us. But you already know that, because you know if I wanted you dead you'd be dead.'' His gaze drifted to the makeshift bandage around Rafe's head. ''That looks nasty. You should have it looked at.''

Rafe looked at Meg. He was pale and sweating slightly, and she realized suddenly that it was taking all his strength to just stand there. ''It's your call, sweetheart. Take them out or trust them?''

''I don't trust either of them,'' she said flatly. She looked at

O'Dell. "I hope you won't take this personally, sir, but I'm going to lock you both in that machine shed over there. You won't be very comfortable, but I'm sure you see my problem."

He inclined his head, mouth quirking in one of those ironic little smiles O'Dell was so fond of. "Not perfect field procedure, but not bad improvisation. Engler said you handled yourself like a pro in North Dakota. From what I've seen over the last three weeks, I'm inclined to agree with his report."

"Just walk toward the shed," she said wearily, gesturing with the Taurus. "Agent Jarvis, you too. And please don't try anything. I might not shoot you, but I can almost guarantee that Rafe is just looking for an excuse to use that shotgun, and I'm in no mood to talk him out of it."

To her surprise, he smiled. "If you don't get yourself killed playing games you're not trained for, Specialist Kavanagh, I'd like to get to know you better. O'Dell told me you were one of a kind."

"You got that right, Slick." Rafe gestured toward the shed with the shotgun. "Move."

The machine shed was made of corrugated iron and looked strong enough to hold a small army, although Meg didn't know how long it would hold O'Dell and Jarvis in. But short of letting Rafe shoot them both and burying their bodies under the pile of scrap metal behind the service station, she didn't know what else to do. If she called the police, or even the FBI, she and Rafe would be behind bars in about thirty seconds flat and probably wouldn't get out until they were on social security. If they got out at all. People tended to disappear when O'Dell got annoyed.

She pulled the door open and gave it a quick once-over, but it was empty except for a pile of folded tarpaulins in one corner. Jonah turned up just then, and she had him bring out a bucket of water and two bowls of his venison stew; then she motioned Jarvis and O'Dell toward the tarps and told them to sit down. "Okay, you've got one hot meal and enough water for a week, if you don't waste it. The tarps will keep you warm." She took a deep breath and looked at O'Dell. "I hope I'm wrong about your involvement in my brother's death, sir. And if I am, I'm really sorry about this. When it's all over, and if you're in the clear, I'll turn myself in to you personally, you have my word.''

"I wish I could convince you to come back to Virginia with me right now and save us all a good deal of trouble," he said with visible irritation. "You're involved in something that's way beyond your scope, and you're doing nothing but complicating the hell out of things."

Then he swung that hard, impatient stare onto Rafe. "I know you'd rather take out your own appendix with a chain saw than work for me again, Blackhorse, but you're in this mess up to your neck whether you want to be or not. So make damn sure you finish it. She's good, but she's not good enough."

"Good enough to take you two out," Rafe reminded him coldly. "Jonah, you got a good lock for this door?"

Jonah did. He produced a length of heavy chain and a padlock the size of a small car, and with Meg's help he closed the door on the two men and secured it. Even Meg was impressed with the result, and her hopes went up a notch or two.

"You okay?" She gave Rafe a worried look.

"I've been better," he admitted in a ragged voice, lowering the shotgun with obvious relief. Jonah grabbed it before it hit the ground, and Meg grabbed Rafe before he did the same. He wavered, staggering a little to one side to keep his balance, but managed to stay on his feet. He leaned heavily on her as they started back toward the house.

"How long do you think that shed will hold them?"

"Couple of days if O'Dell wants it to. Couple of minutes if he doesn't."

"We've got to hit the road."

"Do we have a plan or are we making it up as we go?"

"Making it up. I have a cousin in Canada who'd take us in. She and her husband own a vineyard in British Columbia. The climate's supposed to be pretty good where they are. Ever had a hankering to grow grapes and make your own wine?"

"On a scale of one to ten, I'd give it a three."

"Then I'd say we need a better plan."

"I know where we can go." He stopped, still pale and unsteady, and looked down at her. "I'll be as welcome as Custer at a rain dance, but she'll love you. And I can guarantee no one will ever think of looking for us there. Not even O'Dell." He smiled raggedly. "Especially O'Dell."

And then he passed out.

It started to rain again just as they were leaving Weasel Creek, and within minutes it was coming down in heavy, solid sheets of water that turned the badly paved road into a river. Rafe had come to long enough to tell her how to get to their destination but then had slipped into unconsciousness again, leaving her to navigate a whole lot of unfamiliar territory alone and scaring her to death into the process. She and Jonah had gotten him into the back seat, and he was lying there unmoving, wrapped in blankets. Meg kept glancing at his still form in the rearview mirror, wanting more than anything to see him open his eyes, but he just stayed pale and silent.

She drove straight through, sixteen hours dogged by storms and the utter certainty that O'Dell somehow knew where she was going and was already on her trail. Old Jonah had assured her that his two prisoners wouldn't be going anywhere for a while, but Meg wasn't so sure. And what worried her even more was what would happen to him when they *did* get out.

She'd wanted him to come with them, but he'd just waved her off impatiently. "I'll just tell 'em I had me an attack of that Oldheimers disease and forgot they was in there!" Then he wandered off, cackling with laughter.

And then, finally, she was there. The house loomed out of the clear, star-shot North Dakota night like a ship rigged for sea, ablaze with lights, and Meg sobbed with relief as she wheeled the filthy, mud-caked Ford between a black Jeep Cherokee and a red Chevy pickup.

Leaving Rafe in the car, she ran across the tidily landscaped yard and up four wide flagstone steps to a terraced patio, and then she was at the front door, pounding on it with her fists and screaming for someone, anyone, to help her.

She heard voices inside, filled with alarm, then running foot-steps, and then the door was pulled open and light burst over and around her. She took one look at the woman standing there and burst into tears.

"My Lord!" the woman exclaimed. "You're covered with blood! There's been an accident! Mom? Mom! I need help here...."

"CJ?" Meg sobbed. "Charlene Crowchild?"

"Yes." She took Meg's arm and drew her into the house. "Do I know you?"

"N-no. M-my name's Meg Kavanagh. Your brother's in the car and he's been hurt. He told me to bring him here. That we'd be safe here."

"CJ? Who is it? What's going on?" Another woman stepped into the light. Older than the first, but with the same clear, strong features, the same dark eyes.

"I have no idea, Mom." The younger woman stepped past Meg. "But she says Rafe is in the car and that they need help."

Chapter 11

The room was quiet and smelled faintly of lilacs. Rafe stared at the ceiling, wondering if whatever Fates were up there keeping an eye on him were finished laughing yet. Because all this sure had to be somebody's idea of a bad joke.

The good news was that he'd decided he just might live after all. Even better, if he lay very still, nothing hurt. The doctor CJ had called in had peered and poked and prodded at him, not finding too much wrong. CJ had told him the wound was accidental, and he didn't seem to think otherwise, muttering things about idiots with guns and suggesting, none too politely, that anyone who shot himself in the head while cleaning his own firearm deserved what he got.

But, opinions aside, he seemed competent enough, telling Rafe dryly that his thick skull had saved him, deflecting the bullet before it could do serious harm. And that the worst thing he could expect in the next day or two was a ferocious headache. He'd cleaned the gash thoroughly and then stitched it closed as best he could, considering the bullet had taken a hunk of Rafe's scalp with it. Then he covered the wound with a clean dressing and finished up by jabbing a couple of shots into Rafe's back-side, one a standard tetanus shot and the other a mild painkiller.

One crisis down. Only a few dozen to go.

It made him smile faintly. He turned his head—gingerly—to the left. Meg was still there, standing by the window, staring into the night. The light cast from the small table lamp behind her made her hair glow like a flame, and he found himself just wanting to lie there and look at her, deliberately letting his eyes follow the outline of her cheek and jawline and throat, the curve of her shoulder, the supple line of her back. It had been a long time since he'd looked across the room at a woman and felt that tingle of pleasure, not sexual desire but a comfortable satisfaction at just seeing her there.

Truth was, on those few occasions when he'd wakened to find himself in some woman's bed, he hadn't been able to get out fast enough. It wasn't something he was proud of, but by dawn, the urgencies of sexual need and mutual desire sated, he'd felt nothing but a cold emptiness that awkward efforts at closeness or even conversation just made worse.

But with Meg...

He found himself smiling for no reason at all then, suddenly wanting to hear her voice and have those thoughtful blue eyes looking at him instead of at reflections in a window.

"Hey," he said softly. "How are you doin'?"

She turned and smiled at him, and he could have sworn the room lit up. Still smiling, she walked across and sat on the side of the bed. He took her hand and meshed her fingers with his. She smelled good. English lilacs, maybe. She was wearing a fluffy white bathrobe about five sizes too big and had washed her hair sometime during the evening. It had dried into a nimbus of copper curls, and he lifted his other hand to brush a tendril off her cheek, more for an excuse to touch her than anything. Her skin was warm and silken, and he remembered how she'd felt in his arms last night, all hot satin and soft laughter and a mouth a man could get drunk on.

"Hey yourself, hotshot. How are *you* doing?"

"Good," he replied ungrammatically. "As long as I don't move anything, I'm good."

"Then don't move anything." She bent down and kissed him lightly, gently, on the mouth, but before he could collect his wits enough to do something about it, she'd pulled back. "The doctor says he doesn't know how that bullet didn't crack your skull, but he doesn't think any real harm was done. You're not seeing double or feeling nauseous or disoriented or anything, are you?"

"Nope. Seeing one of everything, don't feel nauseous, and I'm no more disoriented than I always am around you."

"Are you saying I confuse you?"

"You wind me in circles, Kavanagh."

"Well, I have to say you don't do my peace of mind a lot of good, either." She put her palm on the bandaging on his head, frowning as she leaned across him slightly.

She'd caught her lower lip between her teeth, and Rafe found himself staring at it, then at the golden sheen of the skin on her throat, which led his eye down the V of the robe to where it had fallen open just a little.

"Feels okay," she said. "Does it hurt an awful lot? The doctor left some painkillers and said I'm supposed to make you take them." Her smile blossomed and she looked down into his eyes, and Rafe could have sworn his heart had forgotten how to work properly. "He seems to think you're one of those silly macho types who'd rather suffer than admit he needs something for the pain."

"I'll yell."

"Do that." She smiled again, and then seemed to suddenly realize that she was still leaning over him, her mouth only inches from his, and sat up. "You've got a sprained ankle, too, so don't count on running any marathons for a while. Not to mention a wild assortment of bruises and scrapes. We got you cleaned up as well as we could, but I could give you a sponge bath tomorrow if you like."

Rafe had to laugh, his imagination suddenly exploding with erotic possibilities. "Oh, yeah, I think I'd like that a whole lot!"

To his amusement, she blushed like a schoolgirl. Rafe lifted her hand to his lips again and kissed it, running the tip of his tongue between her fingers, his gaze holding hers. The blush deepened and she dropped her gaze, and he laughed again. "I can't believe you're still shy with me, Meg. There isn't an inch of me you haven't seen. And vice versa.'' He ran the tip of his finger down the V of the robe. ''Just out of curiosity, how far south does that blush go, anyway?''

She laughed and snatched the robe closed. ''All the way! And will you behave, please? You're supposed to be an invalid.''

''I might be dented, but I'm still alive. And you're a very beautiful woman I've spent a lot of hours naked with.''

''So you remember that, do you?'' She grinned mischievously. ''I was afraid you'd wake up and decide to come down with selective amnesia to avoid having to deal with morning-after regrets.''

Rafe looked her straight in the eye. ''I don't have any morning-after regrets, Kavanagh, let's get that straight right now. Last night was the best damn thing that's happened to me since…in years.'' Since Stephanie, he'd been about to say. It was true, but he wasn't sure she would want to hear that. Wasn't sure he wanted to hear it himself.

Meg smiled shyly. ''Thank you for saying that. Even if it's not true, it's a nice thing to say. I was wondering if this was going to be awkward….''

''We made love, Meg,'' he said quietly. ''I was *inside* you. There isn't any part of you I don't know by heart, any part of you I haven't touched and tasted and explored. I might be a bastard in a lot of ways, but I don't hit and run. Not with a woman like you. You're…'' What? he thought deliberately. What exactly was she to him? ''Special.''

Except she was so far beyond special it made his head spin.

She looked confused and flustered, and Rafe knew exactly how she felt. He sighed and put his hand on her cheek, and she turned her face to kiss his palm, eyes closed. Rafe felt something pull tight in his chest, something liquid and hot and achingly pure, a yearning so strong it gathered thickly at the back of his throat.

''Are you okay?'' he finally asked, when he was more certain of his voice. ''You still haven't told me how you're doing.''

She smiled a little shyly. ''I'm okay. Better than okay, now I know you're going to be all right.''

"CJ taking care of you?"

Meg gave a peal of laughter. "Your sister is a combination of Mother Teresa, Albert Schweitzer and Arnold Schwarzenegger! And your mother is even more awesome. Five minutes after they got you inside the house, I was bathed, shampooed, clothed and fed. I didn't know what hit me!"

"Just Beth Blackhorse," Rafe said sourly. "A force of nature."

"Why didn't you tell me your family was so incredible?"

"Sounds as though my mother has taken you under her wing like she does all her other strays." He heard the bitterness in his voice and bit it off, wanting to hang on to the good mood he felt when Meg was around.

"I can't imagine what she must have thought, opening the front door and finding a wild-eyed stranger there with her bullet-wounded son and a three-legged dog."

Rafe fingered the dressing on his temple. "Don't kid yourself, she loves every minute of it. We'd fit right into the image she's created of herself as Saint Beth on her holy crusade against the dark forces. The three-legged dog would have been the perfect touch."

Meg was quiet for a long moment. Then she said, quietly, "Why do you do that?"

"Do what?"

"Close yourself off like that whenever you mention your family."

"Was that what I was doing?" He gave her an impatient look he hoped she would take as a warning.

"You're doing it again," she said, still more quietly. "Everything's fine, as long as you can keep the discussion away from personal things. Then you just freeze up."

"My family and I don't have a hell of a lot to say to each other," he said curtly. "I mind my business and they mind theirs, except when CJ is on one of her crusades to turn us into a *real* family, whatever the hell that means."

"Yes, she mentioned something about that." There was a hint of laughter in her voice, and Rafe looked at her sharply. She smiled that serene, nunlike smile he was beginning to recognize meant trouble. "Your mother's birthday is next month and CJ is planning a party. And it's going to be a reunion, too. She's invited your half brother in Montana and his family. Rhett... that's not it. Something Kendrick."

"Jett. Jett Kendrick."

She looked startled. "I'm surprised you remember. You sent him a card a couple of years ago saying you'd spent almost a year tracking him down and would like to get together. But then you dropped out of sight. He's been looking for you ever since. He managed to find CJ—you'd mentioned she's a lawyer and so is Jett's wife, so she found CJ through the internet. CJ, your mom and he have been corresponding ever since."

Rafe snorted. "CJ'll love that, having another brother to drive crazy with all this family bonding." His mouth twisted bitterly. "My mother, too. She's real keen on all this family stuff now, even if it is thirty years too late."

Meg winced slightly. "She's your mom, Rafe."

"She gave birth to me, I'll meet you halfway there. But she sure as hell was never my mother."

Meg didn't say anything, although the frown between her brows spoke volumes, and Rafe lifted his hand to rub it away before he even realized what he was doing. He dropped it to his side again awkwardly.

She wouldn't understand. To her, family was a close-knit clan who stuck together no matter what. To him, it was just a collection of people who got in each other's way.

After he'd joined the Navy, he'd gone ten years without setting eyes on either his mother or CJ. It had been CJ who'd made the first move, of course. He could always count on CJ to stick her nose in, as determined to turn them into a normal, functioning family as he was to avoid any such attempt. She'd tracked him down, as resolute as a bloodhound, and had nagged and schemed until it was easier to give in than fight. He'd gone home with her and had found his mother there, and things had been strained and uncomfortable, although CJ had sworn it was a success.

To be truthful, there had been a while, back when he and Steph were together, that he'd thought maybe CJ was right and they might have a chance to build something of a family. The two of them had gotten almost close for a couple of years, laughing more than they bickered, and he'd even made an uneasy peace with his mother. Then Stephanie had gotten pregnant, and for a while it seemed as though all the hurt from the past was over and he finally belonged somewhere, was part of something.

It was during that time that he'd written the note to Jett Kendrick, at Steph's urging. He was only a half brother, but Steph had said family was family and had talked about blood and water and all the rest of it, and he'd finally given in, laughing, just to get some peace.

Then Steph had been killed and it all unraveled. He'd pushed them all away, wanting nothing more than to be left alone. And after a while it seemed as though everyone from O'Dell to CJ had given up and was going to give him what he wanted.

Or thought he wanted.

"Anyway, CJ wants you there," Meg said.

Rafe shook the past off and looked at her.

"Jett wants to meet you, for one thing, and CJ figures…" She shrugged and met his gaze almost apologetically. "I told her I'd ask you. She says if she asks, you'll tell her to go to hell like you did the last time she talked to you, and then she'll get mad and you'll get mad and you'll both start yelling at each other. Apparently," she added almost delicately, "you do that a lot."

"CJ yells," Rafe muttered, feeling defensive for no reason he could fathom. "I just try to stay out of her way. And for the record, I didn't tell her to go to hell. I told her to—"

"Yes, I know," Meg put in hastily. "I was paraphrasing."

For some reason, it made Rafe laugh. He didn't know how she did it, but she could wind him up like no one he'd ever met and then diffuse it in about thirty seconds flat with no more than one of those serious, wide-eyed looks or a smile.

"I'll tell you what," he said recklessly, "I'll agree to go to this thing if you'll come with me. You can keep CJ and me from killing each other and keep my mother off my case, and if this Kendrick turns out to be a jerk, we can sneak off and make love all day instead." He grinned at her. "How about it? You're always telling me how great this family stuff is. Willing to put your money where your mouth is?''

''Yeah.'' She was looking at him speculatively. ''You're on. And if you try to cop out on me, I'll come up there to Bear Mountain and haul you down at gunpoint.''

The mention of Bear Mountain seemed to bring them both back to the present with an unpleasant jolt. Meg sighed and looked down at their intertwined fingers, lost in thought, and Rafe found himself just looking at her again, amazed, as always, by her presence.

He traced the outline of her cheek with his eyes, thinking with vague amazement that it had been about twenty-four hours ago that he'd made love to her for the first time. He felt a rush of pain somewhere under his breastbone and realized that he would give just about anything to spin the clock back those twenty-four hours and recapture that moment. To relive it and the long, magical hours afterward until the end of time. There had been nothing but the two of them last night. It had been as though the world had ceased to exist for one delirious night and they had been suspended in time and space, just the two of them and the sweet perfection of two people as utterly in tune with each other as it was possible to be.

He suddenly realized she was looking at him, that faint frown marring her forehead again. This time he did reach up and rub it with his thumb to erase it. ''Nothing to worry about for a little while, Irish. No one knows we're here.''

She put her hand on top of his, caressing the scarred knuckles. ''I'm sorry about your trailer, Rafe. I keep thinking about that snapshot of Stephanie you had in the bedroom. And that chewed-up plastic toy of Three's.''

''I have other pictures—at least, CJ and my mother do. It's my truck that chokes me up. I just put a new starter motor in the damn thing, and it ran like a Swiss watch.'' He smiled and rubbed her cheek with his finger. ''Don't sweat it, Irish. That trailer was just a place to hang my hat and stay out of the rain.''

''So you're just footloose and fancy-free.''

''Something like that.''

She shook her head with mock seriousness. ''Gettin' kind of

old for all those wild days and wild ways, Slick. There comes a time when footloose and fancy-free is just another way of saying you can't commit.''

He pretended to wince. ''Ouch. You've been talking to CJ.''

''Nope. Just my own private observation based on watching four of my six brothers do the footloose thing and then suddenly, and I mean practically overnight, meet the right woman, marry, settle down, build picket fences and make babies. Pretty amazing, that old biological imperative to perpetuate the bloodline.''

Rafe didn't need to pretend to wince that time. He thought fleetingly of Stephanie. Of his unborn son.

''Oh, damn,'' Meg whispered. ''Rafe, I'm sorry! Sometimes I just can't believe what I hear coming out of my own mouth.''

He managed a rough laugh. ''For what it's worth, you're right. About the biological imperative, I mean. I was going through life just fine on my own. Never thought I'd want to get married. Was positive I never wanted kids. Then I met Steph at some Native rights powwow thing CJ dragged me to, and that was all she wrote.'' He grinned at the memory. ''She took one look at me and knew I was more trouble than she needed. I took one look at her and knew I wanted to spend the rest of my life with her.''

Meg laughed quietly. ''So what changed her mind?''

''Just my natural charm, I guess.'' He grinned broadly. ''That and the fact I called her almost every day for six months. Trouble was, I was working on an art theft case down in New Mexico, and she was teaching in Montana, so it wasn't until she had a teachers' conference in Albuquerque that we actually got together. We went to dinner and did the museums, but mainly we just talked. We'd just sit in her hotel room for hours, talking about everything under the sun, and then realize it was midnight and we'd forgotten to have supper. So we'd order something in and talk until dawn.'' He smiled reminiscently. ''I kept asking her to marry me, and she kept saying no. Then one morning, real early, I asked her again, and she surprised both of us by saying yes. We were married three weeks later.''

''I knew there was a romantic soul down deep inside that stony exterior of yours!''

''What I can't figure is why some guy hasn't snatched you up long before this.'' He lifted her hand to his mouth and kissed her fingertips. ''Big brothers or no big brothers, you'd be a hell of a catch for any man.''

Meg gave another one of those peals of merry laughter. ''You are such a liar! You've been telling me what an unrelenting pain in the backside I am ever since we met five weeks ago. And you spent the entire time on Bear Mountain threatening to turn me out into the cold, wet night because I was such a nuisance.''

He grinned good-naturedly. ''I've revised my opinion. Besides, being an unrelenting pain in the backside is part of your unique charm.''

''You are so full of it.'' Still laughing, she squeezed his fingers.

''So you're saying there isn't one real man on the entire Eastern Seaboard with the essentials to face down the Kavanagh clan and win the lady?'' He reached up with his free hand and gave a flyaway strand of hair a playful tug.

''Not so far,'' she said easily. ''Although I was sort of unofficially engaged, I guess you could call it, earlier this year.''

Rafe felt his belly tighten. ''What the hell kind of an engagement is that?''

Meg heard what she could have sworn was anger in his voice, and she shrugged offhandedly. ''It was sort of...taken for granted, I guess, that we'd get married.'' She frowned suddenly, thinking about it. ''He seemed to take it for granted, anyway.''

''And the Kavanagh Boys agreed to this?'' he asked in a growl.

''I'm not sure anyone ever mentioned it, if you want the truth.'' That made her frown again. ''That's strange, isn't it?'' she muttered more to herself than to him. ''Royce is the first man I've ever dated that they didn't maim, threaten or run off. I wonder if that means they approve, or...?''

''Or they just figure the guy isn't much of a threat to their baby sister.'' Rafe's eyes held hers with lazy humor. ''And I figure they're right. It raises a few questions about old Royce's well-being when you're supposedly engaged to be married and—''

"Unofficially. There was never any ring or announcement or anything." Meg fidgeted slightly. "We never even really discussed it."

"So what's the matter with him?"

"Matter with him? There's nothing the matter with him."

Rafe's smile widened. "Honey, I was in bed with you the night before last, remember? Divesting you of…what did you call it? Your encumbrance? If old Royce is sound in wind and limb, why was *I* doing the divesting instead of him? Have a problem in the bedroom department, old Royce?"

Meg steadfastly ignored the blush pouring across her cheeks. "You're being vulgar. There's nothing wrong with Royce at all in that…way. We've just never…our relationship hasn't progressed to that point yet, that's all."

"The point it took *us* a couple of hours to progress to, you mean?"

He was grinning broadly now, eyes dark with mischief, and Meg refused to let him bait her. "That was just sex."

"Damned good sex, too."

It distracted Meg from what she'd been about to say in Royce's defense and she felt the blush deepen, feeling inordinately pleased. "You're just saying that to get me all flustered."

Rafe held up both hands as though in surrender. "Hey, I'm just tellin' the truth here. I'm no playboy, but I've been around a bit. Heard things, seen things, done things." His grin widened. "And I can say with some authority that what we had was really good sex."

"I…" She really was flustered now. "Well, I thought it was, but I'm hardly an expert."

"No thanks to old Royce."

"Will you stop calling him *old* Royce! He's no older than you are. And there's nothing wrong with the fact we've never been to bed together, in spite of your snide insinuations. Our relationship is simply based more on respect and…things like that."

Rafe's laugh was soft and decidedly suggestive. "I respect you just fine, Irish. But I still get a definite satisfaction in—"

"Royce works very hard," she put in quickly. "He's busy

with his investments and the company—he's CEO of Packard Industries, which I'm sure even *you* have heard of. When his father retires, he'll be president and—''

''*Ahhh.*'' Rafe smiled knowingly. ''Not exactly a self-made man, then, our Royce.''

''I've been busy with my work,'' Meg went on, ignoring him. ''We just haven't had the time to develop the physical side of our relationship.''

''I'll bet this Royce has two last names and a membership in a yacht club. And a Mercedes. And he pretends to smoke a pipe.'' He laughed at Meg's expression. ''And tennis. I'll bet old Royce is a hot tennis player. When he's not sailing. And investing.''

''You know,'' she said, tongue firmly in cheek, ''I don't think I want to discuss my future husband with you anymore.'' She got to her feet, still clutching her robe closed.

''Future husband, my—'' He thought better of it and just grinned. ''You're no more going to marry some daddy's boy named Royce than fly. You're not the sweet corporate wife type, Kavanagh.''

''Really?'' She arched one eyebrow and gazed down her nose at him. ''And just what *type* am I?''

Rafe let his gaze move over her slowly and suggestively. ''The kind who can walk naked across the bedroom in front of her man and drive him wild with no more than a smile. The kind who slides her body along his, real slow, touching every part of him, and then takes him inside her and makes it last forever. The kind who takes her mouth and—'' He chuckled softly. ''Well, you get my drift.''

Meg, cheeks glowing like hot embers, did indeed.

''Come here, Meg,'' he coaxed, holding out his hand. ''Sit down and keep me company. I'm an invalid, remember?''

''You don't sound much like any invalid I've ever met,'' Meg muttered, thinking she should be playing much harder to get than this. ''No more sarcastic comments about Royce?''

''Not even one.'' He grinned ingenuously. ''Which shows a hell of a lot of willpower, because I can think of hundreds. Wait, wait,'' he protested, laughing, as she made to turn away. ''Ah, come on, Meg! I'm hurt. I might be delirious. You can't hold me responsible for anything I say when I'm delirious.''

Meg hesitated, trying hard not to laugh. ''Including the bit about how good you thought the sex was between us?''

''That part you can believe,'' he shot back promptly. ''I was dead lucid when I got to that part. I have these periods when I'm okay. They kind of come and go.…''

Meg burst into laughter in spite of her best efforts not to, and she shook her head in despair and sat back down beside him.

Rafe looked pleased with himself. He took her hand and wrapped his fingers around hers. ''So, do you and old—Mr. Packard of Packard Industries laugh like this?''

''You promised!''

''That wasn't sarcastic, it was just a general question.''

Meg stared at him suspiciously. Then she sighed. ''No, actually,'' she said after a grudging moment. ''We don't. Royce is quite…serious.'' *Dull* was the word that popped into her mind.

''Hmm.'' To his credit, Rafe didn't say anything, although Meg could tell he was dying to.

She could feel her mouth twitch with another of those treacherous laughs. ''And it's an Acura, actually. Royce's car. You said Mercedes. Actually it's an Acura.''

He thought about it. ''Yeah, that fits. Colored coordinated cell phone, car fax, laptop computer, modem, printer…''

''I don't know about the printer,'' she said doubtfully.

''Trust me, he's got the printer.''

''You really don't like him, do you?'' She had to laugh.

''He's a jerk.'' He reached up and cupped her cheek. ''He's got you in his life and the damn fool's more interested in his stock portfolio and his tennis game than he is in getting you naked and doin' some serious lovin'.''

''There *is* more to a relationship than sex, you know.'' She grinned.

But to her surprise, Rafe didn't grin back. Instead he looked uncharacteristically serious, his eyes moving over her face slowly. ''Trust me, I know that,'' he said quietly. ''But it takes a different kind of investment strategy than Royce is focusing on.''

Meg turned her face slightly to kiss his fingers. ''Such as?''

''Friendship. Finding things to laugh about. Trust. The courage to let each other grow.'' He grinned suddenly and let his hand slip from her cheek, as though finding himself getting too serious and not liking it. ''If you're serious about marrying this guy, send him out to spend a couple of days with me. I'll straighten him out.''

Meg gave a peal of laughter. ''Now you sound like my brothers!'' Still laughing, she took his hand between both of hers. ''For what it's worth, you're right. I never really planned on marrying him. But he dances well and oozes with charm and doesn't slurp his soup, so he was a safe date when I needed one. And I suspect I filled the same need in his date book for pretty much the same reasons.''

''Good.'' He nodded slowly, holding her gaze. ''I'd hate to see you married to some guy who never made you laugh that laugh....''

For some reason that embarrassed Meg, and she felt herself blush again, letting her gaze slide from his. Her mind wanted to play with the fantasy of what it would be like being married to *him*, but she wasn't going there.

She stroked the knuckles of his left hand again, tracing the network of faint white scars.

''You put this hand through a window or something?''

He flexed his fist a time or two, looking at it thoughtfully. ''I punch left handed,'' he said after a time. ''I got most of those in juvenile detention when I was a kid.''

''*Ahhh.* One of those.''

Rafe was still staring at his hand. ''I stabbed a man when I was fourteen. Didn't kill him, but it wasn't for lack of trying. His family wanted me tried in adult court, and I'd have gone down for attempted murder, sure as hell, but the judge said no.'' He smiled bitterly. ''First good turn I ever got from the law.''

Meg was staring at him, trying to keep the shock off her face. But she couldn't have been very successful, because another of those cold smiles twisted his mouth again. ''I was in a foster home—I spent most of my life back then in one foster home after another—and the so-called man of the house was a drunk who liked to hit. He liked to hit his wife, and he liked to hit his own kids, but what he really liked to hit was me.'' He flexed his fist again, staring at the scars. ''Used to call me a red-skinned bastard, then he'd roll up his sleeves and whale the hell out of me. That went on for upwards of six months.''

His face was cold and remote, and Meg realized she was squeezing his hand so hard her knuckles were white. She loosened her grip instantly, then realized he'd never even noticed. He drew a deep breath suddenly, then released it, looking at her again. ''He came home one night, drunk as a preacher's cat, smacked his wife across the room, smacked a couple of the other kids. He was going for the little one—she wasn't quite four, I had no idea why he was always beating on her—and I…'' He shrugged. ''I took one look at his fat face and went for him. Grabbed the bread knife off the counter and took him down. I'd have killed him, too, except the knife blade snapped off, and by then the wife had gone screaming to the neighbors, and they came in and pulled me off him.''

''And she wanted you tried for the attempted murder of the man who beat her and her children?'' Meg stared at him.

''Women sometimes get themselves trapped in impossible situations,'' a quiet voice said from behind her. Meg glanced around as Beth pushed the door fully open and stepped into the room. She smiled at Meg. ''You were raised to be a fighter, so you can't imagine being in that situation, more afraid of leaving than of staying and being beaten.''

''And you ought to know,'' Rafe said coolly. ''You stayed with my old man long enough.''

Meg stiffened, but Beth laughed quietly. ''It's all right. My son and I plow this ground every time we get within shouting distance of each other. It sounds pretty terrifying, but it's our version of mother-son bonding.''

Rafe swore softly and turned away.

''Do you have everything you need?'' she asked Meg. ''Would you like a sandwich or something?''

''No, I'm fine.'' Meg sat there awkwardly. There was a tension in the room, taut and silent, filled with old battles still being fought.

Beth nodded, her smile fading as she looked at Rafe. He refused to meet her gaze, and she looked at Meg again. "I'll leave his nursing in your hands, then. His skull could be hanging by a thread and he'd let it rot off before telling me he needed anything." Then she laughed quietly at Meg's expression. "Sorry. We actually get along pretty well in our own little dysfunctional way."

"Give it a rest," Rafe said wearily. "You've shocked her enough for one night. Meg comes from one of those weird families where everyone gets along. She isn't used to this kind of familial blood sport."

Beth managed another of those offhand smiles, although Meg thought she saw a bit of strain in it this time. "Thanks for checking on me. I found the extra blanket, and there are plenty of towels in the bathroom."

"Good. CJ kept threatening to sell this house when she and her ex divorced a few years ago, but every now and again she's glad of all these bedrooms." She smiled and walked to the door, then glanced at Meg again. "Have a good sleep. Breakfast is whenever you come downstairs, or if you want, you can have it in bed." Her smile widened. "This bed, if you're so inclined. CJ doesn't run bed checks to see who's sleeping where."

Meg felt her cheeks turn bright red and hoped the light in the room was dim enough to hide it. "I, um…thank you. But the room across the hall is fine."

Beth just nodded and slipped through the door, closing it gently behind her. Rafe swore again, dropping his arm across his eyes, and Meg just sat there for an awkward moment or two, not knowing what to say.

"Sorry," Rafe said finally. "She enjoys winding people up."

"Seems to me you both do."

Rafe's mouth twisted in a bitter smile. "Yeah, I guess we're all pretty good at it." Then he reached out and touched her cheek with the back of his hand. "Coming here was a mistake," he said quietly. "I thought it would just be CJ. God knows, she can be bad enough. But if I'd known my mother was going to be here…'' He just shook his head, mouth tight.

But Meg was only half listening. She was thinking of her own family, of the unbreakable bonds between her and her siblings, of the strong relationship she had with her father and mother and the extended family beyond, aunts and uncles and cousins. They spread out from the core like ripples on the surface of a lake, and she wondered what it would be like to be cut off and alone, outside the walls. Her family drove her crazy at times, most of them seeming to think they needed to run her life for her, but that sometimes misguided concern was actually what gave her much of her strength.

''Hands,'' she said softly, realizing she'd said it aloud only when Rafe looked at her questioningly. She laughed. ''Sorry. Someone asked me once what it was like being the youngest of eight kids, and I said it was never being afraid of falling because there were always hands around me to pick me up.''

Rafe's expression grew quizzical. ''You miss them.''

''At a time like this, you bet I do.'' She shrugged her shoulders more deeply into the soft depths of the robe. ''Don't get me wrong. I feel safe enough here, but I wouldn't mind if Michael and Grady walked through that door right now.''

''The cop and the Marine.''

She nodded. ''You'd probably like them. After they stopped beating on you for sleeping with their sister.''

''You weren't planning on telling them about that, I hope.''

She grinned mischievously. ''Seems to me a man would be willing to pay dearly to keep information like that from getting out.''

''What did you have in mind?''

''Nothing you're in any shape to deliver, unfortunately.''

''You'd be surprised.''

Meg laughed right out loud. ''I would be *very* surprised. I take rain checks, though.'' Then she let the smile fade, not wanting to think about that. Odds were that if they survived the next few days and got out of this mess whole, they would go their separate ways—she back to her parents in Boston to lick her wounds and figure out what to do now that she was unemployed,

Rafe back to Bear Mountain to rebuild his home and his life. That one wondrous night was probably all they would ever have.

"Hey."

She looked up and found him looking at her. "Hey what?"

"You were somewhere else."

She nodded and smiled, lifting her shoulders wearily and then letting them drop. "It's late. I should let you get some sleep. It's been a long, bad day."

"Come here." Rafe reached out and grasped the front of the robe in his hand and pulled her gently toward him. It *had* been a long, bad day—the first of many, probably—and he had the sudden urge to just lie there with her in his arms for a while and feel her heart beating against him. To let her warmth seep into his bones and banish the chill that seemed to go marrow deep.

Chapter 12

She came to him easily, lying across his chest and nestling against him, as supple as a sun-warmed cat. Her hair tickled his cheek, and he breathed in the familiar scent of her, that hint of English lilacs that always seemed to be around her.

She felt good in his arms. Right, somehow, all the curves of her fitting to him the way a woman's curves ought to. He thought fleetingly of making love to her but immediately put the idea aside as a bad one. The painkiller the doctor had given him had worn off, and every time he moved his head, lightning bolts of pain shot through him, which wasn't the kind of thing a man wanted to have happen when he was trying to concentrate on pleasing his lady.

The thought made him smile sleepily. His lady. Strange, how things worked out. He'd spent a day with her in North Dakota over a month ago and been hooked like a trout. Then, after weeks of cold showers and hot dreams, he looked up to find her in his life again, and the hook had been set a little deeper.

He thought he'd been unhookable, his heart as smooth and hard as polished steel, impervious to the sweetest lure. But here he was, all tangled up in her and not even putting up a half-decent fight.

"Your mom's pretty remarkable," she said sleepily after a few minutes of companionable silence. "You never told me she and your sister are both lawyers. Or that your mom spent a month in jail recently for calling a judge in district court a sexist, ignorant, rednecked bigot. Or that she's a Native rights activist and a member of the American Indian Movement and was down in South Dakota at Wounded Knee in '73 when your people and the government nearly went to war again. Or that she works with runaways and has set up safe houses for prostitutes all over the Midwest." Rafe felt her chuckle. "My sister Maureen would love her."

"Maureen's the doctor?"

"The lawyer. And a nun."

"Now there's a combination you don't often see."

"The nun part came first, but she got so frustrated trying to fight the system that she got her law degree." She smiled against his throat. "Maureen says she isn't a very *good* nun because she has a lot of trouble with the obedience part of her vows, but I think she does okay. She works in downtown Boston with street people, prostitutes, runaways and so on. Gets a lot of stuff done, too. She opened a women's shelter last year when the city said there was no money. Started up a soup kitchen and homeless shelter from next to nothing, too."

"Doesn't surprise me. When you Kavanagh women decide you want something done, you get it done."

"Mmm." She snuggled against him, sighing. "But we had a lot of breaks when we were growing up. I might be out of line, but from what your mom said, from what you said, I get the feeling that life was anything but a picnic when you and CJ were kids. Makes her success all the more remarkable."

Rafe tightened his arms around her, not wanting to go there. Those memories were still raw, even after thirty years, and he saw no point in hauling them out and rummaging through them. But in spite of his best intentions, he heard himself say, "She was fifteen when I was born, and by that time she'd already had one baby—Jett—by some drunken rodeo cowboy who never knew her name. Her parents made her give him to his old man's people, but she was pregnant again a few weeks later.''

''CJ said there's barely ten months between you and Jett.'' She had her chin on his shoulder, and Rafe could feel her warm breath on his ear, making his toes curl. But even that hurt, so he tried to ignore it. ''She said Jett's dad was white. But your dad was Native, right?''

''Oh, yeah.'' The anger was back in his voice, and Rafe tried to ignore that, too. ''My old man was a walking cliché, the classic good for nothing drunken Indian. My mother's parents were fed up with her by that time and kicked her out, so she went to live with this loser. He drank, and he beat the hell out of her. And me, until I was old enough to see it coming and learned to hide. CJ was born when I was four. My mother was drinking by then, and hooking to keep them in booze. One day a john beat her so bad she almost died, and she wound up in the hospital.''

Rafe rubbed his eyes wearily, wondering why he was boring her with all this. It was old news. Stuff he'd put behind him years ago.

''Go on.'' Her voice was soft with some emotion and she'd gone very still.

Rafe opened his mouth to tell her none of it mattered, then sighed instead. ''The doctor told her if she didn't get off the street and the booze, she'd be dead in a month. He scared her so bad she agreed to go into rehab and dry out and get some help. But she was scared they'd take CJ and me away, so she didn't tell anyone about us. My old man took off, and CJ and me lived on our own for almost a month before my mother let it slip that she had a couple of kids at home.''

''How old were you?'' Meg asked softly.

''Me? Almost eight. CJ was four. We did pretty well, all considered. If we'd been on the rez, we'd have been fine, but in the city we had to take care of ourselves.''

Meg made a soft sound and her hand crept into his.

''Anyway, Social Services found us. Put CJ in foster care with a family who thought she was a gift from God. They treated her like one of their own kids, and she did okay.''

Meg was silent, and Rafe knew she was waiting for the rest. He wished he'd never started the whole sordid story, but knew she would never leave him in peace if he didn't end it. "Me…well, that was another story. I was already a real little badass. If I wasn't fighting, I was stealing or running away. I figured out once that I was in twenty-nine foster homes in seven years." He had to smile, although it had never struck him as particularly funny before. "Probably a record of some kind."

"My God," Meg breathed. "And your mom?"

"Got sober and off the streets. She managed to get CJ back, but by then I was in juvie hall and not much good to anyone. I tried living with them when I got out, but it was no good, and I left after a couple of months before she kicked me out. I banged around for a couple of years until I was old enough to join the Navy, and you know the rest." He turned his head to kiss her cheek. "And that, sweetheart, is *my* happy little family portrait."

Meg started to say something, then thought better of it and subsided into a thoughtful silence, and Rafe found himself wishing he could just take her and leave. Out into the night and far away from here. Away from who and what he was. They could make a new start in some far off place and spend their days and nights making love, needing no one but each other.

Then he caught himself and smiled roughly. It was impossible, of course. None of this was real. They'd come together like gasoline and flame, but that had just been situation and circumstance. She was on a mission to find out who had murdered her brother, and she had a family she would never leave behind, and friends and a life. He was a momentary part of that, allowed inside her boundaries for as long as she wanted him there, but he would never really belong.

He lifted her hand and looked at it, then drew it down to his mouth and kissed the tips of her fingers. She smiled and touched his cheek with her other hand, then lifted her face and put her lips lightly against his. He ran his tongue along the swell of her lower lip, and she smiled against his mouth and touched his tongue tip with hers.

She tasted faintly of mint and honey, and as she settled her parted lips over his and kissed him sweetly and deeply, he felt some of the knots across his shoulders dissolve. Saying nothing, she did something to the robe, and he smiled as it fell open. He slipped his hand inside its warmth and cupped one small, soft-tipped breast.

He felt the nipple harden almost instantly as he caressed it with his thumb, and her breathing seemed to falter slightly. Her kiss deepened, and he ran his palm slowly down her flank and along the rich swell of her bottom, drawing her against him.

She slid her mouth from his and rested her forehead on his cheek, and he could hear her swallow as he slipped his hand between her thighs.

She made a soft little sound in the back of her throat and moved her hips reflexively. And then he was touching her, his fingers just brushing the silken, moist curls at the juncture of her thighs, parting them to caress the folds hidden within. Her breath caught, and she made another soft sound, and as he slipped his fingers slowly into the heat of her, she shuddered and whispered something in a tangled, caught voice.

She was like nothing on this mortal earth, all silk and fire and electricity. He moved his fingers rhythmically within the satin prison of her body, his thumb caressing the very nub of her, and she whimpered, hips moving in tiny thrusts against his hand.

He felt it coming even before she did and brought her to the edge and then gently over, feeling her body contract strongly around his fingers even as she gave a soft, choked cry of satisfaction that he smothered instantly with a deep kiss.

She went quiet after a while, lying spent and panting against his chest, thighs still locked around his hand. He could feel the tremors still running through her and rubbed her back gently in rhythmic circles, thinking absently that he could fall in love with this woman as easily and effortlessly as he'd once fallen in love with Steph.

And then immediately had to remind himself that falling in love with Meg wasn't any more possible than running away with her was.

He doubted he was even capable of it, to be honest. Falling in love with Steph had been surprising enough, but he'd been different back then. Not whole, but not nearly as broken and weary and worn-out as he was now, either. It had been too long. And too much had happened.

So he just cradled her tightly against his chest instead and decided to take this one day at a time for however long it lasted, and when the time came for her to leave, he would go back up to Bear Mountain and try to put her out of his mind once and for all.

"That was kind of a nice ending to a rotten day," she murmured, her voice soft and sleepy. "I'll get up and lock the door in a minute and return the favor...."

Rafe laughed quietly. "Go to sleep, Meg. You're out on your feet, and as much as I'd love to have the favor returned, I just ain't up to it."

"That doesn't sound fair." Her voice was already slurring toward sleep. "Take an IOU?"

"Damn straight, Irish," he whispered. And held her as she slipped into sleep as sweetly as a child.

Meg woke hours later, befuddled and disoriented, and discovered she was still in Rafe's bedroom. Still in Rafe's bed and arms, actually. He had fallen into a deep sleep with his arms still around her, and she could feel the slow, strong thud of his heart against her cheek, as reassuring and eternal as the rhythmic beat of the tide. Someone had covered them both with a wool blanket, and she was warm and sleepy and couldn't recall ever feeling more safe.

Gently, she eased herself up onto her elbow to peer at the clock and was startled to see it was well after ten. She sat up gingerly, feeling as though she'd been run over by a fleet of large trucks. Every muscle throbbed, and she was covered with bruises and scratches from their wild scramble down the mountainside. Groaning, she crept from between the sheets, limped down the corridor to the bathroom and stood under a steaming hot shower until she felt almost human. Then she pulled on the thick terry robe CJ had lent her and hobbled back into her own bedroom, wondering if she was going to be able to salvage any of her clothing.

But there was no need. Someone had set out a pile of freshly laundered underthings for her, and beside them a white cotton T-shirt, a pair of tan slacks and a big dark blue sweatshirt with the words American Indian Movement written in an arch over a warrior on a speckled horse. She pulled everything on gratefully, then shook out her wet hair and made her way downstairs.

Beth was alone in the kitchen, frowning over a legal pad covered with small, tidy handwriting and taking absent sips of coffee from the huge red mug in her hand. She looked up as Meg came in. "Well, you look like hell." She nodded toward the counter. "Coffee's fresh. Cream's in the fridge. Sugar in that cupboard at the end."

"Oh, man…" Meg limped across and helped herself to a gigantic mugful of the coffee. "Intravenous would be better, but I guess this'll do."

Beth snorted with laughter and leaned back in the chair, sweeping her fingers through her long raven hair. Her fingers were covered with silver and turquoise rings that glittered in the sunlight pouring through the kitchen window. She pulled one bare foot up onto the chair and rested her arm across her knee, taking another sip of the coffee. "How's his lordship this morning? Head still in one piece?"

"So far." Meg took another sip of the coffee, very aware of Beth's look of frank curiosity. There was a familiar whimper, and she looked around the end of the counter. Three was curled up on an old Navajo blanket, a dish of fresh water and another of kibble on the floor beside him. "Hey, Three!" Meg knelt down and gave the old dog a hug, and he whimpered with pleasure and tried to lick her face, banging the floor with his tail.

"CJ said he'd found some half-dead dog on the side of the road and had paid a small fortune in vet bills to keep the thing alive," Beth said with amusement in her voice. "And he calls *me* a sucker for every stray that comes along."

Meg just laughed and rubbed the old dog's ears. Then she straightened and looked at Beth. "I want to thank you again for—"

Beth waved it off impatiently. "If you feel obliged to thank anyone, thank CJ—it's her house. I'm just a weekend guest. But there's no need. She's flattered half to death that he came to her for help, if you want the truth.'' She combed her hair back with her fingers again. ''Rafe, as you've noticed, isn't filled with warm fuzzies when it comes to family.''

''None he'll embarrass himself by admitting to, anyway.''

Beth snorted, staring at Meg again through the steam from her mug as she sipped the coffee. ''This is none of my business, but I'm glad he's found someone again. Stephanie's death took him to a very dark place, and I've been worried about him.''

Meg frowned and sat down on the opposite side of the big maple table. ''I think you and CJ might have gotten the wrong impression about Rafe and me. We're not, um…together. I was up at Bear Mountain because I thought Rafe had some information I needed, and then these men came after me and Rafe got shot and…'' She let her protest fade as she saw the amusement in Beth's eyes. ''We hardly even know each other.''

Beth's left eyebrow arched.

''No, really,'' Meg protested, feeling a blush start to pour across her cheeks. ''He's just helping me with an investigation and—''

''Ha!'' Beth whooped with laughter. ''CJ, get in here! I've made her blush! Can you believe it? I swear it's been twenty years since I was around a woman innocent enough to blush.''

''You make me blush routinely,'' CJ drawled, coming in from the dining room. She smiled at Meg. ''Ignore her. I do. Sleep all right?''

''How could she possibly sleep all right crammed in beside Rafe on that narrow little bed? I told you to put them in the back room with the big bed instead of separate rooms.''

CJ rolled her eyes and dropped gracefully into a chair across the table from Meg, giving her waist-length mane of hair a toss. ''Just because they came here together doesn't mean they're sleeping together,'' she said reasonably.

''For God's sake, CJ, pay attention! Watch his face when he looks at her, for crying out loud. He can barely keep his hands off her.''

Still blushing, Meg couldn't quite meet either pair of eyes. ''We're not really…it's awfully complicated, actually.''

''Sex usually is,'' Beth said with an airy wave of her hand.

"And love's even worse, so if you're not already in love with him, think twice."

"Oh, I'm not—"

"Good God, don't fall in love with him!" CJ shuddered dramatically. "I love him, but I wouldn't wish him on my worst enemy. He's...broken."

"CJ..." her mother said with a pained look.

"Well, I'm sorry, but he is." CJ leaned over, took the mug out of Beth's hand and took a sip of coffee, then handed it back to her. "Steph made him whole for the first time in his life, but when she was killed..." She shook her head as she reached into the pocket on her denim shirt and brought out a pack of cigarettes. She took one out, lit it and took a long drag on it, closing her eyes. "I know, I know. I said I was quitting. This will be my first and last of the day, all right?"

"I never said a thing."

"You don't have to. I can hear you thinking."

"That's your conscience."

"I don't have a conscience. I'm a lawyer." CJ gave her mother a broad grin, then leaned back in the chair, sweeping her hair back with her fingers in a gesture that mirrored Beth's.

They were as alike as twins, except for the difference in their ages, and that barely showed. Same glossy fall of long, straight hair the color of crows' wings, same high cheekbones and strong Sioux features, same black, laughing eyes. She could see Rafe's handsome features in both of them and wondered how on earth he thought he could shut himself off from these two women, both as much a part of him as they were of each other.

"Anyway," CJ went on, "it's as though Rafe has shut himself off for good now. He let himself believe he could be happy and then had his heart broken, and he's damn sure not going to let it happen again." She blew out a stream of smoke and eyed Meg through it. "I know I sound as though I hate the guy, but I don't. He's my brother and I love him, as unlovable as he can get."

"You're too impatient with him," Beth said mildly. "He has his reasons."

"Oh, please!" CJ helped herself to another mouthful of her

mother's coffee. "How much longer are you going to let him get away with that mother guilt crap, anyway? Jett did just fine, you'll notice. And I did pretty well. Things weren't peaches, but we survived."

Beth stared into her coffee. Then she took a deep breath and released it, and gave Meg a rueful smile. "What my cynical been there, done that daughter isn't telling you is that she worshiped the ground he walked on when she was a little girl. He was her hero. It broke her heart when they were put in separate foster homes. And later, when I got myself together and made a home with CJ, he broke her heart all over again when he came back for a short while and then left again. For good that time. We didn't see him for almost ten years."

CJ took another drag on the cigarette, then made a face and ground it out in the ashtray. "And what about you, Meg?" She grinned. "We've bored you to tears with our sad little soap opera. What's your life story?"

"Before you start interrogating her, let me feed her or she'll keel over in midstory." Beth unfolded gracefully to her feet. "Meg, we have pancakes, sausage, hash browns, eggs, steak…"

"Wow. Steak and eggs sound great."

Beth and CJ exchanged a nod of approval. "Good. She eats."

"I'll give Rafe credit for one thing," CJ drawled. "When he does pick a woman, he gets it right. None of these scrawny little things who's always fidgeting about her weight."

"God almighty," someone said in a hoarse voice from behind them. "Are you at her already?" Rafe eased himself into the room cautiously, moving as though he'd aged about ninety years in the last twenty-four hours. "She eats like a trucker, swears like a sailor and can outfight most men I've known. Now leave her alone."

"For what it's worth, you bonehead, I like her. A lot." CJ stood up and walked across to the counter. "Sit down, for heaven's sake. You look like death. I'll make you a cup of healing tea and—"

"Coffee," Rafe croaked. "Just coffee."

"I set up the portable sweat lodge yesterday," Beth put in

smoothly. "You could use a good commune with your ancestors."

"I could use a good cup of coffee," he muttered irritably.

"Jett asked me about *hanblecheyapi* the last time he telephoned." CJ gave Rafe a sidelong look. "Seems to me it's something you might want to think about."

"It's a Lakota word that more or less translates as lamenting," Beth said, seeing Meg's puzzled expression. "Your people call it a vision quest. Rafe's half brother has been working at learning more about his Lakota half and feels a few days of fasting and contemplation out on the plains might give him some insights."

Rafe steadfastly said nothing.

"For a half-breed raised white, he's taking to his Lakota heritage like a natural," CJ said. "He and his wife, Kathleen, have a seventeen-year-old son, and I suggested the boy could stay here for a few weeks so I could teach him something about his family and history."

"Spare me the lecture, Charlene. I got enough of my Lakota *heritage* shoved down my throat, along with a few of my teeth, when I was a kid."

CJ looked annoyed as she banged a mug of hot coffee down on the table in front of him. "*Hoka hey,* Macintosh."

Rafe laughed quietly and looked at Meg. "It means it's a good day to die. And a Macintosh is an apple—red on the outside, but white on the inside." He gave CJ a dry look. "My sister the Indian heritage guru is a real joker."

"Hey, we're the family who put the fun back in dysfunctional, right?" She leaned down and planted a kiss on Rafe's cheek. "Marry this Irish warrior, big brother, and all's forgiven. She's too good for you, but she might overlook your shortcomings just to get Mom and me for in laws."

"Don't get too attached to her," Rafe muttered, cradling the mug between both hands, seeking its warmth. His shoulders were hunched, and he felt like walking death. "We're leavin' tonight."

"What?" The word echoed resoundingly, coming in three separate voices. CJ and Beth looked at each other, and Meg looked at him.

He didn't look at anybody. "We're putting everyone in danger. The plan was never to stay. Just to regroup and then move on."

"No." Beth said it with quiet finality, placing her palm flat on the table. "You said yourself that this is the one place where no one would ever think to look for you."

"Which is very flattering, by the way," CJ muttered from the other side of the kitchen, giving him a dagger glare.

Beth silenced her with a look. "You're in no shape to travel, Rafe. And you're certainly in no shape to fight. As ferocious as Meg is, there are limits to what she can do. You need a safe place, and this is it."

"She's circling the wagons," CJ said with an irreverent grin. "War dance at eight."

"Oh, shut up, CJ," Rafe said wearily. "This isn't a joke."

"Rafe, you've dedicated your life to doing the complete opposite of what I think is a good idea," Beth said tightly, "but if you leave here with Meg, I swear I'll call the cops and tell them you're a danger to yourself and everyone around you. Risking your life is one thing, but risking hers is unconscionable."

"And risking yours isn't? And CJ's?"

Beth waved him off impatiently. "I've faced rednecks and skinheads and brainless politicians and white judges who call me a *squaw* behind my back, not to mention armed soldiers with more reason to kill me than whoever's chasing you. So has CJ. At the risk of damaging your male ego, CJ and I can take care of ourselves pretty well. From what I've heard, Meg can handle herself just as well. But she can't watch her own back *and* yours."

Rafe's head was pounding, but he ignored it and opened his mouth to argue, and then Meg's soft voice stopped him in his tracks.

"We have nowhere else to go, Rafe. Until we know what's going on, we'll just be running blind. And you were a good enough agent once to know that means we're dead."

Beth tossed two steaks into a hot cast-iron frying pan, and the kitchen exploded with the scent of grilling beef. "Meg, run this whole thing by me again. I got it in bits and pieces last night, and it never did make sense.''

''It might not make sense this morning,'' Meg said gloomily. ''Rafe, you try.''

Rafe ran it down for them quickly, letting Meg fill in a few details he was hazy about himself. Laid out in detail like that, it had more holes than the Titanic. And he realized they were damned lucky to even be alive.

Beth was frowning when they finished. ''So you're saying you don't know who killed Meg's brother; who burned your trailer and shot at you yesterday morning; whether or not all that was related to her investigation into her brother's death; what, if anything, O'Dell has to do with either yesterday morning's events or Bobby's death; or why this Rick Jarvis character was brought in.'' She lifted both her hands, then let them fall. ''Take any of this to the police and they'll laugh you out of the state.''

''And the hole in Rafe's head?'' Meg asked.

''Some nut on drugs. Someone with a grudge. Mistaken identity.'' Beth shook her head. ''Could be anything. CJ?''

''There might be probable cause on a conspiracy charge, but conspiracy to do what I have no idea. You worked for O'Dell for years, Rafe. Do you really believe he's got bad agents working for him and is covering up the truth about Bobby's death to protect them? Doesn't sound like the O'Dell you used to talk about.''

''People change,'' Rafe said roughly. ''Truth is, I don't know what's going on. I have a feeling Meg accidentally stumbled onto something a lot bigger than her brother's murder and either messed up an internal investigation or triggered one. Problem is, I don't know which side of the investigation O'Dell is on.''

''But surely you can go to someone who can tell you that.''

Rafe's mouth twisted with a bitter smile. ''O'Dell doesn't answer to anyone but the president, and then only when he feels like it. No one will know what's going on. And if someone from outside the Agency is investigating him, I can guarantee they won't be talking.''

Beth looked a little pale.

"There is one person who could find out what's going on," Meg said quietly into the silence. "Someone I trust completely."

"God, maybe," Rafe muttered. "Any of your brothers a priest?"

"I was thinking of someone a little lower in rank than God." She grinned. "Not much lower, in my estimation, but I'm biased. My dad is chairman of the President's Foreign Policy Advisory Committee, and people listen to him. I know O'Dell thinks he's beyond everyday law and order, but he's never tangled with my dad."

Rafe swore in surprise. "Your dad is *that* Kavanagh?"

She just nodded.

"Well, that explains a hell of a lot." He was staring at her with renewed respect. Kavanagh was a straight arrow, incorruptible in a town where it wasn't a question of whether people could be bought but what their price was. The president trusted him without reservation, but most of the party hacks loathed him, because he couldn't be manipulated, intimidated or scared off. And blackmail wouldn't work, because he didn't do things he could be blackmailed for. Rafe had seen press photos of him now and again over the years, a tall good-looking Irishman with a direct gaze and an aura of calm authority, usually with a brood of kids underfoot. One of them had undoubtedly been a little redheaded girl who took after him in more ways than she probably suspected.

"I *love* this woman!" CJ beamed. "I'm telling you, big brother, if you don't grab her up and marry her before some other dude does, you're a bigger idiot than I ever gave you credit for!"

Rafe slept for the better part of the day, much to his disgust. Beth had stuffed them with steak and scrambled eggs with salsa and mounds of golden hash browns and piles of toast, and within half an hour he was down for the count. He'd staggered upstairs and back to bed and had fallen asleep before his head hit the pillow.

He awoke finally to find Meg beside the bed. She was gently sliding the drawers open on the big oak chest beside the bed, rummaging through the contents of each before sliding it closed again and pulling the next one open.

He watched her for a moment or two before she realized he was awake. She winced. "I'm sorry! I was trying to be quiet. Your mom said there are a couple of photo albums in here, but I can't find them."

"Bottom drawer," Rafe told her, yawning. "But don't expect any cute baby pictures of CJ and me. There aren't any."

"Weren't you cute as a baby?" She grinned. "That's hard to believe, considering how gosh-darn cute you are nowadays. Especially with that black eye and your head wrapped up like a mummy."

"You're a cruel woman."

"Only on odd numbered Tuesdays." She bent over and kissed him on the mouth. "Otherwise, I'm a pussycat."

"Mmm." Rafe was quick enough this time to catch her before she could get away. He kissed her back, and she responded eagerly, warm lips parted sweetly above his, her kiss slow and deep and achingly familiar.

It seemed a long while later that she drew her mouth from his and sat upright again, looking sleepy and a little dazed.

"I have an idea." He ran a fingertip along her lower lip. "Why don't you lock the door and come to bed for a while? I'm holding an IOU with your name on it, as I recall. And I feel up to collecting."

Meg smiled slowly. "Are you sure? I'd hate to send you into a relapse and have to explain to that doctor what we were doing when it happened."

"Oh, I'm sure." He slipped his hand over hers, then guided it under the light blanket and sheet to his groin, laughing when her eyes widened. "Convinced?"

"Well, it's certainly a propitious beginning." Grinning mischievously, Meg reclaimed her hand, then walked across and locked the door.

She stood there with her back to it, her eyes dancing. And then, not saying a word, she pulled the sweatshirt over her head. Holding his gaze with hers, she slipped out of the T-shirt, as well, and Rafe caught his breath. She wasn't wearing a bra, and her breasts were as full and lush and dark-tipped as he remembered. He swallowed, hard, when she unbuttoned the waistband of her slacks and drew the zipper down, still holding his gaze. She stepped out of them and the pale pink panties, and stood there utterly and heartbreakingly naked, then raised her hands to pile her hair on top of her head and started to walk, very slowly, toward the bed.

"The kind of woman who can walk naked across the bedroom in front of her man and drive him wild with no more than a smile." Rafe grinned, his pulse starting to hum.

Meg's mouth curved in a delicious and wicked smile as he lifted the sheet for her and she saw that he was as naked as she was. She knelt on the side of the bed, letting her fingertips trail over his belly, and then lower, watching him as he gritted his teeth and groaned very softly.

"The kind who slides her body along his, real slow, touching every part of him," she whispered, doing just that. "And then takes him inside her and makes it last forever."

Rafe groaned as she drew one leg up and over his hip and guided him toward her. He lifted himself onto one elbow and half turned toward her, then grasped her hip with his hand and, eyes riveted on hers, eased himself delicately and smoothly into the honied velvet of her waiting body.

He dropped his mouth over hers to smother her soft outcry, and she moaned into his throat, then arched strongly backward, hands clutching his shoulders. Very aware of the houseful of people below them, Rafe moved slowly and gently. Meg was so ready for him so quickly that he smiled as he rhythmically caressed her breasts with his palm and then dropped his mouth to suckle her strongly, rubbing the pebbled nipple with his tongue until she was half-wild, biting her lip to keep from moaning aloud.

"This isn't going to be fancy," he whispered against her ear as he pushed himself strongly into the heat of her body and felt her lift and enfold him.

"I don't need fancy," she gasped. "I just need...oh, my gosh, yes!"

Then her mouth was under his and she was kissing him urgently and deeply, and he knew it was going to take them no time at all, both of them so needy it was like making love on a volcano. He tried to hold himself back, but Meg wasn't having any of it. Holding her hip tightly, he dropped his forehead onto her shoulder, using every bit of willpower he had to keep from just letting go, silence be damned.

In no time at all Meg gave a convulsive movement and buried her face into the pillow to smother her outcry, and Rafe gritted his teeth so hard he saw stars, trying not to shout his satisfaction for the whole world to hear when it hit him. They collapsed into each other's arms, panting and strangling on swallowed laughter.

"I like your bedside manner, Kavanagh," he whispered when he got his breath back.

"Are you all right?" Still laughing, she looked at him with real concern.

"Can't recall feeling better." He smiled at her. "I'm all right, Meg. Trust me, this is what the doctor ordered."

"The doctor ordered bed rest and aspirin, actually. I don't remember him saying anything about sex."

"I distinctly remember him recommending sex. Lots of sex, actually."

"Uh-huh." She kissed his shoulder, still breathing quickly. "Well, you're going to have to wait for a replay. I came up here thirty minutes ago to look for those albums. Your mom is going to wonder what I'm doing that's taking so long."

"Thirty minutes is not what I'd call taking long."

"Not for this, maybe." She kissed his chest, then gently swung her leg from around his hip and rolled onto her back. She lay there for a smiling, sated moment, then slipped out of bed. "Maybe tonight we can manage more of the same medication," she whispered, smiling. "If the doctor said you need plenty of sex to get well, then I guess I should make certain that you get it."

She paused long enough to take a fast shower before dressing quickly, grabbing the two albums and dashing back downstairs, trying to look as though it was perfectly normal to run upstairs to find a photo album and come down forty minutes later all flushed and freshly showered.

CJ was talking on her cell phone when Meg came into the kitchen. She broke into a wide, cheeky grin but, to Meg's everlasting gratitude, didn't say anything.

Beth glanced up and speared Meg with an amused look. "That didn't take too long."

"Well, no. I mean…I couldn't find them at first, then I stopped to talk to Rafe for a few minutes and…" Realizing she was digging herself deeper with every word, Meg finally had the sense to just shut up.

"A little late-morning talk can be enjoyable," Beth said blandly. She reached for one of the albums. "Okay, there are a bunch of snapshots of Stephanie in this one, and some of the two of them together. Let's pick out the best ones and I'll put them in an album for him. He'll probably say he doesn't give a damn, but one day he'll thank us for this."

Chapter 13

Rafe didn't actually realize he'd fallen asleep again until he woke up, befuddled with dream and slightly disoriented for the moment or two it took him to remember where he was. He'd been dreaming of Bear Mountain and the trailer and Stephanie, except it hadn't been Steph in the dream but Meg.

Now, awake, he tried to catch the tendrils of dream-memories, but they eluded him, tantalizing him with the awareness that whatever the dream had been about, it had left him feeling content and happy. That in itself was rare. Usually his nights were filled with more nightmare than dream, and he often awoke disturbed and unsettled and out of sorts without even remembering why.

One thing for sure, making love with her hadn't been a dream. He and the sheets were still warm and musky, and it made him smile. He stretched with lazy contentment. Sooner or later he and Meg were going to have to come up with some plan to get them out of this mess, but he was damned well going to enjoy this moment of afterglow, and O'Dell and his plots and subterfuge could go to hell.

He lay there comfortably and stared at the ceiling, thinking he'd been doing that a lot lately. There was something to be said for ceilings. You could look at a ceiling and just let your mind wander without anything getting in the way. Like reality, for instance. Take now. During all this enforced ceiling-gazing, he'd found himself daydreaming the most ridiculous things. Like marrying Meg and raising a bunch of kids with her and stuff like that.

Which wasn't anywhere near being possible, of course.

Yet it was strange, how the idea kept flickering through his thoughts as he lay there in the quiet, staring at the ceiling. He could hear her laugh somewhere downstairs. Kitchen, more than likely. For some reason he couldn't figure, women always seemed to congregate in the kitchen, sitting around the table talking about things that could make him blush. It was always the same. You'd hear low voices, and then they'd all erupt into screams of laughter and you'd find them practically falling off their chairs, tears running down their cheeks, but they'd never tell you what had set them off.

They were down there now, all three women, as mysterious and complex as life itself. CJ and his mother had taken to Meg right away, just as they'd taken to Steph without hesitation, the three connecting and bonding in some arcane, female way he would never understand. He could hear their voices, just a murmur of sound. The clatter of dishes as someone cleared the table. A burst of laughter, his mother's this time. Comfortable sounds he hadn't heard in too long to remember. It made him smile again, and the ceiling coaxed his thoughts into a fantastical weaving of daydream and wistful impossibility.

And then he heard the rifle shot.

Meg didn't actually know what had happened at first. There was a sharp crack of breaking glass, and then the plastic cat-shaped clock on the wall behind her exploded and CJ screamed. And only then, finally, did she see the small round hole in the kitchen window above the sink.

"Get down!" She was on her feet even while the rifle shot echoed from the sweeping hills cradling the house, physically dragging Beth and CJ off their chairs and shoving them onto the floor as she was reaching for her weapon.

Which wasn't in the small of her back where it should have been, because it was upstairs in the drawer of the night table by her bed. She swore at her own carelessness and checked to make sure the other women were all right. Beth was on her belly, looking grim, and CJ was staring at the pieces of clock scattered across the floor.

"Somebody shot my cat," she managed to get out finally, picking up a piece of black-and-white plastic that was all that was left of the tail.

"It was the ugliest clock I've ever seen," Beth snapped. "It deserved to get shot. Is the rifle still in the front hall?"

CJ nodded. "I took the bolt out, though—the neighbor's kids come over sometimes, and I didn't want them hurt. It's in the cutlery drawer right behind you, and the shells are in my bedroom closet."

"Very conscientious but not very convenient," Beth said calmly.

"Meg!" It was Rafe's voice, a bellow that echoed more loudly than the distant shot.

"All okay," Meg called back. "It came in the kitchen window. By the retort, I'd say the shooter was almost a mile away, so he's using a top-of-the-line sniper's weapon and scope. And," she added more quietly, "he's damn good."

"I'm coming down."

It was standard operating procedure, one armed agent letting another armed agent know where he was so they didn't shoot each other. Meg winced. "My weapon's in my bedroom," she called.

Rafe didn't reply, but his silence spoke volumes. There was a resounding crash behind her that made her jump. Beth had pulled the kitchen drawer out and it had landed on the floor beside her, spilling cutlery and kitchen gadgets. Beth quickly searched it, then held up the rifle bolt.

"I'll get the rifle," Meg said, already scuttling crablike toward the door into the living room and the front hall closet.

"And I'll get the shells," CJ said tightly.

"Stay down!" Rafe materialized beside her, dressed in a pair of jeans and nothing else. He placed his hand in the center of CJ's back and pushed her flat onto the floor. "Everyone stay on the floor and away from a clear sight line from any of the windows." He tossed the holstered Beretta to Meg, and she fielded it deftly. "See anything?"

"They shot my clock," CJ said plaintively. "They were aiming at Meg, but they missed her and shot my clock."

"Good. I was tempted to shoot the thing a few times myself."

Meg had her weapon out and was on one knee by the kitchen door, her back against the wall. She reached up and turned the lock, then shot the dead bolt home. "Beth, is the front door unlocked?"

"No, I've been keeping it locked since you and Rafe got here. All the windows are locked, too, except for the upstairs bedrooms."

"Okay, so we're locked down." She wetted her lips and looked at Rafe. "I've still got fifteen rounds, you have twelve. And we have a rifle. Not great odds."

"I think you're right about him being a long-range sniper," he said thoughtfully. "And I figure he's solo. No reason to take you out from that distance if he had the manpower to take the house by force."

Meg nodded. "That's what I figure. So how do you want to play this? Based on his limited sight line through that window, he has to be up on that rim of hills behind the house."

"Not anymore." Rafe eased himself to his feet, keeping clear of the window as he slid along the wall. "He doesn't know if he hit you or not. If you're dead, his job is done. If you're not, he knows he'll never get another clear shot at you from up there. Either way, he's got to check it out."

"So you're saying he's on his way down here?"

"I'd bet money on it." He picked up a steak knife from the pile of cutlery on the floor beside Beth and started digging at the small round hole in the decorative brick wall where CJ's clock had hung. "But whatever's going on. I'll lay odds this is the same guy who took those shots at your car on the mountain—aha!'' Using the knife as a pry bar, he gently levered the spent bullet out of the wall. ''Same caliber.''

''This guy's operating parameters are all over the place,'' Meg muttered unhappily. ''Long-range sniper fire, matches and gasoline. The bullet that took you out was a small caliber handgun. And *none* of it's O'Dell's style.''

''Yeah.'' Rafe sounded just as unhappy. ''But one thing's dead certain, we're not staying here. Beth, give one of your sisters in South Dakota a call and tell her you and CJ are coming home to the rez for a while and need a place to stay. You'll be safe there.''

''So will you and Meg,'' CJ said quietly. ''Once you're back on the rez, no one can touch you. Not even O'Dell and his government goons would dare come onto tribal land looking for trouble.''

''And Meg?'' Rafe looked across the room at his sister. ''You know what'll happen if I take a white woman who's technically on the run from the Feds onto the reservation. Aside from giving the Bureau of Indian Affairs a collective coronary—something that ordinarily wouldn't bother me—the Tribal Council and elders will have us stripped naked and staked out on an anthill.''

''It was the Apache who did that anthill thing,'' CJ said solemnly. ''I don't think our people ever did that.'' She shrugged at Rafe's look of impatience. ''So we don't tell anyone she's there.''

Rafe looked at her, then at Meg, his frown deepening. ''You know, she has a point.''

And Meg, who had been kneeling quietly by the back door this whole time, shook her head firmly. ''No way. Bad enough I brought this guy here and am jeopardizing *your* lives. I'm not taking him somewhere with families and kids. I appreciate the thought, CJ, but that's out.''

''We can make sure he doesn't know you're there.''

''Like he wasn't supposed to know we're here?'' Meg asked pointedly.

''Meg—''

''No.'' The one word was as crisp as frozen steel. ''I can't just keep running. My best bet is to set a trap and grab him when he walks into it.''

''Guys like this don't walk into traps.''

''They do if they don't know it's a trap.''

Rafe's gaze drilled into hers. ''Meaning?''

''Meaning we con him. You, CJ and Beth all run for the car, making sure he sees I'm not with you. Odds are he'll figure I'm dead and—''

''And where the hell are you while all this is going on?''

''In here. Waiting for him. If he's gone to this much trouble to kill me, he'll come down to check for a body. And I'll have him.''

''That's the dumbest plan I ever heard,'' Rafe said flatly.

Meg glared at him. ''I don't hear you coming up with a better one.''

''The three of *you* leave, and I stay. CJ, in my coat and a hat you could pass for me at a distance. We can wrap that mane of Meg's under a black scarf so it looks like hair and—''

''And that is the *second* dumbest plan I've heard today,'' Meg snapped.

''Actually it might work,'' Beth said quietly. She looked at Meg. ''Give me ten minutes and I'll turn you into a passable Indian.''

Rafe grinned broadly. ''First time I set eyes on her, she made a pretty convincing Las Vegas peroxide blonde named Honey Divine. A little shy on cleavage, but those blue spandex tights were a work of art.'' The grin widened. ''She's a natural at undercover.''

Beth looked at him, then at Meg, then shook her head. ''I don't even want to know.''

''And if he doesn't take the bait?'' Meg asked. ''If he follows the car instead?''

''We don't have to go far to make it look convincing,'' CJ said. ''I have a friend down in Grassy Butte. Ex-Marine, ex-cop, ex-biker. Spike's a marshmallow, but not someone you want to mess with. In case this guy does follow us, we'll be safe there.''

"I'd like to meet your friend Spike one day," Rafe said mildly.

CJ looked at him in surprise. "Really?"

"Not really," Meg spoke up. "I know that tone of voice. He wants to do the big brother thing and threaten the guy with a slow death if he messes with you. He'll probably suggest that Spike find himself a new girlfriend and maybe even leave the state, because he's not nearly good enough for you and so on and so on."

CJ looked at Rafe again. "You'd do that?"

Rafe looked annoyed. "Hell, no."

But Meg could hear the lie in his voice. And so did CJ. A smile blossomed on her mouth, and she looked like a kid at her first birthday party. "You used to watch over me all the time when we were kids," she said in a shy voice. "No matter what happened, I knew I was safe, because you were there to take care of me."

Rafe didn't say anything, but he did take the time to skewer Meg with a *look what you've gotten me into now* look. "I'm your brother," he growled after a moment, not looking at her. "Are we doing this or not?"

Considering it was a pretty lousy excuse for a plan, Rafe was surprised when the first part of it went off without a hitch. Even after Beth had tucked Meg's hair up under a long black wig, Meg was still too blue-eyed and freckled to pass as Native close up, but she only had to pass for about fifteen seconds at a distance of a mile or so. She, Beth and CJ trotted out to the car and drove off, which was the riskiest part of the whole thing, to Rafe's mind, the three of them easy targets to a trained sniper with a high-powered scope. But the car drove off without incident, leaving him alone in the suddenly still, silent house.

Meg had insisted he take the Beretta, and he got the bolt back into the rifle and finally found the shells that CJ had hidden, but he still felt vulnerable. He checked the windows and doors again, then unlocked the kitchen door that opened onto the backyard and took his position, trying not to think of how many things could go wrong. Odds were one in a thousand that the shooter would take the bait and come down to check his handiwork. And the longer Rafe thought about it, the longer the odds got.

He'd probably seen right through their silly attempts to trick him and was after Meg, CJ and Beth right now. CJ's friend lived about twenty miles away, and a lot could happen in twenty miles. Even the way Beth drove, which was usually twice as fast as anyone else on the road. Meg had the Taurus and a scant twelve rounds and no training. All three of them had more guts than most men, but that wouldn't help them against a government-trained sniper.

And then with no warning at all the kitchen door opened and a man slipped through, and Rafe held his breath and steadied his grip on the Beretta and got ready to spring the trap closed.

Whoever it was moved stealthily and silently. Rafe couldn't get a clear look at him from his vantage point in the living room, but he could see enough to know his prey wasn't taking chances. Footsteps crunched on broken plastic, and then the figure moved into sight, his back to Rafe. He was looking at the bullet hole in the window, then he glanced at the wall behind where Meg had been sitting, took in the shattered clock and the gouge in the bricks where Rafe had prized the slug free. Rafe heard him swear.

And that was when a hand came out of nowhere and settled itself onto Rafe's shoulder and the barrel of a gun kissed the back of his neck, just at the base of his skull. ''Don't even breathe.'' The voice was just a whisper against his ear. ''Put the weapon onto the floor.''

A hundred options flickered through Rafe's mind within the span of a single heartbeat. But under the options lay the reality: He'd been caught like a first-year rookie, and whoever was behind him had a perfect kill shot. Fighting for time, he laid the Beretta onto the floor.

Someone stepped by him, someone lean and silent and deadly, and Rafe's heart dropped like a stone.

Weapon in a two-handed grip, O'Dell eased himself toward the kitchen door, not even glancing at Rafe and whoever was behind him. He watched the man in the kitchen for a moment or two, then stepped through the door in perfect firing stance and said, "It's over. Put the weapon down and your hands behind your head."

There was a startled silence, then a scuffle, then silence again. Rafe heard something heavy thud onto the floor. Still not looking around, O'Dell said, "Okay, it's clear."

The hand disappeared from Rafe's shoulder and the pressure of the gun barrel lessened, then vanished. Swearing, he vaulted to his feet, forgetting his sprained ankle as he spun around. He came down on it wrong and it nearly gave way, and he staggered into the wall as a searing pain shot up his leg, swearing a blue streak as he brought his weapon up to train it on the man who was standing there calmly watching him.

Jarvis smiled a smile as cold as any O'Dell had ever produced, ignoring the gun pointed at his chest. He holstered his own weapon, nodding a greeting. "Blackhorse. That ankle looks like it could use some medical attention."

"What the hell are you doing here?" Teeth gritted, Rafe surreptitiously braced himself against the wall and waited for the pain in his ankle to ease before even attempting to put his weight on it. He thought of Meg and prayed she'd gotten well away.

"Cleaning up some loose ends," Jarvis said pleasantly. "You'll recognize this one." He nodded toward the door as O'Dell came back through, his handcuffed prisoner looking subdued and sporting a bruise along the side of his jaw that darkened even as Rafe looked at it.

"Sweetgrass." Rafe's heart gave a thud and he just stared at the man.

"I knew I should have tracked you down three years ago and killed you," Charlie Sweetgrass snarled in reply. "And I knew you were going to cause me grief the minute they said the woman had gone to you for help."

"They?" Rafe looked at O'Dell. "What the hell's he talking about?"

O'Dell ignored him. "The house clear?"

Jarvis nodded abruptly. "She's not here."

O'Dell's profane oath was uncharacteristically explicit. He leveled a heated glare onto Rafe. "Where is she?"

Rafe had his mouth open to tell O'Dell that Meg was long

gone when a movement in the doorway made them all look around.

"I'm right here." Meg stepped into the room, looking hot and tousled and damp with sweat, as though she'd run a marathon. Her hair was wind-tangled and she was breathing hard, but she held the Taurus like an agent who'd been doing this sort of thing for years, and it was trained squarely on O'Dell's chest. "I am really tired of all this crap. Sir. I want to know why you're chasing me and who *he* is—" this with a nod in Jarvis's direction "—and who's trying to kill me and just what on earth is going on!"

O'Dell didn't even seem to notice the gun. "You're quite right, Miss Kavanagh. I do owe you an explanation. And an apology."

"Put the weapon down, Meg," Jarvis said quietly. "You're in no danger from us." He held both his hands well away from his own weapon. "Spence, from the look in her eye, I'd say you'd better start talking. And talking fast." He grinned at Meg. "After this is all over, I'd like to take you to dinner."

"Not in this lifetime," Rafe said testily. "Back the hell off, got that?"

Meg glared at the two of them. "Will you two shut up? Agent Jarvis, I'd be happier if you'd put your weapon on the floor. You, too, Agent O'Dell. And then you can start telling me what's going on."

O'Dell and Jarvis exchanged a look. Rafe stiffened, but to his surprise both men wordlessly took their weapons out of their holsters and laid them on the floor, then backed away from them.

Meg looked at Rafe worriedly. "Are you okay? You look awful."

"I'm okay. Ankle's acting up, that's all." Trying to hide the full extent of the pain, he hobbled over and picked up the Beretta. "Your plan worked like a charm, Irish. Beth and CJ?"

"At Spike's. I made them let me out about a mile down the road and ran all the way back." She gave him a wide grin. "It's not that I didn't think you could handle things by yourself, but you're not at your best these days."

O'Dell snorted.

Meg looked at him coldly. "I have always had the utmost regard for you, sir, but I really am losing my patience."

To Rafe's surprise, O'Dell laughed softly, his expression gentling as he looked at Meg. "You know, if I were about thirty years younger…" Then he laughed again and gestured toward an armchair. "Sit down, Blackhorse, and get your weight off that ankle. It looks broken."

"Just a sprain," Rafe replied through gritted teeth, although he was beginning to doubt that. He did, however, sit on the arm of the chair. He was feeling woozy and light-headed, and his stomach was roiling unpleasantly, and he didn't want to pass out and leave Meg alone with Jarvis and O'Dell, both of whom could kill her with the flick of a finger. They reminded him of chained tigers, condescending to lie quietly and pretend they were under control, when in reality everyone knew they could break their chains with a single tug and wreak havoc.

"I can sum most of this up with one name," O'Dell said. "Baxter Pollard."

Rafe exchanged a quick glance with Meg.

O'Dell smiled faintly. "I see the name rings a bell. We've been trying to nail him for years, with no luck. Then your lady put a paper trail together that led right to him, and we've been tracking him ever since."

"You got access to my computer?" Meg sounded annoyed.

"Not without considerable effort on the part of your friends in Information Retrieval," he drawled. "I'm going to have to institute a fail-safe so we don't get locked out of our own system by some overly zealous young gnome. The security codes and traps you put on your computer were very impressive. We may wind up using some of them on our main system."

Meg just shrugged. "That's what you pay me for, remember?"

O'Dell looked as though he wanted to remind her that he wasn't paying her to keep him out of his own computers, but then he seemed to think better of it and just shrugged, showing more self-control than Rafe would have thought he had.

Instead he drew a deep breath, gray eyes glittering with sudden anger. "I have a leak in my organization," he said in a rough voice, as though the admission were torn out of him. "Pollard found out what you were doing, and also knew you were capable of bringing him down, given enough time. So he sent Mr. Sweetgrass out to get rid of you."

"But how did he find us *here?*"

"He convinced the old man at Weasel Creek that he was with the FBI and had been sent out to help protect you from CIA assassins."

"The CIA assassins being you and Jarvis," Rafe said disgustedly.

"None of this explains a thing," Meg said impatiently.

"O'Dell screwed up," Rafe muttered. His head was spinning but he ignored it. "He knew you'd made a connection between Sweetgrass and Pollard and decided to let you run with it and see what else you came up with. He used you as bait, basically. Except Sweetgrass was better than he figured, and you almost wound up dead."

"Miss Kavanagh was never in that much danger," O'Dell said quietly. "She's had someone on her every step of the way. That's why I brought Jarvis in from Special Ops. He's the best there is."

"Except Sweetgrass has nearly shot her twice and almost toasted us both alive up on Bear Mountain. If this is your best work, Jarvis, you have a way to go."

"And my brother's murder?" Meg asked.

"Sweetgrass. Your brother's identity was leaked, his cover blown, and Sweetgrass, or Pollard himself, had him killed."

Meg's expression was bleak. "And this leak...it's a gnome, isn't it?" O'Dell hesitated, and Meg sighed. "We're the only people in your organization who have access to all the information. Everyone else works on a needs-to-know basis. But we have it all."

"Randall Cruse."

Meg blanched. "Randy? Randy betrayed my brother?" She looked stunned. "We had lunch together almost every day. How could he...?" She shook her head, and the gun wavered. Then, abruptly, she lowered it and sat in one of the armchairs with a thump. "I don't believe this."

"Believe it," Jarvis growled. He walked across and carefully eased the weapon out of her hands. "He's been selling information for over a year, compromising a dozen or more long-term undercover operations. I've spent the last two weeks getting our men out and plugging leaks and running damage control. It's a damn mess."

"But it's over now, right?" Meg looked up. "I can go home to my family now?"

"Yes," O'Dell said quietly. "It's over."

Over.

A simple word, Meg thought. Four letters. Two syllables. Yet it felt like the weight of the world. She rested her forehead against the cool glass of the bedroom window and stared, unseeing, into the night.

She was supposed to be happy. Supposed to be doing cartwheels all the way back to Boston, her brother's murderer exposed and on his way to prison, O'Dell's agency more or less back to normal, her life out of danger. She was even still employed, which was pretty astonishing, considering she'd accused her boss of covering up a murder and trying to kill her. And that she had held him at gunpoint not once but twice, and had locked him in a machine shed.

But she wasn't happy. And she didn't feel like doing cartwheels.

Sighing, she turned away from the window and looked around at Rafe. He'd drifted into a light sleep finally, his left leg elevated slightly on a pile of pillows and the covers pulled back to keep the weight off his bare foot, it and the ankle above it swollen and purple with bruising.

The afternoon had been chaotic, with O'Dell's people coming in and out and someone going down to Grassy Butte to bring CJ and Beth home, and O'Dell trying to debrief everyone and getting absolutely nowhere. Even Rick Jarvis had been short-tempered and uncooperative, unhappy about not being able to find the rifle Sweetgrass had used.

Sweetgrass was admitting to trying to kill her and wounding Rafe and even to setting fire to the trailer, but swore up and down that he hadn't shot at her, either on Bear Mountain or here at the house. Meg couldn't imagine why he was arguing about it, considering they had him cold on all the other things, but, unlike Jarvis, she didn't care. She was just glad it was over.

"For someone who just got her life back, you don't look too happy."

Meg smiled and strolled across to the bed. "I thought you were down for the count." She sat on the side of the bed and he reached for her hand automatically, his fingers braiding with hers.

"Been better." He grinned sleepily and lifted her hand to his mouth and kissed her knuckles, each in turn. "I was afraid I'd wake up and you'd be gone."

"Not yet." The two words felt like lead in her chest. "O'Dell wanted me to go back with him, but I—" She shrugged and stroked his hand. "I wanted a chance to thank CJ and Beth. And to say goodbye properly. And to thank you. And say... goodbye." The word stuck in her throat and made a lump, and she had to swallow hard.

Rafe didn't say anything. He just looked at her for a long moment, his dark eyes troubled and thoughtful, then he pulled her down so she was lying across his chest, her head tucked under his chin. "You're a hell of a woman, Mary Margaret Kavanagh," he murmured.

"I'm sorry for stirring everything up again," she said quietly. "I thought if you found out who sent those two goons up to Bear Mountain, Gil Gillespie and the other one, that it might help you get some closure. But all it did was open old wounds, and I'm sorry."

Rafe had both strong arms wrapped around her, and she heard him sigh, his breath warm along her cheek. "I thought I'd feel something," he said after a long while. "Anger. Hate. Something. But when Sweetgrass admitted he'd sent Gillespie up there after me, I felt nothing."

"I don't think he intended for Gillespie to kill Stephanie, for what it's worth. I know that doesn't change things, but you did get the right man."

"Gillespie was unarmed when I killed him." Rafe's voice

was hoarse. "O'Dell tried to stop me, and I damn near killed him, too. Would have, if two other agents hadn't grabbed me and held me down long enough to get the gun away from me." He was quiet for another long while. "I always blamed O'Dell. When I realized Gillespie was after me and had headed for Bear Mountain to wait for me, I knew Steph was in danger. I called O'Dell and told him to get a chopper up there to get her out of harm's way. And he did that. But he was too late. She was already dead. I always figured he delayed getting her out on purpose, that he was using Steph as bait to bring Pollard out into the open."

"And now?" Meg kissed the hollow of his throat.

"It was easier to blame O'Dell than to blame myself," he said softly. "I was the one who screwed up. I was working deep undercover, and no one should even have known about Steph or Bear Mountain or any of my real life. But Steph was pregnant, and I'd made some phone calls to her. God, I knew better! Even when I was talking to her, I knew I was putting everyone in danger. Me, the rest of my team, Steph, the baby."

His arms tightened, and Meg could hear him swallow. "Sweetgrass traced the calls. No one blew my cover, Meg. I blew it myself. I got Steph killed because I forgot the first rule of being a good undercover agent, and I got my wife and baby killed. And I wanted to kill someone in return, so I shot an unarmed man who was begging for his life, and I would have shot O'Dell, and then I would have shot myself. Except that didn't happen and I've had to live with it."

Meg didn't know what to say, so she said nothing, just kissing his throat again. And after a little while Rafe sighed deeply and buried his face in her hair. "But it's over. Finally. I can't even hate O'Dell anymore, as much as I *want* to hate the bastard."

The frustration in his voice made Meg laugh quietly against his throat. "He has that effect on people, doesn't he? I think it's that calm way he has of just letting you make a fool of yourself that does it."

Again Rafe was quiet for a long while. "He was…like a father to me, in some ways. Not really—hell, you know O'Dell. He's about as fatherly as a chain saw. But there was something about him that always made me want to do my best, and I guess in some weird way I turned him into this father figure in my head. So when he couldn't stop Gillespie from killing Steph, it was like all those fathers I had when I was growing up who never kept their word.''

Another betrayal of trust, Meg thought. Another betrayal of love.

And if she told him that *she* loved him? That the reason she was still here, lying in his arms instead of on a plane with O'Dell, Virginia bound, was that she didn't want to leave him, ever?

She would never know, she realized with weary sadness, because she couldn't tell him. A couple of nights of lovemaking wasn't a commitment for a man like this, and if she tried to press it, she would only hurt both of them. So she was going to be smart and just leave without saying anything and keep this time with him in a special place in her heart, the one reserved for her very first true love.

Smiling a little at her own whimsy and swearing she wasn't going to cry, she eased herself out of Rafe's arms and sat up. She was out of reasons to stay. If she hung around much longer, he was going to start to suspect she had taken things much too seriously and was hoping for some kind of declaration of a love he didn't feel. It would get awkward and uncomfortable and embarrassing for both of them.

A soft knock at the bedroom door made them both look around. It was CJ, looking apologetic as she pushed the door open just wide enough to pop her head in. ''I hate to disturb you, Meg, but there's someone here who wants to see you. Says he's with the Agency.''

''Damn.'' Meg shook her head. ''I guess I…'' She shrugged, unable to bring herself to say it.

CJ ducked out of the room and closed the door, and Meg took a deep breath, telling herself ferociously that she could do this. ''I have to go, Slick,'' she said carelessly. ''You have been…outrageous and wonderful and I'm going to miss you forever, but it's time for me to go now.''

Rafe smiled easily. "You promised to come back to Beth's birthday party, remember."

"Oh, yeah." Meg smiled just as easily, knowing they were both lying but deciding maybe it was better this way. She bent down and kissed Rafe on the mouth, intending to leave it at that, but he drew her close and kissed her with a deep, satisfying thoroughness that made her head spin, so when she finally did draw away she was breathless and utterly rattled.

"I gotta go," she whispered shakily. "Keep this sort of thing up, Agent Blackhorse, and I'll do something foolish like fall in love with you, and then where will we be?" She laughed lightly to show him she didn't mean it.

"Ditto." Rafe's smiled faded and he touched her cheek, his eyes holding hers searchingly, then dropped his hand to his side. "Stay in touch, Specialist Mary Margaret Kavanagh. And watch your back now that I'm not going to be around to do it for you, okay?"

"Okay." Another swift kiss, and then she wheeled away and was out the door and down the stairs, the tears that had been threatening for hours finally spilling down her cheeks. She blinked them back furiously and walked into the kitchen to find Adam Engler standing by the door, looking impatient.

"Adam? What on earth are you doing here?"

"O'Dell wants you back in Virginia ASAP," he said tightly.

Meg nodded. "Yeah, okay. Let me say goodbye to my friends first, and I'll be right with you."

Adam didn't say anything all the way out to the car when they finally left a few minutes later, which suited Meg just fine. It was taking every ounce of control she had to keep the tears back—she'd nearly lost it entirely as she'd said an emotional goodbye to Beth and CJ—and she didn't feel like talking to anyone about anything.

It was only when they were a couple of miles down the road that she finally looked at him and smiled faintly. "What did you do to annoy O'Dell so badly he sent you all the way out here to baby-sit me?"

He just shrugged, not looking at her.

He didn't seem inclined to say anything else, so Meg let it

drop and just stared out the window, trying not to think. She would get through the next few days, and then the next few weeks and months, and gradually the ache in her heart would heal.

The car started to slow, and she brought herself out of her reverie and looked around. They were in the middle of nowhere, as far as she could tell, but Adam suddenly swung the car off onto a narrow, unmarked side road. Meg frowned as the car wallowed along the rutted trail, headlights strobing the darkness ahead of them. She caught glimpses of a half-collapsed barbed wire fence and a few straggly bushes and tufts of long, dry grass and nothing else.

They hit a particularly deep hole and Meg slammed against the shoulder harness of her seat belt so hard it nearly knocked the wind out of her. "At the risk of sounding unadventurous," she said with a laugh, "can I ask where on earth you're taking us?"

"Right here." Adam braked abruptly, and the car slowed to a stop, rocking on its springs as he cut the engine. The headlights lasered through the night, eerie in the sudden stillness, and then he reached down and turned them off and they were suddenly enveloped in the utter darkness of a moonless prairie night.

Chapter 14

"Adam?" Meg's internal alarms were starting to go off, and she looked at him in confusion.

"You couldn't leave it alone, could you?" he said calmly. He reached into his jacket. "All you had to do was leave it alone, Meg. Just accept my report of the night Bobby died, accept that it was an accident, and leave it at that." He pulled his hand from under his jacket and leveled his gun at her. "But you just had to keep digging and digging."

Meg stared at the gun stupidly. "Y-you killed Bobby," she finally whispered numbly.

"I needed money. Lots of money. Marilyn, my wife, wanted new living-room furniture and trips and clothes, and she said that either I gave them to her or she'd find someone else who would." He was speaking calmly and quietly, as though they were discussing nothing more complicated than the morning news. "It was easy at first. Pollard knew someone was on to him, and I traded information for money—he changed shipment dates around, changed suppliers, buyers, never following a routine that Bobby could pin down to use against him."

"Bobby said something wasn't right."

Adam made an impatient gesture. "Your brother was always such a damn straight arrow! He found out what I was doing, and when I told him my problems, that it was no big deal, he went ballistic." He looked at Meg in frustration. "He was going to take me to O'Dell, Meg. I mean, it was nothing, right? I knew O'Dell would get Pollard on something else, so what harm was there in getting some money out of him before that happened? He was just a crook. It wasn't as though I was taking money from some honest guy."

Meg just stared at him. "And you killed my brother to buy your wife new *furniture?*"

His eyes turned cold. "You wouldn't understand, of course. You're just like he is. Worse, even, with your perfect little rules for your perfect little world. You've always had everything handed to you, and you don't know what it's like, needing money for things. Afraid of losing someone so bad—" He took a deep breath and motioned with the gun. "Get out. I'm finishing this here and now."

"Y-you were the one shooting at me!"

"I tried to warn you away from Blackhorse, to scare you off so you'd just put the whole thing to rest. But of course you wouldn't. I was going to finish you both off up at the trailer, but then Sweetgrass turned up and I took off. I figured if he took care of you, I'd be rid of the problem and my hands would be clean."

"You'll never get away with this in a million years! My God, Adam, CJ and Rafe and Beth all know you came here to get me. Unless you're going to kill them." She went as cold as glass and just stared at him, feeling sick and numb. "You're not—"

"Don't be stupid," he snapped. "And I'm not actually going to kill you, either." He smiled. "Not with this gun, anyway. You're going to commit suicide, Meg. With your own weapon. Which I want you to slide out and give to me right now."

"I can't—"

"Do it!"

Mind spinning, trying to think herself through and out of this, Meg did as he ordered. He put the Beretta in the pocket of his sports jacket, released his seat belt, then hers, and gestured toward the door. "Get out."

Again she did as told without arguing. The night air was cold and crisp, the sky littered with stars. "No one will ever believe that I killed myself, Adam," she said quietly, trying to sound calm. "I have no earthly reason to commit suicide. And O'Dell's not that stupid."

"He'll believe it when he finds the suicide note you left." He smiled through starlight. "You're depressed over Bobby's death. Despondent over your failed love affair with Blackhorse."

"What?" Meg's voice lifted.

He shrugged. "Poetic license. It reads well."

"You're crazy." She took a step backward. If he wanted her death to look like suicide, he had to kill her with her own weapon. That meant he couldn't afford to shoot her with *his* weapon. Theoretically, anyway. In reality he could shoot her with any damn thing he wanted and make up a story later to explain it. But as she took another half step backward, she hoped he wouldn't figure that out until a split second too late.

He frowned, as though realizing she was up to something, and lifted his gun. "Stay there!"

"Kill me with your weapon and you'll never be able to explain it," she said quickly. To her everlasting surprise, he seemed to think about it, then swore and lowered his own weapon fractionally while reaching into his jacket pocket for hers. And in that heartbeat, Meg was gone.

She literally sprang sideways, then sideways again, then sprinted into the night, praying she didn't fall off a cliff and end it then and there. Once her eyes had adapted to the dark, she could see pretty well, but she was still running blind. They seemed to be in a ravine of some type, the rim well above her head, but there were plenty of trees and bushes to give her cover, and she ran as quickly as she dared, desperately trying to get her bearings. Then she tripped over something and went down like she'd been shot, landing so hard she knocked the wind out of her lungs.

Dazed, she just lay there for a moment or two. Someone was crashing through the undergrowth to her left, and she hugged the ground, realizing that if she stayed very still and very quiet, odds were good he wouldn't find her. The noise stopped finally, and a silence as thick as velvet seemed to trickle around her, broken only by her own harsh breathing and the cry of some night bird. After a few moments she got to her feet and stood there, straining to hear something that would tell her where Engler was. Then he stepped right in front of her and her heart nearly stopped.

"That was stupid," he chided her gently. "I'm not doing this because I *want* to, Meg, you should know that. But I know you won't stop your investigation into Bobby's death and—"

"I thought Charlie Sweetgrass killed Bobby," she said wearily. "So does O'Dell. It would have been over, Adam."

He blinked. "You're lying."

"No, I'm not. Even Rick Jarvis thinks it was Sweetgrass." She found herself smiling for no reason at all. "So you blew it again, Adam. O'Dell will never believe I killed myself, because as far as we all knew, the case was solved. And Bobby's killer was going to jail."

He stared at her, as though undecided. And then a tree branch came swinging out of the night behind him with deadly and silent intent, catching him across the back of his head so solidly that he staggered forward and fell to his knees, stunned, the gun flying out of his hand and landing right in front of Meg. She snatched it up and trained it on his chest just as Rafe limped heavily out of the darkness.

Adam stared up at her, eyes widening as he saw the gun. Widening even more as he saw her expression. "Don't... please...."

"Don't do it, Meg," Rafe said very softly. "It's not worth it. Trust me, I know."

She wasn't going to kill him, she knew that. But it was an odd feeling, holding a gun on a man who had caused her so much pain and knowing she *could,* theoretically, pull the trigger and end it there. But it wouldn't bring Bobby back, and it wouldn't ease her parents' grief, and it wouldn't do a single thing to mend her own sadness.

"I'm not going to kill him," she said quietly. "I'm going to do something much worse.'' She smiled at Adam almost gently. ''Bobby was my brother. But more than that, he was one of Spence O'Dell's men. And so was Damon Christopher. So when you killed them, you didn't just killed my brother and his partner, you messed with O'Dell. And I have to say, I really, really would not want to be in your shoes right now.''

Engler's moonlit face turned as white as bone.

Only when she finally had him on his feet, secured with his own handcuffs, and had her own Beretta safely retrieved, did she look at Rafe with a sense of wonder. ''How on earth...?''

''Jarvis.'' Rafe's mouth tightened. ''He called the house about five minutes after you'd left. The fact that he never found the rifle Sweetgrass fired at you was still bothering him, and he dug out your notes and saw that Engler had been on Bobby's team. He ran a check and found that Engler was a crack rifle shot in field training. Sniper quality. Called the house to talk with you, and when I said you'd left, and who with, he went nuts. I jumped into CJ's truck and took out after you.'' He grinned. ''I could see your car lights for miles and just drove like hell.''

The mopping up took forever. Three days, at Rafe's count. Three days of endless questioning and note taking and statements, first for O'Dell and then for the Feds and then for the local cops, who had somehow or other decided they needed to be in on it. He'd had about five minutes with Meg in all that time, and although he'd told himself that it was better that way, that they'd already said goodbye, by the time he and Three finally got to the top of Bear Mountain three weeks later, he was missing her more than he'd thought he could ever miss anyone again.

Missed her eyes and her voice and the sound of her laugh. Missed glancing around and seeing that tangle of flame-colored hair, missed arguing with her, missed holding her in the night. Even Three seemed to miss her, moping and whining around the tent as though holding Rafe personally responsible for all the ills of the world.

Rafe swore and wiped his forehead with the back of his arm. It was hot and dry, and the ashes from the burned-out trailer kept catching in his throat, making him cough. He'd cleared most of the mess away, dragging everything into one big pile and smoothing the scorched soil where the trailer had stood, halfheartedly readying it for a new one.

When he got around to buying a new one. That was something else he hadn't done yet. He and Three were camping out in a tent for now, but if they were going to stay up here, he needed something permanent by winter.

If they were staying. He'd come back up here with nothing else in mind but starting over, but in the week he'd been working on cleaning up the mess, he had started to realize his heart wasn't in it.

The trailer was gone, but that wasn't all that was missing. He'd stood in the frame of the house, trying to call up the memory of Steph's laughing face as he contemplated finishing it and moving straight in and skipping the trailer part altogether. But Steph wasn't there. And the house felt empty, cold, the ribs of timber rising against the blue sky just wood, all the promise they'd once held gone. And after a while he'd walked back out, knowing that part of his life and those dreams were gone, too.

Which didn't leave a hell of a lot. Wiping the sweat from his forehead again, Rafe looked around the clearing at all his worldly possessions. A new truck. A fly rod. And a three-legged dog.

It made him laugh, for some reason. You're a piece of work, he told himself deliberately. You could have had the best damn thing that ever happened to you since Steph, but you let her get away from you.

Beth and CJ still weren't talking to him over that one. "Go after her, you bonehead!" CJ had shouted at him impatiently. His mother hadn't said a thing, but she hadn't needed to. One look at her expression had told him all he needed to know, and he'd sworn at both of them and told them to mind their own business and limped out and away, telling himself they were wrong.

Except he was starting to think that maybe they hadn't been wrong at all. Even Three seemed to have an opinion about it, fastening a frowning look at him now and again, as though wondering what he was waiting for.

And what *was* he waiting for, if it came to that? He looked around at the ruin of what he'd once thought was all he needed. This mountaintop had been a home once. After that had died with Steph, it had become a place to run to—a place, he'd hoped, to die. Except it hadn't let him die. It had taken him into itself and had purified and strengthened him and given him a purpose. *Hanblecheyapi:* lamenting. Seeking peace, he'd found himself. And later, if CJ was to be believed, it had become a place to hide.

Whatever it had been, it held nothing for him now. It had done what it had needed to. It was time to move on.

Rafe straightened his back, wincing, and looked around him again. He'd buried the scorched rubbish from the trailer. Nothing was left of it but the pile of wood and bits and pieces, and they would break down soon enough under the combined alchemy of wind, rain, snow and summer's heat. The frame of the house he would leave there, a memorial to a woman he'd once loved. Someone might find it up here one day and think what a perfect place it was for a home, looking over valley and mountain range, and build their own home on that same spot.

"Yo, Three!" The old dog looked up as Rafe shouldered the shovel and walked toward his new pickup truck. "Come on, dog. We've got to go to Virginia and find us a gnome."

She heard the whispers first. A susurration of sound that seemed to have its origin somewhere in the front of the vast, still, dimly lit room that was her realm. There were maybe twenty people in here at any one time, hidden behind computer consoles, the only sound the hum of hard drives and the sighing of the air conditioning. Now and again there would be a soft rise and fall of voices, muted and private, but this was different. And it was moving toward her.

Frowning, Meg looked up from her computer monitor again. Matt Carlson was standing at the end of her desk, looking over the curved, mock suede half wall that divided her spacious work area from the one next to her. He'd come down as he did every

Friday morning, with a copy of the *New York Times* crossword puzzle and a big mug of latté, but he was just standing there with a look of stupefaction on his clean-cut face.

"Matt?"

"Well, now I have for damned sure seen everything."

Meg looked at him impatiently. "What is it? What's going on?"

"It's him," he said with awe in his voice. "Here. They said he'd never come back here."

"Who?" Frowning again, Meg waited impatiently for him to reply. But when he just continued to stare at whatever had captured his—and apparently everyone else's—attention, she got to her feet and stood on her tiptoes to see over the wall divider. "What *is* it?"

"A legend," Matt said with a laugh. "A real, honest to God legend!"

"A what? This is—oh, my gosh." She just stared at the apparition striding toward her, tall and wide-shouldered, dark eyes flashing with irritation as he wove his way through the maze of half walls and desks and glowing computer terminals.

He spotted her then. And headed straight for her with an expression of grim determination. Matt, in a misguided attempt at bravado, held his ground. "This, um…this is a restricted access area. No one is authorized to enter this area without the proper security clearance and coded badge and—"

Rafe got to within about a foot of him, then stopped, eyes narrowing. "You," he said with soft ferocity. "Move."

Matt moved.

Meg realized she was gaping and closed her mouth, unable to take her eyes off him. He was fit and healthy, the scar on the left side of his head still noticeable, but not badly so. It gave him a reckless aura of total disrepute that probably had something to do with the twenty pairs of eyes that had followed his progress through the huge, high-ceilinged room and were now riveted on the two of them.

"Ex-Agent Blackhorse." Her mouth was dry, and she inclined her head slightly, her heart cartwheeling like a pebble down a mountainside.

"There are going to be about fifty armed agents down here in the next minute or two," he said by way of greeting. "I bluffed my way through the first couple of levels, bullied my way through the next couple, and punched my way through the last one. I figure O'Dell is on his way down here by express elevator, so I don't have a lot of time to finesse this."

"I...see," Meg whispered, not seeing at all.

"Mary Margaret...Meg. I love you, damn it," he said in a ferocious growl, as though not happy about having to admit it. And considering the audience he had, it was no wonder. Twenty pairs of eyes were trained on them like laser scopes, rapt with curiosity.

Meg just stood there and stared at him. "C-could you say that again, please?"

Something softened around his eyes then, and he relaxed suddenly, the tension going out of his shoulders. He laughed softly. "I said I love you, Meg. I think Three does, too, but he'll have to wait and tell you himself. No, don't say anything—I have maybe thirty seconds left before all hell breaks loose, and I want to get this said."

Meg closed her mouth again and just gazed at him, wondering if she was awake or asleep but afraid to pinch herself in case it was just a dream. Because if it *was* a dream, she wanted it to last a little while longer.

He took a deep breath. "I'm no bargain, but you already know that. I loved Steph like crazy, and I know I love you like crazy, too. I don't know if that's enough for you, but it's about all I've got to offer. I'm out of a job, unless I go back to being a retrieval expert, but you were right about that being a low rent bounty hunter. I've got some money put away—not a lot, but a bit. I don't have a place for us to live, and everything I own fits in my hip pocket, except for a new fly rod and Three. And a truck. I did buy myself a new truck." There was a shout somewhere in the corridor and the pounding of running feet. "Okay, this is the deal. I love you and want like hell to marry you. But I'll understand if you say no, okay?"

The shouts were getting louder, but Rafe didn't even look around. "Take as long as you need to give me an answer. And if it's no, I swear I'll never bother you again. But I didn't want you comin' back here and marryin' old Royce without telling you how I feel.'' He took another deep breath and straightened his shoulders. "And that's about it."

"Yes."

A frown flickered across his forehead. "Yes, what?"

"Yes, I'll marry you."

He looked slightly stunned. "I thought you'd need more time to—"

"Freeze right there! Hands on your head! Now!"

"You know," Meg said, reaching up and grabbing the front of his shirt and pulling him toward her, "CJ is right. You really *are* a bonehead."

"Specialist Kavanagh, move away from—"

"Oh, shut up!" Meg released Rafe and wheeled toward the man. "Back off, Agent! Put your weapon up and back off now!"

He blinked and took a step backward. Then he caught himself and braced his gun hand more firmly. "I said—"

"Back off, Agent," a quiet, familiar voice said from behind the row of armed men circling them. "It's all right. I'll vouch for this man's security clearance."

The man snapped to attention so abruptly that Meg could have sworn he gave himself whiplash. "Yes, sir, Special Agent O'Dell, sir," he said all in one breathless rush. The circle of weapons vanished as one, and within a heartbeat the circle of hard-eyed agents and security personnel had melted away. Leaving just one tall, flinty-eyed figure staring unsmilingly at them.

"You care to explain what the hell you're doing here?"

"Asking me to marry him," Meg said evenly.

O'Dell just moved that cool gaze back to Rafe. "That right?"

Rafe flexed his shoulders, feet firmly braced. "Yeah."

O'Dell nodded slowly, the barest hint of what Meg would have sworn was a satisfied smile just brushing his lips before it vanished again. "And your answer, Specialist Kavanagh?"

"Well, I said yes." Her bravado was evaporating as swiftly as O'Dell's crack security team had. "Which probably means

I'm fired. I know your rules about gnomes marrying and making themselves vulnerable to threat and blackmail and—''

"They're my rules, Specialist Kavanagh," O'Dell drawled. "I get to break them when I want to."

Meg didn't say anything, not entirely sure if that meant she was still employed or not.

O'Dell looked at Rafe for a long, still moment. "You sure about this?"

"I'm sure."

"Kavanagh's a pain in the backside most of the time, but a lot of people around here are fond of her. Very fond of her. Most of them carry guns and know a variety of ways to make a man disappear. They won't be happy if she marries you and you mess up and she gets hurt."

"I'm not going to mess up."

O'Dell just nodded after another long moment. Then he held his hand out. And after another long moment, during which Meg held her breath, Rafe put his own out and shook it.

And that, finally, was when Meg decided she wasn't dreaming after all.

Epilogue

It had been a very strange, very busy and very satisfying day, all in all.

Meg smiled beatifically and gazed around her parents' huge backyard, enjoying an unexpected moment of quiet and solitude. Her mom and dad had gone overboard on the flowers—the entire yard was one mass of flowers and white satin ribbon. Even Three was sporting a red rose in his collar. Someone—one of her brothers, most likely—had put a bow tie on the old dog, and he looked positively handsome—if you overlooked the cake crumbs and icing all over his muzzle.

It had been a perfect wedding. There had been a variety of last minute crises, of course. Father Reilly had taken a wrong turn and gotten lost, and the caterer had forgotten the baked salmon, and the cake had been mistakenly delivered to the house down the road. But Maureen and the rest had worked it all out, and she and Rafe had been married under a bright blue sky, surrounded by family and friends.

And O'Dell, who wasn't technically part of either group. But he had come anyway, seemingly genuinely pleased by the invitation and looking so incredibly handsome in black tie that he'd spent the day being deftly pursued by at least a half dozen of her mother's friends, most of them shrewd-eyed mothers with unwed daughters and at least two of them equally shrewd-eyed divorcées with no such encumbrances.

It was an eclectic group. Her parents and brothers and Maureen and loads of family and personal friends and assorted wives and husbands and offspring. Beth and CJ were there, and, to Meg's delight, so was Rafe's half brother, Jett Kendrick, who was the spitting image of Rafe and a heartbreaker in his own right. He'd come all the way from Montana with his wife, who turned out to be as warm and funny and down-to-earth as she was beautiful. It had been Rafe's idea to ask Jett to be his best man, bridging what might have been a vast distance between them with a simple gesture worthy of any diplomat.

Jett and Kathleen's son, Jody, was there, too. Seventeen and as handsome as sin, he'd acquired a trail of adoring young women almost as long as O'Dell's, and Meg had finally taken pity on him and sent Patrick to rescue him.

And there were a few Agency people there, as well. Matt Carlson and some of her fellow gnomes, and the mysterious Rick Jarvis, who was cutting a dashing swath through the eligible women that even O'Dell couldn't match. She'd invited him on a complete whim, and he'd seemed as surprised and pleased as O'Dell. Even old Jonah was there, another whim. Hair slicked down and resplendent in a new suit, he seemed to be enjoying himself thoroughly.

"Queen of all she surveys," someone murmured behind her. Two male arms slid around her waist, and a warm mouth browsed leisurely along her nape.

"You'd better hope my husband doesn't catch us," she murmured in reply, leaning back against the wide male chest that went with the arms. "Do I know you?"

"I think we've met," Rafe whispered with a soft laugh. "And it's a good thing your husband has a sense of humor." He gave her a squeeze and nipped at her earlobe. Then he cradled her against him and kissed the top of her head. "So, Mrs. Black-horse. How's married life so far?"

"Tolerable." Meg laced her fingers with his and rested her

head against his chest. "It's been, what? Two hours? No regrets so far."

"That's good, 'cause I don't think that ring's returnable."

"Neither is the wife that goes with it," Meg reminded him with a soft laugh. She tipped her head back to look at his chin. "The bruise is fading nicely. And I noticed that Grady's fist is starting to heal. You two made up and shaken hands yet?"

"Yeah." Rafe sounded amused. "He told me a couple of minutes ago that he figured I'd do as a brother-in-law, then invited me fishing. Is that a good thing, or can I expect to have to swim home?"

Meg laughed. "No, that's a good thing. He likes you, actually. He told me so himself."

"Then why did he sock me on the jaw?"

"Oh, he had to do that." Grinning, she looked up at him again. "Family honor." Still smiling, she went back to watching the crowd milling around the gardens. "I saw you talking to Spence. Did he ask you to come back and work for him again?"

"Yep."

"And?"

"I told him it was up to my wife."

"Training unit?"

"Yep."

"Then your wife says it's fine with her. But you can tell him that your wife also said that if he sends you out on a field assignment and gets you shot, she will make life very, very unpleasant for him."

Rafe laughed aloud. "Oh, I suspect he knows that already." He gave her another hug. "And you? He says that field agent job is open if you want it."

Meg shook her head. "Nah. All that running around with guns chasing bad guys is overrated. I'm going to have my hands full getting this wife business figured out."

"Well, you're doing pretty fine so far."

"All two hours of it." Laughing, she turned in his embrace and looked up at him. "I have something for you."

He gave her a slow, lazy grin, his eyes warm and teasing. "That sounds promising."

"Cool off," she said with a grin. "This is from your mom." Meg reached into the tiny pocket on her brocade jacket. "Hold out your left wrist."

"Handcuffs," he speculated with a raunchy grin.

"You wish. Be serious—this is important." Gently she held up the narrow braided leather thong that Beth had given her. And even more gently, she wrapped it loosely around Rafe's wrist and secured it with a tight knot. "She made this for you before you were born," she said quietly.

Rafe looked at it thoughtfully, fingering the red-and-black beads that Beth had inexpertly threaded into the braid over thirty-five years ago. "Did she tell you we talked last night?"

Meg nodded. "She said you called her Mom for the first time since you were a kid. That it made her cry."

Rafe just nodded, still looking at the thong. "Lot of stuff's been said that can't be unsaid."

"You were angry. Hurt. She understands that."

"I never understood why she never came and got me out of those foster homes," he said after a long moment, touching the beads again. "I never knew until years later how tough it must have been for her back then. How tough *she* had to be just to survive."

"It's going to take her a long time to get over her guilt," Meg said quietly.

He smiled. "She did say I have good taste in women, though."

"Well, I'd agree with that." Meg gazed up at him wonderingly, feeling happier than she'd ever been in her life. "Am I going to wake up tomorrow morning and find this has all been a dream?"

"You're going to wake up tomorrow morning well loved," he said with a slow, incendiary smile. "Beside your husband. Who's going to make love to you again, more than likely. And would love nothing better than to sneak you out of this garden and into a bedroom and out of that pretty outfit you're wearing and make love to you right now."

Meg felt her heart give a ridiculous little leap. "We do have the honeymoon suite at the hotel reserved..."

"Then how about we start saying our fond farewells to all these folk and mosey on over there and see what happens?"

"That," she said softly, "sounds like a wonderful idea." She paused then, and reached up to touch his cheek, still trying to convince herself that this was real. That *he* was real. "I love you," she whispered.

And Rafe, gazing down into the small, heart-shaped face gazing up at him, felt his heart turn clear over. "You fill me up, Mary Margaret Kavanagh. I was emptied out up there on Bear Mountain, and you just seem to fill up all those empty spaces and make me feel whole again."

Her eyes grew warm and loving, and she laughed very quietly. "A fourth-century bishop named St. Hilary—who's the patron saint against snakebites, in case you ever need to know, by the way—wrote 'Everything that seems empty is full of the angels of God.'"

"Old Hilary might have been hot stuff in the snakebite department," he said quietly, "but she knew spit about heartbreak and lonely." He touched her cheek with his fingertips, always mildly amazed that when he touched her, his fingers connected with warm, soft flesh. It all seemed unreal—the love in her eyes, the ring on her finger that he'd put there a scant two hours ago. Then he smiled and replaced his touch with a kiss. "You start saying goodbye and I'll bring the car around. Call me selfish, but I'd really like to spend some time alone with my wife."

"A plan your wife endorses enthusiastically." She rose onto her toes and planted a warm kiss on his chin. "See you in a couple of minutes."

Rafe was still grinning like eight kinds of a fool as he made his way through the garden—deftly skirting well-wishers left and right—and down the long curved driveway to where he'd stashed the rental car. It had been Meg's idea, renting a small import instead of using either of their own vehicles for their final getaway, and as he walked by Meg's blue Chrysler, parked at the curb as a decoy, he was glad he'd listened to her. Someone—her brothers, no doubt—had filled the thing with about a million inflated balloons.

He was still shaking his head and wondering if he was ever

going to get used to finding himself dropped into the middle of a family of lunatics when he spotted Spence O'Dell leaning against a tree at the edge of the big front yard, smoking a rare cigarette.

"Those things'll kill you."

"Most things can." O'Dell blew out a stream of smoke, then tossed the cigarette onto the sidewalk and ground it out under his shoe. He shoved his hands back into his pockets and leaned a shoulder against the tree, looking relaxed and very un-O'Dell-like. "Great day for a wedding."

"Great day for this one, anyway." Rafe looked at the other man for a moment or two, then snorted and shook his head again, smiling. He held out his hand, and after an amused moment, O'Dell took it and shook it firmly.

"Congratulations. You found yourself a good woman. I figure she'll keep you on your toes, but you could use that."

Rafe's smile turned wry. He turned his face up to the sky and closed his eyes for an instant or two, feeling the sun's heat. "So how did you do it, O'Dell?" he asked, not looking at the other man.

"Do what?" O'Dell looked so innocent it made Rafe's teeth ache.

"Put the idea into her head that I had information that could help her find Bobby's killer."

O'Dell's gray eyes were as calm as glass. "I don't know what you're talking about. She made the connection herself."

"Exactly," Rafe said comfortably. "There was no need for her to track me down. All she had to do was take the information to you. But somehow or another, she was led to believe that I had information I hadn't put into my original field reports. Information she needed."

"You think I had something to do with her heading up to Bear Mountain?"

"I know damned well you did." Rafe smiled again, not even feeling angry. "I know you, O'Dell, remember? I know how that manipulative mind of yours works. When Meg came back from Dakota talking about me, I figure you saw a chance to shake me up a bit. So you put the idea into her head that I had answers she needed and let her bulldog nature do the rest.''

''And why would I do that?'' O'Dell asked lazily. ''Send one of my best gnomes to hell and gone out to chase you down?''

''I don't know for sure. Maybe you saw the same thing in her that I did and figured we'd fit. Maybe you were just bored down in that office in Virginia and decided to throw us together and see what happened.''

O'Dell gave a noncommittal grunt. ''I strike you as the kind of man who gives enough of a damn to waste my time playing matchmaker?''

''No more than you strike me as the kind of man who gives enough of a damn to camp out on a mountaintop in early spring to watch over some falling-down drunk who'd hit bottom so hard he didn't care if he lived or died.''

Something shifted deep in O'Dell's glacial-gray eyes, a warming perhaps, a hint of what a rash man who didn't know better might think was genuine affection. ''Interesting story, but I don't know what you're talking about,'' he said easily.

Rafe just smiled slowly, his gaze holding O'Dell's. Then he touched his finger to his forehead in a lazy salute and started back down toward the car again. ''You take care of yourself, O'Dell. I'll see you in a month or so. And thanks.''

There was a quiet chuckle behind him. ''Anytime.''

And Rafe, his heart soaring, just threw his head back and laughed, thinking about the long, sweet days ahead with the woman he loved. No more wild days or wild ways, he thought with satisfaction. Just a contented man and his family and a life that seemed to be working out just fine after all.

* * * * *

If you enjoyed what you just read,
then we've got an offer you can't resist!

Take 2 bestselling love stories FREE!
Plus get a FREE surprise gift!

Clip this page and mail it to Silhouette Reader Service™

IN U.S.A.	**IN CANADA**
3010 Walden Ave.	P.O. Box 609
P.O. Box 1867	Fort Erie, Ontario
Buffalo, N.Y. 14240-1867	L2A 5X3

YES! Please send me 2 free Silhouette Intimate Moments® novels and my free surprise gift. Then send me 6 brand-new novels every month, which I will receive months before they're available in stores. In the U.S.A., bill me at the bargain price of $3.57 plus 25¢ delivery per book and applicable sales tax, if any*. In Canada, bill me at the bargain price of $3.96 plus 25¢ delivery per book and applicable taxes**. That's the complete price and a savings of over 10% off the cover prices—what a great deal! I understand that accepting the 2 free books and gift places me under no obligation ever to buy any books. I can always return a shipment and cancel at any time. Even if I never buy another book from Silhouette, the 2 free books and gift are mine to keep forever. So why not take us up on our invitation. You'll be glad you did!

245 SEN CNFF
345 SEN CNFG

Name _____ (PLEASE PRINT)

Address _____ Apt.# _____

City _____ State/Prov. _____ Zip/Postal Code _____

* Terms and prices subject to change without notice. Sales tax applicable in N.Y.
** Canadian residents will be charged applicable provincial taxes and GST.
   All orders subject to approval. Offer limited to one per household.
   ® are registered trademarks of Harlequin Enterprises Limited.

INMOM99   ©1998 Harlequin Enterprises Limited

INTIMATE MOMENTS®
™ Silhouette®

SUZANNE BROCKMANN

continues her popular,
heart-stopping miniseries

*They're who you call to get you out of
a tight spot—or into one!*

Coming in November 1999
THE ADMIRAL'S BRIDE, IM #962

Be sure to catch Mitch's story,
IDENTITY: UNKNOWN, IM #974,
in January 2000.

And **Lucky's story** in April 2000.

And in December 1999 be sure to pick up a
copy of Suzanne's powerful installment
in the **Royally Wed** miniseries,
UNDERCOVER PRINCESS, IM #968.

Available at your favorite retail outlet.

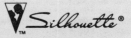

SILHOUETTE'S 20ᵀᴴ ANNIVERSARY CONTEST
OFFICIAL RULES
NO PURCHASE NECESSARY TO ENTER

1. To enter, follow directions published in the offer to which you are responding. Contest begins 1/1/00 and ends on 8/24/00 (the "Promotion Period"). Method of entry may vary. Mailed entries must be postmarked by 8/24/00, and received by 8/31/00.

2. During the Promotion Period, the Contest may be presented via the Internet. Entry via the Internet may be restricted to residents of certain geographic areas that are disclosed on the Web site. To enter via the Internet, if you are a resident of a geographic area in which Internet entry is permissible, follow the directions displayed on-line, including typing your essay of 100 words or fewer telling us "Where In The World Your Love Will Come Alive." On-line entries must be received by 11:59 p.m. Eastern Standard time on 8/24/00. Limit one e-mail entry per person, household and e-mail address per day, per presentation. If you are a resident of a geographic area in which entry via the Internet is permissible, you may, in lieu of submitting an entry on-line, enter by mail, by hand-printing your name, address, telephone number and contest number/name on an 8"x 11" plain piece of paper and telling us in 100 words or fewer "Where In The World Your Love Will Come Alive," and mailing via first-class mail to: Silhouette 20ᵗʰ Anniversary Contest, (in the U.S.) P.O. Box 9069, Buffalo, NY 14269-9069; (In Canada) P.O. Box 637, Fort Erie, Ontario, Canada L2A 5X3. Limit one 8"x 11" mailed entry per person, household and e-mail address per day. On-line and/or 8"x 11" mailed entries received from persons residing in geographic areas in which Internet entry is not permissible will be disqualified. No liability is assumed for lost, late, incomplete, inaccurate, nondelivered or misdirected mail, or misdirected e-mail, for technical, hardware or software failures of any kind, lost or unavailable network connection, or failed, incomplete, garbled or delayed computer transmission or any human error which may occur in the receipt or processing of the entries in the contest.

3. Essays will be judged by a panel of members of the Silhouette editorial and marketing staff based on the following criteria:

   > Sincerity (believability, credibility)—50%
   > Originality (freshness, creativity)—30%
   > Aptness (appropriateness to contest ideas)—20%

   Purchase or acceptance of a product offer does not improve your chances of winning. In the event of a tie, duplicate prizes will be awarded.

4. All entries become the property of Harlequin Enterprises Ltd., and will not be returned. Winner will be determined no later than 10/31/00 and will be notified by mail. Grand Prize winner will be required to sign and return Affidavit of Eligibility within 15 days of receipt of notification. Noncompliance within the time period may result in disqualification and an alternative winner may be selected. All municipal, provincial, federal, state and local laws and regulations apply. Contest open only to residents of the U.S. and Canada who are 18 years of age or older, and is void wherever prohibited by law. Internet entry is restricted solely to residents of those geographical areas in which Internet entry is permissible. Employees of Torstar Corp., their affiliates, agents and members of their immediate families are not eligible. Taxes on the prizes are the sole responsibility of winners. Entry and acceptance of any prize offered constitutes permission to use winner's name, photograph or other likeness for the purposes of advertising, trade and promotion on behalf of Torstar Corp. without further compensation to the winner, unless prohibited by law. Torstar Corp and D.L. Blair, Inc., their parents, affiliates and subsidiaries, are not responsible for errors in printing or electronic presentation of contest or entries. In the event of printing or other errors which may result in unintended prize values or duplication of prizes, all affected contest materials or entries shall be null and void. If for any reason the Internet portion of the contest is not capable of running as planned, including infection by computer virus, bugs, tampering, unauthorized intervention, fraud, technical failures, or any other causes beyond the control of Torstar Corp. which corrupt or affect the administration, secrecy, fairness, integrity or proper conduct of the contest, Torstar Corp. reserves the right, at its sole discretion, to disqualify any individual who tampers with the entry process and to cancel, terminate, modify or suspend the contest or the Internet portion thereof. In the event of a dispute regarding an on-line entry, the entry will be deemed submitted by the authorized holder of the e-mail account submitted at the time of entry. Authorized account holder is defined as the natural person who is assigned to an e-mail address by an Internet access provider, on-line service provider or other organization that is responsible for arranging e-mail address for the domain associated with the submitted e-mail address.

5. Prizes: Grand Prize—a $10,000 vacation to anywhere in the world. Travelers (at least one must be 18 years of age or older) or parent or guardian if one traveler is a minor, must sign and return a Release of Liability prior to departure. Travel must be completed by December 31, 2001, and is subject to space and accommodations availability. Two hundred (200) Second Prizes—a two-book limited edition autographed collector set from one of the Silhouette Anniversary authors: Nora Roberts, Diana Palmer, Linda Howard or Annette Broadrick (value $10.00 each set). All prizes are valued in U.S. dollars.

6. For a list of winners (available after 10/31/00), send a self-addressed, stamped envelope to: Harlequin Silhouette 20ᵗʰ Anniversary Winners, P.O. Box 4200, Blair, NE 68009-4200.

Contest sponsored by Torstar Corp., P.O. Box 9042, Buffalo, NY 14269-9042.

PS20RULES

ENTER FOR
A CHANCE TO WIN*

Silhouette's 20th Anniversary Contest

Tell Us Where in the World
You Would Like *Your* Love To Come Alive...
And We'll Send the Lucky Winner There!

Silhouette wants to take you wherever
your happy ending can come true.

Here's how to enter: Tell us, in 100 words or less,
where you want to go to make your love come alive!

In addition to the grand prize, there will be 200
runner-up prizes, collector's-edition book sets
autographed by one of the Silhouette anniversary
authors: **Nora Roberts, Diana Palmer,
Linda Howard** or **Annette Broadrick**.

DON'T MISS YOUR CHANCE TO WIN!
ENTER NOW! No Purchase Necessary

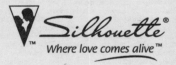

Silhouette®
Where love comes alive™

Name:

Address:

City: State/Province:

Zip/Postal Code:

Mail to Harlequin Books: **In the U.S.**: P.O. Box 9069, Buffalo, NY
14269-9069; **In Canada**: P.O. Box 637, Fort Erie, Ontario, L4A 5X3

*No purchase necessary—for contest details send a self-addressed stamped envelope to:
Silhouette's 20th Anniversary Contest, P.O. Box 9069, Buffalo, NY, 14269-9069 (include
contest name on self-addressed envelope). Residents of Washington and Vermont may
omit postage. Open to Cdn. (excluding Quebec) and U.S. residents who are 18 or over.
Void where prohibited. Contest ends August 31, 2000.

PS20CON_R